∞ DELTORA ∞
SHADOWLANDS

Books 1-3

Emily Rodda

SCHOLASTIC INC.

New York Toronto London Auckland Sydney
Mexico City New Delhi Hong Kong Buenos Aires

Cavern of the Fear, ISBN 0-439-39491-0,
Text and graphics copyright © Emily Rodda, 2002. Graphics by Bob Ryan.

The Isle of Illusion, ISBN 0-439-39492-9,
Text and graphics copyright © Emily Rodda, 2002. Graphics by Bob Ryan.

The Shadowlands, ISBN 0-439-39493-7,
Text and graphics copyright © Emily Rodda, 2002. Graphics by Bob Ryan.

12 11 10 9 8 7 6 5 4 3 2 1   5 6 7 8 9/0

Printed in the U.S.A.   23

This edition created exclusively for Barnes & Noble, Inc.

2005 Barnes & Noble Books

ISBN 0-7607-6604-5

First compilation printing, February 2005

Contents

Cavern of the Fear v

The Isle of Illusion 145

The Shadowlands 297

DELTORA SHADOWLANDS

CAVERN OF THE FEAR

Contents

1 Secrets 1

2 Dangerous Times 6

3 Shadows 14

4 By Order of the King 23

5 Meetings 32

6 Treasure 40

7 Doran the Dragonlover 47

8 Discoveries 55

9 Grains of Truth 62

10 Pursuit 69

11 A Friend in Need 77

12 Mysteries 85

13 Gold and Scarlet 92

14 The Giving 100

15 The Bargain 108

16 The Fear 115

17 Nightmare 121

18 Rainbows 129

19 The Hand of Fate 135

1 ~ Secrets

The flickering lamp made an island of light in the darkness. The wrinkled hand moved slowly across the page.

Outside, the city of Del lay silent, wrapped in sleep. Even those who had long lain awake, grieving for their lost loved ones, had at last fallen into uneasy slumber. The writer's lamp was hidden. The only lights visible in Del burned in the palace on the hill. Lights to comfort the guards who stood watchful by the stairs. Lights that guided two shadows as they slipped through the palace grounds and into the most hidden of its doors.

Soon it would be dawn. But the writer worked on. He had lost all track of time. He had been alone so long that for him day and night had almost lost their meaning.

He ate when he was hungry, and slept when he was tired. And in the long stretches of time between, he wrote, his expert hand rarely faltering, his world shrunk to his secret island of light . . .

The Shadow Lord's tyranny over our land has been ended by the magic and power of the Belt of Deltora. We are free once more, and our king is the same young hero who, with two brave companions, restored the stolen gems to the Belt and brought it home to Del.

The rejoicing of the people can well be imagined. My own rejoicing is no less. But after all I saw in the sixteen years of Shadow Lord rule, and long before that, I am still wary.

The Enemy is defeated but not destroyed. He and the creatures of his sorcery have been driven back across the mountains to the Shadowlands, but I fear he has human servants, too, and they are still among us.

I must therefore remain in hiding until I am certain that the treasure I have protected for so long can be delivered safely to the palace. I try to wait patiently, continuing my work as always, but I confess it is difficult.

Since I have been alone I have been able to make only short visits to the marketplace for news. I dare not stay longer in the sun, though I have grown very weary of this long, lonely time of waiting.

But the treasure must be guarded. That is the most important thing. There will be time enough for sun and news when the treasure is in King Lief's hands.

I fear I have wandered from my point. This has been happening more and more, of late, and must not continue. My feelings are of no importance. I must restrict myself to my main purpose, which is to paint a word picture of Deltora in this time of tumult.

The Shadow Lord has been banished, but now another battle has begun — a battle against the famine, misery, and devastation he has left behind him. Of all the evils facing us, the most terrible is our growing understanding of how many of our people have been taken to the Shadowlands as slaves.

The farms of the northeast and the west have been emptied of people. The best fighters of the Mere and the Plains have been taken. With only one exception, so has every member of the Jalis tribe who was not slaughtered at the time of the invasion. Thousands have gone from Del itself.

The land can be healed and the rivers cleansed. Crops can be sown once more. Houses and workplaces can be repaired. All over Deltora the work has already begun. But the prisoners in the Shadowlands are out of our reach, and their families and friends cannot be comforted.

The marketplace buzzes with talk. There is a growing clamor for a rescue attempt to be made. It has become so loud, of late, that I am sure it is being fermented by Shadow Lord spies. It would suit the Enemy very well for Lief to lead an army across the border. What better way to lay hands on him?

So far, I am thankful to say, Lief has refused even to consider an invasion of the Shadowlands. He must be as aware as I am that without a powerful weapon to combat the Shadow Lord's magic, such an attempt would be a fruitless waste of life.

Yet how his heart must ache when the people cry out to him, and he must deny their hopes.

If only he knew that I could help him! If only he knew I even existed!

They say that he has begun to keep away from crowds, leaving the day-to-day affairs of the kingdom to his mother, Sharn. He spends much of his time alone — shut up, it is said, in the palace library. He shuns even the trusted companions of his quest — Barda, chief of the palace guards, and Jasmine, the wild girl from the Forests of Silence. The only one with whom he spends time is the onetime leader of the Resistance — the stern man all still call Doom.

Perhaps he is searching for some clue as to how he can save the prisoners. Or perhaps he haunts the library because it is safe, and he has realized that he is in constant danger.

Remember, dear Reader: the Belt of Deltora was created by Adin, Deltora's first king, in ancient times. Adin united the seven tribes of Deltora against the Shadow Lord, persuading each tribe to add its talisman, a gem of great power, to the Belt.

And ever since, Adin's heirs by blood have been the only ones for whom the Belt shines.

Lief is Adin's heir. Still little more than a boy himself, he has as yet no child to wear the Belt in his place, should accident or treachery befall him. He has no brother, no sister. His death would lay Deltora open to the Enemy.

Even now, I am certain, the Shadow Lord is hatching plans to lay hands on our land once more. The slaves in the Shadowlands are the bait for one of his traps. But he never relies on just one scheme. A simple plot may succeed where a cunning one fails — and what could be simpler, or quicker, than the thrust of a dagger?

I must not think of these things. I must keep up my spirits, as I pray King Lief is doing. It is vital that he is not driven by frustration to act foolishly. Too much depends on his safety.

I am tired now, and must sleep. The lamp is failing, and my old eyes also. Perhaps I will wake to find that my long wait is over.

I pray that it will be so, for all our sakes. I must show the king what I have to show, before it is too late.

I must tell him, at last, of the Pirran Pipe.

2 – Dangerous Times

As soon as Lief entered his bed chamber, he sensed that danger lurked within it. He glanced down at the Belt of Deltora. Light from the candle he held flickered on the gems set in their medallions of steel.

The rich red of the great ruby, the glowing green of the emerald, had dimmed. The Belt was warning him.

Lief's stomach tightened. He drew his sword. His tired eyes searched the shadows.

He saw nothing. The room looked exactly as it had when he left it that morning. The barred windows were bare, and there was no trailing cover on the bed. Everything that could have concealed an enemy had been removed weeks ago.

Yet there was danger. He knew it.

He moved forward cautiously, ears straining for

the slightest sound. The moon, sinking in the sky as dawn approached, cast its light into the room. The shadows of the window bars fell darkly across the bed.

Lief set the candle on the bedside cabinet. He stretched out his hand and, with one sharp movement, stripped the blanket from the bed. The white sheets and pillow gleamed unmarked in the moonlight.

"Show yourself!" he muttered.

Nothing stirred. He looked around the room again, his thoughts raging. What use was a king who was a prisoner of his own fears? Who could not do what his people most wanted him to do?

He froze as a faint piping sound, a single note, piercingly sweet, filled his mind. The sound lasted for only a brief moment. Then it was gone.

Lief shook his head to clear it. The sound had come to him before. Once in the library, once here in his bedchamber only a week or two ago.

He had mentioned it to no one. His mother and friends were already worried enough about him. If he had ringing in his ears, it was because he needed rest. And he could not afford to rest. Not until . . .

But he could not hide away from the people for too much longer. The calls for an attempt to rescue the Shadowlands slaves were becoming louder. Soon the people would begin to feel that their hidden king cared nothing for them. Slowly their trust in him would grow less, and at last vanish altogether.

Lief knew this as well as he knew his own name. His own father, kept away from the people, had lost their trust. That was how the gems had been stolen from the Belt, and the Shadow Lord had triumphed.

He gripped his sword more tightly. It will not happen to me, he told himself. Why else have I been working day and night, but to find a way out of this trap? Tomorrow . . .

At the thought of the morrow, he looked longingly at the bed. Perhaps, after all, his nerves had been playing tricks on him.

At that very moment, he heard a tiny scratching, so faint that he was not sure it was real. It seemed to have come from right beside him.

Slowly he slid the point of his sword into the edge of the smooth, white pillow. Gently he tilted the pillow upward.

And there, crouching beneath it, was a Plains scorpion, purple striped with black, and as big as a man's fist. Alerted by the sudden movement, the scorpion reared up, its deadly stinging tail curved to strike.

With a shout, Lief flicked the pillow out of the way. Feathers exploded from its torn side as he smashed the flat of his sword down onto the bed. The scorpion, half-crushed, still struggled to attack. Panting, shuddering with disgust, Lief hammered it again and again, till finally it was still.

The door flew open and Doom, sword in hand, burst into the room. He stopped, staring at the oozing purple mass that stained the white sheet.

Lief sat down heavily on the edge of the bed. Feathers drifted around him, settling on his hair and shoulders. He tried to smile. "I had a visitor," he said.

"What is happening?" Jasmine was standing in the doorway. Kree, the black bird who was her constant companion, fluttered behind her. The small furred creature she called Filli blinked sleepily on her shoulder.

Jasmine's green eyes were gleaming as brightly as the dagger in her hand. She moved into the room, taking in the situation at a glance.

"A Plains scorpion," she said grimly. "That certainly did not come here of its own accord. But how — ?"

"Go back to bed, Jasmine," Lief broke in. "I am sorry you were woken. All is well."

"All is *well*?" exclaimed Jasmine. "Lief, if you had put your head on that pillow . . ."

Lief shrugged. "Fortunately, I did not." He did not say how nearly he had done so.

Jasmine went to the window and tugged at the bars. They came away in her hand.

"The bars have been sawn through, then replaced!" she said. "So that is how the assassin entered." She glanced at the sky and her eyes narrowed.

Lief exchanged glances with Doom. They both

knew what Jasmine was thinking, now that her first alarm had passed. What had Lief been doing all night, that he should come to his bedchamber for the first time as dawn approached?

"I have been wakeful, but I feel tired now," Lief said. That, at least, was true, he thought ruefully. He ached for sleep. He pulled the stained sheet from the bed. He would lie on the bare mattress and be glad of it.

"We will leave you in peace, then," said Doom, moving to the door.

Jasmine knew the words were meant for her. The man they all still called Doom was her father, but over the past weeks he had become as hard to talk to as Lief himself. Every day he was surrounded by people. Every night he disappeared on mysterious business of which Jasmine knew nothing.

He left the room, but Jasmine made no move to follow. This was the first time she had seen Lief alone in weeks. She was determined to speak to him.

But Lief would not look at her. He began to unlace his boots. "I must have a few hours rest, Jasmine," he said pointedly. "We leave for Tora in the morning."

"*Tora?*" Jasmine stared at him, thunderstruck. "Lief, you cannot leave Del now! People are clamoring to see you. You *cannot* run away!"

"I do only what I must," Lief muttered. "If you choose to think of it as running away, I cannot stop you."

Filled with unbelieving rage, Jasmine stormed out of the room. She heard the door close behind her, and the key turn in the lock.

The hallway was deserted. Doom had returned to his bedchamber, and no one else had stirred.

Suddenly Jasmine felt suffocated. She longed for the open air.

She hurried to the great staircase and began to run down, her bare feet making no sound on the cool marble of the floor. If only she had someone to talk to! But she did not.

Barda had taken troops to the city of Noradz, to free the people from their cruel leaders, the Ra-Kacharz, and to collect food for the hungry of Del. Jasmine would have gone with him, but the Noradz people feared Filli, and she could not leave Filli behind. So she had stayed.

Sharn and Doom were always busy. And Lief seemed to have lost all trust in her. He kept secrets he would not share. And now he was running away altogether, to Tora, the great city of the west.

Certainly, he would be safe there. No evil could survive in Tora, which was guarded by its own magic. But surely he did not believe he could hide forever?

Or perhaps he did. Lief had changed. The old Lief, the Lief Jasmine knew, was brave, and eager for action. She was not sure that she liked the new Lief — the secretive, prudent, kingly one — at all.

She reached the ground floor, and the burly

guards at the bottom of the stairs moved aside to let her pass. If they thought it odd that she was up so early, they did not say so. In truth, Jasmine thought grimly, they probably expected her to act strangely.

Many tales were told of Jasmine. How she was a fearless fighter who had grown up alone in the dreaded Forests of Silence and could speak to trees and birds. How her mother had died in the Shadowlands. How her father had been injured so badly as to lose his memory, but had escaped to return to Deltora and become Doom, the feared leader of the Resistance.

Uncomfortably aware of the guards' curious eyes upon her, Jasmine threaded her way between the huddled bodies of the hundreds of people who slept on the floor of the vast entrance hall.

The people came seeking help and, above all, hope. All day they waited patiently in line to see Sharn and her helpers. When night came they slept where they had been standing, so as not to lose their places. Many had been there for weeks.

Jasmine moved carefully, hoping that no one would wake. She dreaded meeting the eyes of those whose loved ones were in the Shadowlands. What could she say to them?

I am sorry. The king says we can do nothing.

The thought of the slaves filled Jasmine with shuddering horror. The loss of freedom was to her worse than death.

With relief she reached the huge entrance doors and slipped outside into the dawn. A lone horseman was approaching the palace at a gallop. As he came closer, Jasmine saw, to her surprise and joy, that it was Barda.

She ran to greet him as he pulled the horse to a halt, but stopped short when she saw the grim lines creasing his tired face.

"Barda, what is wrong?" she exclaimed.

"I bring bad news," Barda said shortly. "Noradz is empty. The food has been destroyed. And all the people have been taken — to the Shadowlands."

3 - Shadows

Lief sat at the great table in the palace kitchens, fighting down rage as he listened to Barda's story. Doom sat opposite him, his face as usual showing no emotion. Beside Doom was Jasmine, her head bowed.

Barda had learned of the Noradz people's fate from Tom, the strange shopkeeper he, Lief, and Jasmine had met on their journey through the north.

"When I found the city deserted I went to Tom," he said. "I knew he could tell us what had happened, if anyone could. He says the Ra-Kacharz were seen marching the people towards the border. It was only days before the Shadow Lord's defeat."

Jasmine lifted her head. "Those people were helpless," she said bitterly. "Among them was the girl Tira, who saved our lives. And still we do nothing! We sit here and *talk*! While thousands of souls all over Deltora are willing and able to — "

"Jasmine!" Lief's stomach was churning. "We cannot march on the Shadowlands. The Shadow Lord's sorcery is too mighty to be defeated on his own ground."

"But the Belt — " Jasmine began.

"The Belt was made for defense, not attack," Doom broke in. "The gems cannot be taken beyond Deltora's borders. Can you have forgotten that, Jasmine?"

Jasmine *had* forgotten it, but she paused for only a moment. "Then we must invade the Shadowlands without the Belt," she said stubbornly. "Deltorans are suffering there in slavery, perhaps in torment — "

"I know this, Jasmine! Not an hour passes that I do not think of it!" cried Lief, jumping to his feet. "But I cannot send thousands of other Deltorans to their deaths in a hopeless quest to save them. I can do nothing until I find a weapon we can use against the Shadow Lord. I cannot and I *will* not! Do you understand?"

Jasmine's mouth was a thin, hard line. "I understand only too well, Lief," she said coldly. "We are to give the prisoners up for lost, while you go into hiding in Tora. Well, I will have no part of it!"

She turned and almost ran from the room. With a muttered curse, Barda went after her.

Lief slumped back into his chair again. "She does not understand. Doom, I must tell her — "

"You must *not!*" Doom leaned forward urgently, gripping Lief's arm. "You must follow the plan in absolute secrecy. It is so important, Lief. It is the *most* important thing. You know it!"

Lief gritted his teeth, then slowly nodded his head.

☀

Meanwhile, Jasmine could no longer hear Barda calling her name. He had gone outside, thinking she would surely make for the open air. She was glad of that. She did not want to be found and soothed. She wanted to stay angry. At least anger was a feeling she understood.

She made her way to the great dining room. She was sure that at this hour it would be deserted.

She was annoyed, therefore, to find that the dining room was not empty at all. Hunched on one side of the huge table was the hulking, savage figure of her old enemy, Glock. Facing him on the other side was the one person she liked even less — Jinks, the malicious little man who had once been a palace acrobat.

Both men were wearing a heavy glove on one hand. Each had a small wooden cage, a mug of ale, and a pile of coins at his elbow.

Between them, wrestling on the polished wood, were two huge spiders. One was spotted brown. The other was darker, with a splash of yellow on its back.

16

At the sound of the opening door, Glock and Jinks turned sharply, but relaxed when they saw who it was.

"Why, it is the king's wild little friend, hero of the quest for the Belt of Deltora," Jinks jeered. "To what do we owe the honor of this visit, my lady?"

As he spoke, the spider with the yellow back flipped its opponent over and leaped on top of it, fangs bared.

"Win to Flash?" bawled Glock in excitement.

"Win to Flash!" Jinks agreed resentfully. He pushed his pile of coins to Glock's side of the table.

Glock snatched up the winning spider in his gloved hand and thrust it into its cage.

The spider which had just escaped death jumped up and threw itself against the cage bars.

"Be still, Fury," said Jinks, pulling it away none too gently. "You will have your revenge soon enough."

"Have you nothing better to do than gamble on fighting spiders?" Jasmine demanded in disgust.

"*You* seem to have nothing better to do than watch us, weakling," growled Glock. "Just take yourself off!"

Jinks cleared his throat. "I hear the king is going to Tora," he said, his face alight with mischief. "Are you accompanying him, my lady?"

"No I am not!" snapped Jasmine.

Smiling, Jinks pulled a roll of parchment from his coat and pretended to study it. "That does not surprise me, under the circumstances," he murmured.

Jasmine burned to know what he meant, but was determined not to ask.

"Lief should not be going to Tora," mumbled Glock, filling his mug with ale again. "He should be raising an army to invade the Shadowlands — making plans to rescue my people!"

"Ah, well, you are the last of the Jalis, my lumbering friend, and the Jalis have always been fools for fighting," said Jinks, looking down his nose. "But do you really want to join the rest of your tribe in slavery across the mountains?"

"I would not be captured," growled Glock. "I am Glock, the greatest Jalis fighter. I am protected by a powerful talisman, passed down to me by my family through the ages."

"Oh, indeed!" jeered Jinks.

Glock fumbled under his stained shirt and drew out a small, faded cloth bag which hung on a string around his neck.

"See here!" he shouted, pulling the bag open and tipping a carved lump of wood, three stones, a few tiny twigs, and a scrap of shriveled purple into his enormous hand. "The talisman of a goblin killed by one of my ancestors. A stone from the belly of a Diamond Serpent, and two more from a dragon's nest. Herbs of great power. And the flower of a Gripper."

"Oh, I see!" Jinks' small eyes were glittering with amusement. "So you would be safe in the Shadowlands, would you? You could lead our army to victory?"

"Of course!" said Glock, in a calmer tone, carefully tipping the heap of objects back into the bag. "And so I have told Lief, again and again. But he will not listen!"

"Ah, he has more important things in mind, just now," said Jinks, with an all-knowing air.

"You know *nothing* of what is in Lief's mind, Jinks!" flashed Jasmine, very irritated.

Jinks darted a spiteful look in her direction. "There you are wrong, my lady. I know what I hear."

"You talk like a fool! And stop calling me 'my lady'!" Jasmine exclaimed.

Jinks pursed his lips and went back to studying his parchment.

The silence lengthened, and at last Jasmine's curiosity got the better of her pride. "Well? What have you heard?" she demanded.

Jinks smiled slyly. "Why, everyone knows that Lief is going to Tora to find a bride," he said.

Jasmine felt her face grow hot. "That is ridiculous!" she cried. "Lief is far too young to marry."

Jinks looked her up and down, from her tangled black hair to her bare brown feet.

"Such ignorance is to be expected, no doubt, in one who grew up in a forest, instead of at the palace, as I did," he said, his lip curling. "But I had thought you would have known, since you are such a *great* friend of the king's. Why, rumor has it that your own father has been helping him choose the best of the royal jewels for his bride."

Glock muttered something under his breath and drank deeply, though he had plainly had too much ale already.

"The kings and queens of Deltora always marry young," Jinks went on, in a lecturing tone. "It is their duty. Lief must produce an heir as soon as possible — a child to take his place should he die."

Jasmine did not answer. Of course, what Jinks said made sense. One life was a fragile thing to stand between Deltora and the Shadow Lord. But Lief to marry! Why had he not told her?

Aware of Jinks' sharp eyes upon her, she struggled to keep her face from showing any feeling.

Jinks pushed the parchment towards her. "See here, if you do not believe me," he said. "This is one of the old papers our king has been studying. I made arrangements to . . . ah . . . *borrow* it from the library this morning. I like to keep up with affairs of state."

"With gossip, you mean," growled Glock, burying his nose in his ale once more.

Jasmine glanced at the parchment. It was covered in names, lines, and symbols. At the top was a title in flowing script.

The Great Families of Tora

"You see?" crowed Jinks. "Lief will choose his queen from one of the *best* Toran families."

Glock snorted. "Why go all the way to Tora for a wife? he slurred. "There are plenty of pretty girls in Del."

Jinks looked at him with disdain. "Lief is following ancient ways," he said loftily. "Adin himself married a Toran, and his children did the same. Adin was a wily bird. He knew the value of keeping strong links between east and west."

"The Torans say that Adin married for love," retorted Jasmine.

Jinks sniggered knowingly. "No doubt the Toran lady in question was highborn, well read, and very beautiful," he said. "I daresay Adin was pleased enough with his choice. As Lief will be in his turn."

Glock guffawed into his mug, spattering the table with specks of foam.

Jasmine could not bear their company anymore. She left the room and made for the kitchen.

But before she could reach it, she was stopped by the sound of Sharn's voice.

"Jasmine! Barda was looking for you," Sharn called, hastening towards her. "Now he has gone to his rest, for he rode all night. And Lief and Doom said to say goodbye. They have just left for Tora."

Seeing Jasmine's frown, and misunderstanding it, Sharn smiled kindly. "They will be quite safe, Jasmine. Toran magic will speed their journey. They may have arrived even now. They will be back in a day or two."

"Bringing someone with them, I believe," Jasmine answered in a hard voice. "A young lady, of high birth."

Sharn's eyes widened. "Who told you that?" she asked sharply.

Jasmine shrugged. "I cannot remember now," she lied. "It is true, though, I imagine?"

Sharn hesitated. "I can tell you nothing," she said at last. "I am sorry."

That was answer enough for Jasmine. She gave a small nod, and turned to go.

Sharn bit her lip. "Do not be angry with Lief, Jasmine," she pleaded. "He is only doing what he must — what is his duty."

"Oh, I understand," said Jasmine coolly. "I understand completely."

4 ~ By Order of the King

By the time Jasmine reached the great stairway, she had made up her mind. She could stay in the palace no longer.

"We will go back to the Forests where we belong," she murmured to Filli and Kree. "I am tired of palaces, and rules — and kings."

There was a tightness in her chest and a dull ache in the pit of her stomach as she began to climb the stairs.

Something stopped her and she looked down to see a thick silver rope strung across the stairway. She had been so lost in thought that she had gone past the second floor where the bedchambers were.

Ahead was the library floor — forbidden to all except Lief, Doom, and Sharn.

The very sight of the rope barrier annoyed Jasmine. On a sudden, defiant impulse, she crawled under it. If Jinks could disobey the rule, then so could she.

At the top of the stairs was a large, square space. Two huge palace guards sat against the far wall. Half-finished mugs of ale stood on a table between them.

Jasmine half-turned, ready to retreat. But the men did not move or speak. They were asleep.

Jasmine smiled wryly. No doubt the ale was a gift from Jinks. This was how he had "arranged" to steal Lief's parchment.

She looked around. To her left was a high, arched door marked LIBRARY. But to her right, a broad hallway led towards the back of the palace. It was barred by yet another silver rope.

So this floor held more secrets than the library. What secrets?

Kree fluttered anxiously as Jasmine crept past the guards, ducked under the rope, and moved swiftly into the dimness of the hallway. He had never trusted this shadowy palace, where trees did not grow and the sky could be seen only through windows. And here he felt especially uneasy.

At first, Jasmine found the hallway disappointing. There were storerooms on the right-hand side. All were filled with books and papers except the last, which was blackened and empty. There had plainly been a fire there long ago.

That was no loss, I am sure, Jasmine thought bitterly. There are more than enough old books in this place.

The wall on her left seemed totally blank. But at the very end, she found something strange.

An archway opened onto a short corridor. But the corridor ended in a wall of roughly laid bricks, upon which there was a notice. Jasmine felt a strange tingle of excitement. She ran to the wall and slowly spelled out the words on the notice.

SEALED BY ORDER OF THE KING

So. Here was another of Lief's kingly secrets.

Obeying an urge she could not explain, Jasmine pressed her ear against the bricks.

Thump! Thump!

The sound was coming from the other side of the wall! Jasmine closed her eyes, listening intently.

The muffled throbbing grew stronger, stronger, pounding like a great heartbeat. The rough bricks grew warm under Jasmine's cheek. The sound filled her mind, vibrated through her body.

Thump! Thump! Thump!

The notice fell down. Tiny pieces of mortar began dropping from between the bricks, pattering to the floor like hailstones. The bricks grew hotter, hotter . . .

Suddenly, Jasmine's need to reach the source of the sound became overwhelming. Forgetting all about the sleeping guards and the need for silence, she beat the wall with her fists.

The bricks seemed to tremble. Mortar showered from between them, falling onto Jasmine's feet.

Kree clucked warningly. Filli squeaked in fright.

"It is all right," Jasmine soothed. But she was trembling as she pulled out her dagger and began to scrape more of the crumbling mortar away.

Thump! Thump! Thump!

The bricks shuddered, moving in their places with harsh, clinking sounds. Jasmine staggered back as one came free and fell to the floor. Behind the hole it had left was a heavy brass doorknob.

Lief and the Belt have gone. Now is our chance. Come to me . . .

The thought was clear, so clear. Like a voice. The summons was urgent. It could not be denied.

More mortar was falling by the moment. Jasmine put away her dagger and began tearing at the bricks, pulling out one, then another. Now she could see the deeply carved wood that surrounded the doorknob. The gap in the wall was just big enough for her to crawl through.

Come to me . . .

Jasmine twisted the doorknob. The door swung smoothly open. Ignoring Kree's warning cry, she squeezed through the hole into the room beyond.

When she was inside, she stood, staring.

What was this place? It was quite different from anything else she had seen in the palace. The walls were smooth, white, and gleaming, and so was the floor. There were no windows, yet there was light — harsh, white light that hurt her eyes.

Suddenly she knew without question that she should not be here. Filli whimpered. Kree shrieked a warning from the hallway. Jasmine spun around, but already the door was closing behind her. Before she could reach it, it had shut with a small, final click.

Thump! Thump!

Jasmine froze. The sound was deep, throbbing, and loud — so loud it drowned out every thought. Slowly she turned away from the door.

The sound was coming from the center of the room. From something that was shrouded in a heavy black cloth. Drawn by a force she had no will to resist, Jasmine stumbled towards the black shape, stretched out her hand, and pulled the cloth away.

Thump! Thump! Thump!

Underneath the cloth was a small table. Its surface was thick, curved glass, rippling like water. Jasmine stared. The sound filled her body and her mind. The moving surface seemed to draw her. She bent over it, staring into its transparent depths.

Slowly the throbbing sound died away. The ripples began to swirl and color, becoming grey as smoke with rims of red. In the center of the ripples was a core of darkness.

"Jasmine! It is you!"

The voice drifted from the swirling darkness — young, sweet, and warm.

Jasmine caught her breath. "Who are you?" she whispered. "How do you know my name?"

"I knew you would hear me, Jasmine," sighed the voice. "I called and called."

"Who are you? *Where* are you?" Jasmine bent low over the table, straining to see beyond the darkness.

"Where I was born," sighed the voice. "The other slaves grieve for Deltora, but I have known no home but this."

Jasmine gripped the edge of the table to steady herself. "The Shadowlands," she murmured.

"Yes," whispered the voice. "Yes, of course, but I must make haste. If I am discovered using the crystal . . ."

There was a choking sob. Then the voice began again, though more unsteadily than before.

"I must not cry. I must be brave, as you are, Jasmine. Our mother told me that. She said that in the Forests you feared nothing. You — "

Jasmine's heart seemed to stop. "*What* did you say?" she breathed. "*Our mother?*"

The young voice ran on, the words tumbling over one another.

"Mother said you would help us. Before she

died, she told me. She said that I must somehow reach the crystal and call you. She said I would know when it was time. And I did, Jasmine! I did!"

Jasmine was panting as though she had been running. "How did you know?" she whispered.

"Red clouds swirled back over the mountains. There was thunder, and terrible anger. The creatures moaned and gnashed their teeth."

"Wait . . ." Jasmine begged wildly. "Tell me — "

But the voice was excited now. "I knew what the anger meant. You defeated the Shadow Lord, didn't you, Jasmine? You — and the other, the son of our father's friend. The one who will not listen to me. Who sealed away the crystal, so you could not hear me . . ."

"Lief," said Jasmine through lips that were stiff, and hard to move.

"Yes. He does not want you to know me. He fears the Shadow Lord. But I did not give up hope. Mother said you would not know you had a sister, for I was just beginning when she was taken from the Forests, but I should tell you . . ."

Jasmine tore herself away from the table, her head reeling. She could not take this in.

"Jasmine, are you still there?" The young voice was suddenly sharp with panic.

Jasmine took a deep, shuddering breath. She leaned forward and looked into the swirling, smoky surface of the table once more.

She concentrated — searching, searching — and

then, deep in the black core, she saw a face—a girl child's face, surrounded by a tangled mass of black hair. Pointed chin, wide, frightened green eyes . . . It was like looking in a mirror, but a mirror that reflected her own image as it was years ago.

"I am here," Jasmine said huskily.

"You must hurry," the girl whispered. "We are to be put to death, all of us, very soon. The Shadow Lord has decreed it. It is revenge for what you and the ones called Lief and Barda did to him. Please—oh!"

The image in the blackness wavered and faded.

"I must go," the voice said rapidly. "I hear them."

"Wait! What is your name?" Jasmine called.

"Faith. My name is Faith." The voice was very faint now. The image had disappeared, overcome by swirling greyness, which was itself fading away.

"I will find you, Faith!" Jasmine shouted desperately. "Do not despair! I will find you!"

✳

Jasmine was still shaking as she ran down the stairs to the ground floor and began pushing through the crowd.

People stared as she passed. Some called to her, but she did not hear. A dark, clever-faced man caught her arm. She shook off his hand and hurried on.

She reached the doors and saw that the crowd had spilled onto the steps and down into the garden.

She ran towards the gates and out into the road beyond.

She had to find a peaceful place where she could think clearly. But where could she go?

Then an idea came to her. Lief's old home—the blacksmith's forge! It was not far from the palace, and it would offer the peace she needed.

She set off, moving swiftly through the long grass at the side of the road. Her shocked mind was seething with wild plans. So it was that she did not hear the furtive footsteps behind her, or feel the eyes of the one who was following.

5 – Meetings

In a beautiful, light-filled room in the marble city of Tora, Lief took the hand of the gentle young woman whose great dark eyes were fixed on his own. There were three other people in the room, but Lief spoke to the girl as though they were alone.

"You are willing, Marilen?" he asked softly.

Half eager, half afraid, the girl glanced up at a tall man whose hand rested protectively on her shoulder. She looked so like him that he could only be her father.

The man hesitated. "Toran magic will not protect Marilen so far away in Del," he said at last. "She is my only child, and very precious to me."

Doom, who had been standing behind Lief, stepped forward. "Marilen is precious to the whole of Deltora now," he said firmly. "She will be well guarded."

"Whatever I have will be hers," added Lief, more quietly. "And my mother will treat her as her own."

The man bowed his head. "Her own mother would have been very proud, this day," he murmured.

Marilen turned back to Lief. "I am willing," she said. "It is a great honor. I will try to be worthy."

"You will not have to try, Marilen." A grey-haired woman moved to the girl's side.

It was Zeean, the Toran leader who had nearly lost her life in the final conflict with the Shadow Lord in Del. Her scarlet robe shone like a jewel in the sunlight reflecting from the white walls of the room.

"This day will do much to undo the evils of the past," she said.

She gestured at the scrolls of parchment scattered on a nearby table. "It is not the way of Torans to keep old writings. We left that to the librarians of Del. A mistake, perhaps. But we will study these carefully now."

"Indeed," agreed Marilen's father fervently.

"Thank you," said Lief. "And there is something more that —"

"Perhaps we should leave Marilen to prepare for her journey?" Doom interrupted smoothly.

Zeean smiled. Bowing to Marilen and her father, she led the way out of the house, and into a vine-hung courtyard where a sparkling fountain played.

"And so, Lief?" she asked, when she had settled herself by the fountain's edge. "What did you want to ask me, that even Marilen must not know?"

Lief leaned forward. "The prisoners in the Shadowlands, Zeean. Is there a chance — any at all — that Toran magic could help us set them free?"

Zeean's brow creased as she shook her head. "I am sorry. Our power within Tora is great, but outside our boundaries it is very limited. It could not aid you in a quest to the Shadowlands."

She sighed as Lief's face fell. "I fear you must accept that there is nothing that would do so, Lief. According to legend, the only thing the Shadow Lord ever feared in his own domain was the music of the Pirran Pipe."

Lief's mind was suddenly pierced with sound. A single, piping note, almost unbearably sweet. Tears sprang into his eyes. He gaped at Zeean, unable to move, unable to speak.

The sound died away, and he became aware that Doom was shaking his arm and calling his name.

"I am all right," he managed to say. He blinked at Zeean. "This — Pirran Pipe. Tell me . . ."

"The Pipe's magic was a thing of legend, not truth, I think, and I know little of it," the old woman said, her face troubled.

"Still — tell me, please!" begged Lief.

Zeean glanced at Doom, then nodded uncertainly. "The Pirran Pipe is — or was — a flute, or pipe, of great magic and power. It is said to have existed in the lands beyond the mountains long, long ago. Before they became the Shadowlands."

"So — this Pirran Pipe existed *before* the rise of the Shadow Lord?" Doom asked.

"Indeed. I heard of it as a child. From a Jalis traveler I met by the river. It was part of a tale he told me as he caught fish for his dinner. But what the tale was . . ." Zeean thought carefully, but finally shook her head.

"I am sorry. It was so long ago. I remember only what I have told you, and the strange, rough looks and speech of the man. Also, that he said — " She smiled. "He said that the tale was first told to a girl child of my own years, by a black bird."

"Then it was one of the Tenna Birdsong Tales!" exclaimed Doom. "Ancient Jalis folk stories. I have heard Glock speak of them."

"I would not have thought Glock a very reliable source of information," Zeean said dryly. "But if these Birdsong stories are of the Jalis, you can soon find out about the Pirran Pipe. The folk tales of all the seven tribes are in the first volume of *The Deltora Annals*. Adin insisted that — "

She broke off as Lief groaned with frustration. "What is wrong?" she asked.

"All the volumes of *The Deltora Annals* were burned in the time of King Alton, my grandfather," said Lief flatly.

"*Burned?*" Zeean's face, usually so calm, filled with startled horror. "But the *Annals* contained Deltora's oldest history! It was the only record — "

"Indeed," said Lief. "But it was burned, nonetheless, on the orders of King Alton's chief advisor, Prandine." His face twisted as he spoke the hated name. "The palace librarian who was forced to carry out the order was a man called Josef. He threw himself on the flames, rather than live with the knowledge of what he had done."

"Terrible!" Zeean breathed. "Why burn the *Annals*?"

"Because a land which does not remember its history can never learn the lessons of its past," said Doom soberly. "I fancy those old books contained things the Shadow Lord wanted forgotten. Among them, perhaps, the Tenna Birdsong Tales. One in particular . . ."

Lief looked up quickly. "The tale of the Pirran Pipe?"

"Why not? There are those who claim that many of the old folk tales are based on truth," said Doom. His lean, sun-browned face was taut with excitement.

"You cannot surely have it in your minds to try to find the Pirran Pipe?" Zeean shook her head in disbelief. "Why, that is madness. If the Pipe ever existed at all, it surely exists no longer. Its country has become the Shadowlands! And, whatever the Shadow Lord feared, it did not defeat him."

"We do not yet know the whole story," said Lief. "There may have been a reason — "

"Indeed," Doom broke in. "We must return to Del with all speed, as soon as Marilen can be ready.

We must speak to Glock. He may not be the most reliable storyteller we could find, but he is the only Jalis left alive in Deltora. The only one who might be able to tell us what we need to know."

✳

Far away, at the forge in Del, morning shadows still lay across the cottage and the overgrown herb garden.

Jasmine felt her tight muscles beginning to relax as the peace of the place enfolded her.

When he first became king, Lief had declared that he would not live in the palace, but would go back to the forge, where he had spent his childhood.

But the move had been delayed, and delayed again. And now — well, now Lief was to take a Toran bride, so of course it would never happen.

Jasmine had seen the marble, fountains, and fine things of Tora. She could not imagine a lady from that place living in a humble dwelling.

So the move to the forge had all been a dream and a lie. As her faith in Lief had been.

She stared sightlessly at the peeling paint of the cottage door. Because Lief was determined not to invade the Shadowlands, he had decided that she must never know about her sister. So he had sealed the room. How had he *dared* to make such a decision?

No wonder he has been avoiding me, Jasmine thought. No wonder he cannot meet my eyes.

By Order of the King . . .

Feeling her anger rise again, she turned her back

on the cottage and walked across the yard to the forge itself.

She peered into the place where the great fire had once burned. The heavy hammers, tongs, and bellows lay close at hand, as though waiting for their owners to return. It was strange to think that Lief had once worked here, helping his father to make horseshoes and ploughshares for the people of the city.

But something else was strange, too, and at last Jasmine saw it.

The forge had lain idle for almost a year. The tools should have been covered with dust. But they were not. And — was it her imagination, or did the metal of the forge seem warmer than it should?

Jasmine looked around. An old chair stood nearby. Its back was dusty, but the seat was partly clean, as though, perhaps, a jacket or cloak had been thrown over it not so long ago.

And on the ground behind one of the chair legs was a folded scrap of paper. It showed no sign of the yellowing of age. So it had been dropped recently. Probably it had slipped from the pocket of the garment that had been thrown over the chair.

Jasmine picked up the paper and unfolded it.

EPPN–GPSHF 22, UPOJHIU –M

The letters and figures made no sense at all to Jasmine. But she was sure of one thing: Lief had written the note. She had seen his writing too often to be mistaken. This was some sort of code. Yet another secret.

She threw the note to the ground in irritation.

"It seems you are displeased," said an amused voice behind her.

6 ~ Treasure

Snatching her dagger from her belt, Jasmine spun around. A man was standing watching her. It was the dark, clever-faced man who had tried to talk to her in the entrance hall of the palace. He must have moved as silently as a cat, Jasmine thought, for neither she nor Kree had heard him approach.

The man smiled, white teeth flashing against his brown skin.

The smile made him look younger than Jasmine had first thought. In fact, it was hard to tell what age he might be. His body was lean, but strong. His face was unlined. His hazel eyes were clear and amused. His straight black hair was long, and tied back in a band.

He took a step towards her.

"Keep back," Jasmine muttered warningly, holding her dagger so that it flashed in a shaft of sunlight.

The man stopped, and held his arms away from his body to show that he held no weapon. "I mean you no harm," he said, without the slightest sign of fear. "I have a favor to ask of you."

"Speak, then," said Jasmine, admiring his coolness in spite of herself.

"I have a friend who has something of great value to give the king," said the man. "I have been waiting in the palace on his behalf for many days now. I followed you in the hope that you would help us."

Jasmine laughed bitterly. "If you think I have influence with Lief, you are very much mistaken," she said. "You would do better to go back to the palace and stand in line again."

The man raised one eyebrow. "I have had enough of standing in line," he said.

Jasmine nodded slowly. She recognized in this man a fellow spirit. Someone who disliked rules, and who went his own way. But the last thing she needed now was to become entangled in another problem connected with the palace. She had to plan, to prepare . . .

"Let me take you to see my friend, I beg you," the man said. "The treasure he has been guarding is priceless. Believe me, the king will be grateful."

Jasmine had no wish to earn Lief's gratitude. She wanted never to see him again. Yet . . . if this man was speaking the truth, and his friend's treasure was indeed valuable, it would cause a great sensation in the palace.

And a sensation was what she needed. She was too well known to travel all the way to the Shadowlands border without being recognized. If Sharn heard of what she was doing, she would try to stop her. But if Sharn's attention was diverted, even for a day or two . . .

"What is this treasure?" she asked abruptly.

The stranger shook his head. "That is for my friend to tell," he said. "He has suffered much to guard it."

Jasmine watched him narrowly. Could he be trying to lure her into a trap?

"You have no reason to trust me," the man said, as if reading her mind. "I do not ask you to do so. Walk behind me with your dagger in my back, if you wish."

Jasmine made her decision. She nodded briskly. "Lead on, then," she said. "But I warn you. One false move and I will not hesitate to kill you. And whatever this treasure is, it had better be worth my while!"

＊

As the stranger led her into the heart of Del, Jasmine told herself that she had been right to trust him. When, however, he stopped at the burned-out shell of an old pottery, she shook her head.

"Do you really expect me to enter that place with you?" she exclaimed. "I am not so foolish."

The man sighed. "No doubt you have good reason to be suspicious. But I am the last person likely to be a threat to your safety. Fighting and weapons do not appeal to me in the slightest. My friend lives within."

"Tell him to bring the treasure out to me," Jasmine ordered abruptly.

"He will not do that," said her companion. "He does not believe Del is safe."

Tired of the argument, Kree squawked loudly, left Jasmine's shoulder, and flew into the air.

Jasmine nodded. "Kree will follow you," she said. "I will wait until he brings me word that all is safe."

The man looked up at the circling bird, and gave a low whistle. "So the stories are true," he murmured. "You *do* talk to birds."

Jasmine did not answer. The man shrugged and climbed through a gap in the ruined wall. Kree soared after him. Soon both of them had vanished from view.

Minutes crawled by. Suddenly nervous, Jasmine looked behind her, but the street was deserted.

Then she heard a harsh cry and saw a black streak racing towards her, dark against the sky.

Filli chattered excitedly and scurried out from under Jasmine's collar. "Yes, Filli, it seems that we are to discover treasure after all," Jasmine said. Despite everything, she felt a small thrill of excitement.

She climbed into the pottery, and began picking her way through the blackened rubble inside.

The stranger was waiting for her beside a gaping hole in the floor near the back of the building. With him, sitting on a large chest made of woven cane, was a frail, white-haired old man. Seeing Jasmine approach, the old man struggled to his feet.

When she reached him, and he was able to see her clearly, he looked rather surprised.

"Are you *sure* this is a lady of the palace, my boy?" he asked, in a piercing whisper.

His companion smiled. "There is nothing more certain," he said. "This is Jasmine, who helped King Lief restore the Belt of Deltora. We are greatly honored by her presence."

Jasmine squirmed, and darted him a furious look. His smile did not waver.

The old man nodded gently. "Of course, times have changed," he murmured. "We do not have the leisure for plaited hair, fine clothes, and trinkets now. So much the better, perhaps."

With great dignity, he bowed low to Jasmine. "Thank you for agreeing to see me, madame," he said. "I have come out to greet you, for I fear the steps of our home are very steep."

He waved his hand at the hole in the floor, and Jasmine realized that it was in fact a trapdoor that led down to a deep cellar.

She had hardly taken this in when the old man was speaking again. "I have waited long for this moment," he said. "May I present myself? I am Josef, once Palace Librarian to King Alton. I — I wish to give you these."

His hand trembled as he lifted the lid of the chest on which he had been sitting.

Jasmine looked down, and her heart sank. She had thought of many things the treasure might be. But she had not thought of this!

The chest was filled to the brim with old books, all bound in the same pale blue cloth, all the same size, and all with exactly the same gold lettering on the front.

The Deltora Annals

She raised her head to look at Josef once more. He had drawn himself up, plainly waiting for a reaction.

"*The Deltora Annals*?" she repeated stupidly.

A smile transfigured the old man's wrinkled face, making it glow. "Of course you are shocked," he said gleefully. "You believed the *Annals* to have been burned in their storeroom, many years ago. And I with them. But I played a little trick on Prandine, you see. Yes, so I did."

He laughed. "I could not disobey his order openly. But neither could I bear to burn Deltora's history. So I set a fire in the storeroom, and left a note saying I had put an end to myself. Then I, and the *Annals*, escaped the palace to hide and wait for happier times."

His eyes were sparkling. "And we survived, as you see — of later years with the help of Ranesh, my apprentice, who brought you here. Is it not wonderful? Will not the young king rejoice?"

Jasmine forced a smile, and nodded. She did not want to disappoint the courteous, excited old man. She would help him and Ranesh take the old history books to the palace.

But she was sure, absolutely positive, that no-one would care about them at all. Least of all Lief.

7 ~ Doran the Dragonlover

Jasmine had often said that she would never understand the ways of the palace. She was even more sure of it when she saw how Josef was greeted.

On seeing what was in the cane chest, Sharn shrieked with amazement and delight. And she was not the only one. In moments the great entrance hall was ringing with the voices of people cheering.

Jasmine stood silently by, shaking her head in bewilderment, waiting for her chance to slip away.

"Thank you for helping us," a voice said in her ear. The man she now knew as Ranesh was beside her.

"It was nothing," Jasmine said, shrugging.

"You did not realize the importance of the *Annals*, did you?" Ranesh persisted. "I saw it in your face when Josef opened the chest."

"Old books are not what I think of as treasure, certainly," Jasmine answered shortly.

Ranesh laughed. "When I met Josef, years ago, I would have agreed with you. I was just a ragged orphan, then — living by thieving in the streets of Del. I thought Josef was an old fool to have given up life in the palace for the sake of a few old books. Now — I feel differently."

His sharp hazel eyes softened as they looked at the old man bowing to the admirers crowding around him.

"It is good to see Josef receiving the honor he deserves," he murmured. "I owe him much. He taught me to read and write. He gave me a home. He taught me to live without stealing — well, almost!"

His white teeth flashed in another smile. "After the pottery was raided by the Grey Guards, and the kind people who had fed us were taken, we were often very hungry. Occasionally, I admit, I persuaded myself that what Josef did not know would not hurt him, and went back to my old ways to feed us both."

"You were lucky to survive the raid yourselves," said Jasmine.

Ranesh's smile disappeared. "The Grey Guards did not find the cellar, and the fire did not touch it either. It grew warm, though. For a time I thought Josef and I would be roasted like ducks in an oven — and *The Deltora Annals* with us."

"Would it really have mattered?" Jasmine sighed. "About the books, I mean," she added hastily, as the man raised an eyebrow.

"I think so," he said. "They are not just dry history, you know, but a day-by-day account of events in the kingdom for many centuries. Every volume is full of tales, sketches, maps — "

"*Maps*?" Jasmine asked, suddenly alert.

"Of course," said Ranesh, glancing at her curiously. "Are you interested in maps?"

"If they show me how to reach places I want to go," said Jasmine cautiously. "And if I can understand them."

Ranesh grinned. "Then you should look at my favorites, in Volume Five. They are only rough sketches, but I would trust them with my life. They were made by Doran the Dragonlover."

He looked at Jasmine to see if the name meant anything to her, and, seeing that it did not, went on:

"Doran was a famous traveler who explored Deltora from the coasts to the Shadowlands border. He always wrote in the *Annals* with his own hand. He said he could not trust the librarians to do it, for they introduced errors by making his words too polite and his map lines too neat. Doran was a great character, and a man of many talents, who . . ."

Jasmine was no longer listening. She had begun to think rapidly, calculating the best way of gaining some time alone with the *Annals*. Doran's maps sounded just what she needed, if she was to find the fastest, most secret way to the Shadowlands.

"Jasmine?" It was Sharn's voice. Jasmine looked up.

"Jasmine, would you be so kind as to take the *Annals* to the library and stay with them for a time?" Sharn asked quietly. "I would like Josef and Ranesh to take some refreshment, but Josef will not rest until the books are safe, under the eye of someone he trusts."

Rather startled that her wish had been granted so immediately, Jasmine agreed willingly. In moments she was running up the stairs while a palace guard followed, carrying the chest of books.

Sharn took Josef and Ranesh into the kitchen where a meal had been prepared for them. She returned to her duties with a far lighter heart than she had begun them that morning. How overjoyed Lief would be to hear of the unexpected return of the *Annals*!

It was also wonderful to see Jasmine happy. The girl seemed relieved, for a time at least, of her misery over the fate of the prisoners in the Shadowlands.

And that means, Sharn thought gratefully, that *I* can be relieved, for a time at least, of the fear that she will do something foolish.

✳

As soon as the palace guard had put down the chest and left the library, Jasmine searched rapidly through the *Annals* until she found the one marked 5.

As she picked it up, it fell open at a page with no ruled lines, and covered in untidy printing. Jasmine guessed it had been opened at this place many times before. The page was signed *Doran*.

My recent journey to the Os-Mine Hills was
disastrous. I went there hoping to find a dragon's
lair, having read the Tenna Birdsong ~~tale~~ legend 'The Girl
With the Golden Hair' in volume 1 of the Annals. My
foolish quest resulted only in a bloody nose, a sore head
and a shivering fever caused by sleeping the night
through while soaked to the skin.

I have no memory of what brought these
calamities about. I cannot have fallen foul of a
dragon, for I still live. I cannot have met with a
granous, for I still possess all my fingers and toes.
No doubt I merely slipped and fell into some foul
stream, cracking my stupid skull.

The rhyme below was spinning in my head
when I awoke from my daze. It ~~may after some~~ is clearly
~~clue or be merely~~ the product of a rattled brain.
~~I must find out.~~   SONG OF THE DEAD

'Above our ~~land~~ heads the tumult rages
Struggle echoes through the ages
There the strife will never cease
But here below we ~~dwell~~ rest in peace
Where ~~timeless tides~~ tides of time swamp memory
Our sunless prison makes us free.
The gem-glow lights our ~~rocky~~ earthy walls
And dragons guard our shining halls.'

NOTE: I AM NOW CONVINCED
THAT THE OS-MINE HILLS ARE
HIGHLY DANGEROUS & OF NO
INTEREST TO THE TRAVELLER.

DORAN

Doran the Dragonlover might have been a man of many talents, Jasmine thought, but he had plainly not valued neatness. He had scribbled down his report, and a verse, then corrected them both at a later date, using a different pen and darker ink.

Tears were burning in Jasmine's eyes as she read the last words of the verse and thought of her mother, dead in the Shadowlands. Yet . . . it seemed to her that something about the rhyme did not quite ring true.

Frowning, she read the whole page again. The more she looked at Doran's hasty corrections and added lines, the more she became convinced that they were intended to conceal something. Curiosity buzzed in her mind like an annoying insect.

Quickly she sorted through the books she had unloaded on the library table, searching for Volume 1.

✳

An hour later, Josef came hobbling into the library, leaning on Ranesh's arm and exclaiming with delight on seeing his old place of work once more.

He was delighted to see Jasmine sitting at a table on which several volumes of *The Deltora Annals* lay scattered. One volume was open in front of her, and she had plainly been taking notes from it.

"Can I help you, my dear?" he asked, hurrying forward.

"Thank you, but it is not necessary," said Jasmine, hastily closing the book and stuffing the paper on which she had been writing into her pocket.

She pushed her chair back, and stood up. "I must leave you," she said. "There are things I must do."

"Why, of course!" exclaimed Josef, patting her arm. "You run along. Ranesh and I have much to do also. We have been asked to stay in the palace, to care for the *Annals* and the other books! Is it not wonderful?"

"Indeed it is," said Jasmine warmly. She was very glad that the old man's devotion had been rewarded. Besides, she owed him much. She could hardly contain her excitement as she thought of the paper she had in her jacket pocket.

She hurried to the door, then turned back. She was almost certain that she was right in what she had worked out, but it was best to be quite sure.

"Josef," she said, as casually as she could. "If *Annals* writers changed their minds about what they had written, were they permitted to tear out the page?"

Josef looked shocked. "Oh, certainly not!" he said. "Small *corrections* could be made, under supervision. But that was all. Why do you ask?"

"Oh, no particular reason," Jasmine answered carelessly, but her heart was racing as she left the library. Nodding brightly to the guards who had replaced the ones she had crept by that morning, she ran down the stairs to her bedchamber.

It was a matter of moments to pack her belongings. The vine growing on the wall outside her window was sturdy. It supported her easily as she swung herself out and began to climb down.

She had almost reached the ground when Kree squawked a warning. Jasmine looked down and groaned. Glock was standing below, glaring up at her.

"What do you think you are doing, Miss?" he growled.

8 ~ Discoveries

It was deepest night when Lief and Doom returned to Del with Marilen. Like thieves, the three slipped into the silent palace by the kitchen door.

Sharn was sitting at the table, waiting for them. She jumped up, her face wreathed in relieved smiles.

"You are really here!" she cried. "When your message came that you would be back so soon, I could hardly believe it."

She hastened to settle Marilen by the stove with a mug of hot soup. Then she drew Lief aside. "I have much to tell you!" she whispered. "There is wonderful news, but bad news as well."

Doom's voice interrupted them. "I am going to wake Glock," he called from the door. "We should talk to him at once."

"Why *Glock*?" Sharn demanded. "What has he to do with — "

"I will tell you later, Mother," Lief said in a low

voice, as Doom left the room. "Give me your news. The bad news first, while we cannot be overheard."

He nodded towards Marilen, who was leaning towards the stove, warming her chilled hands. The girl looked delicate, defenseless, and very tired. If she was frightened on her first night at the palace, she might beg to return to Tora. Such a request could not be denied, so it was vital that it was never made.

"Guards reporting for duty on the third floor this afternoon found that the two men they were to replace were asleep, and would not wake," Sharn whispered. "We believe they were given a powerful sleeping potion in some ale."

Lief felt the chill that always came over him when he thought of the third floor. "The sealed room!" he whispered. "Had the wall been — ?"

Sharn nodded reluctantly, seeing lines of worry deepen on her son's face. "The mortar between the bricks had crumbled away, and some of the bricks had fallen. But the hole was small, and the door beyond was shut fast. Perhaps the intruder was disturbed before he could enter."

"We must just hope that is so," Lief muttered. "Has the damage been repaired?"

"Of course," his mother answered.

She glanced at the drooping figure of the girl in the armchair. "Poor child. What a place she has come to! And she is so young . . ."

Lief smiled ruefully. "No younger than me," he reminded her. "Or Jasmine."

"Oh!" Sharn exclaimed. "That reminds me! The good news! *The Deltora Annals* have been returned to us. And it was Jasmine who brought it about."

She had expected her son to be pleased. But even she was startled at the sudden, disbelieving joy that lit his face. Before she could ask him to explain it, however, Doom strode back into the kitchen, his face like thunder.

"Glock is not in his bed!" he muttered. "No doubt he is snoring under a table in some tavern in the city."

"Let him snore!" Lief grinned. "We do not need him any longer!"

✳

Soon afterwards, Lief and Doom were being excitedly welcomed by Josef. His white hair ruffled, the folds of his borrowed night robe flapping about his thin legs, he seized one of the books lying on the table.

"I had no idea your majesty would be back so soon!" he cried, flipping pages rapidly. "There is something I must show you! Something of great importance."

"I would like to see everything in its turn, Josef," Lief said hastily. "But just now I have some research of my own that — "

He heard a slight sound behind him and turned to meet the shrewd, hazel eyes of a dark man with a humorous twist to his mouth.

This, Lief knew, must be Ranesh, Josef's apprentice. How silently he had approached! Unlike Josef, he had taken the time to dress before leaving his room at the back of the library. Perhaps that said something about the difference in their characters.

Ranesh was a man who would not rush to anyone's bidding. He was a man who would weigh his decisions carefully. A man whose real character would be difficult to know.

A man like Doom, thought Lief, glancing at his friend.

Doom was watching the newcomer. Lief knew that he was trying to decide if Ranesh was to be trusted.

"We should have tidied this table before going to our beds, I know," Josef was chattering, still searching his book. "But I wished to clean the shelves before arranging the *Annals*. I fear the library has been sadly neglected. Then I became very tired, and — "

"Of course!" Lief said, in a frenzy to have time alone with the precious books. "I am sorry that our arrival woke you, Josef. And you, too, Ranesh. Please return to your rest. We are quite able to — "

"Ah, here it is!" Josef cried. He placed the open book on the table and pulled out a chair. "Read, your majesty!" he begged. "And here — " He pushed forward paper and a pencil. "You can take notes with these, if you wish, as young Jasmine did this afternoon."

"*Jasmine*?" Lief exclaimed. "She was *reading*?"

"Oh, yes!" Josef nodded. "She was taking notes from the *Annals*."

"From Volume One," Ranesh put in. "I happened to notice before she closed it."

Ah, yes, you *would* notice, Ranesh, thought Lief. There is not much those sharp eyes miss, I fancy. He glanced at Doom's expressionless face, knowing that Doom was wondering, as he was, whether Jasmine had somehow also heard of the Pirran Pipe.

"Now, your majesty," urged Josef, waving at the open book. "Will you read — ?"

"Certainly I will, Josef, but only if you and Ranesh leave us," said Lief, trying with all his might to keep his voice casual and unhurried. "I will not be able to concentrate if I know I am keeping you awake."

Josef hesitated, his eyes flicking from the open book to Lief's face and back again.

"We will speak again soon," Lief added, forcing a smile.

At last Josef nodded. Plucking at Ranesh's sleeve to make sure his assistant followed his lead, he bowed and shuffled away.

Soon Lief and Doom heard the sound of their mumured goodnights, and doors closing at the back of the library.

"At last!" Lief breathed. "Now — to find this tale."

He swung round to the table. The book lay open at the place the old librarian had been so anxious for him to see.

Lief glanced impatiently at the yellowed pages, the small, exquisitely neat writing. A name caught his eye. He gasped and stared.

"Doom!" he whispered. "Look!"

THE TALE OF THE PIRRAN PIPE

Long, long ago, beyond the Mountains, there was a green land called Pirra, where the breezes breathed magic. Jealous shadows lurked on Pirra's borders, but the land was protected by a mysterious Pipe, which played notes of such beauty that no evil could take root within sound of its voice.

The Pipe was played morning, noon, and evening by the people's chief, the Piper, who was the finest player in the land.

One dark winter's night, the Piper of those days passed away in her sleep. The next day, three great musicians offered themselves as her replacement. They were called Plume the Brave, Auron the Fair, and Keras the Unknown.

The three played in turn before the people, as was the custom. Plume's playing was so stirring that the crowd cheered. Auron's music was so beautiful that her audience wept. Keras created sounds so haunting that all who heard them were rapt in wonder.

When the people voted to choose their favorite, each player received an equal number of votes. The three played again, and again. But each time the result was the same.

Night fell, but the testing went on. The people, who had by now separated into three groups according to their favorite, grew tired and angry. But each person wanted his or her own choice to become Piper, and would not vote for another.

At last, long after midnight, when the vote was called equal for the thirteenth time, the three groups turned furiously upon one another, using their magic to insult and injure.

A man in a hooded cloak stepped forward. He was tall, but bent with weakness, as though the long day and night of music had been almost beyond his endurance. Each section of the crowd thought that he was one of its own, for he had spent time with all three, urging its members to hold firm.

"I have a solution, my friends!" he cried. "Let the contestants share the honor of being Piper. The Pipe is made from three parts which fit together. Let Plume, Auron, and Keras each take one part of the whole."

And so tired, so angry had the people become that they agreed. They gave Plume the mouthpiece of the Pipe, Auron the middle stem, and Keras the endpiece. Then, because they still had bad feelings for one another, the three groups went their separate ways, each group following its own favorite.

The hooded man rubbed his hands, well satisfied, and slipped away like a shadow before the rising of the sun.

The dawn broke with no sound of music and the long day passed in silence, for the three rival groups were far apart, and no one piece of the Pirran Pipe could play alone.

Shadows crept into Pirra. Trees withered in their shade and flowers wilted. Little by little the Shadows swallowed up the green fields, the pleasant villages, while every moment the dread power cloaked within them grew stronger.

Too late, the three groups realized their danger. Shadows now rolled dark between them. They could not reach one another to make the magic Pipe whole. And at last, seeing that their land was lost, they were forced to to use the last of their magic to escape, and save themselves.

So it was that the green land of Pirra became the Shadowlands. Its people, still blaming one another for their ancient loss, dwell to this day on three separate islands in a strange and secret sea.

And the Pirran Pipe, forever divided, is heard no more.

9 - Grains of Truth

Doom drew back from the table. "So — the Shadow Lord played the same trick on Pirra as he did on Deltora. He divided the people, made the land's protection useless, then invaded."

"The Pirrans allowed him to do it," Lief muttered, rubbing his hand over his eyes. "As we in Deltora did in our turn. He used their anger, their stubbornness, their ambition, their weakness . . ."

"Your majesty!"

A white figure was hobbling slowly towards them from the back of the library. Josef.

"Forgive me, your majesty," the old man mumbled, as he drew closer. "But I forgot — "

Lief scrambled to his feet and held out his hand. "Forgive *me*, Josef," he said. "You were trying to tell me of the Pirran Pipe, and I would not listen."

Josef's face lit with an eager smile as he took the offered hand. "You have read the Tale, then?" he whispered. "You believe it contains a grain of truth?"

At Lief's nod, he hurried on. "I am sure that each of the Pirran tribes would have treasured its own part of the Pipe, and kept it safe. So if the Pirrans still exist, the three parts of the Pirran Pipe exist also."

"I am as sure of it as you are," said Lief. "And I know the Pipe can help us, for I have heard its voice."

Josef stared at him, awestruck. "You must understand, your majesty," he ventured at last, "that the Enemy has the Shadowlands too firmly in his grasp now for even the Pirran Pipe to drive him out of it. All the Pipe could do, I believe, is weaken him."

"I understand," Lief said firmly. "Do not fear, Josef. All we hope for is time — time to get our prisoners out! But first we must find the Pirran Islands."

"Yes!" Josef cried. "That is what I had forgotten to tell you!" Swiftly he seized volume 5 of the *Annals* and expertly riffled through the back pages. In a very short time he had found what he was seeking: a series of maps.

He pointed to a small sketch above another, much larger, map of the western sea.

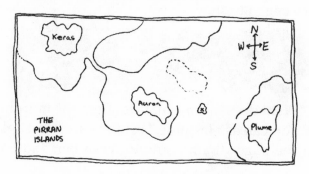

"There is no signature, but I strongly suspect this sketch was made by Doran, our greatest explorer," Josef said. "He certainly drew the larger map below. I recognize his hand."

"Thank you, Josef." Lief's heart was too full to say more. The map was so simple as to be almost useless. But to him it proved one thing at least. The Pirran Islands were not just a legend. They existed. And that meant they could be found.

Josef beamed. "It is my pleasure to be of service," he said. He bowed, turned, and tottered back to his room.

Lief reached for the paper and pencil. "I will copy this map," he said. "Perhaps we can find others with which to compare it."

He looked down at the sheaf of paper in front of him. Now that it was in better light, he could see that the top page bore indented marks caused by Jasmine writing heavily on a sheet of paper above it.

He rubbed the side of the pencil tip lightly over the white surface. As he had hoped, the grooves in its surface began to show as white lines.

"What does this mean, I wonder?" he murmured.

"You can ask Jasmine," said Doom, barely glancing at the page. "I am going to wake her, and Barda, too. If they are to accompany me on this voyage . . ."

Lief looked up quickly. "Accompany *us*, you mean," he said. "I am going with you. Do you really think the Pirrans will give up their greatest treasure to anyone other than the king of Deltora?"

Doom frowned. "You are right," he said at last. "The king must be the one to ask the favor. But you must agree to this, Lief — Jasmine, Barda, and I will be the ones to take the risks, if risks there be."

Lief nodded reluctantly. Doom lightly touched his shoulder, and left him.

Alone, Lief stared again at Jasmine's strange words. They made him uneasy. *O-M hills* must mean the dangerous Os-Mine Hills, to the north of Del. But what the rest meant he could not imagine.

Ranesh had said that Jasmine was reading Volume 1 of the *Annals* — the very book open before him now. Lief began turning pages, finding more Tenna Birdsong Tales. *The Tale of the Three Knights. The Seven Goblins. The Dragon's Egg* . . .

Then he found something else. Caught between two pages was a small black feather.

Kree! Lief imagined the great black bird sitting on the book as Jasmine read. He imagined Kree fluttering back as Jasmine closed the book hurriedly, on Josef's approach. And a feather falling, to be trapped between the pages.

He read the story on the open double page with a growing sense of dread.

THE GIRL WITH THE GOLDEN HAIR

Once there was a maiden called Alyss, whose only beauty was her long golden hair which shone like the sun. Though her eyes were small, her nose was very long and her ears were as big as bats' wings, her golden tresses were so beautiful that she had many admirers. She encouraged all except one, a youth called Rosnan, who was as plain as she.

One day, Alyss was combing her hair, to the delight of all who watched her, when a great, golden dragon swooped from the sky and carried her off.

All her handsome admirers wept, and gave her up for lost, but Rosnan took his sword and followed the dragon to its cave in a valley of the Os-Mine Hills. Seeing him, the dragon snarled and breathed fire, but Rosnan stood firm.

"Free Alyss, great dragon!" he cried. "Take me instead!"

The dragon laughed — a truly terrible sound that made even the vine weaver birds in the trees above fall silent. "You will not do!" it said. "Have you golden hair to line my nest? I do not think so."

With that, it flicked its tail and sent Rosnan sprawling, the sword falling, useless, to the ground. "Run, Alyss!" shouted Rosnan, as he prepared for death. "Save yourself!"

But Alyss picked up the fallen sword and, with a single sweep, cut off her hair. "Take it!" she cried to the dragon, holding out the golden silk, so long and thick that it filled her arms. "But let him live!"

The dragon turned away from Rosnan, and its eyes shone with pleasure as it took the hair. "Thank you," it said, "I will."

Then Alyss saw herself in the mirror of the dragon's eyes, and was so horrified at her ugliness that she screamed and ran. She ran deep into the dragon's cave and down, down under the earth, into the caverns where the goblins dwell. Calling after her, Rosnan followed, but Alyss did not stop, for gold light gleamed in the cavern walls, tormenting her and reminding her of what she had lost.

They fled — Alyss in front, Rosnan behind — through the sunless world below the world, where the seas of forgetfulness crawl. They fled so far that they forgot why they were fleeing, but they went without harm, for they were so ugly that the goblins mistook them for a pair of their own.

The gleaming gold changed to red that glowed like the setting sun. Then came glimmering rainbows, and the green of the forest after rain. And still the chase went on.

But when the color faded to the grey of dusk, and the darkness of deepest night was ahead. Alyss feared to go further, and stopped. Then Rosnan caught up with her and took her in his arms, saying that to him she was the most beautiful girl in the world. Which was nothing but the truth, for he loved her with all his heart.

And Alyss looked at him and saw a soul that was honest, brave, and true. And her heart melted within her.

The goblins saw their love, and wondered at its power. A few traveled to the world above, seeking the same happiness for themselves, though never finding it. But the lovers were never seen under the sun again, and only the birds know that, deep in the world below the world, they lived happily ever after.

Lief sat for a moment, deep in thought. Then he heard a sound from the door. Doom and Barda were striding towards him, grim-faced. He knew what they had come to tell him before they spoke.

"Jasmine has gone, hasn't she?" he asked dully.

They looked surprised, but did not ask how he knew.

"Her bed has not been slept in." Barda rubbed his forehead angrily. "She slipped away yesterday, no doubt, while I was asleep. I should have expected this! By now she will be in the Forests. And alone!"

Lief shook his head. "Not alone," he replied. "If I am right, Glock is with her. And they have not gone to the Forests, but to the Os-Mine Hills. I believe — I am sure — that Jasmine thinks she has found a secret way to the Shadowlands. Underground."

10 ~ Pursuit

Marilen shivered and wrapped her cloak more closely around her. It was not yet dawn, but Lief knew that she was shuddering not with cold, but with anxiety she was trying desperately to disguise.

"Do not fear, Marilen," he said gently. "You need do nothing but wait. Doom is staying here, to prepare for a journey. He will watch over you. And Barda and I will soon return."

He hoped that she would not ask him where he was going. Even in Tora, she might have heard the evil stories of the Os-Mine Hills. He smothered a sigh of relief as she nodded silently.

"I had not planned to leave you so soon," Lief went on carefully. "But I do not think that Jasmine will return for anyone but me, for I am the one who offended her."

"I do understand, Lief," Marilen said in a low voice. "And you must not think I am a coward, who will always panic as soon as you leave her sight."

Torn between fury at Jasmine's stubbornness, and a terrible fear for her safety, Lief was impatient to be gone. But there was one thing left to ask.

"Very few people know that we returned with Doom last night, Marilen," he said. "Most think we are still in Tora. It is safest if they continue in this belief for now. Will you remain out of sight while I am gone? Mother will see to your meals."

Marilen raised her eyes to meet his anxious gaze. "Do not worry about me, Lief," she said quietly. "I will occupy myself in the library."

Lief smiled, hiding his doubts. He had not remembered the library. But he could not bring himself to forbid it to Marilen.

As he left her, he told himself that all would be well. The guards would not allow Marilen to stray into the forbidden hallway. And Josef could surely be trusted to keep her presence secret.

What of Ranesh? Doubts stirred again, but Lief forced them out of his mind, and hurried down the stairs.

He was approaching the kitchen, where he had arranged to meet Barda, when he heard a muffled scream. He quickened his pace and as he threw open the door a startling sight met his eyes.

Barda had Jinks by the collar, and was shaking him. Jinks, wearing a red nightshirt, his mouth smeared with jam, was howling, trying to kick the big man's legs.

"You knew they had gone, you miserable worm!" Barda was thundering. "Yet you said *nothing*!"

"Am I Glock's keeper?" screeched Jinks. "He is old enough and ugly enough to look after himself. And as for that green-eyed minx he went with — "

His voice broke off in a high-pitched squeal as Barda jerked him upward, nearly strangling him.

"Barda, put him down!" Lief begged. "He will wake the whole palace!"

Barda swung around, hauling Jinks with him. Jinks' eyes widened. "I did not know you were home, your majesty!" he spluttered. "Call off your bear, I beg you. He has gone wild!"

"I can go wilder yet, Jinks," growled Barda. "Do not tempt me. Would you care to explain to 'your majesty' why you were stealing food while the rest of us tighten our belts and eat only our fair share?"

"I am in delicate health," Jinks whimpered. "I need frequent small, tasty morsels to keep body and soul together."

"Indeed?" said Lief coldly.

"I found him guzzling jam," said Barda, looking at Jinks with contempt. "To get himself out of trouble, he accused Glock and Jasmine of being traitors."

"It was very wrong of them to set out for the Shadowlands when your majesty has forbidden it," whined Jinks to Lief. "Why, torn as I was between loyalty to them and loyalty to your majesty, it is no wonder that I became dizzy, and needed a taste of sweetness."

Barda snorted. Lief moved closer to Jinks. "Glock and Jasmine are free to go where they wish," he said.

"We are simply concerned for their safety. Do you know the way they have taken?"

"They did not take the trouble to inform me," Jinks snapped, forgetting that he was supposed to be ill.

His face creased into a furious scowl. "That animal Glock cares nothing for anyone else's comfort! My fighting spider lost to his in our last contest, and is mad for revenge. She kept me awake all night, beating at her cage. That is why I needed — "

"Jinks!" Lief began in exasperation. But Barda's voice, tight with excitement, drowned him out.

"Glock took his spider with him, then?" he snapped.

"Yes," said Jinks sullenly. "And what if he is away for weeks? Or never returns at all? What am I — ?"

He squeaked as Barda began to haul him towards the door. "Where are we going?" he cried in panic. "Not the dungeons, surely? It was just a few spoonfuls of jam! Your majesty! Stop him! Have mercy!"

"Be silent!" growled Barda. "I am not taking you to the dungeons, you fool. You are going to dress and put your spider on its chain. Then you are coming with us."

✳

The journey to the Os-Mine Hills was the strangest Lief had ever made.

Barda held the whining Jinks on the saddle in front of him. Jinks held the end of a long, fine chain. And at the other end of the chain, scurrying in front of the horses, was a huge, spotted brown spider called Fury.

"Fighting spiders cannot stand defeat," Barda

explained to Lief as they rode. "A losing spider will not rest until it has tracked the victor and forced it to fight again. Fury will follow Glock's spider's scent to the end of the earth, given the chance. She is our best hope of finding Glock — and Jasmine — quickly."

It was soon clear that Lief had been right in believing that Jasmine was aiming for the Os-Mine Hills. Without hesitation, Fury was leading them towards those ragged peaks regarded with dread by all in Del.

She moved so fast that the horses, picking their way over the rough ground, could hardly keep up with her. When she was forced to stop, she fought furiously to continue.

At night she beat ceaselessly against the sides of the cage in which Jinks kept her while he slept. Not that Jinks, or either of his companions, *could* sleep. It was truly astonishing that a single spider, however large, could make such a din.

The second day brought them to the first low, rocky ridges of the Os-Mine Hills. The way was even more difficult for the horses now, and Fury strained on her chain as the pace of her followers slowed.

"We might do better on foot," said Barda, as his horse stumbled for the third time in an hour.

"No!" Jinks squealed. He squirmed in the saddle, his face a picture of fear. "This is Granous country! Have you not heard the stories?"

"Of course," Barda said grimly. "But so has everyone else. That is why there are no trails through this wilderness. On foot we can at least follow Fury more safely."

Jinks opened his mouth to argue, but his words were never spoken. For abruptly a grey shape streaked from the bushes in front of them, sharp, yellow teeth snapped, and the horses reared, shrieking with pain and fright, tumbling their startled riders to the ground.

✳

As Lief slowly came to his senses, he became aware that he was sitting on the ground, tied to a tree at the edge of a clearing. Something was panting close to his face. Its hot breath was foul.

Lief opened his eyes and saw grinning jaws, grey, matted fur, a wet, snuffling black nose. With sinking heart he realized that this must be a Granous. And there were more of them — several more, by the sound of the other mutterings and gigglings in the background.

The creature which had filled his vision moved back and squatted on the ground. Now Lief could see its companions — four of them. All had the same evil grins on their faces. Every now and then, one of them would snap its yellow teeth unpleasantly.

Lief struggled to free himself, but at once realized that it was impossible. His ankles were tied to pegs that had been driven into the ground. His wrists were lashed to heavy logs of wood that lay on either side of him. His sword was still at his belt, but he could not reach it.

Turning his head, he saw that Barda and Jinks were tied exactly as he was. Barda was still shouting furiously. Jinks' jaw was gaping, his eyes mad with fear, the remains of Fury's chain dangling from his wrist.

Fury's chain must have broken when Jinks fell, thought Lief. She will catch up to Jasmine and Glock without us. Perhaps she already has. Again he vainly struggled against his bonds. They were only vines, but were as strong as the heaviest rope.

"Free us, Granous, or it will be the worse for you!" roared Barda.

Their captors laughed uproariously. " 'It will be the worse for you!' " mimicked one. "Oh, I am so afraid!"

"This is Lief, king of Deltora!" Barda growled, jerking his head at Lief. "You dare not harm him!"

"We care nothing for kings," sneered the first Granous, who seemed to be the leader. "The dragons have gone. These are *our* hills now."

It grinned at Lief, and bowed mockingly. "But if you are a king, *you* can be the one to play the Twenty Questions game with us. We have never matched wits with a king before."

Its shaggy companions grinned, snuffled, and snapped their jaws. A chill ran down Lief's spine.

The first Granous moved closer, rubbing its hands together. Tufts of grey fur covered the backs of the hands. The fingers were thin as wires, tipped by nails that were long, yellow, and rimmed with grime.

Lief stared in fascinated horror. His own fingers tingled at the thought of those hands grasping his, the sharp teeth moving closer . . .

"Rules are simple, king," said the Granous, grinning horribly. "We ask question, you answer. If answer is wrong, you pay the price. One finger from you, and one from each of your friends. Yes?"

Jinks began to wail piteously.

Fighting for calm, Lief concentrated on the birds chattering in the trees that surrounded the clearing. No doubt they were Os-Mine vine weaver birds, of which he had learned as a child. Their famous net-like nests strung many of the treetops.

He breathed deeply, feeling Barda's eyes upon him. He knew that Barda was hoping against hope that the gems of the Belt of Deltora would help them now. The topaz that sharpened the mind. The amethyst that calmed. The diamond that gave strength . . .

He swallowed. "What if I will not play?" he asked.

The Granous shrugged. "If you do not answer in the time it takes to count twenty, you lose. And you each give a finger. Then we ask another question. And so on. You see?"

Lief saw only too well.

"And if I answer correctly?" he asked.

"Then no finger is taken," said the Granous. "And we ask another question. At the end of twenty questions, you are all free to leave us." Its face split into another hideous grin. "If you can," it added. "For when the fingers are finished, we begin on the toes."

Jinks' wails grew louder.

11 - A Friend in Need

The head Granous placed a small wooden board on Lief's lap. The board was very old, and beautifully crafted. Many squares of wood, each one bearing a painted letter, had been arranged upon it in rows.

O	A	L	J	G	E	T	I	N	B
V	T	E	W	N	R	P	O	J	E
P	U	N	F	I	S	A	Z	E	N
I	B	A	S	E	N	N	D	T	T
Q	U	I	P	V	A	T	S	E	O

"Where did you get this?" Lief exclaimed.

"We have had many visitors before you, king!" the Granous giggled. "Now! Your first question is — what are the only useful things about you? The answer is hidden on the board. It may run up, down, sideways, or all three. Go!"

At once, the other Granous began to clap and chant. "Twenty. Nineteen. Eighteen . . ."

Lief stared at the board. The letters seemed to swim before his eyes. He blinked, trying to clear his head, searching desperately for a starting point.

Words seemed to jump out at him. GET. TIN. BENT. BASE. PAN. But they led nowhere.

Up, down, sideways, or all three . . .

". . . Fourteen. Thirteen. Twelve . . ." The counting was growing louder.

Lief glanced desperately at Barda. Barda, squinting at the board, trying to make the letters out at a distance, shook his head. Beyond him, Jinks, his face fixed in concentration and shiny with sweat, was staring straight ahead. But then Lief saw that one of the acrobat's hands, narrowed to a claw, was moving — twisting rapidly.

Jinks was trying one of his old tricks. And this time it was not for the entertainment of others or for a bet, but to save his life. He was trying to slip out of his bonds while the Granous were not watching him. Lief looked quickly back at the board, his heart thumping.

The Granous leader pretended to smother a yawn, tapping its gaping mouth with its hand. The wicked teeth were razor sharp. Sharp enough to shear through flesh and snap through bone.

The only useful things about you . . .

An idea flashed into Lief's mind. Feverishly he searched the board.

"Six. Five. Four . . ."

And suddenly, there was the answer, coiled within the mass of letters, crooked as a snake.

"Ten fingers and ten toes!" Lief shouted.

The chanting stopped, dissolving into a chorus of disappointed groans.

Lief risked another glance at Jinks. The little man had managed to free his hand, and was cautiously feeling for the dagger at his belt.

"No doubt you think you are very clever, king," said the first Granous sulkily. "We will see. Here is your second question. Listen carefully."

It folded its hands over its belly, and recited:

A king dined with his sister,
His friend and his friend's wife.
All of them were greedy beasts
Who loved food more than life.
At last three pies alone remained.
There wasn't any knife.
How did they all have equal shares,
And save themselves from strife?

The chorus of counting began again. Lief tried to forget about Jinks and concentrate on the rhyme.

Three pies. No knife. Equal shares for four people. It sounded impossible! But he knew that such apparently impossible puzzles always contained a simple trick.

The chanting of the Granous pounded on.

". . . TWELVE. ELEVEN. TEN . . ."

"Lief!" Barda whispered urgently. "Perhaps one of the four was killed by the others. The verse says they loved food more than life."

Lief shook his head. "It says they *all* had equal shares," he whispered back. "All of them. The king, his sister, his friend, and . . ."

A thought stirred in the back of his mind.

". . . FIVE! FOUR! . . ."

Barda cursed under his breath.

"THREE! TWO! . . ."

"The king's sister was married to his friend!" Lief cried. "*That* is how the pies were equally divided. There were only three people at dinner all the time!"

This time the counting broke off in howls of frustration. The head Granous scowled as the others began shouting at him, criticizing his choice of questions.

Lief slumped back, pretending relief, and slid his half-closed eyes in the direction of Jinks' tree.

The acrobat had gone! The vines with which he had been bound were lying loose on the ground. He must be even now creeping through the bushes behind Lief and Barda, dagger at the ready to cut their bonds.

Hurry, Jinks! thought Lief. The Granous were still arguing, paying no attention to the prisoners. Jinks would never have a better chance than this.

Barda drew a sharp, hissing breath. His eyes were fixed on a rocky hill that could just be seen over the trees on the other side of the clearing. Lief followed his gaze.

A small figure was scrambling up the hill. Jinks!

Far from remaining to save his companions, Jinks was running away as fast as he could.

One of the Granous suddenly screeched and pointed. "Prisoner escaped!" it howled. Instantly the whole group plunged off into the bushes, following the acrobat's scent.

"I hope they catch him, the vile little worm!" muttered Barda, struggling violently against the vines that bound him. "How could he leave us here?"

A vine weaver bird flew down from the tree above Barda and perched on the log to which his right hand was tied. It put its head on one side, and regarded him with a sharp black eye.

It nodded as if satisfied. Then it hopped onto his wrist and began pecking at the knotted vine.

"Lief!" Barda whispered in astonishment. "Look!"

The knots were loosening! The bird's long, expert beak was doing what all Barda's strength could not.

In moments, his right hand was free. The bird began working on the knots that bound him to the tree while he sliced through his other bonds with his sword.

He scrambled stiffly to his feet, and staggered over to cut Lief loose. Then, with the vine weaver swooping ahead of them, they both stumbled out of the clearing and into the undergrowth.

The bird darted on, plainly expecting them to follow. Even when the ground began to climb steeply it did not slow, whistling impatiently whenever they paused for breath.

At last they reached the top of the hill and slumped to the ground, panting. The air was filled with bird calls, and when Lief raised his head he saw why.

Not far below them was a thick mass of treetops, ringed by the peaks of other grey hills. Birds in their thousands were busily weaving their nets or feeding on the yellow berries that covered the trees.

Lief and Barda's guide darted around their heads, calling urgently.

It is foolish to think that the bird is leading us to Jasmine, Lief told himself as they followed it down to ground level. Jasmine is searching for a valley, not a high-ground forest.

But hope still flickered as he followed Barda into the trees, his feet sinking deep into the thick carpet of rotting leaves that covered the forest floor.

Then he saw, just ahead, dozens of birds swooping around a small bush which was thrashing violently from side to side for no apparent reason. The vine weaver sped toward the place.

And there, her chain caught around the bush, was Fury.

She was living up to her name — twisting and lunging, her huge fangs snapping. Her trailing chain had become tangled around the bush, and was holding her fast.

Lief swallowed his disappointment. The vine weaver, it seemed, thought one good turn deserved another. It had freed them. Now it wanted them to remove this unwelcome visitor from its forest.

In moments Barda had untangled the chain. The instant Fury felt it loosening she made a wild dash foward, almost jerking him off his feet. Lief felt hope flare all over again.

"She is still following a scent!" he shouted over the excited shrilling of the birds. "Glock's spider must have passed this way!"

With a call of thanks to their relieved vine weaver guide, they plunged after Fury into the trees.

As they moved deeper into the forest it grew darker and more silent. The only living creatures to be seen were fat, gold-colored moths that blundered about in the dimness like stray scraps of sunlight.

For a long time, Fury did not pause. Then, abruptly, she stopped. She rose up on her back legs, her fangs clicking together, her front legs frozen in the air.

"What is she doing?" Lief whispered.

He and Barda moved cautiously forward. Several of the big yellow moths were fluttering close to the ground just beyond where Fury was poised.

"She must be hungry," said Barda.

Fury lowered her front legs once more and began creeping toward the moths. She had almost reached them when Lief noticed something odd.

There were more moths than before. Yet he had not seen any new ones fly down to join the crowd.

Then he realized what was happening. The moths were fluttering around a hole in the ground. And more moths were rising out of the hole every moment.

"They must lay their eggs down there," murmured Barda. He shouted in annoyance as Fury suddenly jumped forward and scuttled into the hole, disappearing deep inside.

The moths scattered, bumbling out of the way. Barda tugged vainly at the spider's chain, cursing it and ordering it to come back. But Lief's heart was thumping as he threw himself to the ground, scraped the disguising piles of leaves away from the sides of the hole, and peered into its depths.

When he looked up his eyes were shining.

"Barda!" he exclaimed. "Barda — you are not going to believe this!"

And without another word, he swung his legs into the hole and followed Fury.

12 - Mysteries

Barda bent over the hole, roaring furiously. But Lief, rapidly disappearing into the gloom, merely shouted to him to follow. Fury plainly had no intention of returning to ground level either. The chain around Barda's wrist was pulling violently.

There was only one thing to do. Barda scrambled into the hole himself, cursing under his breath. What was the boy doing? What had he seen in this foul burrow?

Dirt and rotted leaves showered his face as he lowered himself through the earth, clinging to the tree roots that netted the sides of the hole. His feet scrabbled for footholds. His hands ached. When he looked up, he could see only a faint glimmer of light.

"Take care!" Lief's muffled voice floated upwards.

"You are a fine one to speak of taking care!" Barda shouted back.

A moment later, his feet broke into open space.

He kicked out wildly, searching for a foothold. Something grabbed his ankles, and he yelled.

"I have you!" Lief called. "Wait!"

With relief, Barda felt his feet guided to a firm surface. Slowly he lowered himself out of the tunnel.

The first thing he saw was Lief's face, wild with excitement and streaked with dirt. Then he moved his eyes downward. And stared.

He was looking down at a vast space filled with thousands of huge grey poles that stretched from floor to ceiling. A gurgling stream lined with pale ferns wound its way through the poles, disappearing into the dimness.

Then he realized what he was seeing, and his jaw dropped.

"Why, they are giant trees!" he breathed. "This is a forest! A forest beneath a forest! How could this be?"

"I think the vine weaver birds must have caused it," said Lief, touching the matted web of branches and vines above his head. "Once they lived in the tops of these trees, weaving their nests and eating berries. Over time, the forest canopy became so thick and tangled that it was almost solid. The berries the birds dropped did not fall to the ground, but were caught in old nests and the forks of branches."

"So the seeds took root, watered by the rain, and young trees grew on top of the old," said Barda. "And after hundreds of years . . ."

"After hundreds of years," Lief finished for him,

"there was no sign of the old forest left. No sign of the valley in which it grew. Only the trees, the moths, and the birds above knew the secret."

Barda became aware that Fury was tugging once more on her chain. She had moved down the tree as far as she could, and was now rearing and scrabbling in frustration because she could go no further.

"We still do not know if Jasmine and Glock are here, or just Glock's spider," he said.

Lief grinned. "What trees and birds know, Jasmine soon knows also," he said. "She and Glock have found this place, there is no doubt. Look!"

He pointed. And there, tied around the trunk of the tree and dangling almost to the ground, was a rope.

❋

It did not take long for Lief and Barda to reach the ground using the rope, but even this small delay drove Fury to distraction. The moment she was free to do so, she set off at a great pace along the stream.

This time, Lief and Barda hardly needed her to show them the way to go. The ground was almost covered by fragile white fungus and patches of brittle fern. The tracks of two people were plainly visible — one set of heavy, large prints, one set of lighter, smaller ones.

The air was heavy with the smell of earth and mold. There was no sound but the gurgling of the stream. The trees rose silent and ghostly around them, their trunks blotched with tongues of yellow fungus from which hung squirming bundles of fat caterpillars. Clearly the moths from the forest above used the hidden valley as a safe nesting place.

Now and then Lief or Barda called Jasmine's name, but no answering cry reached their ears. Slowly a feeling of dread began to grow in Lief. Were they too late? Words from *The Girl with the Golden Hair* echoed in his mind.

She ran deep into the dragon's cave and down, down under the earth, into the caverns where the goblins dwell . . .

"Dragons have been extinct in Deltora for hundreds of years," said Barda, as if reading his mind. "If there is a dragon's lair in this valley, it is empty. The forest would never have been covered over if this was not so. The dragons would have kept the canopy open, by flying out to hunt every day."

"And the goblins?" muttered Lief. "Are they extinct also?"

"If they ever existed," said Barda. "My mother used to tell a story of seven goblins who prowled the countryside north of Del. But the tale always began, 'Once upon a time,' as fairy stories do."

"I have heard Glock claim that one of his ancestors fought and killed a goblin," said Lief.

Barda snorted. "I have heard Glock claim many things," he said.

They rounded a bend in the stream and saw ahead of them a rocky cliff, rising behind the trees like a wall. The stream ended in a small, deep pool at its foot.

"We have reached the forest's edge," whispered Barda. "This must be the base of one of the hills we saw when we looked down from the other side."

Lief nodded, his skin prickling as he saw that the footprint trail led away from the stream, and into a vast, dark cave in the cliff.

Fury dashed ahead of them as they crept towards the cave's entrance. It was heavily fringed with ferns, and somehow this made it look even more like a gaping, toothless mouth. Inside, it was black as night and silent as the grave.

"Lief," Barda breathed. "The ruby . . ."

Reluctantly Lief pulled his cloak aside to reveal the jeweled belt. The rich red of the ruby seemed only a little dimmer.

"If there is danger, it is slight," Barda said, visibly relaxing.

Lief wet his lips. "I think we should still take care," he said slowly. "The belt may not be as powerful here as it is on the surface. And look at Fury."

Barda glanced downward. The huge spider was standing motionless and wary at his feet.

They lit a torch. Then, shoulder to shoulder, swords drawn, they moved into the cave.

The torch lit the ground immediately ahead, but thick darkness surrounded its warm, flickering glow. It was as though they were floating through a black sea in a small bubble of light.

Lief felt as though he were moving in a dream. The air was heavy and warm. And slowly, slowly, a strange, musky smell was growing in strength.

"There is something alive in here," he breathed.

As he spoke, the torchlight flickered on something ahead. Something huge.

Scales gleamed golden amid dancing shadows. Teeth and claws glimmered white. A tail lay coiled, thick with spines as sharp as needles. Folded leathery wings netted with spiderwebs trailed in the dust.

Dragon!

A deep, ancient dread welled up in Lief, turning his legs to jelly. He heard Barda draw a quick breath.

The dragon did not stir. All that moved was the torchlight flickering over its huge form.

"Its eyes are shut. It is asleep — or dead," Barda hissed.

"Not dead, I think," said Lief, struggling to calm himself. "But not asleep either, or it would have sensed us and woken. This is some sort of enchantment."

Fury began to creep to the left. As Lief and Barda went after her, the torchlight began to flicker on the cave's rocky wall. Soon they saw that there was a narrow space between the wall and the dragon's head.

This then, was to be their path. Already Fury was crawling doggedly through the gap. Taking a deep breath, Barda moved after her, looking straight ahead.

Lief began to follow. He knew that he, too, should keep his eyes to the front, but he could not. He turned and gazed, fascinated, at the terrible head, so near that he had only to stretch out his hand to touch it. And as he stared, the dragon's great, golden eye opened.

Lief froze. His mind went blank. There was no fear, no hope, no thought. There was only the dragon's eye, and his own face mirrored there — pale, weak, and small, floating in a cold, flat sea that was gold as the topaz in the Belt of Deltora, deep with ancient memory.

For a long moment the eye held him. Then, slowly, it closed once more.

Released, almost sick with shock, Lief lurched on to where Barda was waiting for him.

"Why did you stop?" Barda whispered. "Are you mad, Lief, that you would risk — ?"

Lief brushed past blindly. Blackness yawned ahead, but that was better than what lay behind him. Cool air fanned his face, chilling the sweat on his brow. All he could think of was to get away — hide himself.

He heard Barda hurrying after him, felt Barda trying to hold him back. There was another gust of cold air. The torch flared and went out.

Lief stumbled, righted himself, and stepped forward into — thin air. There was a split second of disbelief. And then he was falling, dragging Barda with him, plunging down, down into darkness.

13 ~ Gold and Scarlet

Deep, chill water. Holding him down. Up! Up! Breathe! His lungs almost bursting, Lief fought his way to the surface. He floundered there, taking great gulps of air, looking blindly around him through a blur of water.

"Barda!" he shouted desperately.

Barda . . . Barda . . . Barda . . . Echoes answered him — a thousand echoes, calling and whispering from every direction.

There was a sudden splashing nearby. Dizzy with relief, Lief heard Barda gasping and coughing.

"Barda! I am here!" he called, struggling towards the sound.

Here . . . here . . . here . . .

As his eyes began to clear, Lief saw the shape of Barda's head, dark against water that moved like pale, liquid gold. He saw the soft glow of gold all around him, gold shining from the walls of a vast cavern that seemed to have no beginning and no end.

Gold as the dragon's eye, as the dragon's scales. Gold as the great topaz.

This was the cavern through which Alyss fled in ages past. This was the place Jasmine had sought. The beginning of the underground way to the Shadowlands.

But the old tale had not mentioned one important detail. The cavern was flooded. And . . . Lief's stomach turned over.

And Jasmine could not swim.

Through a haze of misery he saw Barda's arm reach out and catch hold of something that was bobbing in the water beside him. For a terrifying moment Lief thought that it was a body. Then he realized that it was only a log of wood.

He looked up. The shimmering roof of the cavern curved high above him like a golden sky. The hole through which he and Barda had fallen was just a small, blurred patch of darkness. He could barely see it. There was no way he and Barda could reach it.

Barda paddled over to him, half leaning on the log. "This will keep us afloat for a while at least," he panted. "Until we find another way out. Or . . ."

Or what? Lief thought, as his companion's voice faltered. Until finally the wood grows waterlogged, and sinks? Until we grow too exhausted to hold on to it any longer?

"The water may be more shallow further on," he said huskily. "Let us try."

As he spoke, he saw movement out of the corner of his eye. Something small and dark was wriggling towards them through the rippling water. Lief could hardly believe his eyes when he recognized the tangle of flailing legs and angry red stare for what they were.

"Fury!" he exclaimed, as the spider reached the log.

Fury climbed laboriously from the water, still trailing a short length of chain. She reached the top of the log and crouched there glowering, the picture of rage.

Barda shook his head in disbelief. "I thought that at least I was rid of you, spider," he growled.

All the same, Fury's appearance had cheered both of them. Supporting themselves on the log, they began to paddle slowly forward.

At first they spoke to one another, marveling at the mysterious beauty of the place, even joking about Fury's continued sulking. But as the hours passed the talk grew less, and at last they were silent.

It was the silence of exhaustion, cold, and the gradual disappearance of hope. Lief's legs were numb. He no longer had the strength to paddle. He put his head down on the log, feeling its strange, spongy softness under his cheek.

"Lief, hold on! You must not die . . ."

Barda's voice seemed very far away. Lief could not answer. His mind was drifting, floating. As he was drifting on this shining water. As his reflection had floated on the surface of the dragon's eye . . .

✳

Lief swam slowly up from the depths of a fainting sleep with no idea of how much time had passed. He opened his eyes. And blinked.

The golden light had changed to scarlet. The very air seemed stained with red. He could hear the splashing of water, and had the sense of rapid movement.

Slowly it came to him that he was in the bottom of a boat. Barda was lying beside him. And sitting in the center of the boat, dipping paddles into the water in fast and perfect time, were two strange-looking creatures.

Their bodies were small, but human. Probably, when they stood up, they would be about as tall as gnomes, though they were far less stockily built. But they seemed totally hairless, and their heads and faces were dog-like, with long muzzles and large pointed ears.

At first Lief thought they were dressed in red, and that their skin was red, too. Then he realized that this was an illusion caused by the scarlet glow. In fact, the creatures' skin was deathly pale, with the softness common to crawling things that live beneath the earth.

Lief shuddered. These must be goblins, the ugly, spiteful creatures of old tales, though they did not look as he had imagined.

Unwilling to reveal that he had woken, he watched through half-closed eyelids as the goblins paddled silently, their pale eyes staring straight ahead.

It occurred to him that they were hurrying. There was urgency in their movements, in their set faces. It must have taken some time for them to load

Lief and Barda into their boat. Now, it seemed, they were late, or in some kind of danger.

It was always said that goblins were creatures of evil will. Yet this pair had saved him and Barda from drowning, even though they could ill afford the delay.

Perhaps the goblins' evil reputation was false. Perhaps the few Deltorans who had seen goblins in past ages had feared them simply because of their strange appearance.

But as the thought came to him, Lief felt for his sword. It was missing. He turned his head and saw that Barda's sword, too, was gone. Squinting through the soft red light, he caught the glimmer of metal at the goblins' feet.

He and Barda had been disarmed. Was this just caution on the goblins' part? Or did it mean something more sinister?

A low, rasping sound, like rock grating on rock, echoed through the cavern. The goblins both paused, their ears quivering, their faces alert.

One murmured to the other. Then they both began paddling even faster. The rippling of the water against the boat grew louder as the craft picked up speed.

The rasping sound came again, there was a distant thundering crash and suddenly, shockingly, the nose of the boat rose sharply then dipped again. Lief gasped as cold water slopped over the sides and poured over him. Barda stirred and groaned.

The goblins glanced at them but did not stop paddling for a second. The boat rose and fell sickeningly once more. And now Lief could see great waves of red water heaving around them, clearly visible over the sides of the boat and becoming larger every moment.

It was as though they were caught in a storm, yet there was no wind. There was only that menacing rasping noise and the dull thundering that was growing louder, and which Lief now recognized as the sound of waves crashing on land.

Land!

He tried to sit up, but fell back again immediately as the boat rose over yet another wave, and slid down the other side. Wallowing in cold, foaming water he struggled to get up again.

"Be still!" cried one of the goblins angrily.

He and his companion were almost knee-deep in swirling water, but still they were paddling with the same fierce concentration as before. Huge red waves were towering over the boat on all sides now, but the goblins looked only ahead, their long noses twitching, their pale eyes staring shortsightedly.

And then, quite suddenly, came a sound and a feeling that made Lief shout with relief. The bottom of the boat was scraping on land.

The goblins threw down their paddles, leaped into the water, and began dragging the boat out of the waves, calling for help.

Bruised, shaken, and shivering, Lief and Barda crawled to their knees. The goblins were pulling the boat onto muddy land that rose out of the swirling water. Other boats were nearby, tied to what at first seemed strangely shaped trees, but which Lief soon realized were huge, branching scarlet fungus.

Dazed, Lief looked around him, trying to take in what he was seeing. Hills of red and brown fungus trees, a few nearest the water broken or uprooted by the force of the waves. Orderly fields where rows of some sort of crop showed above streaming water. And beyond the mud of the shore, a village. Waves had crashed over the low wall that surrounded it, and the streets were flooded.

Several goblins were running from the village, crying out in relief and welcome. Lief and Barda's rescuers, whose names seemed to be Clef and Azan, had plainly been anxiously awaited.

But at the sight of Lief and Barda, there was even greater rejoicing, and eager hands helped them out of the boat.

"Get them to safety, quickly," said Azan, bending to retrieve the swords from behind the boat's seat.

Jostled in the center of the group, Lief and Barda were hurried towards the village. As they reached the wall the rasping sound came again, this time rising to a high, harsh note that was painful to the ears.

To Lief's surprise, the goblins slowed, and their tense faces relaxed a little. After a moment, he realized that waves were no longer crashing against the walls. The crisis, it seemed, was over. At least for the moment.

They entered the village and began splashing through empty, flooded streets lined with dwellings.

The houses were all dark red or brown. Many had been damaged by the storm. In other cases, doors had simply burst open, allowing water to stream into the rooms beyond. Brightly painted bowls and pots, small pieces of furniture, even bedding and clothes, drifted in the flood.

Clef peered angrily from side to side as they hurried though street after street. "This is worse than ever I have seen it!" he growled at last. "Why has Worron not proceeded with The Giving?"

"There has not been time," the goblin beside him said nervously. "The ceremony of preparation had to be begun again for the new Gift, and it is not yet completed."

"What does that matter?" called Azan from behind. "That last call was the final warning. Are ceremonies more important than our lives?"

Barda gave a muffled exclamation. Lief glanced at him quickly.

But Barda had not been listening. He was looking over the goblins' heads, towards an open space at the end of the village where a crowd had gathered.

In the center of the space, clearly visible as the crowd surged forward to greet the newcomers, was a tall cage. It was backed by a high wall and surrounded by a complicated pattern of red stones.

And standing inside the cage, their hands bound behind their backs, were Glock and Jasmine.

14 - The Giving

With a roar, Barda felled the goblins closest to him and swung around, intent on pushing his way towards Azan and the swords. Lief sprang to help him. But before he had taken two steps, there was a brilliant flash and he was frozen to the spot.

At the same moment, the cavern was plunged into darkness. Trembling and blind, his arms and legs refusing to obey his will, Lief stood helpless while confusion reigned around him. The air was filled with cries and moans.

Slowly, very slowly, a little light returned — the faintest red glow, like the promise of sunrise.

Lief began to make out shapes and movement. Barda was standing rigidly nearby, as motionless as Lief was himself. The goblins who had been knocked to the ground were struggling to their feet, with others helping them.

"Bind the creatures, and make haste!" ordered a

new voice. "I cannot hold them for long and keep the light also."

With dismay, Lief felt his arms pulled behind his back and his wrists tied together. His ankles, too, were tied, though not so tightly that he could not walk. He saw that Barda was receiving the same treatment.

"Why were they not bound before, Clef?" the new voice demanded irritably. "Surely you realized that the Longhairs would fight when they saw the Gift?"

"How could they see them from such a distance?" Clef sneered. "Do they have a magic eye?"

"If you had listened when the old tales were told, boy, you would know that Longhairs have unnaturally far sight," snapped the other. "You have endangered us all by your carelessness."

"And you, Worron, have endangered us all by your delay!" Clef retorted furiously. "The Giving should have been accomplished long ago. Azan and I were fighting for our lives on the sea while you dallied here, daring the anger of The Fear and allowing the village to be — "

"Do not try to turn attention from your own fault!" cried the goblin called Worron. "And if you do not respect me, Clef, you can at least respect my office and call me by my proper title."

Clef kept sullen silence, but through the dimness Lief saw his lips draw away from his teeth in a snarl.

Worron waited for a moment, then raised his voice again. "I will now release the Longhairs so that we can have more light," he said. "Hold them firmly."

The cavern slowly brightened and Lief felt his arms and legs tingling as movement returned to them. Someone seized his shoulders from behind, and he was turned around. Barda was pushed into place beside him.

Standing before them was a wrinkled goblin wearing a long scarlet robe and a tall, stiff head covering studded with red stones. This, it seemed, was Worron.

Worron leaned forward to peer at the prisoners then abruptly drew back, shuddering slightly and wrinkling his nose. Plainly he found Lief and Barda extremely ugly to look upon, and did not like their smell either.

"Bring them to the Giving Bay," he said. "The ceremony must continue at once. The Fear is growing impatient."

With a swish of his robes, he turned and began hobbling back towards the open space.

Pushed from behind, their arms gripped tightly, Lief and Barda shuffled after him.

Dwarfed by the hulking figure of Glock standing behind her, Jasmine pressed her face against the bars of the cage. Lief's heart lurched.

Kree was sitting on Jasmine's shoulder, and Filli was peeping from her collar. Jasmine's hair was damp and tangled. She looked just as she had looked when Lief first saw her in the Forests of Silence.

But then she had been free. It was agony to see her imprisoned.

Jasmine's eyes were wild as they reached the cage.

Clearly she could hardly believe what she was seeing.

"Lief! Barda! What are you doing here?" she burst out. "How — ?"

"Silence!" bellowed Worron. He opened the cage door and beckoned impatiently for Lief and Barda to be pushed inside.

"What are you doing?" shouted Clef angrily, as the order was obeyed. "Surely you do not intend to use all the Longhairs in the one Giving?"

"Indeed I do," said Worron. He looked down, clicked his tongue in annoyance and bent down to replace some of the red stones which had been pushed out of place.

"But that is madness!" growled Azan, pushing his way through the crowd to stand by Clef's side. "The Fear demands only one Gift each year. If we keep three of these Longhairs for the future, our people will not have to draw lots for three more Givings!"

Many in the crowd nodded and murmured agreement.

Worron shook his head disdainfully. "We cannot keep Longhairs in safety. They are as vicious as they are ugly. Besides — if The Fear is well pleased, it may not demand another Giving for a long time."

"It is far more likely that it will demand four Gifts instead of one in the future!" cried Clef.

Rumblings of discontent began as Worron continued to tidy the stones, not bothering to reply.

"What are they talking about?" whispered Lief. "What is The Fear?"

"It is death," growled Glock.

Wordlessly Jasmine turned and nodded towards a panel in the wall that loomed behind the cage. Lief's stomach lurched as he saw what was carved there.

It was a picture of a terrible sea-beast with ten writhing tentacles. The beast had a screaming goblin in its grasp. It was tearing him apart.

"The Fear is in a cavern called The Glimmer not far from here," Jasmine murmured. "Every year it demands a living sacrifice. If the people delay, it beats the water and creates great waves that flood the island and destroy the village. They do not dare to defy it."

Lief turned and stared in horror at the murmuring crowd gathered outside the cage. He saw Worron straighten and hold up his hands, then press them to his mouth. Silence fell instantly.

Slowly moving his hands forward, the fingertips touching, Worron began a curious, high, wordless singing. Slowly the other goblins joined in. The sound rose and swelled, strangely powerful and thrilling.

"The oldest ones among them draw lots, to see who will be The Gift," muttered Glock. "This year it was to be that old crone there."

He pointed at a bowed and wrinkled goblin who was clutching Clef's arm, urging him to join the singing. Clef frowned and moved away from her, towards the cage. Shaking her head at him, she followed.

"Her name is Nols. They were preparing her for the Giving when Glock and I arrived here," Jasmine added in a flat voice. "One of their fishing boats had plucked us, half drowned, from the water. If it had not been for Glock risking his own life by holding me up, I would have perished long before."

Glock snorted. "Risking my life?" he jeered. "Why, I could have held twenty of you, weakling! My talisman protects me from drowning."

"Indeed!" said Jasmine dryly. "Will it protect you from The Fear also?"

Glock ran his tongue over his lips and fell silent.

"They cheered when they saw us," Jasmine went on, looking out at the crowd. "We thought we were welcome. But they were only rejoicing because Nols is much loved, and they had found strangers to take her place."

She groaned. "We tried to scare them into freeing us by saying we were not alone. We had no idea it was *true*! Oh, why did you follow us?"

"We did not want to, but what else could we do?" said Lief sharply, to hide the pain in his heart. "You were rushing headlong into danger — and dragging Glock with you!"

"Glock forced me to bring him!" Jasmine snapped. "He threatened to have me stopped if I did not."

"I thought you knew what you were doing," snarled Glock. "That was my mistake. I fell into water. My fighting spider, which cost five gold pieces, escaped. And now I am about to be sacrificed to a monster."

"Why did you take this risk, Jasmine?" Lief sighed. "*The Girl with the Golden Hair* told of goblins in the underground, and made clear they were to be feared."

Jasmine shook her head stubbornly. "A man called Doran the Dragonlover came here. He visited at least twice, and for him it was a place of peace and beauty."

"How can you know this?" Lief demanded.

"I read it in the *Annals*," Jasmine said. "After his first visit, Doran wrote a verse about these people. After the second, he changed the verse, to disguise the meaning of what he had written."

"Why?" asked Barda bluntly.

"Don't you see?" Jasmine exclaimed. "Doran wanted the secret kept. He thought *we* were a threat to the goblins, not the other way around."

"Then Doran was a fool," growled Barda.

"You must not say that!"

The companions saw the old woman, Nols, glaring at them through the bars of the cage.

"You must not speak ill of Doran in this place," she repeated in a lower voice. "He was a friend to us in ages past. Before The Fear grew."

"Come away, Grandmother," muttered Clef, pulling her back.

"They said an evil thing of Doran," complained Nols. "I could not let it pass."

"Doran is only a character of legend," said Clef impatiently. "It does not matter what they say of him."

"Doran was not a legend!" exclaimed Nols. "Was it not Doran who told us to beware of Longhairs and other creatures from above? Was it not Doran who said that some of them were servants of the Shadow Lord? How else did we know?"

"Doran was real enough. And he was right to warn you," Jasmine burst out urgently. "But we are the Shadow Lord's enemies, not his friends."

The two faces, old and young, turned to look at her in surprise.

"We came here only to find the secret way to the Shadowlands," Jasmine hurried on. "Many of our people — our loved ones — have been taken captive by the Shadow Lord. We must reach them, and save them. We must! Before it is too late." Her voice trembled as she said the last words.

Lief and Barda glanced at her quickly, surprised by the desperation in her voice. Jasmine had always been determined to free the slaves. But this strong feeling seemed far more personal. And why had she said "before it is too late"?

The expression on Nols' wrinkled face had changed from anger to something like pity.

"If that is true, your journey was always in vain," she said, shaking her head sadly. "The Glimmer is the only gateway to the far seas, and it has been sealed by The Fear."

Jasmine bowed her head, biting her lip. As she did so, the singing in the background rose to a climax, then died away.

"Clef! Nols!" Worron called harshly. "Get back! The Giving is about to commence."

15 - The Bargain

Clef took his grandmother's arm and pulled her gently away. At the same moment, the carved panel behind the cage began to slide silently aside.

Through the gap the prisoners could see a narrow band of shore and a sheet of scarlet water. On the other side of the water the cavern ended in a natural wall of high, sheer rock, gleaming red. And in the rock, directly opposite the cage, yawned the entrance to a cave.

Ropes attached to the top of the cage spanned the water and led directly into the cave. Lief saw, to his horror, that several members of the crowd had taken hold of one of the ropes. The cage lurched and began moving towards the water.

"Stop!" Lief shouted. "We can help you! Use us not to feed The Fear, but to destroy it!"

The goblins pulling the rope hesitated.

"Do not listen to the Longhair!" roared Worron. "The ceremony must continue!"

The cage jolted and began to slide again.

"We are warriors!" Lief shouted. "Together we have defeated many monsters — some of them the servants of the Shadow Lord. Free us, return our weapons, and we will rid you of The Fear forever!"

Again the cage stopped moving. The goblins who had been pulling the rope began arguing in low voices.

"I say we let them try!" called Azan from the middle of the crowd. "They are Longhairs — tall and strong and skilled in battle. Their weapons are of steel. If they could destroy The Fear — think what it would mean to us!"

"No!" Worron's face was twisted with anger. "Are you mad? If we free the Longhairs, they will turn on us, and the power is not strong enough to hold them all."

"We will not harm you — we swear it!" called Barda. He pointed to Lief. "This is the king of Deltora. The magic belt he wears is proof of it. Did Doran tell you no tales of its power?"

Many in the crowd pressed forward curiously as Lief pulled aside his cloak to show the belt at his waist. Plainly they had indeed heard of the Belt of Deltora.

Worron's eyes narrowed with suspicion as he, too, peered through the bars of the cage.

"It resembles the belt in the tales," he said slowly. "But I see no magic in it."

"Perhaps your feeble eyes are not worthy, goblin!" roared Glock, ignoring Barda's efforts to quiet him.

Lief's heart sank as he saw Worron's face harden and draw away.

"You see?" Worron cried, turning to face the crowd. "Longhairs lie and cheat as easily as they breathe. Did you hear what that one called me? Does it not remind you that Longhairs killed the traitors who went to seek the sun in ages past, calling them 'goblins' to excuse the slaughter?"

Glock's lip curled. "If you are not goblins, what are you?" he muttered under his breath.

"We are not liars, Worron!" shouted Jasmine, desperate to undo the damage Glock had done. "We will keep our word! We have good reason to do so. We need to pass through The Glimmer. We need to reach the other side. And for that we must face The Fear in any case."

"I believe she is speaking the truth," quavered Nols. As heads turned in her direction, she lifted her chin and continued more loudly. "Whatever you say, Worron, we cannot turn our backs on the chance to rid ourselves of The Fear. Such a chance may never come again."

"And if the Longhairs betray us?" sneered Worron. "If they run, steal boats, and take to the seas? What of The Giving? We have already had the final warning."

Nols looked at him proudly. "I was the chosen Gift before the strangers came here. If they fail us, I will take their place in the cage."

"If Nols is willing to trust them, then so am I!" called a high-pitched voice in the crowd. Many other voices shouted agreement.

But Worron shook his head, frowning. "The Fear cannot be destroyed," he said, folding his hands. "The sacrifice it demands is hard, but suffering is the way of the world. And if The Glimmer is sealed, so much the better. We have no wish to know those who live on the other side."

"Now we come to it!" shouted Clef passionately. "A hundred deaths or one, it is all the same to you, Worron. As long as nothing changes!"

He ran to the cage and began opening the lock.

"Stop!" Worron shouted in rage. He raised his hand. There was a flash, the light dimmed, and Clef was struck motionless.

There was a moment's tense silence. Then Nols walked slowly to her grandson's side.

"Free him, Worron," she said quietly. "Or we will take back the power we gave you."

Worron bared his teeth. "You cannot — "

"We can," said Nols. "We can, and we will."

Struck dumb with fury, Worron's eyes raked the crowd. He saw no sign of support there. Instead he saw anger, determination, and — hope.

Sulkily he raised his hand again. The light returned to normal. Clef stumbled slightly, shook himself, and without a word began fumbling once more with the lock on the door of the cage.

In moments the door was open. One by one Lief, Barda, Jasmine, and Glock hobbled to freedom. They stretched their arms and legs in relief as Clef and Azan cut their bonds. Others in the crowd brought their weapons.

"Now we will see," sneered Worron, standing well back.

"I think I will warm my sword on him before we go," Glock muttered, flexing his cramped hands.

"Save your sword for the beast!" snapped Jasmine. She measured the distance to the cave with her eyes. "How best should we reach it?"

"I have a plan," Lief began. "The cage — "

"I know what you are thinking, and I agree," Barda interrupted. "But you are no part of this, Lief. You must go to high ground and wait."

Lief shook his head. "I cannot do that. I will not." The thought of Marilen waiting anxiously at home flashed into his mind, but he thrust it away.

"Do what Barda says, Lief," said Jasmine. "You have no choice."

"You will go to high ground or be carried there," growled Glock. "You must be protected."

"It is too late for that!" Lief exclaimed. "No one here is safe now. If we fail to kill The Fear, it will destroy the village. And there is no way out of this cavern."

Clef, Nols, and Azan had been watching them anxiously. Now they came closer. "Please delay no further," muttered Clef. "The Fear will any moment grow tired of waiting."

Still the companions hesitated, Lief glaring defiantly at the rest.

Kree screeched and flapped his wings. Jasmine looked up, alert.

"The thing in the cave is stirring," she murmured.

But the goblins knew it already. They were all shuddering and drawing back. Some of the children had begun to cry.

Lief leaped past Barda and swung himself onto the top of the cage. "Make haste!" he shouted.

Seeing that he had taken matters out of their hands, Glock, Jasmine, and Barda clambered after him.

"Take the ropes!" Lief called to Clef and Azan. "Pull us over to the cave!"

As Clef and Azan ran to do his bidding, a harsh, grating call sounded over the water. It was low and full of menace. Foam-flecked waves began to surge from the cave. Water splashed against the wall and flooded through the open panel into the cage and beyond.

"You see?" Worron hissed to Clef. "Your defiance and your grandmother's foolishness will be our death!"

Clef made no reply. Shoulder to shoulder with Azan, he was heaving on the rope. The cage slid down the shore and reached the water. A few in the crowd cheered.

"Our torches are lost, and the cave is dark," Lief called. "Can you light it?"

"Worron can," Clef called back. "If he is willing. He has all our power in his hands." He turned his head to where Worron stood scowling furiously. "Will you light The Glimmer, Worron?" he asked. "If it is what the people want?"

"No, I will not!" Worron shrieked in a frenzy of rage. "How dare you ask it of me? You have chosen to go against my orders. You will all die because of your folly. And I will not lift a hand to help you!"

Another fearsome cry sounded from the cave. The crowd retreated in panic. Even Clef and Azan took a stumbling step backwards, and the rope slackened and sagged.

But Nols stood her ground. "Keep pulling!" she shouted. Clef and Azan gripped the rope and heaved once more. The violently rocking cage with the four companions clinging to its roof was lifted clear of the waves and began moving away from the shore.

Lief looked back. Foam swirled around Nols' ankles as she stared at Worron, her face filled with contempt. Her voice floated clearly across the water.

"Since you were chosen I have followed you loyally, Worron, despite my doubts. But now you show your true colors. You are a tyrant and a coward! You . . ."

"The old crone's tongue is as sharp as yours, weakling," Glock sniggered to Jasmine.

"Hold your own tongue, Glock, or I will tear it out by the roots!" flashed Jasmine. Satisfied at having stirred her to anger, Glock snorted with laughter and was still.

And so it was that Nols' final words came to their ears loud and clear. Words that hit Lief and Barda like thunderbolts.

"I withdraw my trust in you, Worron," Nols cried. "You are not fit to lead the Plumes. You are not fit to be Piper."

16 ~ The Fear

Stunned, Lief stared back at the shore and at the crowd gathered there. Suddenly he was seeing the land for what it was — an island.

"The secret sea!" he breathed. "We found it, and we did not know! And that island, the people — "

"Goblins," growled Glock.

"No!" Lief exclaimed hoarsely. "Pirrans! The descendants of the Pirrans who followed Plume. The owners of the mouthpiece of the Pirran Pipe!"

"I never dreamed the islands could be anywhere but in the open sea," gasped Barda.

"None of us did," said Lief. "Doran disguised his map well, by drawing another, of the western sea, beneath it. Yet, if we had thought carefully about the story, we might have guessed the truth."

"What are you talking about?" Jasmine demanded. "What truth?" But to her annoyance neither Lief nor Barda seemed to hear her.

"The Pirrans had no time to think," Lief murmured. "The Shadow Lord was upon them. They had to hide — disappear from his sight — at once! So they simply commanded the earth to swallow them up. And down below they found another world. A world of which even the Shadow Lord knew nothing."

Clinging one-handed to the cage, he pulled out his copy of the map and shook it open.

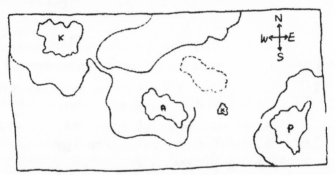

"The lines are not tide-lines," he said slowly. "They are cavern walls!"

"And if that is so, we are — here." Barda pointed midway between Plume Island and a gap in the line that ran around it. "And that gap is The Glimmer. Though why it has that name I do not know, for it is as black as night."

Lief stuffed the map back into his pocket. "If we succeed in this, one piece of the Pirran Pipe will be ours! The Plumes will not be able to refuse us. And the way will be open for the journey to the other islands."

"I have no idea what you are talking about," said

Jasmine sharply. "But I *do* know that if we do *not* succeed in this, we will all be dead."

She turned to face the cave that yawned before them. The water had stilled, and now lapped peacefully against the rock wall.

"The Fear has heard or felt the approach of the cage," she said. "It is quietly waiting for its Gift."

"Then it is about to get a shock," said Glock, grinning savagely and drawing his heavy sword.

"It could be *we* who are shocked," said Jasmine.

Glock puffed out his chest. "This beast may terrify those puny goblins, but it will be no match for a Jalis warrior. I will slay it single-handed."

"We had better make a plan, just in case you need help," said Jasmine dryly. "Barda?"

"The Fear expects The Gift to be caged, so will approach without fear," said Barda. "We can take it by surprise. Glock, Lief, and I have swords, so we will see to the tentacles. While the beast is distracted, you, Jasmine, will attack its body from behind. Agreed?"

Lief and Jasmine glanced at each other and nodded. Glock snorted impatiently.

"The Fear lives underground, so no doubt it hunts by touch, hearing, or even smell, rather than by sight," said Jasmine. "But we need to see. We need light."

Lief glanced over his shoulder to the shore. Nols and Worron were still in argument. The crowd was hesitating, looking nervously towards the cave.

"If Nols fails to convince the people to join her, there

will be no light," he said. "We cannot depend upon it."

The cave gaped before them now. As the cage lurched into its mouth, Lief felt a draught on his face — a chill, sour breath that raised the hairs on the back of his neck.

In moments, the light from outside was just a dull glow. Then there was no light at all. The cage came to rest, settling with a creak into thick, sour-smelling blackness. Shallow water lapped gently against its base.

It was very still, very quiet, very dark. And in the darkness, something stirred.

"Ready," whispered Barda.

Lief held his breath. His sword hand was slippery with sweat.

There was a slithering sound, like the sound of a great snake coiling over rock. And a delicate rippling, like a giant eel writhing through water.

But the sounds seemed to be coming from all around them. They were echoing from the cavern walls and roof, echoing from every direction, so it was impossible to tell where they had begun. The darkness was alive with slithering and splashing.

The companions turned one way, then the other, jostling each other in their confusion.

"Where *is* the thing?" hissed Glock. "Curse this dark!"

The cage jolted as something prodded the bars on one side.

"There!" Barda whispered. But almost immediately there was a second jolt, this time from the other side.

"It moves swiftly," Glock growled. "We will have to separate. I will — "

"No!" Jasmine's voice was very quiet. But something in her flat, even tone sent a cold trickle of fear down Lief's spine. He heard her take a deep breath.

"I think — " she began.

But she never finished what she had been about to say, for at that moment red light began to gleam from the cavern walls. And as the light grew brighter, the companions saw The Fear.

Lief heard Glock cursing under his breath, saw Jasmine's eyes darken, felt Barda's body stiffen, fought his own terror.

The Fear was not on one side of the cage or the other. It was not above them, or below them.

It was everywhere.

Gigantic tentacles like the twisting trunks of vast trees filled the cavern from wall to wall, from floor to roof. The cage suddenly seemed tiny — dwarfed by the great mottled coils that wound above and around it.

At the end of every tentacle wriggled bundles of slimy white threads tipped with vicious hooks. Some of these were already sliding delicately through the bars of the cage. Others were slithering like worms over the dripping cavern walls as the tentacles from which they grew writhed into position.

And on the far wall of the cavern, visible only in glimpses as the tentacles moved, was the heart of the horror. A bloated mountain of slimy, billowing flesh hulked there, overflowing from a shell so ancient, so thick and crusted, that it seemed part of the rock itself.

The creature's tiny eyes were invisible. Its hideous hooked beak gaped greedily as its tentacles explored its domain. Perhaps it had already realized that the cage was empty. But it could sense that prey was near.

It was in no hurry. It knew there was no escape.

"The plan!" muttered Glock. "What are we to — "

Lief felt an insane urge to laugh. Plan? The plan was a joke. The plan had been based on knowledge that was so out of date as to be worse than ignorance.

That carving on the panel — how long ago had it been made? Two hundred years? Five hundred? More?

Why had they not expected this? For centuries, The Fear had been left unchallenged. It had been un-seen, even by its victims. It had been known only by its terrible cries, and the waves with which it flooded the land.

And in the darkness, it had grown.

Lief became aware that Glock had crawled to his feet, and was lumbering towards the nearest coiled tentacle, his sword raised high above his head.

"Glock! No — " roared Barda.

But he was too late. With a savage shout, Glock brought the sword down with all his strength. The mighty blade struck the tentacle with the sound of an axe on stone — and snapped in two.

17 - Nightmare

G lock stared, stunned, at his broken sword. He seemed unable to believe what had happened. He did not react to the rasping growl that echoed around the cavern. He did not move as the bruised tentacle shifted.

"Glock! Beware!" Jasmine screamed.

The tip of the tentacle lashed upward, striking like a snake. Slimy white threads caught Glock around the neck, the hooks burying themselves deep in his flesh. He fell to his knees, screaming in agony. In an instant the tentacle had whipped around his body, and he was being lifted into the air.

Jasmine darted forward.

"No, Jasmine!" shouted Lief.

But Jasmine either did not, or would not, hear. With Kree shrieking above her head, she leaped to the rising tentacle as once she had leaped from tree to tree in the Forests of Silence. She clung motionless for a moment, then, thrusting her dagger between her teeth, she began to climb, her fingers digging into the hard, slimy surface.

"Your dagger will be useless against it, Jasmine!" cried Barda. "Glock is lost. Save yourself!"

But Jasmine had already reached Glock's limp body and was climbing over it, to the tentacle's tip. The tip was bent, the white threads stretched taut as they kept their strangling, stinging hold around the groaning man's neck.

Jasmine snatched her dagger from her mouth and slashed at the roots of the white threads. One by one the threads fell away, thick, green liquid bubbling from the ragged wounds.

The Fear bellowed in rage. The injured tentacle writhed. Its grip on Glock loosened and he fell like a stone. Jasmine jumped after him, shouting to Kree.

Rigid with horror, Barda and Lief looked down. They caught sight of Jasmine's dark head break clear of the water, saw her stagger upright among the heaving mottled coils of the beast. She was dragging Glock by the shoulders, holding his head out of the water.

Shrieking, Kree swooped at the tip of the injured tentacle, stabbing at it, darting aside as it lunged for him. He could not hope to save Jasmine. All he could do was try to distract the beast, and give her time to save herself.

Did Glock still live? Lief could not tell. But his heart seemed to rise to his throat as he saw a jagged slash of silver in the churning water.

Glock's huge hand still gripped his sword as

though, alive or dead, he would never let it go.

The Fear's terrible, earsplitting roars echoed around the cavern. It thrashed the water, and Glock and Jasmine disappeared in a whirlpool of foam. Great waves swelled and rushed towards the cavern entrance, and into Lief's mind flashed a picture of the Plumes waiting on the shore.

The tentacles around the cage tightened and the bars cracked like twigs. The tentacles above Lief and Barda began uncoiling and writhing downwards, their pale undersides ribbed like the belly of a snake.

The light flickered, and went out.

"Jump!" Barda roared.

Lief leaped for his life as the cage collapsed beneath him. He hit the foaming water and went under. He tumbled helplessly in the deathly chill, his mouth and nose filled with the taste and smell of the beast. Splinters from the shattered cage and the bones of long-dead victims of The Fear swirled with him in the stinking froth.

His right shoulder slammed against something solid, and agonizing pain jolted down his arm. Blindly he reached out with the other hand, felt rock under his fingers, and managed to haul himself to his feet.

He had been swept against the cavern wall. Shivering and panting, water foaming to his waist, he clung to the rock. His eyes were tightly closed, but slowly he became aware of wavering light against his eyelids. Somehow, as waves pounded their island, a little band of Plumes had managed to summon up their power once more.

Lief forced his stinging eyes open and, through a flickering red haze, saw a scene of nightmare.

Vast, thrashing tentacles filled the cavern. The water heaved and boiled with their writhing. One of the tentacles, the one Jasmine had attacked, twisted more wildly than the rest, its blunted tip jerking horribly, spattering the walls and roof with thick blobs of slimy green.

Lief shrank back, and only then realized that he was clutching a thick rock shelf that jutted from the cavern wall at water level.

Slowly, painfully, he hauled himself onto the ledge. He crawled to his feet, flattened himself against the rock and began searching desperately for some sign of Jasmine, Barda, or Kree.

But he could see nothing. Nothing but the coiling tentacles, quietening now, beginning to search more patiently, more thoroughly. The threads at the tips of the nine uninjured arms wriggled, stretched, and pulsed like hideous worms as they probed the rocky walls, combed the dark red water. Seeking, seeking . . .

How many crushed, drowned bodies were drifting just below that scum-covered surface, waiting to be found? Was Glock there? Barda? Jasmine?

Lief closed his eyes, fighting down the despair that threatened to engulf him. He tried to block everything from his mind but the need to survive. Cautiously, wincing with pain, he moved his injured arm.

Only then did he realize that his hand was not only numb, but empty. His sword was gone.

Forcing down panic, he made himself think. He was certain that he had been gripping the sword when he hit the water. He could remember the feel of the hilt in his hand as he was being tumbled about in the foam.

But then he had crashed against the rock — against the rock ledge on which he was standing now. He peered into the dark, foam-flecked water lapping at his feet. His stomach lurched as he saw the long, slow turn of pale, ribbed flesh.

One of the beast's tentacles was writhing just below the ledge. If he had still been standing there . . .

The tip of the tentacle broke the water's surface. Lief watched in fascinated dread as the worm-like fingers stretched towards the ledge, touched it, and began to ooze forward.

He stood rigidly still, hardly daring to breathe. If he tried to edge away, the fingers would sense movement and lash out, as they had lashed out at Glock. But if he stayed where he was, the fingers would soon reach his feet. Then they would creep up to his ankles. And as soon as they felt warm flesh . . .

"Be very still."

The voice was just a breath. Stiffly, Lief turned his head to the right and saw Barda edging out of a shallow hole in the cavern wall, only an arm's length away.

Barda was dripping and bedraggled. His face

was smeared with blood, and blood matted his sodden hair. But his sword gleamed as he raised it high.

Lief looked down again. The toes of his boots were covered in a mass of squirming, hooked threads. Cold sweat broke out on his brow. His stomach churned with revulsion.

The threads oozed forward. The tentacle tip from which they grew rose higher from the water, nodding horribly . . .

"Go!" roared Barda, and struck, his blade slicing cleanly through the white threads, a hairsbreadth from their roots.

Slipping and sliding on the uneven footholds in the wall, Lief scrambled aside. The water beneath the ledge began to heave and bubble as though it were boiling.

"Get behind the shell!" he heard Barda shouting.

Lief glanced over his shoulder. Huge coils of the injured tentacle were heaving upward, bursting out of the water in cascades of spray. The jerking, blunted tip, oozing slime, was dashing itself against the ledge where he had been standing.

Barda was hurriedly squeezing back into his shallow hiding place. But he would not be safe there for long. Nowhere would be safe for long.

The beast was screeching ferociously, its tentacles pounding the water once more. The light began to flicker. A wave crashed into Lief, throwing him to his knees, jarring his injured arm which throbbed agonizingly. Gasping, he crawled on, half in and half out of the water.

He could not move back. He could not stay where he was. His only choice was to move on.

For long, agonizing minutes he crawled, expecting every moment to be snatched into the air. But at last he realized that the water beside him was calming. The rock shelf had broadened. Bleached, white bones lay in heaps all around him. He dared to look up.

He had reached the end of the cavern, the heart of The Fear.

Now he could clearly see what lay behind the huge mass of tentacles. He could see the cruel, tearing beak. He could even see the small, pale eyes staring vacantly ahead. He could see the shapeless body and the vast, stone-like shell which rose halfway to the cavern roof, dull blue, ridged with the growth of centuries.

The shell had become part of the cavern wall. The Fear could not move. But it did not need to. Its mighty arms were more than long enough to reach every corner of its domain. No prey could escape it.

A small movement on the shell caught Lief's eye. He stared, and almost cried out.

For the movement was Jasmine! Jasmine was crawling up the stony blue ridges, dagger in hand.

As if Jasmine felt Lief's gaze she looked down. Their eyes met, and her face broke into a broad smile.

Perhaps she saw Lief's joy at seeing her alive. Perhaps she felt joy of her own. But she did not speak. She simply pointed downwards, lifted her hand to Lief, palm outwards, and climbed on.

His heart beating wildly, Lief looked to where she had pointed. He saw Glock slumped against the shell, his broken sword still clutched in his hand.

Glock was breathing in shallow, painful gasps. Great, swollen wounds burned scarlet on his neck and face. Kree was standing motionless beside him, as though on guard.

By the time Lief looked up again, Jasmine had reached the top of the shell. As Lief watched in terror, she jumped lightly onto the billowing flesh that spilled from it, lay facedown, and began to wriggle forwards.

The Fear's tiny eyes showed no sign that it felt her. Perhaps it did not. Or perhaps it thought no more of Jasmine than a human would think of a crawling fly.

Half sliding, half crawling, Jasmine moved on until she was just behind the beast's eyes. Deliberately she raised her dagger. Lief stood, paralyzed, helpless, unable to do anything but watch.

His heart leaped as Jasmine thrust the dagger down with all her strength, burying it to its hilt between the creature's eyes. But then, with a thrill of terror, he saw those pale, vacant eyes roll back and fix on Jasmine's face. He saw Jasmine stare, unbelieving, as the dagger sprang back in her hand, rejected by the rubbery flesh it was supposed to pierce.

Then, with a strike so fast that it was like a blur, a tentacle whipped backwards, curled around Jasmine's body, and snatched her, screaming, into the air.

18 ~ Rainbows

A black shape streaked upward. It was Kree, his golden eyes fixed and savage. He did not attempt to attack the vast coil that held Jasmine, but instead swooped fearlessly at the tentacle's tip, stabbing and tearing at the hooked white fingers that wriggled there.

But this time The Fear did not loosen its grip. And more tentacles were curling back, their tips whipping through the air, striking at the darting bird, reaching for Jasmine's dangling feet.

Lief plunged wildly forward, aware of nothing but Jasmine's peril. He seized a bone from the scattered pile on the rock and, left-handed, threw it as hard as he could into the squirming maze of tentacles above his head.

The bone hit one of the tentacle tips. The tentacle jerked and recoiled. Shouting savagely, Lief threw another bone, then another.

From the corner of his eye he glimpsed a figure

moving near him on the ground. He could not pause to see who it was. A tentacle was coiling directly towards him. He spun a bone at it, and caught it on the tip. Some of the white threads curled back, jerking and oozing slime.

Lief shouted in triumph. But the sound died on his lips as another tentacle reared up from the churning water in front of him. It lashed at him with such speed that he barely saw it before it had wrapped itself around him. His head spun as he was swung off his feet, struggling and kicking.

The tip of the tentacle which was holding him bobbed beside his shoulder. White stubs waggled there, dripping slime. This was one of the arms that had been injured. But, injured or not, it had him. He could feel its coils tightening around his chest, crushing his ribs, squeezing the life from him.

Struggling for breath, he was swept up into the squirming center of the tentacle mass. And it was then that he heard a bellowing cry from below.

And saw, in the very midst of the place where the tentacles began, directly in front of the beast's gaping beak, the hulking, swaying figure of Glock.

Glock had crawled from hiding. Crawled, ignoring agony, ignoring fear, into the center of the terror.

Now, bent and staggering, he raised his shattered sword. "So you tear us apart, and cast away our bones!" he roared. "You like your meat soft, do you? Well, see how you fancy this!"

And he fell forward, plunging his arm and the jagged stump of his great blade straight down the beast's throat.

A ghastly, bubbling roar echoed through the cavern. The tentacle holding Lief seemed to freeze in the air. Then it began to shudder and jerk. Lief heard Kree screech, felt the coil that held him loosening, felt himself slipping. His fingers scrabbled on the slimy, ridged skin of the tentacle's underside as he plunged down into the water.

He rose to the surface spluttering and swung around, frantically trying to see Jasmine among the foam and the twisting coils of the beast.

"Lief! Here! Make haste!"

Barda was splashing towards him. Barda was seizing him by the waist and hauling him recklessly over the squirming tentacles towards the rock.

Lief struggled weakly. "Jasmine!" he choked.

"She is safe! There, see? By the shell!" Barda shouted.

Lief twisted his neck, blinking through a haze of water. He saw Jasmine kneeling by the heaving body of the beast.

Jasmine's hair was streaming with water and blood. But she was alive. Alive!

Filli was clasped in her arms. Kree was on her shoulder. As Lief watched, she raised her head, looked straight at him, and then up, above his and Barda's heads.

Her face changed. She stumbled to her feet.

"Lief!" she shrieked. Lief himself looked up and suddenly understood.

Above his head great tentacles were curling inward. And they were swaying, like great trees about to fall.

To fall!

Lief twisted free of Barda's clasp and began clawing his own way through the water, heedless of the pain in his arm. Together he and Barda struggled forward. Together they reached the rock, sprawled to safety, just as the giant tentacles began crashing down, carving great furrows in the water. Water shot to the roof and rained down again, pounding on the rock, beating on the quivering, dying body of The Fear.

And then, quite suddenly, it was over, and there was silence.

Lief, Barda, and Jasmine crawled to their feet. Nothing moved in the cavern but the water lapping against the rock. Red light flickered feebly. The tentacles, already paling to shades of grey, lay half-submerged, like the trunks of vast, drowned trees.

And Glock lay still, crushed beneath the mass of mottled flesh at the heart of The Fear. Only his head and shoulders were free. His eyes were closed.

They clambered over to him, and knelt by his side.

"Glock," said Lief softly.

Glock's eyes opened. They were glazed, but a small spark burned deep within them.

"It is dead, then?" he asked.

"Yes," said Barda quietly. "You defeated it, Glock. Single-handed. As you always said you would."

Glock nodded slowly. "That is good," he said. "I thought — there is one place where the beast is not protected. One place. If only I can reach it. If only . . ."

The light in the cavern was slowly brightening. The jewel-like color fell on Glock's face. "I am dying," he murmured, almost in wonder. "But that is good also. For what use is a Jalis without his sword arm?"

"You will fight again, Glock," said Lief.

Glock's mouth twisted into a mocking smile. "Not in this life," he said. His eyes shifted to Jasmine's face. "The girl knows. She does not lie to me, or to herself. She knows I am finished."

Jasmine met his gaze. Her eyes were burning with unshed tears, but she moved her head slightly in a nod.

"I have called you weakling more than once, girl. But that — was sport," the dying man said huskily. "You have the heart of a Jalis. Take my talisman from my neck. It is yours now. May it serve you well."

Jasmine's eyes widened, but she did not stir.

A flicker of impatience crossed Glock's face. "Take it!" he muttered. "Take it now, so I may see it in your hands."

Jasmine reached forward and did as she was told.

Glock stared at the small, faded bag, and again his mouth twisted into a smile. "You may think that it

133

did not serve *me* so well," he said. "But remember this. The dearest wish of a Jalis is to die fighting in a great cause. And that I have done."

The light in the cavern grew brighter, brighter, and suddenly it seemed to Lief that rainbows began to dance within it. Blinking, dazzled, he looked up.

His eyes had not been deceiving him. Visible at last, on the other side of the slowly collapsing body of The Fear, was the mouth of a tunnel. And from the tunnel streamed rainbow light that mingled with the cavern's scarlet so that it seemed that the very air was shining.

"The Glimmer," Jasmine whispered.

A faint sound reached their ears. The sound of the Plumes cheering wildly on the shore. They had seen the light.

"Lief." Glock's voice was very low. Lief bent over him.

Rainbows played on Glock's ravaged face. "The way to the Shadowlands is open," he murmured. "Now — you can find my people. You can bring them home."

Lief nodded. His heart was so full that he was unable to speak.

"When you find them," the dying man said, "I would like you to — tell them of me."

Lief found his voice. "I will tell them, Glock," he said. "I swear it."

Glock nodded slightly with satisfaction. Then his eyes closed, and he spoke no more.

19 - The Hand of Fate

The island had been battered mercilessly by The Fear's rage. But the Plumes were singing as their boats carried Lief, Barda, Jasmine, and Glock to the shore, skimming over the water like brown leaves swept by the wind.

And as the boats landed, the song rose in joy until it seemed to fill the vast cavern. The words echoed from the glowing walls, rolling in waves of beauty over the scarlet sea.

Above our land the tumult rages
Struggle echoes through the ages
There the strife may never cease
But here below we dwell in peace.
Where timeless tides swamp memory,
Our sunless prison makes us free.
The gem-glow lights our rocky walls,
And dragons guard our shining halls.

"It is not a song of death, but of life," said Jasmine softly as the last, pure notes drifted on the air. "I knew it was so."

Lief and Barda glanced at her curiously, but did not question her. Her eyes were fixed on the boat which Nols herself had guided — the boat in which Glock's body lay, shrouded in scarlet.

"So Glock will remain here," Jasmine sighed. "It seems strange . . ."

"Your friend will be honored among us," said Nols, stepping forward and putting her small hand on Jasmine's arm. "He will lie with the Pipers of Plume, and never be forgotten."

Jasmine thought for a moment, then smiled slightly. "Glock would like that," she said. "He would like to take his place with chiefs."

Nols bowed. "Our debt to him, and to you, can never be repaid. We have little enough to give, but whatever we have is yours. Boats for your journey. Food. Light, as far as we are able to supply it . . ." She paused, waiting.

Lief took a deep breath. This was the opportunity he had been hoping for, but now that it had come he almost feared to take it.

"There is one thing which only you can give us," he said slowly. "It is a treasure we dearly need — though only for a time. The mouthpiece of the Pirran Pipe."

Nols stepped back, a stricken look on her face.

The people behind her murmured and whispered.

Dismayed, Lief glanced quickly at Barda and Jasmine. Barda was frowning in angry disbelief. Jasmine, who still knew nothing of the Pirran Pipe, was simply confused.

"I know we ask a great deal," Lief said, keeping his voice steady with difficulty. "But I beg you to consider our request. If we are to save our people from the Shadow Lord we must make the Pipe whole again. It is the one thing the Shadow Lord fears. The one thing that may give us time to — "

Nols held up her hand to stop him. "You do not understand," she said, her voice trembling. "It is not that we *will* not give you the mouthpiece of the Pipe. It is that we *cannot*. It was lost long ago."

It was like a blow to the pit of Lief's stomach. He stared at Nols, unable to speak.

"Not lost — stolen!" said Worron's sharp voice. He stepped forward, still an imposing figure in the long red robe and scarlet headpiece he had not yet put aside. "The symbol of the Piper's leadership was stolen from the people by the Seven Traitors — the wicked ones who left the safety of our seas for the world above."

"It was in ancient times, when the Plumes' time in the world below the world had not been long," said Nols, more quietly. "The people of those days were not accustomed to the caverns, as we are. It is written that the rebels planned to find a place of safety, then return and lead the Plumes back into the sun. But they never returned."

She sighed. "Doran the Dragonlover told our ancestors that they had all lost their lives. He knew a tale of it. It was an old tale often told, he said, by the members of a savage Longhair tribe called Jalis, whose own ancestors had done the killing."

"Yes." Worron's eyes narrowed maliciously. "The Seven Traitors were destroyed, and the mouthpiece of the Pipe with them, no doubt. So if the Pipe is what you have come here to seek, Longhairs, your journey, your time, and your friend's life, have all been wasted."

Into Lief's mind came the memory of Glock grinning over a mug of ale. Glock, the last of the Jalis. His eyes suddenly burned with tears, and he looked quickly away.

He saw that Jasmine had taken the little cloth bag from her neck, and was opening it. Plainly she, too, was thinking of Glock.

Lief turned back to Worron. "It is our loss, certainly, that the three pieces of the Pipe cannot be joined once more," he said, struggling to keep his voice steady. "But The Fear is dead, Worron. The Plumes are free of it. So nothing has been wasted."

"Indeed it has not," said Clef loudly. "We — "

He broke off, staring. Lief saw that Nols, too, was staring. And Worron. And all the Plumes crowding behind them.

But they were not staring at him. They were looking at Jasmine — or rather, at the dusty, oddly shaped piece of wood that Jasmine was holding in the palm of her outstretched hand.

There was a moment's stunned silence. Then Nols reached out and took the wooden object reverently. Slowly she crouched and dipped it into the water. The dust of centuries loosened and lifted away in a fine cloud. And when she stood up once more, the thing in her hands seemed to glow — a small miracle of shining wood and strange, carved patterns.

"The mouthpiece of the Pirran Pipe!" she whispered.

Worron's mouth was opening and closing like the mouth of a fish. "Where — ? Where — ?" he stuttered.

"Glock had it all the time," Jasmine said calmly. "It was part of the talisman passed down to him by his family. He had no idea it was anything more than a lucky charm. Neither did I, until a few moments ago — and even then I only suspected the truth."

Wisely, she said no more. She wanted Glock buried in state with the Pipers of Plume. She knew better than to admit how his ancestors had come by the object that the crowd was pressing forward to see.

Nols' face was alight with joy. "It is a miracle!" she cried. "Our treasure has been returned to us. Now we can pay our debt to you."

Lief, looking down at her beaming face and at

the joyous faces clustered around her, wondered how he ever could have thought these people were ugly. He wondered, too, at the chance that had brought the mouthpiece of the Pirran Pipe back to its rightful owners.

And, finally, he wondered if it was not chance at all, but something else.

He turned to Barda, who was still staring at the gleaming mouthpiece in amazement. "We have reached our first goal, Barda," he murmured. "And the way is open to our second. According to the map, the island of Auron is next."

Barda shook his head slowly. "First we must find our way back to Del. Doom is waiting for us there, with supplies, fighters — "

"No!" cried Jasmine fiercely. "There can be no delay! Time is running out! We must — "

She broke off as Lief and Barda turned to her.

"Why do you say this, Jasmine?" Barda demanded.

Jasmine wet her lips. "I heard . . . heard that the Shadow Lord was going to kill the prisoners. Very soon."

"Birds told you this?" Lief asked sharply.

Jasmine hesitated. It was not in her nature to lie. But she did not want Lief to know that she had entered the sealed room, that she had spoken to the sister he had tried to keep from her.

She knew she could not bear to see the look on

his face as he tried to deny, or explain, his deceit and betrayal of trust. She preferred to put it out of her mind. To focus on the task at hand. To lose her thoughts in action.

So she pressed her lips together, and nodded.

"Then we must go on — the three of us," said Lief instantly.

"No!" Barda growled. "You, at least, cannot — "

"I can," said Lief firmly. "And I think it was always meant that I should."

"But you are Deltora's king!" cried Jasmine. Lief was saying just what she had wanted him to say. Yet, suddenly, she found herself filled with doubt.

Lief met her anxious gaze squarely. "I have thought of this long and hard," he said. "I am the king, but I am still Lief. I must do what I must do."

"No!" Barda protested, but Lief shook his head.

"I cannot be a prisoner," he said. "That is what happened to the kings and queens of our past, and it was their ruin. It was not what Adin intended when he created the Belt of Deltora. He — "

Feeling a light touch on his arm, he turned to see Nols looking up at him.

"I asked Azan to arrange sleeping quarters for you, on the high ground, where it is still dry," Nols said. "Your wounds must be tended, and you must rest. Ah, Azan!" She smiled welcome at the young Plume who was running, panting, towards her. "Is all well?"

Azan shook his head, his face furrowed with anxiety. "No! I fear — I fear all is *not* well," he stammered. "The only dry sleeping quarters have been overtaken by two hideous monsters, the like of which I have never seen before."

Nols looked alarmed. Azan looked piteously at Lief, Barda, and Jasmine. "They are fearsome — as large as my head, with huge fangs, eight legs, and red eyes. And they are fighting with one another savagely, as though they will never stop!"

The companions glanced at one another. "I think we are familiar with the beasts," Barda said reluctantly. "Leave them to us."

Azan's face broke into a relieved smile. "I will take you to the house!" he said eagerly, darting away.

"Ah, what it is to have heroes among us!" beamed Nols.

"Indeed," said Lief glumly, as he, Barda, and Jasmine, with Kree fluttering overhead, trudged after Azan. "And if we can defeat The Fear, surely we can control Fury and Flash."

"I would not count on it," Barda muttered.

Jasmine turned to Lief. "What were you telling us, when Nols interrupted you?" she asked.

Lief hesitated. He had thought again about what, in his excitement, he had been about to say. "Whatever it was, it does not matter," he lied. "If we three survived the quest to restore the gems to the Belt of Deltora, why should we not survive this?"

"*This* will end in the Shadowlands," said Barda gravely. "And all depends on the Pirran Pipe. We have its first part by a miracle. What of the second and third?"

Lief turned to look back at The Glimmer, shining across the scarlet sea. What perils lay beyond that mysterious gateway? That he could not know. But as he looked, he heard again in his mind that clear, sweet music, beckoning him.

"They are waiting for us," he said simply. "I know it. All we have to do — is find them."

DELTORA SHADOWLANDS

THE ISLE OF ILLUSION

Contents

1 The Rainbow Sea 149

2 Warnings 158

3 Reunion 167

4 Trapped 175

5 Hope and Fears 183

6 Dread 191

7 Truth and Lies 198

8 The House of Penn 208

9 Troubles 215

10 The Dome 223

11 Arach 232

12 Suspicion 240

13 Treachery 249

14 Leap of Faith 258

15 The Isle of Illusion 268

16 Terror 278

17 Peace 287

1 ~ The Rainbow Sea

L ief and Barda were silent as they paddled the frail boat through the world below the world. Jasmine sat in the front of the boat with Filli on her shoulder. Her eyes were fixed on Kree, who was flying ahead. In her hand was the tiny map that was their only guide to their next goal — the island of Auron.

Above their heads the soaring roof of the great cavern shimmered with opal light. The rippling water surrounding them was like liquid rainbows.

"To think that this wonder exists below Deltora!" Barda murmured, finding his voice at last. "I still cannot quite believe it."

"Nor I," said Lief. "The caverns of the Plumes — the gold and the scarlet — were beautiful enough. But this place . . ."

Jasmine moved restlessly. "Beauty is all very

well," she muttered. "But we do not know where we are!"

She held up the battered map. "Ranesh said he would trust Doran the Dragonlover's maps with his life. But there are no landmarks drawn here. Just four islands, a dotted line which could mean anything, and a few cavern walls."

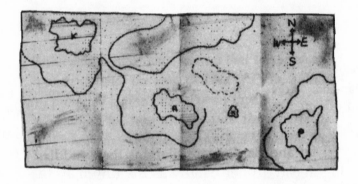

Lief stared at the map, remembering the excitement with which he had traced it in the palace library in Del.

Little had he dreamed then that the Pirran Islands were not in the open sea, but hidden beneath Deltora itself. Little had he dreamed that a short journey to the Os-Mine Hills in pursuit of Jasmine was to lead him into this far longer and more dangerous quest.

With a pang, he thought of home. His long absence must be causing great anxiety. Not for most of the people, who believed their king was still safe in Tora. But for those few who knew he was not.

Doom. His mother. The old librarian, Josef. Josef's assistant, Ranesh. And the girl, Marilen.

Most of all, Marilen. What must she be feeling now? Frightened? Lonely? Bitterly regretting that she had ever agreed to leave Tora?

Doom had promised her father that she would be closely guarded. But spies, traitors, and assassins were everywhere, as Lief himself knew only too well.

Into his mind came the memory of the first attempts on his life. Both were in the great entrance hall. First, a frenzied, babbling woman had tried to strike him down with a knife. When her attack had failed, she had turned the knife upon herself and died without giving any reason for what she had done.

Not long afterwards, a man who could walk only with the aid of crutches — a man called Moss, a trusted palace guard before the time of the Shadow Lord, Barda said — had seized Lief by the throat as Lief bent over the blanket where he lay.

The choking grip was like iron. It had taken three guards to break it. And then, as Moss was being taken away, someone in the jostling crowd had stabbed him in the back. That person had never been found.

After that, Lief had kept away from crowds. But he had learned that nowhere in the palace was truly safe. Even his own bedchamber.

And why? Why? Lief thought, as he had thought a thousand times before. Why would any Deltoran act as a servant of the Shadow Lord?

Impatiently, he pulled his mind back to the present. "Doran could not draw landmarks if none existed, Jasmine," Barda was saying, lifting his paddle from the water and stretching his aching back.

"Do not wake Fury," Jasmine warned.

Barda glanced quickly at the cage hanging from his belt. But Fury the fighting spider had not moved.

"It is more important not to wake Flash." Lief nodded at the second cage, resting in the bottom of the boat. "Flash was the loser in their last battle. He is the one who thirsts for revenge."

"We are fortunate that the movement of the boat lulls them to sleep," said Jasmine.

"Indeed, for nothing else does," Barda growled. "If only we could have left them behind! This boat is cramped enough without giving room to caged spiders."

"I do not blame the Plumes for refusing to keep them," said Jasmine. "Who would want two beasts who think of nothing but fighting each other?"

Filli snuffled agreement. The huge spiders made him nervous.

They fell silent once more, gazing around them.

Unbroken water met their eyes on every side. The cavern wall through which they had passed to reach this glittering sea was lost in the hazy distance. There was no sign of another.

"At least we know where we are in Deltora," said Lief at last. "When we first went underground in the Os-Mine hills, the cavern walls and roof shone gold like the topaz, the Del tribe's talisman. But by the time we reached the island of Plume, the cavern walls were shining red."

"So we can guess that Plume lies below Deltora's northeast — the land of the Ralad people, whose talisman is the ruby," said Barda.

Lief nodded. "And now we are in the territory of the opal. We must be moving west, beneath the Plains. And the island of Auron is near, I am sure of it."

He broke off as sweet, piping music filled his mind — the music of the Pirran Pipe, calling to him through time. The sound had come to him before, but it was more compelling now. Because now he possessed the mouthpiece of the Pipe itself.

The mouthpiece hung around his neck. It was muffled in a red cloth bag and hidden beneath his clothes. Yet he could feel its power, as once he had felt the magic of the Belt of Deltora.

He could feel, too, its yearning to be joined once more with the other two parts of the Pipe, from which it had been separated so long ago.

"Lief! Barda!"

Lief jumped slightly as Jasmine's voice broke the spell of the music. He saw that she was holding out her arm to Kree, who was swooping towards her.

"Kree sees land ahead!" Jasmine called excitedly. "Land!"

Land . . . Land . . . Land . . . murmured the echoes.

Lief's heart beat faster as he and Barda plunged their paddles into the rainbow water and the boat began moving forward once more.

*

Far away, in the palace in Del, Josef the librarian sighed. The day was still young, but comparing the official library catalogue to the books actually on the shelves was a sad and tiring task.

Many books were missing. Some might have been put away on the wrong shelves. But most, Josef suspected, had been quietly removed and destroyed, because they contained things that the Shadow Lord had wanted Deltorans to forget.

At least I was able to save *The Deltora Annals*, Josef thought, glancing at the pale blue books standing in pride of place near the library worktables. So King Lief was able to read of the Pirran Pipe, the only thing which can help him save the prisoners in the Shadowlands. And he could see Doran's map, which will lead him to the three parts of the Pipe when he returns from the Os-Mine Hills.

When he returns . . . Josef's brow creased. Now he came to think about it, where *was* Lief? Surely he should have returned long ago.

The old librarian's stomach knotted with sudden fear. Why, Lief and the Belt of Deltora were the land's only defenses against the Shadow Lord. What if . . . ?

Ringing laughter disturbed the library's silence. Startled and angered, Josef shuffled forward, but stopped when he saw where the sound was coming from.

His apprentice, Ranesh, was bending over the table where sat Marilen, the young Toran visitor who had spent many hours in the library of late.

Marilen had several weighty books open in front of her, but she was looking up at Ranesh, her eyes dancing. As Josef watched, Ranesh murmured something, and the girl laughed again.

Josef hesitated, very troubled. He was not wise in the ways of the world, but he had been young once. Something about that laughter, and the look on Marilen's face, warned him that this situation was not as it should be.

Lief had asked Josef to make Marilen welcome in the library, but not to speak of her to others. Marilen was a very special guest, Lief had said, but her presence in the palace must be kept secret — at least until his return from the Os-Mine Hills.

Josef had smiled discreetly. He had not been in the palace long, but already he had heard the rumors that Lief had gone to Tora to choose a bride. He had no doubt as to who this beautiful, highborn young lady called Marilen was.

Now this same young lady was laughing with Ranesh in a way that did not seem at all fitting. And Ranesh was surely leaning far too close to one who was the future queen of Deltora.

Josef felt panic rise within him. Nothing but harm could come of this. Harm for the girl who had been put in his care. And terrible harm to Ranesh, who Josef loved liked the son he had never had.

Bitterly, Josef blamed himself for being so wrapped up in his work that he had failed to see what was happening under his very nose. He had paid no attention to how much time the two young people were spending together.

I must stop this at once, before it goes too far! he thought wildly. I must speak to Ranesh. Send him away, perhaps. Just for a time. Until—

At that moment, Ranesh looked up and his eyes met Josef's. His teeth flashed in a seemingly casual grin. But Josef knew his apprentice too well to be deceived. Josef recognized the gleam in those dark eyes.

It was the gleam of defiance. Josef remembered it from the days of the Shadow Lord's rule, when Ranesh had often slipped back into their cellar home below the old pottery with bread, cheese, or fruit under his jacket.

Josef, weak with hunger, had always eaten what he was given. But he had felt uneasy, nonetheless. He knew that Ranesh, once a homeless orphan surviving alone on the streets of Del, would not hesitate to steal to feed them both.

"Did we disturb you, Josef?" Ranesh called. "I am sorry. But Marilen and I have just discovered that we are both from the west. She is from Tora, I from Where Waters Meet. Is it not strange?"

"I am going down to the kitchen for a warming drink, Ranesh," Josef said stiffly. "Please join me as soon as you can. I wish to talk to you about — about an important matter."

He turned abruptly and hobbled out of the library. Nodding to the guards, he started moving carefully down the stairs.

Josef had never felt less like a warming drink. His fears had made him far too warm already. But he knew that the kitchen would be a safe place to talk to Ranesh, for Marilen never ventured below the library floor. Her meals were all carried up to her bedchamber by Sharn, Lief's mother.

It is a lonely life for a young girl, Josef thought. No wonder she enjoys Ranesh's company. And he must be flattered and pleased by the admiration of one so beautiful and highborn. But it will not do. No, it will not do.

Clinging tightly to the banisters, he began to move a little faster. Oh, let Lief be safe, and let him return soon, he thought desperately. Then there will be no need for me to send Ranesh away. Lief's return will solve everything!

2 - Warnings

L ittle knowing the trouble that was brewing in Del — more trouble than even Josef suspected — Lief was paddling as fast as he could towards the land ahead.

The island was shimmering in the distance. Bright pink and yellow weed grew thickly in the shallows that surrounded it. Several times Lief thought he glimpsed movement on the shore, but it was difficult to be sure.

"I can see small buildings, I think," said Jasmine, squinting into the rainbow haze. "Not like the houses of the Plumes, though. Much simpler dwellings, shaped like cones. Of course, they could be rocks . . ."

"Indeed they could, and probably are," Barda growled. "If the map is accurate, and our course has been straight, this land is not Auron, but the small island to its east. The one marked with a cross."

"We should keep our wits about us, in any case," said Jasmine. "Remember what Clef and Azan said."

Lief remembered only too well. The people of Plume had given their part of the Pirran Pipe gladly. But they had warned the companions that the people of Auron would not do the same with the Pipe's stem.

The Plumes had nothing but hatred for their ancient enemies. They wanted to attack Auron and take the second part of the Pipe by force. Their anger had flared when Lief disagreed.

The Plume leader, the Piper, Nols, had frowned. And the young Plumes, Clef and Azan in particular, had argued violently.

"The people of Auron will use their magic against you without pity!" Clef cried. "To enter their territory unprotected would be madness! They are as savage as the monsters they breed in their seas."

"The Aurons *breed* monsters?" Barda exclaimed disbelievingly.

"Indeed! There are many old tales of it," Clef insisted. "We have long believed that The Fear, the beast you killed, was sent by the Aurons to prey upon us."

Azan nodded agreement. "And they will never give up their part of the Pirran Pipe. Never, while they live. What is more, they will take *our* part of the Pipe from you, and keep it for themselves!"

"No. It will be safe with us," said Lief steadily.

"Your promises are useless," cried Azan. "Once the Aurons see you in one of our boats, they will slay you as viciously as they would slay three defenseless Plumes."

"We are not defenseless!" Jasmine snapped. "And how do you know what the Aurons would do? The way between your sea and theirs has only now been opened after hundreds of years. Their feelings about you may have changed."

"Why should they?" Clef asked shortly. "Our feelings about *them* have not changed."

The arguments had continued for days, but at last the companions had been allowed to leave alone. Plume was far behind them now. Their memories of their friends' warnings had not faded, however. If anything, they had grown stronger.

Lost in his thoughts, Lief jumped as Jasmine jerked back with a hiss, reaching for her dagger.

"What is it?" Barda demanded urgently.

Jasmine pointed. Lief and Barda craned forward, and at last saw what her sharper eyes had seen before them.

A ragged shadow was surging towards them, just below the surface of the gleaming water.

Lief's heart hammered in his chest as he threw down his paddle and drew his sword. The thing streaking towards them was large — large enough to upset the boat. It was closing in with amazing speed, changing shape as it came, great arms spreading . . .

A small, sleek head broke the surface. Then there

was another, and another. The next moment, all the companions were laughing with relief.

The shadow they had so feared was not a single beast at all, but a group of small, plump creatures with tiny eyes and long whiskers. The little animals frolicked around the boat, playfully butting one another and making tiny chittering sounds.

They were covered with smooth, silvery-grey fur and had fin-like paddles instead of arms and legs. They seemed to breathe air, but were as at home in the water as any fish.

"The island ahead might be their breeding ground," said Barda, picking up his paddle again. "Ah, I long to stretch my legs. I am cramped to death in this boat."

He looked around. "Are my eyes playing tricks on me, or has the light dimmed a little?" he asked.

Jasmine lifted her head from her delighted study of the animals. "I had not noticed, but you are right!" she said, in tones of surprise. "It is as if a cloud has passed over the sun. But there are no clouds here."

"The Plumes did warn us that their magic could not light the caverns all the way to Auron," said Lief.

He felt a chill as the words left his lips. He had assumed that where the Plumes' magic failed, the Aurons' magic would take over.

But what if he had been wrong? What if the light failed altogether?

They moved forward once more. The little grey creatures accompanied them for a time, but as the boat neared land and finally crossed the broad band of pink and yellow weed, they dropped back. The next time Lief looked behind him, they had disappeared.

The island certainly did not look inviting. It was bare and bleak, its barren clay riddled with holes like a pockmarked face.

The gleaming mud of the narrow shore was rippled with ridges created by the tide. Beyond the shore, on slightly higher ground, were straggling groups of the lumpy, cone-shaped objects Jasmine had seen from afar. They seemed to be made of dried mud, but were surely not big enough to be dwellings.

There was no sign of life at all.

The movement I thought I saw must have been a trick of the light, Lief told himself.

And yet he felt danger. The silence, broken only by the soft lapping of water on mud, seemed heavy with menace.

Jasmine was also uneasy.

"I do not like this place," she said in a low voice. "Filli and Kree do not like it either. I do not think we should land after all."

"I see nothing to fear," Barda said irritably. He moved his cramped legs restlessly and the toe of his boot overturned Flash's cage. Flash woke, and at once began leaping and plunging, beating against the cage bars.

"Now see what you have done, Barda!" Jasmine scolded. "Now Fury will wake as well, and we will have no peace."

"Fury had better not wake, or it will be the worse for her," growled Barda. "I am a patient man, but my patience is being sorely tested at present."

Lief did not want to set foot on the island. But he wanted a quarrel even less. "Let us land, just for a few minutes," he suggested. "We need not stray far from the water."

Jasmine glowered at him. "My injured arm is paining me," Lief murmured, taking refuge in a small white lie. "I would be grateful if you could paddle in my place for a time, Jasmine. And it will be safer to change seats on dry land."

"Why did you not say so before, Lief?" Jasmine demanded. "Of course we will land, then."

How tactful I am becoming, Lief said grimly to himself, as he and Barda began paddling once more. I am learning the ways of the palace all too well.

This thought made his mind fly again to home. How he longed to know what was happening there! Had Marilen had word from her father? Was she safe and well?

I cannot know these things! he told himself impatiently. It is useless to fret, and probably needless. As long as no one knows Marilen is in the palace, or who she is, she will be safe.

He looked up, frowning, and caught Jasmine's

eye. He made himself smile, but the grin must have looked forced, for she did not smile back.

Jasmine knows me too well, Lief thought. She senses that my mind is full of things she knows nothing about, and it annoys her. But this is one secret I cannot tell — to anyone.

Looking at Jasmine's closed face, an immense feeling of loneliness swept over him. He wished with all his heart that the easy companionship they had once shared would return. But he knew that while he had to guard his tongue and his thoughts, this could not be.

In time, I hope, Jasmine and Barda will know all, and surely then they will forgive me for my silence, he thought. Surely they will understand that it was not that I did not trust them. I would trust them both with my life!

They reached the shore and together pulled the boat out of the water. Flash was still raging in his cage, and they decided to leave him where he was. Fury had not yet woken, and for this they were grateful.

Barda stretched his limbs with relief. "Ah, it is good to be on land again — even such miserable land as this!" He looked around, then began to stride towards the cone-like shapes they had seen from the boat.

"Do not go too far!" Jasmine called after him.

"Do not fear," Barda shouted back, his temper

much improved by freedom from the boat. "I simply want to look at these cones. They interest me."

He had moved only a few more paces, however, when he stopped dead. Silently, without turning around, he beckoned. Lief and Jasmine hurried to his side.

"There," Barda breathed, pointing.

Movement could be seen inside the holes that scarred the bare earth around the cones. As the companions watched, heads began to poke cautiously from the holes — smooth, round heads with huge, blinking eyes and two short, slim tubes where nose and mouth should be.

"What are they?" whispered Lief, fascinated.

"Some sort of worm, or grub, by the look of things," Barda answered, peering at the holes. "Ah, yes! They have decided we are safe. They are coming out of hiding."

Sure enough, the creatures were all slowly easing their way out of their holes. As Barda had guessed, they looked like giant caterpillars, with long, pale bodies divided into plump segments, and six stubby legs that scrabbled in the mud as they crept along.

Filli chattered nervously and Kree squawked.

"They do not look dangerous," said Jasmine. But she felt for her dagger all the same.

"This may be where the legend of the Auron monsters came from," Barda murmured. "Perhaps the

Aurons breed these things for food. They are fat enough. And standing upright they would be as tall as Nols, at least."

As he said this, the creatures nearest to them did in fact raise their bodies from the ground and stand balanced on their back legs. Their front and middle legs waggled comically in the air, their huge eyes blinked shortsightedly.

"We had better leave them to their island," said Lief. "We seem to be disturbing them."

He glanced over his shoulder to see how far away the boat was, and received a shock. More of the giant grubs were rearing up behind him. Their bodies glistened with wet mud. Fresh, oozing holes in the rippled shore showed how they had approached without being seen.

"Barda! Jasmine!" Lief whispered, reaching for his sword.

A grub leaned slightly forward. A jet of bright yellow mist hissed from the tube just below its eyes.

Lief jerked backwards, but too late. The mist was already in his eyes and nose, stinging and burning.

He heard himself crying out in shock and pain, felt himself staggering. There was a moment of flashing, spinning color.

Then there was nothing.

3 – Reunion

ad Josef known what was happening to his king, he would have been filled with terror. As it was, by the time he at last entered the palace kitchen, he felt only dread at the thought of his forthcoming talk with Ranesh.

The big, homely room was deserted except for one thin old woman. She was standing at the stove with her back to the door, stirring a great pot of stew. Piles of bowls stood nearby, waiting to be filled for the crowds in the entrance hall. Marilen's tray lay lonely on another counter, already set with napkin, knife, and fork.

Dismally, Josef hobbled to the table and sat down to wait for Ranesh.

The old woman did not turn to greet him. This surprised him, for all the people he had met in the palace before this had been very friendly.

He coughed politely, but still the cook made no response.

Have it your own way, then, you cross old dame, thought Josef with irritation. I have more than enough to think about without caring for your conversation.

Just then, the woman put down the spoon and turned from the stove. Catching sight of Josef, she jumped violently and shrieked.

Josef leaped in his seat, almost as startled as she. Then, as she began to laugh with embarrassment at her fright, pressing her hand to her chest to still her racing heart, he received another shock.

He knew this woman! He knew that laughter. Knew that face. It was sadly changed since last he saw it long ago. But beneath the ugly scars that marked the cheeks and brow, and the lines of suffering and grief, it was still a face he had known and loved.

He stumbled to his feet.

"Amarantz!" he cried. "Why — why, Amarantz of the pottery, it is you! I did not know you!"

The woman stared at him, bewildered, for a moment. Then her eyes widened in amazement.

"Josef!" she exclaimed with a sob, flinging herself into his arms. "I never thought to see you again!"

"Nor I you!" Josef babbled, almost overwhelmed by joy. "How did you escape? What of the others?"

But Amarantz said nothing, and at last Josef drew a little away from her and looked searchingly into her face. "Amarantz, why do you not answer?" he asked.

The old woman smiled sadly and shook her head. "I am sorry, Josef," she said. "I see your lips move, but I cannot hear you. I am stone deaf."

From the pocket of her apron she drew a small slate and a piece of chalk. She pressed them into Josef's hands.

Josef took the chalk and wrote.

DEAF? HOW?

Amarantz shrugged. "The Grey Guards marched us to the Shadowlands border. I could not move fast enough for their liking. They called me old and useless — said I would slow their way through the mountains. They beat me until I was senseless, and left me to die."

She touched the scars on her face and her mouth twisted with remembered pain. "I was tougher than they thought. I survived — but the beating had destroyed my hearing. Not that this mattered to me. I had already lost everything I cared about. I have lived — or existed, rather — wandering in the north ever since. I came back to Del only a few days ago."

Josef rubbed the slate clean with his sleeve, and wrote again, with unsteady hand.

THE OTHERS?

A shadow seemed to pass over Amarantz's face as she stared at the words. "The others — my sons, their wives, my grandchildren . . . and our friends in the resistance — " Her lips trembled. "If they still live, they are slaves in the Shadowlands. Beaten, tormented slaves. You and Ranesh were lucky, Josef."

Her voice broke, and she bowed her head.

Josef patted her arm awkwardly, filled with helpless grief and pity. Guilt, too, because he and Ranesh had been spared while disaster had fallen on those who had sheltered them.

After a long moment, Amarantz scrubbed at her eyes with her apron and straightened her shoulders. "I must not give way now," she murmured. "I have a mission here, and weakness will not help me."

Seeing Josef's puzzlement, she lifted her chin. "Why do you think I made the long, hard journey back to Del after all these years?" she demanded. "It was because I knew that Sharn would remember me from the old days. Lief, too, perhaps, though he was only a small boy when I used to visit the forge to get shoes for Dolly, our old horse. Do you remember Dolly, Josef?"

Josef nodded, his chest aching with memory.

"I saw Sharn this morning," Amarantz continued. "She offered food and money freely, of course, but that was not what I wanted. I begged for work in the palace. I need to be here, though I did not tell her why."

She lowered her voice. "I am going to speak to Lief, Josef. Find him alone, and make him understand that he must — he *must* — lead an army of rescue to the Shadowlands, whatever his doubts. The people cry out for it, and he does not listen. But surely he will listen to me! An old friend — who has lost so much."

Josef stared at her in dismay. But Amarantz did not seem to notice his expression. Her own face had brightened. "Why, Josef, I remember now," she cried excitedly. "You were once the palace librarian! In the north it is said that Lief spends his days in the library. You could take me to him!"

Josef felt desperate. He could not tell Amarantz the truth. But she had to know, at least, that he could not take her to Lief. That Lief was not in the palace.

There is no help for it, he thought. I will have to tell her the lie that everyone else believes.

He took the slate and wrote.

LIEF IS IN TORA

The old woman's eyes opened wide. "The king has fled to Tora?" she cried. "I did not hear the news." Her voice rose to a wail. "This cursed deafness! I did not know. Tora!"

Aimlessly she turned from the stove and stumbled towards the door that led to the outside air. As

Josef watched helplessly, she reached for the door-knob, then let her trembling hand fall.

"What am I thinking? I cannot reach him there," she mumbled. "So it was all for nothing. There is no hope. No hope." She pressed her hands to her face and began sobbing in an agony of grief.

Josef could not bear it. He hobbled to her side, tapped her arm to gain her attention, and scribbled on the slate.

HE WILL RETURN SOON

"No!" moaned Amarantz. "He knows that in Tora he will be safe. Why should he return?"

Throwing caution to the winds, Josef wrote again and thrust the slate in front of her streaming eyes.

LIEF MUST RETURN. HIS TORAN BRIDE IS HERE. UPSTAIRS. SECRET. TELL NO ONE.

Amarantz stared, and slowly her terrible sobbing died away. She took a deep, shuddering breath.

But before she could say a word, the door behind her was flung open. An enormous, roughly dressed figure wearing a cap of fur burst into the room, hauling another, much smaller, figure after it.

"Where is Doom?" the tall stranger roared. "Bring him at once!"

Frantically, Josef wiped his sleeve over the slate, rubbing out the chalked words.

He was shaking, sweating all over.

Who were these people? Had they seen the message on the slate? Was that why they were asking for Doom? To report Josef's treachery? To have him thrown into prison?

"What are you gawping at, old fossil?" roared the giant stranger, tearing off the fur cap to reveal a shaved skull painted with swirling red designs. "Move your skinny shanks! Tell Doom that Lindal of Broome is here, and that he must see her. At once!"

The stranger was a woman! His head reeling, Josef turned to do as she asked. But at the same moment the door which led to the front of the palace opened a little, and Ranesh's dark, watchful face appeared in the gap.

At the sight of a newcomer, the small stranger held out his hand pathetically. "Help me, I beg you, kind sir!" he quavered. "A little food . . . a sip of ale . . ."

Lindal thrust him away from her with a snort of

contempt. He squeaked and dropped to the floor, rolling on the stones and moaning piteously.

"I found this puny, whining fellow by the side of the north road," the giant woman roared. "He has terrible news of the king!"

Josef's heart seemed to leap into his throat. He saw Ranesh's eyes gleam with sudden fire.

"I tried to save him!" wailed the rolling figure on the floor. "I fought like a demon till the end. But what could one poor, starving acrobat do against so many Granous? What could poor Jinks do?"

4 ~ Trapped

While Jinks told lies of him in Del, Lief was struggling in the grip of a terrifying nightmare. He was trapped in a coffin. He was trying to beat at the coffin walls, but his arms and legs would not move. He was trying to open his eyes, but his eyes were sealed. He was trying to scream, but could not make a sound.

Somewhere, Kree was screeching. But closer, much closer, there were other sounds — small slapping, scratching sounds which filled Lief with dread.

Desperately he tried to wake, to free himself from the horror that had engulfed him. But every time he struggled towards consciousness, the dream dragged him down once more.

Then Kree screeched again, and this time the harsh sound was loud — loud enough to jolt Lief into true wakefulness.

He forced his sticky eyes open. He saw the tip of a black wing as Kree soared upward again, out of his view. And then, with a pang of pure terror, he realized that the dream had been real.

Or almost real. He was not lying in a coffin. He was upright. But his legs were pressed together and his arms were pinned to his sides. He could not move his head. His nose was filled with the smell of mud. His mouth was choked with it.

At first, he did not understand what had happened to him. Then he remembered.

The island, with its rippled shore and strange, cone-shaped rocks. The grub creature leaning forward, huge-eyed. The jet of yellow mist . . .

His bleary eyes focused on a tall cone standing directly in front of him. Giant grubs were crawling all over the cone, moving busily up and down.

Dimly Lief realized that they were building. They were bringing clay from the ground, mixing the clay with liquid that dribbled from their tube-like mouths, and patting the resulting mud onto the sides of the cone.

His gaze moved to the cone's tip and his stomach churned as he glimpsed Barda's head and face, almost covered by a lumpy helmet of thick, dried mud.

One of the grubs was working there. With its stubby front legs it patted and smoothed the sticky clay mess into a gap beside Barda's mouth. It waited for a moment as the mud lightened and hardened with amazing speed. Then it hurried down to the ground again.

Lief fought down panic as he realized that he himself was imprisoned as Barda was. A thick shroud of dried mud encased him from head to toe.

He could still breathe through his nose, and he could still see. But he knew that would not last long. His skin crawled as he heard a scrabbling sound near his ear. Out of the corner of his eye he saw a large-eyed head nod towards him. He felt a horrible wet coolness on his cheek as new mud was pressed into place.

The grub which had been working on Barda's mouth climbed the cone again, crawling over the mass of its fellows, who were adding to a lump of clay near the middle of the cone. Fury's cage, Lief realized.

Small, familiar sounds were coming from beneath the lump. Fury was awake, and raging. The yellow vapor had not affected her. Perhaps it worked only on warm-blooded creatures.

But even a fighting spider cannot live without air for long, Lief thought. Soon Fury will die. Like us.

He realized that Kree had stopped screeching. Had Kree finally accepted that he could not attack the grubs for fear of being stunned by the yellow mist himself? Had he, perhaps, been caught on that last, desperate swoop?

Or — Lief felt a chill run through him — or had Kree sped away in despair because he had seen Jasmine, and Filli with her, smothered in choking mud?

The cones within his view were far too small to contain Jasmine's body. A few had been broken open.

The one standing beside Barda had several holes in its center. Through the gaps, silvery-grey fur gleamed. Lief guessed that inside the cone was the preserved body of one of the little sea moles the companions had seen farther out to sea.

No doubt the moles are the grubs' usual prey, he thought. The herd we met would not follow us to the island, but other herds, no doubt, are not so wise. And the young, the weak, the lost, and the injured would often be washed to shore.

A mud grub crawled up to the scarred cone. It lifted its front feet from the ground and grasped the cone firmly. It stuck its mouth tube into one of the gaps in the clay. Its body rippled as it drank.

Lief felt sick. So this was to be their fate. To die sealed within a coffin of clay, and then for months to be a food supply for the grubs. With all his might he tried to flex his arms, move his legs, twist his neck — anything to crack the walls that imprisoned him.

But he could not move a muscle. His legs were pressed too tightly together. His arms were held too firmly by his sides. The grubs had done their work too well.

With a shudder he felt the return of the grub that had been covering his face. He shut his eyes to block out the sight of its bobbing head, its blank stare, as fresh mud was patted onto his cheek, close beside his nose.

Then, suddenly, the patting and smearing stopped, as though the grub had been disturbed in its work.

Lief opened his eyes. The grub had moved out of sight, leaving its task only half completed.

It was clear that something unusual was happening. The grubs working on Barda's cone were turning their heads, wriggling urgently. And the one feeding on the dead sea mole was pulling abruptly away from its meal, brown liquid dribbling horribly from its mouth tube.

The next moment, the grubs on Barda's cone were scattering in a cloud of yellow vapour. A ferocious, yellow-backed brown spider had hurled itself into their midst, fangs snapping viciously.

Lief stared. Flash! But how could this be? Flash had been trapped in his cage at the bottom of the boat.

Somewhere above, Kree screeched triumphantly.

Lief's heart leaped as he realized what had happened. Kree had opened the cage door. Kree had known that Flash, free at last, would have only one thing in mind: to reach Fury, wherever Fury might be.

Huge as he was, the giant spider seemed small compared to the grubs. But the grubs had no weapon except the yellow mist, which seemed to have no effect on Flash at all. And he had huge fangs, eight spiny legs, enormous strength, and a fierce will to win.

Grubs fell writhing to the ground as Flash bit and tore at them, ripping between times at the clay over Fury's cage. Already a few bars of the cage had been exposed, and Fury herself, desperate for air, was throwing herself against them, inflaming Flash even more.

More grubs were streaming into Lief's view every moment. It looked as if the whole colony was rushing to defend the cone in which Barda was trapped. The cone's lower half was covered in a seething mass of bodies. Flash was wreathed in swirling yellow mist as the newcomers attacked her in the only way they knew.

It is fortunate that the mist is not rising, or Barda would be unconscious again in a moment, Lief thought. Then all Flash's work would be of no use.

But would it be of use in any case? The widening hole around Fury's cage would not help Barda break out of his prison. The hardened clay around the big man's arms and legs was untouched.

Then Lief felt something. The clay that cloaked his own left hand was being tapped strongly by something hard and sharp.

Lief guessed what it was, but did not let himself believe it until Kree's beak broke through the clay and stabbed his wrist.

Never had Lief felt pain so joyously.

Another two taps and the clay covering his hand had cracked away completely. Violently Lief scrabbled at the edges of the hole, making it larger. Then, as Kree began work on his other hand, Lief felt even more vibrations — a scratching and scraping near his foot.

"Lief!"

With wild joy, Lief recognized the whispering voice. Jasmine was crouching by his right side. He could not see her, but he could feel her dagger chipping at the hard shell that imprisoned him.

Jasmine was alive! Kree must have rushed to free her as soon as the grubs left her to defend Barda's cone.

"As soon as you feel my dagger against your boot, begin to kick," Jasmine whispered. "We may not have much time."

Lief felt movement near his chin and, squinting downward, saw a small grey shape. His fur spiked with mud, Filli was nibbling and clawing furiously at the clay that swathed Lief's neck.

Lief felt the point of Jasmine's dagger against his foot and began kicking towards it, feeling clay crumbling away. He felt her start work on the other side. He felt clay crack from his right hand and wrist as Kree's sharp beak broke through.

His left arm was already free to the elbow. He could bend it. And, thanks to Filli, he could move his head from side to side once more.

He struggled desperately, his eyes fixed on the squirming mass of grubs at the base of Barda's cone. Absorbed by their struggle with Flash, the grubs still had not noticed what was happening behind their backs.

But at any moment, surely, one of them would turn and give the alarm. Then all would be lost.

Lief closed his eyes and took a deep breath, summoning up all his strength. He imagined the clay as an egg, enclosing him. Then, with every muscle in his body, he pushed outward, willing the shell to crack.

5 ~ Hope and Fears

There was a long moment of tension. Then, suddenly, the clay shell simply shattered, falling in great chunks to the ground.

The grubs at the base of Barda's cone turned, huge blank eyes staring. They remained absolutely still for a single moment, then reared up, twisting and turning, heads bobbing. Some began scrambling rapidly towards Lief.

Lief staggered, off-balance. His left foot was still trapped. He kicked violently, fumbling for his sword.

"Lief! Cover your face! They will try to spray you again!" he heard Jasmine shout.

Lief glanced around, sword in hand. Jasmine, her mouth and nose covered by a scarf, was scooping Filli from the rubble. Covered in clay dust, chattering frantically, Filli leaped to her shoulder and dived under her collar.

Then Jasmine was darting away without a backward glance, lunging towards Barda. Three grubs reared up, blocking her path. She dodged aside, covering her muffled face. The grubs sprayed yellow mist after her, but did not attempt to give chase.

The grubs approaching Lief had also stopped. It seemed to have been decided between them that all their energies should be devoted to protecting Barda, their remaining, and finest, prize.

With his free hand, Lief snatched at the hem of his cloak and dragged it up, winding the cloth around his face so that its dusty folds covered his nose. He kicked away the last of the clay and staggered forward.

Flash was taking no notice of the panic around her. She had completely uncovered Fury's cage now, and the two spiders were trying to fight through the bars. The cage was swinging violently, chipping away more clay every moment. Lief could clearly see Barda's jacket, his belt buckle — even the hilt of his sword.

The grubs had stopped trying to mend the gap. Now they were concentrating on Barda's face, no doubt aware that the sooner he was dead, the sooner they would be left in peace.

Barda's eyes were open. He was staring straight at Lief.

Lief knew what those eyes were saying.

Leave me. Take the boat and go. You cannot help me.

Lief shook his head violently. He took another step.

Too close. A grub reared up at him. He jumped away, pressing his cloak hard against his face to avoid the burst of spray that would make him a prisoner once more.

Dagger in hand, Jasmine was warily circling Barda's cone, keeping a good distance from the thrashing grubs that guarded it. Lief ran to her side.

"Kree and I cannot get near him, Lief," Jasmine muttered. "They spray as soon as we try. If only we had a tool with a very long handle. Then, perhaps, we could smash the clay from a distance. But we brought nothing like that with us, and the boat's paddles are far too short and frail to be of use."

Lief ran over the contents of the boat in his mind and reluctantly decided that Jasmine was right. There was nothing of use in the boat. Nothing but food, water, sleeping blankets, bailing buckets, rope . . .

Buckets! Rope! An idea struck him like a bolt of lightning.

"There is another way to break the clay," he said, gripping Jasmine's arm. "Come with me."

He told her his plan as they raced to the boat. They snatched up a coil of rope and the buckets used for bailing. They filled the buckets with water, hurried back to the place where Barda stood, and dashed the water onto the base of the cone.

The grubs there reared and hissed, but did not

retreat. Flash and Fury, their hard, spiny bodies wet and glistening, fought on as if nothing had happened. The water streamed off the hardened clay and sank quickly into the softer earth beneath.

"Quickly!" Lief gave Jasmine one end of the rope, keeping the other end in his own hand. They set off rapidly in opposite directions, their arms held high, circling the cone once, twice, like children playing a game. Loops of rope tightened around the cone, just above Fury's cage. Confused, the grubs hissed at the loops and began running up and down, trying to cover them with clay.

Jasmine and Lief came together on the shore behind the cone.

"Now!" Lief breathed. And pulled his end of the rope with all his strength.

He heard Jasmine groaning with effort as she, too, heaved with all her might. He heard the blood pounding in his ears. He heard Kree screeching above his head.

And then, at last, he heard the sound he had been waiting for — a sucking, squelching sound, as the soggy earth beneath the cone released its hold. Slowly, the cone began to tilt towards him.

He shouted in triumph, and heard Jasmine's voice joining his own as together they ploughed backwards, the lines of rope straining between the cone and their aching hands.

Then, quite suddenly, the cone was toppling. The

grubs were scattering in confusion and panic. And Lief and Jasmine were staggering back, falling, sprawling, as the cone fell crashing to the ground.

Lief scrambled to his feet. Dust hung in a low cloud above the ruins of Barda's prison and the bodies of crushed and dying grubs. Barda himself lay groaning amidst the rubble. Rearing and twisting frantically, the surviving grubs were coming out of hiding and hurrying towards him, yellow vapor already puffing from the tubes below their eyes.

Lief and Jasmine ran to Barda and dragged him to his feet. Dazed, confused, he stumbled between them towards the boat.

Lief saw, to his amazement, that Flash was still clinging to the cage attached to Barda's belt. Covered in dust, almost as dazed as Barda himself, the spider had stopped fighting with Fury, and was hunched like a bundle of sticks against the cage bars.

"Make haste!" Jasmine urged, glancing behind her.

Lief looked over his shoulder in turn and saw that the grubs had disappeared from sight. But the area around the patch of rubble was pitted with holes. The beasts were tunnelling towards them.

The companions reached the boat and Lief and Jasmine hauled it down to the waterline. All around them the wet mud was beginning to bubble as grubs came to the surface.

"In! In!" shrieked Jasmine, pushing at Barda

feverishly. He tumbled into the boat and lay there mumbling and groaning as his companions splashed into the muddy water, hauling the boat behind them.

In seconds, pale heads began emerging from the sand. But Lief and Jasmine were already scrambling into their craft and taking up the paddles. They were paddling furiously away, into ever deeper water.

Only when they had crossed the band of bright seaweed that ringed the island did they look back. The shore they had left behind them was squirming with grubs and veiled in a thick yellow haze. And in the background were the shapes of the lumpy, twisted cones, pale against the dim sky.

✳

A very different sky, sunny and blue as forget-me-nots, was visible through the window of the palace bedchamber where Jinks the acrobat lay.

But Jinks was not interested in the view. He was interested only in the delicious broth being fed to him by Sharn, and in telling the story of his heroic but vain efforts to save Lief from death.

"Of course I would never have left him, had I not seen him die. I would willingly have laid down my own life for my king!" he wailed, rolling his eyes. "And for his friend, poor brave Barda, too, though Barda was often thoughtlessly cruel to me, rest his soul."

His freshly bathed hands clutched the sheet of the soft bed to which he had been carried. His eyelids fluttered as he opened his mouth to receive the spoon-ful of broth that Sharn was holding out to him. He swallowed, sighed, and opened his mouth again.

Sharn forced back the tears that were burning be-hind her eyes. She tried to concentrate on Doom's last words to her, before he set off for the Os-Mine Hills with the giant woman, Lindal of Broome.

"I know Jinks of old, Sharn," Doom had said, pressing her hand. "He will say and do anything that serves his purpose. Parts of his story are true, no doubt, but not all. Lief may be in danger, but he still lives, I am certain of it. We will find him, never fear."

Sharn gave Jinks the last spoonful of broth and shook her head slightly. She wished she could share Doom's certainty.

No doubt Doom believes Lief is alive because the Shadow Lord has not invaded Deltora, Sharn thought. But even the Shadow Lord is not all-knowing. His spies have told him that Lief and the Belt are safe in Tora, and he believes it. His attention is not focused on us. For now. But that could change at any time. Any time . . .

She put aside the empty bowl. When she turned back to the bed, she saw that her patient's eyes were closed, and that he was breathing slowly and evenly. Jinks had fallen asleep, it seemed.

Sharn shut her own eyes. Her head was throb-bing.

She knew she should get up and go downstairs.

There was so much to do. There were still crowds of people in the entrance hall. And by now Marilen would be waiting in her room for her midday meal. Her tray would have to be fetched from the kitchen. Then the poor girl would have to be told, as gently as possible, of the news Jinks had brought. Sharn dreaded the very thought of that.

I will stay here and rest, just for a little while, she said to herself.

Jinks opened his eyes a crack. He peered out from under his eyelashes and saw Sharn still sitting quietly beside him, her head bowed. He almost cursed aloud in annoyance.

What was the woman doing, just sitting there? Did she have no work to do? He had expected her to creep out of the room as soon as she thought he was asleep. Not go to sleep herself!

He considered groaning to disturb her, then decided it would be unwise to do this immediately. After all, he had just pretended to fall peacefully asleep.

Be patient, Jinks, my boy, he told himself. You do not want to make her suspicious, do you? Wake her later if you need to, but for now keep your eyes shut and your mouth closed. And while you are doing that, you can use that mighty brain of yours to make your plan perfect.

6 - Dread

Every nerve in Lief's body was telling him that all was not well in Del. Paddling in the dimming light, with Jasmine beside him, the spiders mercifully sleeping in their cages at the bottom of the boat, and Barda resting in the stern, he had tried to relax. But the feeling of dread had been growing for the past hour. It was impossible to ignore.

He had tried telling himself that it was caused by the gloom through which the little boat was moving. Where once there had been shimmering rainbows, now there was only sullen dullness.

But he knew that this was not the whole answer. The words "Danger" and "Del" kept stealing into his mind hand in hand, tormenting him.

"I do not like this," muttered Barda, breaking the long silence. "I fear the Aurons have sensed us, and

191

have dimmed the light so as to be able to take us unawares."

Lief made no reply.

Jasmine turned to look at him. "You are plainly not with us, Lief," she said coldly. "Could you not speak of what is on your mind, for once?"

Lief sighed. "I keep feeling there is trouble in Del," he said, giving in to the temptation to voice his thoughts. "I would give much to be able to tell Mother and Doom and — and others in the palace who may be worrying — where we are."

"It is a little late to think of that," snapped Jasmine. She knew only too well who Lief meant by "others." He meant the girl he was to marry. The girl he had chosen from "one of the best Toran families," as Jinks had put it, to be his queen.

How can he think I do not know of her? she thought resentfully. *Everyone* is gossiping of the marriage plans, according to Jinks.

Then she realized, with a start, that Lief had said "others *in the palace*." So his bride-to-be was already in Del! Lief had brought her with him when he returned from Tora.

Then he left her almost at once, to pursue me, Jasmine thought. And he has not returned. How she must hate me for that. And Sharn and Doom must hate me, too, for delaying the marriage that was to give Deltora an heir, make it safe.

For the first time she faced the fact that her hasty

192

rush to the Os-Mine Hills might have disastrous results for her country.

Because of me, Lief is in danger, she thought. And that means that Deltora is in terrible danger, too. I have my reasons for trying to reach the Shadowlands. The best of reasons! A little sister I never knew I had. A sister who is depending on me to save her. But I did not intend others to suffer by my actions.

Guilt pierced her heart. And the guilt made her angry.

"I did not ask you and Barda to come rushing after me, Lief!" she said harshly. "If you had not, I would be dead, certainly. But Deltora would have been safe. And your . . . your friends . . . would have had no need to fear."

Lief frowned. To him, Jasmine's anger seemed quite unreasonable. Why should she flare up like this, when all he had said was that he wished he could send a message home?

"Surely I have told you often enough, Jasmine, that, far from blaming you for anything, I am *grateful* to you!" he exclaimed. "If we had not followed you we would never have found the Pirran Islands."

Receiving no reply, he grew even more irritated. "As soon as you told me that the Shadowlands prisoners were in danger I agreed to move on at once, did I not? Without returning to Del to get help? What more could you ask of me?"

Jasmine sniffed.

"When you two have finished sniping at one another," growled Barda from the stern, "you may care to look at what is ahead."

Lief's stomach tightened as he obeyed. A large, low, spreading shape was slowly becoming visible through the dimness. It was very close. They had come upon it all unknowing.

"Land!" he breathed.

"Yes," Barda muttered. "And this time it may well be Auron. In this gloom we might easily have rounded a cavern wall without seeing it. We had better be prepared."

✳

At the same moment, in Del, Sharn was roused by the sound of Jinks moaning. She had no idea of how much time had passed since she began to doze, but she knew very well that the moans were intended to attract her attention.

She looked down at Jinks.

"Are you in pain?" she enquired, a little impatiently. "Perhaps you need another dose of my herbal cure? I know the taste is not pleasant, but — "

"Oh no, my lady!" Jinks cried hastily "The pain has quite gone, thanks to you. But I am still as weak as a baby, and my memories torment me!"

Sharn looked concerned. Jinks fluttered his eyelashes and sighed.

"Please do not feel you have to stay with me," he whispered pathetically. "I need only a good, long sleep. This evening I could perhaps force down a little ale, if you would bring it to me. A glass or two might settle my nerves."

"I will leave you then," said Sharn, rising to her feet. "Sleep well."

Sharn was no fool. She was certain that Jinks was pretending to be far more unwell than he was, so as to be assured of a soft bed, plentiful food, and tender nursing. He had a few cuts and bruises, and his feet were blistered. That was all.

But it suited her that the acrobat should stay where he was for now. It was vital that the news he had brought to the place did not spread and reach the Shadow Lord's ears.

The other people who had been in the kitchen when Jinks arrived would be no problem. Lindal was with Doom. Josef and Ranesh had been sworn to secrecy, then taken back to the library. They would not be permitted to venture downstairs again until Doom's return.

And Amarantz? Amarantz, completely deaf, had not heard a word Jinks had said.

I admit I am grateful for that, Sharn thought. Amarantz is a good cook and a willing worker as well as a good friend. I would be sorry to have to hide *her* away upstairs.

She put her hand to the knob of the bedchamber door. But as she did so the knob turned, the door opened, and Marilen hurried into the room.

"I heard your voice, Sharn," Marilen began. "I have been looking for you everywhere! I must — "

"Marilen — why are you here?" cried Sharn, trying to shield the girl from the bed. "Please, I beg you, go back to your room. I know you must be hungry, but I will bring your tray to you as soon as I am able."

Marilen stood her ground. "Doom brought me my meal before he left," she said shortly. "I must speak with you, Sharn. It is very urgent. I — "

She broke off as she caught sight of Jinks, who had struggled to a sitting position so as to see her more clearly. "Doom told me that a man called Jinks is claiming that Lief is dead," she said abruptly. "Is this he? Is this Jinks?"

"Indeed, my lady, to my great grief," whimpered Jinks. With a tiny groan he fell back on his pillows, his hand to his brow. His eyes, alive with curiosity, gleamed as he watched Marilen between his fingers.

"You are a liar!" the girl snapped. "Why are you playing this trick?" She was holding herself very straight. Her voice was filled with contempt. Her beautiful face was stern.

She has grown up very rapidly in the past weeks, thought Sharn, with something of a shock. How is it that I have not noticed? Oh, why did Doom have to tell her? I did not know he had seen her before he left.

"Has this man been left alone at any time since

he arrived in the palace, Sharn?" Marilen demanded. "Even for a moment?"

Sharn shook her head. "Please leave us, Marilen," she said in a low voice. "I must go downstairs now, but I will come to you as soon as I can."

Marilen hesitated, then nodded. "Please hurry. I will be in the library," she said. With another contemptuous glance at Jinks, she turned and stalked from the room.

"Poor young lady," murmured Jinks. "My news has affected her deeply, it seems."

"All who fear the Shadow Lord must be deeply affected, Jinks," said Sharn, struggling to keep her voice even. She left the room, the door closing with a soft click behind her.

The moment he was alone, Jinks threw back the covers and scrambled from the bed. He padded to the door on his bandaged feet and twisted the knob.

The door was locked. He was a prisoner.

Jinks frowned. Here was something unexpected. Sharn, for all her soft words, did not trust him.

This did not suit his plans at all.

"You think you have me where you want me, my lady," he muttered aloud. "But you will find that Jinks is not so easily outwitted."

Quickly he began to search the room.

7 - Truth and Lies

Far away, in the secret sea, Jasmine leaned forward, peering at the land ahead. She murmured to Kree, who spread his wings and soared into the air. The companions watched as the bird sped low towards the dark, mysterious mass.

Suddenly, something shot upwards from the water. Kree seemed to stop dead in mid-air. And the next moment the boat was rocking violently as Jasmine leaped to her feet, shrieking. For Kree was plummeting, wings fluttering helplessly, into the sea.

"Jasmine!" roared Barda. "You will have us over!"

Lights flared in the darkness ahead. There was the sound of shouting, and splashing.

Jasmine threw herself down, seized her paddle,

and plunged it into the water. "Lief, help me!" she cried. "Make haste! Kree will drown!"

"No!" Barda roared. "Turn the boat! Get us away!"

But Lief paid no heed to either of them. He had dropped his paddle and was reaching for his sword. Dozens of long, pale forms were streaking through the water towards them, like enormous spears veiled with foam.

"Beware!" he shouted. And had no time to say more. For in seconds the attackers were upon them, surging from the water amid fountains of spray.

Lief gripped his sword, knowing that to use it would be fatal. The boat was surrounded by a ring of huge, sharp-fanged silver eels. Their wicked mouths gaped wide, streaming with water. And hunched on the neck of each one was a wild-eyed, dog-faced being clothed in grey animal skins. The beings' hands, tat-tooed from wrist to fingertip, held long, thin spears of sharpened bone, poised to strike.

A dripping black bundle was thrown carelessly into the boat. It was Kree. The bird struggled pitifully at Jasmine's feet, one wing trailing. With a cry, Jas-mine bent to him. The spear arms drew back.

Lief never knew where the words came from. Pure instinct brought them to his lips. "We are the people of Doran the Dragonlover. Do not harm us, tribe of Auron," he gasped.

The eels stared glassily, without understanding. But the strange beings on their backs stirred. Lief was conscious of pale, slitted eyes measuring him.

"Doran sent you to us from above?" one of the Aurons asked at last.

Her voice was like a song, like water rippling over stones. But there was warning in it.

Do not lie.

Lief swallowed, aware that at any moment a spear could plunge into his heart. "Doran is long dead, as you must know," he said carefully. "His words, written in an old book, led us to you."

"What do you seek?" asked another of the Aurons. And again the voice was full of melody, with an undercurrent of threat.

Tell the truth.

"Many of Doran's people are prisoners of the Shadow Lord," said Lief. "To save them, we need the Pirran Pipe."

There was a soft, sighing sound like a wind skimming over water. The spears were lowered a little.

"The Pipe is in three parts," said the first Auron to have spoken.

Do not lie.

Lief nodded. "We already have one part," he said quietly. "We have come to beg you for the second, though we were told you would not give it."

The Auron glanced at her friends. Then she

turned back to Lief. Her tattooed hands tightened on her spear, and slowly turned its point downward.

"You were told truly," she said. "Come with us."

✳

As their boat was towed to shore, the companions saw, to their astonishment, that the "island" was not an island at all. It was a mass of rafts, bound together to form one vast platform crowded with mud-brick dwellings.

The edge of the platform was thronged with people. Many held torches that smoked and flickered, giving off an oily, fishy smell. Small children, yawning and rubbing their eyes, hid behind the adults' legs. Older children stood in groups, very upright and stern, short bone spears at the ready.

Behind the crowd rose a low tower open on all sides. At the top of the tower stood two shadowy figures. One of these was wearing long robes and a tall headdress.

The Piper of Auron, Lief thought. Keeper of the stem of the Pirran Pipe. He watched as the Piper turned and spoke. He saw the companion hesitate, then finally bow. An instruction, it seemed, had been given and accepted.

"This is Auron?" Barda muttered, as they clambered out of the boat.

Lief looked about him. Everywhere there were signs that the people had been woken by the intruders. The newly lit torches. The heavy-eyed children.

201

The doors of the dwellings hanging open, as if the inhabitants had rushed out in alarm.

"It is certainly a place where Aurons *live*," he murmured back. "But it cannot be Auron itself. The map makes it clear that Auron is a true island."

"Then where are we?" Jasmine demanded. She had climbed up beside them and now stood looking around warily, Kree cradled in her arms.

"I think this platform is the dotted outline on the map," Lief whispered. "Doran used a broken line to show that its position is not fixed. It is anchored now, but no doubt it moves around when the people wish it."

"Why do they not live on their island?" Jasmine demanded fiercely, not troubling to lower her voice. "Are they so savage and careless that they have made it unfit to support life?"

Lief nudged her violently, but it was too late. Many in the crowd had heard her, and were frowning and muttering among themselves.

Jasmine's eyes flashed green fire. "I do not care what they think!" she spat. "They struck Kree down for no reason. Who would do such a thing to a creature who meant no harm?"

"Those who did not *know* he meant no harm," said a quiet voice beside Lief. "Those who have never seen a bird in their lives, and who have learned, through bitter experience, that what is unknown may be deadly."

Lief swung around. A pair of shrewd eyes met his own. Instinctively, he knew that this was one of the figures he had seen in the tower. The Piper's companion.

"My name is Penn," the Auron said. "I am the history-keeper of the rafts. The Piper has appointed me to be your host."

"Our jailer, you mean!" flashed Jasmine.

Penn smiled, showing two rows of chipped, pointed teeth. "Whatever I am, I am all you have," she said simply. "It would be wise for you to follow me, now, to a safe place. The crowd's mood is growing ugly."

✳

As Lief, Barda, and Jasmine followed Penn through the narrow pathways of the rafts, Jinks ran on tiptoe through the hallways of the second floor of the palace.

The long, strong hairpin he had found at the back of a drawer had helped him escape from his own bedchamber. Now it was time to carry out his plans.

He knew he had plenty of time. Even if Sharn came upstairs again, she would not stop on the second floor. She would go straight up to the library to see what that Toran spitfire, Marilen, wanted.

There was no doubt in his mind that Marilen was Lief's bride-to-be. How exciting it had been to see the message on the slate that old fool had been holding up in the kitchen!

And now Jinks had seen the girl for himself. A

pert little minx she is, too, he thought resentfully. How dare she call me a liar? As it happens, I *am* lying. But for all she knows, I am telling the honest truth!

He reached the last door in the hallway and began to work on the lock with his hairpin. Lief probably *is* dead by now, in any case, he thought. But whether he is or not, my pleasant life in the palace is over. It is very unfair, but there it is.

He closed his eyes, jiggling the lock, as his thoughts ran over familiar ground. Yes, Jinks, he told himself, you must face facts. If Lief is alive, he will return and tell everyone that you abandoned him. Then you will be finished. And if Lief is dead, the Shadow Lord will come, and the palace itself is finished.

With satisfaction, he heard the lock give way with a gentle click. He entered the room, carefully closing the door behind him.

A blue cloak hanging on a hook in one corner told him that the room was Sharn's. Good! Rapidly, Jinks began to go through shelves and drawers.

I will search all the rooms and take what I fancy, he thought. By the time the losses are discovered I will be riding west on a stolen horse, my saddlebags stuffed with valuables. And in the west I will find a nice, safe hiding place where a rich acrobat who is not too choosy about his friends can enjoy a well-earned retirement.

Closing the last of the drawers, he saw with annoyance that his search had yielded only a few coins, a topaz brooch, and a gold chain upon which hung a locket containing a tiny portrait of King Endon, Lief's father, as a young man.

Jinks snorted in disgust. Why, the king's mother still dressed like a blacksmith's wife! Where were the jewels, gold rings, and ropes of pearls he had expected to find?

Shaking his head, he hurried out of the room and moved to the next door.

Do not fret, Jinks, my boy, he told himself, inserting his handy hairpin into the lock. The girl Marilen's room must be here somewhere.

The gossip was that Lief had chosen the finest of the royal jewels for his bride. But Marilen had not been wearing anything of value when Jinks saw her. So the jewels must be hidden away in her room. What a prize *they* would be!

The lock clicked under the pressure of his fingers, and he entered the second room.

It looked almost as bare as the first. But on a low table by the fire was a tray holding a bowl of stew, a salad, some bread, and, best of all, a small golden-brown cake in a silver paper case.

Jinks hurried to the table, reached for the cake, then drew back. A folded paper was lying beside the tray. Clearly it had not yet been read, for its wax seal was only partly broken. Eyes sharp with curiosity, Jinks opened it.

My dearest Marilen,

We in Tora can no longer share your thoughts. The distance that separates us is too great. But your last letter made me uneasy, for it said nothing of your feelings, or of Lief. I fear there is something troubling you—something that you cannot, or dare not, put into words. I pray that all is well.

I am writing to say that Zeean and I will be travelling to Del within the next few days. I know you will be delighted by this news, my dear, and will tell all those who need to know of it.

Your loving father

Jinks grinned in delight. So he had stumbled on Marilen's room already! He should have realized it at once, because of the tray. The spoiled wench had stormed off to find Sharn, leaving her meal untouched.

He grabbed the cake and gobbled it down with relish.

Now, to find the jewels! He looked around, enjoying the moment. Then, with shock and disbelief, he felt a stab of pain, agonizing pain, in his stomach. Gasping, he doubled up, clutching his belly as the pain stabbed again, and again. He tried to call out, but could manage only a croaking whisper.

Agony gripped him. He fell writhing to the floor, his fingers clawing on the thin rug, his heels kicking at the table.

The table tilted. The tray slid over the edge.

By the time it hit the ground, Jinks was dead.

8 - The House of Penn

Thoughts of Del had again begun nagging at Lief as he followed Penn through the maze of narrow walkways that ran between the crowded dwellings of the rafts. But they were driven from his mind the moment he, Jasmine, and Barda entered the history-keeper's hut.

The hut was small but pleasant, despite the strong smell of fish oil that drifted both from the stove burning in one corner and the shell lamp fixed to a wall.

A sleeping hammock covered with a patchwork rug of grey skins hung from hooks fastened to the low ceiling. There was no other furniture at all, but the floor was covered with a beautiful mat woven in soft sea colors.

Three of the smooth, pale walls were covered with hanging baskets in which rolled parchments, clothes, and other belongings were neatly arranged. The door wall was bare except for a hook upon which Penn invited Lief to hang his cloak, a curtained window, and a small wall-hanging woven in a strange, bold pattern.

Below the wall hanging was a large blue bowl filled with water. Inside the bowl, two small, upright sea creatures swayed amid fronds of silver weed. They were very like sea horses in shape, but glittered with every color of the rainbow.

"My companions, Tresk and Mesk," said Penn, leaning over the bowl. Plainly, by the way she cooed and smiled at the little creatures as they bobbed up to nuzzle her hand, bubbling eagerly, they were very dear to her.

She looked anxious as Filli crept out from under Jasmine's collar and ran down to the edge of the bowl to investigate.

"Filli would not harm them," Jasmine assured her. But Penn did not relax until Filli was safely back on Jasmine's shoulder again, nibbling at a dried berry from Jasmine's pocket.

After that, Penn busied herself in making her guests welcome. She could not have been more helpful, or more agreeable.

She took down the hammock and stored it away, to make more room. Then she supplied Jasmine with everything necessary to care for Kree's injured wing. All the while she asked questions about Deltora and the companions' present journey, listening alertly to their answers.

Finally, once Kree was resting comfortably, she brought large snail shells of strong, oily soup to her guests.

"It is not to your taste, perhaps?" she asked anxiously, as she watched them drink.

"Oh, no, it is very good," Lief assured her, trying not to wrinkle his nose. He felt something hard on his tongue and removed it. It was a shrivelled claw. He stared at it with repulsion, wondering what horrible creature it had come from.

Penn looked grave. "You would be wise always to speak the truth on the rafts," she said gently. "As a keeper of history, who has read much of what Doran taught our ancestors, I am familiar with your people's ways. But in this I am different from most. Even politeness, which in the world above, I believe, is thought good, is no excuse for lies here."

She gestured to the wall-hanging which had fascinated Lief ever since he entered the hut.

Lief, Barda, and Jasmine stared at the bold symbols, and at last saw the word concealed within them.

"Truth," Lief murmured.

Penn nodded. "Beauty is important to us, as befits followers of the Piper Auron," she said. "But we believe that nothing can be truly beautiful unless truth dwells within it. Lies and pretense have been the ruin of our people in the past. Now our children are taught from their earliest days that truth is all-important, and lying is the greatest sin."

She smiled slightly. "So, tell me. Are you really enjoying the meal you have been given?"

"Well, if you want the truth, while I am grateful for your kindness, I find it repulsive!" growled Barda, putting down his shell.

"And I," said Jasmine, doing likewise.

Lief sighed. "Truly the most unpleasant brew I have ever tasted," he agreed.

Penn's smile broadened. "It is written that Doran felt the same at first," she chuckled. Quickly she drained her own shell, crunching the dregs with relish.

"And now," she said, with obvious reluctance, putting the shell aside, "it is my task to tell you why we cannot help you."

Lief leaned forward. "Could we not speak to your Piper? Our cause is just, and we would have your part of the Pirran Pipe for only — "

Penn raised her arm, which was covered in complicated tattoos almost to the elbow.

"Do not waste your breath in argument," she

said bluntly. "The Piper knows why you are here. The guards who were not needed for towing your boat landed long before you and informed him."

She sighed at the expression on Lief's face.

"The Piper wishes you to know that we would give you anything you asked, if we could. Your kinsman Doran spent much time on the rafts in ages past. He gave our ancestors many gifts, including the gift of fire, without which our lives today would be miserable beyond words."

Barda frowned. "Then — "

Penn shrugged. "Do you think that we would live like this if our part of the Pirran Pipe was with us?" she sighed. "Do you think we *choose* to drift the seas, spending half our lives searching for materials to mend the rafts? Do you think we *choose* to live in darkness, when our souls long for light?"

Lief struggled with warring feelings of disbelief and bitter disappointment. He knew the second part of the Pipe was near. He could feel it! Yet he knew also that Penn, whose people valued truth above all things, could not be lying.

"The stem of the Pipe is lost, then?" he asked in a level voice.

"Lost to us," said Penn. "It is on the island of Auron. And that is lost to us, also."

"*Lost?*" Jasmine shook her head impatiently. "*How* lost? Has it sunk into the sea? Has it been overrun by the monsters you bred to — "

"Monsters *we* bred?" cried Penn. Pale eyes flashing, all stiffness forgotten, she jumped to her feet. "Who has told you this lie?" she thundered, looking down at Jasmine angrily.

Then her face changed. Her eyes narrowed, and her wide mouth hardened. "Ah, of course," she hissed. "Those accursed Plumes, who could not speak the truth if their lives depended upon it. Who would stop at nothing to smear our name to descendants of Doran!"

"If the Plumes were lying, they did not know it," snapped Jasmine, refusing to be cowed. "They told us only what they truly believed."

Penn glared at her for a moment. Then, slowly, her rage seemed to die, and her face relaxed. "I am sorry for my anger," she said, walking to the window, pulling aside the curtain, and staring out at the dimness. "I was wrong to blame you. The Plumes are clever deceivers."

Jasmine looked as if she was going to argue further, but Lief spoke quickly, before she had the chance. Hope was again flaring in his heart. For if the second part of the Pirran Pipe was on Auron, it could surely be won, whatever the danger that guarded it.

"Tell us, Penn, I beg you, why you say Auron is lost," he urged.

Strange, high, echoing calls began to drift through the window, filling the room, growing louder every moment.

Penn turned around. Her face was shadowed with weariness and something more. Despair, perhaps.

"Dawn is being sung by the Piper," she said. "The time of sleep is over. Not that any of us have *had* our proper sleep, this night."

"I am sorry — " Lief began, but Penn waved away his apology and walked to the hanging baskets on the back wall. She selected two small, ragged pieces of parchment, then moved to the door.

"Come," she said. "Your boat may now leave the rafts with safety."

"We cannot leave!" exclaimed Jasmine, glancing protectively at Kree. "Kree must rest further. He is still weak."

"The bird may remain where he is," said Penn, her serious face relaxing a little as she regarded Jasmine's earnest face. "In his condition he will not trouble Tresk and Mesk, and you will be back before the Piper calls down the night. To swim would be faster, but not for you, I suspect. I am taking you to Auron."

Lief's heart jolted with excitement. He glanced at Barda, whose face was bright with triumph.

Penn's shrewd eyes seemed to dim as she watched them. "I do not look forward to the journey," she murmured. "I had hoped to avoid it. But you must see the island for yourselves. Only then will you understand the truth."

9 ~ Troubles

Not another word would Penn say. In silence she led the companions through the walkways. Curtains twitched aside as they passed, and faces filled with curiosity, fear, or resentment peered out.

The back of Lief's neck burned. "We are not welcome here," he muttered.

"Why should you be?" said Penn calmly. "You invaded our waters in a Plume boat, carrying the Plume part of the Pirran Pipe, to mock us. You brought fearsome creatures with you. You accused us of making Auron unfit for life. And you are very large and ugly, and smell unpleasant."

"An attractive list of qualities," said Barda dryly. "I wonder how you could bear to have us in your home, Penn."

Penn shrugged. "As I told you, I have read of

your people. That was why the Piper chose me for this task."

They reached the edge of the platform where their boat still rocked gently, tied up with a few others. Stony-faced guards moved aside at a word from Penn to let them pass.

The water was alive with huge, ferocious-looking eels like the ones the guards had been riding. They were cruising just below the surface, twisting together lazily.

Trying not to look at them, Lief, Jasmine, and Barda climbed into the boat, taking great care not to slip. Penn followed, quite untroubled. Then she caught sight of Fury and Flash, still asleep in their cages on the floor of the boat.

"I had forgotten them, when I suggested we take your boat," she murmured nervously. "Their cages are strong, I suppose?"

"Very strong," Lief assured her, taking up his paddle.

Penn shuddered and untied the boat, turning her head as she did so to stare at the eels, which she plainly found quite restful to look upon.

She pointed west. "That way," she said in a low voice. "Keep a straight course. And please paddle gently. I do not distrust your word, but I would prefer that your beasts did not wake."

The boat moved away from the platform. Ahead was dim, open sea. And Auron.

✳

A world away, in Del, the sun was sliding slowly down towards the horizon.

Sharn had been in the entrance hall for far longer than she had intended. Many, many people were waiting to speak to her.

One of these was Barda's deputy, a Resistance fighter called Mobley, who wished to report a death. Pieter, the brother of one of the helpers in the entrance hall, had died horribly when two Plains scorpions escaped from a box he had hidden under his shirt.

"We think it was Pieter who put the scorpion in the king's bedchamber, ma'am," Mobley said. "In the old days he was a roof-mender. He could have easily climbed to the king's window and cut the bars. Also, we found this in the scorpions' box. Maria says it is her brother's writing."

He showed a scrap of paper.

> the King must die the King must die the King must die the King must die the King must die the King must die the King must die the King must die the King must die the King must die the King

"But why would Maria's brother feel this way?" Sharn exclaimed, amazed and distressed.

Mobley shrugged. "Who knows? Like many other folk, he and Maria lost each other the night the

Shadow Lord took over the city. They only met again by chance, when Pieter wandered into the palace a few weeks ago. He was thin as a rail, had no memory, and suffered from headaches, bad headaches that gave him no peace."

He paused. "It was a terrible thing Pieter did, ma'am, but as I saw him lying there it came into my mind that if things had been different, I could have gone the same way as he did. I, too, lost my family in the troubles. It was only joining up with the Resistance that kept me sane, I think."

Sharn hurried upstairs at last, and went directly to the library. There she found Marilen sitting at one of the tables. Josef, looking harried and distressed, was checking books nearby, with Ranesh silently assisting him.

When Marilen saw Sharn, she stood up at once. Her face was very pale. "We will talk in my bedchamber, if you please," she said formally.

They moved down the great staircase in strained silence. As they reached the second floor, and the guards who barred the stairs stepped aside to let them pass, Marilen swallowed and seemed to make a great effort to calm herself.

"Forgive me, Sharn, if I seem to be behaving oddly," she whispered. "I went to the library for comfort while I waited for you. But I must speak to you in privacy. Josef and Ranesh — especially Ranesh — must not hear what I have to say. And

I believe it is dangerous to speak aloud out here."

She hastened towards the hallway which led to her own room. Sharn followed, greatly troubled. What had made Marilen think the hallways were not safe? This floor had been searched very thoroughly for listening devices.

But even stranger was Marilen's determination not to speak where Josef and Ranesh might hear. Sharn had assumed that the girl wanted only to discuss the report of Lief's death. But Josef and Ranesh knew about that already.

What else could she have to tell me? Sharn thought. And why does she say that Ranesh, in particular, should not know of it?

Marilen had reached her door and drawn out her key. But when she put the key in the lock, she drew back.

"It is already unlocked," she whispered.

Before Sharn could stop her, she had twisted the knob and thrown the door wide. There was a moment's horrified silence. Then Marilen gave a single, piercing cry and buried her face in her hands. Sharn simply stared, shocked and silent.

Jinks lay sprawled amid a small wreckage of broken china and spoiled food. His eyes stared sightlessly at the ceiling. His mouth was twisted in a snarl of agony. From the pocket of his trousers spilled part of a fine gold chain with a locket hanging from it.

Sharn looked down at it. "My locket," she said

219

slowly, trying to make sense of what she was seeing. Then, pulling herself together, she moved past Marilen and knelt by Jinks, feeling for his pulse.

After a moment she stood up. "He is dead," she said evenly. "He must have been more badly injured than we, or he himself, thought. His heart — "

"No," said Marilen. "Poison." She stooped to pick up a crumpled silver paper case from the floor. She held it out to Sharn, her face very pale.

"Poison!" Sharn gaped at her.

"That was what I was going to tell you, Sharn," said Marilen, the words at last tumbling out. "As soon as I uncovered the tray, I knew I must not eat the food."

"But — but — " Sharn ran a trembling hand over her brow. So many questions were rushing through her mind. She managed to blurt out one. "Marilen, how could you know?"

Marilen shrank back, wrapping her arms around her body, as though to protect herself from attack. Then she seemed to find the strength to answer. She unfolded her arms and lifted her chin. "I am a daughter of Tora," she said.

"I, too, am a daughter of Tora," said Sharn, staring at her. "Or, at least, my ancestors were Toran, so I was always told. But can Toran magic sense poison?"

"All I can tell you is that I knew at once that there was poison in the meal, and I did not eat it," replied Marilen quietly.

She gestured at the rigid body on the floor. "The man Jinks came here to steal. He stole once too often, and it was his death. But *I* was the intended victim."

Sharn forced her face into a calm she did not feel. Her mind was racing. "Do you wish to leave here, Marilen?" she asked at last. "Do you wish to return to Tora?"

She waited tensely for the answer.

But Marilen shook her head. "No," she said firmly. "That would be to give in to our enemies. Whoever tried to kill me may not know exactly who I am, but at least wishes to make trouble between Deltora's east and west. And who could that be, but a servant of the Shadow Lord?"

"You are right," murmured Sharn, impressed and moved by the girl's courage.

"So there is a spy in our midst," said Marilen. "A spy who has somehow discovered that I am here."

She glanced at the body on the floor. "I thought it was Jinks, but plainly that is not so," she added coolly.

Sharn swallowed. She felt almost timid, facing this girl who seemed to have changed into a strong woman in a matter of days.

"You suspect — Ranesh?" she asked quietly.

Marilen colored to the roots of her hair. It was as though, in a moment, she had become a young girl again.

"Oh, no!" she gasped. "How can you say such a thing? Ranesh would never seek to harm me. On the contrary, if he was to find out my life had been threatened, he would . . . he would do something foolish, I am sure of it. So he must not know."

She turned quickly away, pretending to straighten the tie at her waist.

Ah, thought Sharn. So that is how things stand. Well, this complicates things even further.

A wave of immense weariness washed over her.

Lief, where are you? she thought. Oh, where are you?

10 ~ The Dome

L ief was paddling towards the island of Auron, his mind filled with music. His shoulders were aching, but he was no longer aware of it. He could only think of the sound, which was growing stronger every moment.

"Lief, what is the matter?" asked Jasmine. Lief glanced at her. Her familiar face wavered in front of his glazed eyes like a face in a dream.

"He feels the magic of the Pirran Pipe," Penn said from the front of the boat. She leaned forward and tapped Lief sharply on the knee. "Lief! Wake!" she commanded.

The tap, and the piercing voice, went some way towards cutting through the dreamy haze that clouded Lief's mind. He blinked and murmured. Penn put her hand over the side, scooped up some water, and threw it at him.

Lief gasped as the cold drops spattered over his face. Suddenly he was fully conscious again. Conscious, but confused and furiously angry.

"Why did you do that?" he shouted, glaring at Penn and roughly shaking off Jasmine's restraining hand.

"It was necessary," said Penn calmly. "I have not brought you all this way to have you miss your first sight of Auron."

Breathing hard, Lief wiped the water from his eyes. Slowly his wild anger died. He realized where he was, and what had happened.

"I am sorry," he mumbled, filled with shame.

"The fault is mine," said Penn, still in that same calm voice. "I should have warned you, but I was taken by surprise. The Pipe's spell is more powerful than I have ever felt it, no doubt because of the mouthpiece you carry. I have been struggling with it myself."

Only then did Lief see that her own face was wet, and that her small, tattooed hands were bleeding where she had driven her sharp nails into the palms.

"There is something ahead," Jasmine exclaimed, pointing into the gloom.

For a few moments there was silence. Then Lief and Barda cried out at the same moment as they saw what Jasmine had seen. A faint glow showed through the dimness.

"That is Auron," said Penn, her voice trembling a little. "Go gently, now. We must not cross the line."

"The line?" cried Lief. "But can we not land? Penn, we *must* land. We must see . . ."

"You will see enough, do not fear," Penn muttered.

The boat crawled forward. A strange, unpleasant odor began to creep into the companions' nostrils — a thick smell of decay that seemed to stick to their clothes, to sink into their skin, and cling to their hair.

Then they began to hear the gentle sound of lapping water. Other sounds, too. Soft, squelching sounds, and a sort of clicking, like the creaking of stiff joints.

The glow grew a little brighter. It spread until it was almost filling their view. Lief squinted at it, trying to see through it to the island. He saw nothing but a vast, high dome of dim light. And, to the left of the light, just where he would have expected to see it, a rugged cavern wall jutting out into the sea.

"There is the line," breathed Penn. "Stop!"

The companions tore their eyes from the light and looked down at the water ahead.

A broad band of bright pink and yellow sea-weed floated directly in front of the boat. The band stretched away to left and right, curving to encircle the glowing dome and the odd, milky sea that surrounded it.

"You plant this weed as a warning?" exclaimed Barda. "Ah, if only we had known this before!"

But Penn was intent on Jasmine and Lief. "Turn the boat so its side faces the island," she ordered. "And, for your life, do not let it drift into the warning zone."

So urgent was her tone that Lief did not even think of disobeying her. And the glaring pink and yellow of the weed, clearly visible even in the gloom, brought back memories that were their own warning.

"Now, look," Penn said quietly. "Look carefully, and understand."

Lief stared. And as his eyes grew accustomed to the light, as they searched vainly for the shapes of rocks, hills, or anything he could recognize, his spine began to tingle.

There was nothing to be seen beneath the dome. The dome was a barrier of shimmering energy that hid everything beneath it.

Oily, shallow water, lightly steaming, lapped the dome's base, where pitted lumps of some thick substance moved sluggishly in the tide and unseen things squelched and chewed. Everything seemed covered by a milky haze, like mold. The foul smell rolled over Lief in waves.

He heard Barda curse softly and Jasmine murmur in disbelief. Despair settled over him like a dull grey cloud.

He twisted in his seat to look at Penn. She was

staring fixedly at her hands folded in her lap.

"The dome is sealed by magic," she muttered. "It cannot be penetrated."

She raised her head. "Do you understand?" she said softly. "We of the rafts are exiles. Our ancestors were expelled from the dome long, long ago."

"Why?" Barda asked bluntly.

Penn hunched her narrow shoulders. "They were dangerous. They were sick of pretense," she muttered, speaking haltingly as if every word was being forced from her. "They wished — to make a life outside, in a place that was not what they were used to, but which had its own savage beauty."

Lief, Barda, and Jasmine looked around uncertainly. It was difficult to understand how anyone could find beauty in this overwhelming gloom.

Penn looked around also, her eyes glazed with sorrow. "When first the rafts were made, the cavern walls shone like stars of a thousand different colors," she whispered. "The eels danced in a glittering rainbow sea. The writings say that it was beautiful beyond words."

She sighed deeply. "Even when I was a child, it was still a shadow of what it had been. I well remember the colors. But now, they are gone."

Lief, Barda, and Jasmine thought of the exquisite opal beauty through which they had sailed when first they left the territory of the Plumes. The dazzling colors that had faded as the Plumes' light failed.

Then, they had thought that the Aurons had dimmed their own light for some evil purpose. Now they knew differently.

"What happened?" Jasmine asked.

Slowly, almost unwillingly, Penn took out the two scraps of parchment she had brought from the hut. She handed them to Lief with the lantern.

"Part of the story is here," she muttered. "I wrote it, in simple form, for the children of the rafts. I brought these because — because I knew you would have questions, and it would give me pain to answer them."

Again she looked down at her hands. Her body was rigid, and her mouth was pressed into a hard line.

Lief and Jasmine looked at the first piece of parchment. Barda crept forward to look over their shoulders.

How the Rafts Came to Be

When the three Pirran tribes fled their ancient land after the coming of the Shadow Lord, they found refuge on islands in an underground sea. The Isle of Auron was well separated from the enemy islands of Plume and Keras. It was large, had natural water, and was covered by fast-growing fungus trees from which boats and dwellings could be made. When lit by the magic of the people, the cavern in which it lay shone with every color of the rainbow.

Some Aurons found a strange, wild beauty in the

island and the shining caverns. But most saw only ugliness, and at once began creating illusions of the lost beauties of Pirra. After a time, they went farther. They wove a great spell, creating a dome which covered the island, containing the magic and making the illusion complete.

But there were those who did not agree with what had been done. These Aurons, our ancestors, wanted to live in a world that was real, however strange, rather than to exist in a dream created by their own minds.

Lief put down the first piece of parchment, and took up the second.

And so our ancestors were stripped of their magic and cast out as traitors. Eeran, the Piper of those days, swore that if they went in peace, so blood would not be spilled inside the dome, the caverns would always be filled with light. And our ancestors believed him, and left without a murmur.

They made rafts of driftwood lashed together with ropes of dried weed. They built mud houses, learned to live the life of the shining sea which was their home and were happy.

For many years, Eeran's promise was kept. But then, not long after the coming of Doran, the bringer of fire, the light began, very slowly, to dim. Now, centuries later, our realm is as you see it.

The dome-dwellers continue to expel all things that threaten their idea of beauty, including their dead. Thus they feed the creatures which breed around the dome. And those creatures are hunted by the Arach, those monsters of nightmare which once hid deep in caves, away from the light, but now nest in the warmth and dimness of the dome sea.

The dome is protected by the magic of the Aurons within it, and the stem of the Pirran Pipe. We, who are without magic, cannot penetrate it. Many have tried and died in the attempt.

We must all prepare for a time when the light is gone altogether. We must learn to find our way in dark water, and to know by touch the warning lines which must never be crossed. We must continue to save every scrap of wood, to mend the rafts cleverly, and to hate waste.

Then we will survive.

Lief looked up to meet Penn's grave eyes. He handed back the parchments, saying nothing. What was there to say?

But Jasmine's eyes had narrowed. "What are these Arach?" she asked abruptly.

At the sound of the name, Penn stiffened and glanced from side to side. With a stifled cry she half rose from her seat, then fell back.

"What have I done?" she gasped. "Oh, Auron, forgive me! In my distress I forgot to watch. We are drifting over the line!"

The companions looked down. Pink and yellow

weed was all around them. It was lush and thickly branched, floating just under the surface of the water. Before they could gather their wits, the boat's prow had nudged out of the weed and into the milky water beyond.

And by the dome, something stirred. There were sounds. Sucking, creaking sounds that chilled the blood.

"Back!" muttered Penn, her eyes wild with panic. "Make haste! Oh, make haste!"

Lief and Jasmine began back-paddling frantically. Their paddles splashed uselessly, snagging on the ragged blanket of weed. The boat swayed awkwardly from side to side, but did not move.

Without another word, Penn threw herself into the water and began clawing at the weed, flinging great trails of it aside, trying vainly to clear a path.

Two huge shadows, two vast, lumpy bodies each swaying on eight thin, jointed legs, rose dark against the glow of the dome. Red eyes gleamed as the beasts sprang forward and began running towards the boat, running with terrifying speed over the surface of the water.

"Over the side!" Penn shouted. "Swim! Swim for your lives!"

11 - Arach

Without hesitation, Lief caught Jasmine in his arms and tumbled with her into the weed-filled water.

Surfacing, he heard Barda splashing and shouting somewhere behind him. He shouted back, then, holding Jasmine tightly against his chest, he struck out, kicking aside the sodden cloak that clung around his legs, fighting his way through the weed.

Jasmine was gasping, choking, trying to speak.

"I know what you want to say, and you can save your breath," Lief panted. "I will not leave you."

Barda came up beside him. Supporting Jasmine between them they clawed through the matted growth, struggling forward with painful slowness.

"What are you doing? Make haste!" screamed Penn from the dimness beyond the weed. Then, amazingly, she was leaving safety, plunging towards them, cutting through the water and weed like a fish.

Her head bobbed up in front of them, pale eyes wide with terror. She reached for Jasmine.

"Where is she injured?" she demanded.

"Not injured. Cannot swim!" Lief panted, and saw the history-keeper's jaw drop in stunned amazement.

Then she was swimming away, pulling Jasmine expertly along with her. And Lief and Barda were thrashing behind, hearts pounding, chests aching, through the weed and, at last, out into the open sea.

There Penn stopped and turned, treading water, supporting Jasmine easily with one arm.

"Why have you stopped?" gasped Barda.

"We are safe here," said Penn. "Arach do not hunt beyond the weed. The dome waters are their territory." Then her face twisted with pain. "Ah, no!" she wailed. "Ah, what wicked waste!"

There was a sound like crackling dry leaves. Panting, the breath rasping in his lungs, Lief turned himself around in the water.

The Arach had halted at the edge of the seaweed band. One of them had seized the boat. It was lifting it high into the air, crushing it like paper. The other was fighting for a share, tugging at the frail craft, scrabbling inside it, looking for prey.

Lief stared, dumbfounded. The Arach were like

vast, deformed spiders. Their bloated bodies were covered by glossy black shell, as though plated with armor. Their long, thin legs looked like wires of steel, prickling with spurs and spikes. Their armored heads seemed nothing but greedy red eyes and dripping fangs.

With a dull, angry roar, the second Arach jerked violently, tearing the boat in half. Provisions, buckets, the lantern, and two small objects that Lief realized were the cages of the fighting spiders, sailed high into the air, scattering and falling with dull splashes.

Fury's cage plunged into the water just in front of Lief. Fury was scrabbling desperately inside. Lief grabbed for the cage and lifted it up, gasping as he worked at keeping himself afloat with one hand.

This is madness! he thought. I cannot save myself, let alone this spider. But he could not bring himself to let the creature drown before his eyes.

Neither, it seemed, could Barda leave Flash to his fate. Barda was floundering towards the other cage, reaching out for it as though his life depended upon it.

"The Arach have had enough," muttered Penn.

Lief looked up and saw the monsters creeping back to the dome. The shredded remains of the boat lay scattered on the weed bed.

Without warning, Penn plunged her head under the water. Jasmine, still clasped firmly in her arm, spluttered in panic. Bubbles rose in a great stream around Penn's head and Lief thought he could hear a strange, muffled cry.

"What is she doing?" shrieked Jasmine. But Penn was already lifting her head, shaking it to clear her eyes.

In moments there was a swirling movement in the water around them. Then Lief, Barda, and Jasmine were shouting in shock as four giant eels surged up from the depths, wicked mouths gaping horribly.

"Take hold of their necks," said Penn. "They have come in answer to my call. They will carry us home."

✳

In a shorter time than Lief would have believed possible, they were back at the rafts. Never had he felt such speed. Never would he forget that journey — the spray beating against his face, the desperate clinging to the slippery neck of the eel.

To his shame, he had to be hauled off the eel's neck and onto the platform by the guards. He could do nothing to help himself. His legs and arms would not move. His head was spinning. The children who ducked and played like fish in the water at the platform's edge stared and giggled. The workers mending nets and weaving rope nearby sniffed in amused contempt.

Barda was in the same state as Lief himself, and Jasmine little better. Together, bedraggled, unsteady on their feet, and sick at heart, they shuffled after

Penn to her hut, trying to ignore the sharp-faced, silent crowd which had gathered to watch them.

The hut door was standing open. Inside, a bent figure in long robes and a tall silver head-covering stood waiting. So old, wrinkled, and toothless was the face below the head-covering that if Penn had not already spoken of the Piper as "he," Lief would not have known if he was facing a male or a female.

Penn ushered the dripping companions into the hut and closed the door behind them. "Do not mind the water," she murmured. "This floor has been drenched more times than you could count."

Jasmine darted at once to where Kree sat by the stove. She knelt down and lifted poor, shivering Filli from her shoulder to share the warmth. Lief and Barda took the cages containing the motionless spiders over to her, then returned to Penn's side, trying to stiffen their trembling legs.

"Well?" asked the Piper. And even in his exhaustion Lief thrilled with wonder at the sound of the voice — smooth, rich, and sweet as wild honey.

Penn folded her hands, then spoke flatly, as if delivering a report. "Tall and brave they may be, with weapons of steel," she said. "But in the water the males, Lief and Barda, are helpless as newborn babes, and the female, Jasmine, cannot swim at all. They would have no hope of taking the Arach by surprise, or evading them."

She turned away. "I have done all you require of me, Piper, and it has cost me dearly," she muttered. "But you must abandon your hopes."

The Piper closed his eyes as though in pain. "Did you tell them of my belief, Penn?" he asked softly.

Lief and Barda glanced at each other, then at Penn. What was this?

Penn was hesitating. "No," she said at last. "Once I saw that they could not swim, I felt there was no need to torment them further."

"Tell them now," said the Piper. It was not a request, but a command.

Penn moved restlessly. "The Piper believes that if you could reach the dome, the mouthpiece of the Pirran Pipe would give you entrance," she said, without looking at Lief and Barda. "He believes that the stem of the Pipe within would call to it and draw it through the magic screen. The Piper hoped — "

"I hoped many things." The Piper opened his eyes and fixed Penn with a steely stare. "It seems my hopes were in vain."

But Lief had clutched Barda's arm. And Jasmine had jumped up from the floor and hurried over to them, her face alight with hope.

"Why did you not tell us this before, Penn?" she demanded. "If we can penetrate the dome we can — "

"You cannot *reach* the dome!" cried Penn. "You saw the Arachs! And there are many more! Their webs net the waters of their territory. The moment you enter it, the moment you touch a web, they will sense you."

"There must be a way," growled Barda. "There is always — "

"There is *no* way!" shouted Penn, eyes blazing. "In a boat, should we be so mad as to give you one, you would last only a few moments. To have any hope at all of reaching the dome you would have to swim to it underwater, beneath the webs. And you are not capable of that! Nothing is more certain."

"The eels!" Jasmine exclaimed. "They could surely tow us beneath the webs. We could hold our breath for that time. They swim so fast . . . "

Penn sighed. The Piper smiled thinly. "It could be done," he admitted. "If the eels could be persuaded to enter Arach territory. But they cannot. It has been tried many, many times. They will not do it."

He shook his head in disgust. "We knew that you would not be able to swim as we can," he muttered. "It is written that Doran could not defeat even our youngest children in a race. But never did we consider such weakness as this!"

He glanced back at Jasmine. "And one of you cannot swim at all! It is — beyond belief!"

"I grew up in a forest where the only water was a shallow stream," snapped Jasmine, heartily sick of being criticised for something she could not help. "How could I learn to swim? Any more than you could learn

238

to climb a tree, Piper! Or Penn could learn to swing on a vine!"

Lief gave a sharp exclamation. Jasmine swung round to him, scowling. "I do not care what you say, Lief!" she raged. "Palace manners might do for you, but they will not do for me. I will not be polite to these people any longer!"

But Lief's face was alight with excitement. "Jasmine, you have it!" he exclaimed. "Do you not see? You have told us exactly what we must do!"

12 - Suspicion

It did not take long for Lief to explain the plan that had suddenly come to him. "You see?" he finished triumphantly. "We do not use our weaknesses, but our strengths!"

"It is — incredible!" the Piper exclaimed, his cold eyes shining. "It would never have crossed my mind that such a thing could be done."

"I am not surprised. A more harebrained idea I have never heard!" snorted Barda.

"We can do it!" Lief urged.

"We can try. And it is worth the chance," said Jasmine. "Unless, of course," she added dryly, "the Piper is wrong, and the mouthpiece of the Pirran Pipe will not allow us to penetrate the dome."

Penn buried her face in her hands. The Piper gripped her arm. "You must not weaken now, Penn,"

Lief heard him muttering. "They can do what we cannot. They could be our salvation!"

He turned to Lief, his hard, ancient face wearing a mild expression that Lief could not quite believe in.

"We will give you what help we can," he said. "If you gain the stem of the Pirran Pipe, it will be yours to keep for as long as you need it. All we ask in return is that you use your best efforts to convince the dome-dwellers to return the light to the caverns."

It will be yours to keep for as long as you need it . . .

Those words were carefully chosen, Piper, Lief thought, studying the cold face. You speak the truth, I am sure. But for how long will we *need* the stem of the Pipe, once it is actually out of the dome? Once it is where you can lay your hands on it? No one needs anything after they are dead. Is that your plan?

He moved his gaze to Penn's bent head. The Piper told Penn to make friends with us, he thought. So that we would want to help her people as well as ourselves. And of course she succeeded. In spite of herself.

Penn had carried out her orders reluctantly. That had been plain from the start. Perhaps she did not believe that the dome could be penetrated by the mouthpiece of the Pipe, and feared encouraging the visitors to go to their deaths.

Or perhaps Penn knew very well that once they had gained the Pipe, they would be betrayed.

"Please do not blame yourself for our decision, Penn," he said aloud. "We are doing only what we must."

Penn did not raise her head.

"You accept my terms, then?" the Piper asked.

Lief met his eyes squarely. "We will do all we can to help you once we are inside the dome, Piper. We cannot promise success. But I swear that we will beg the dome-dwellers to return your light as earnestly as we beg them for the stem of the Pirran Pipe."

The Piper bent his head. "I ask no more of you than that," he murmured. He remained utterly still for a few moments, as though in the grip of strong feeling. Then he looked up, his face calm again.

"You must dry yourselves and rest," he said. "I will have a boat prepared. Penn? A moment, if you please."

Penn scurried after him as he swept to the door. They went outside, and Lief saw them speaking in low voices.

"That Piper makes me uneasy," said Barda, walking to the stove to warm his chilled hands. "He reminds me of people I knew in the Palace, in the old days. He is a schemer, and he is bending Penn to his will."

"I think he is using us to gain the stem of the Pipe for himself," Lief said. "The raft-dwellers' magic, the magic that should be the birthright of every Pirran, is trapped inside the dome. But the stem of the

Pipe has its own power — power which would light the caverns and do much more."

Barda nodded agreement. "It must seem to the Piper that fate has brought us to him, as once it brought Doran when he was needed most."

"I agree, but —" Jasmine's brow was creased in thought. "But why bother to deceive us, when surely there is a simpler way to gain magic? Why not seize the part of the Pipe we already have?"

Lief's hand rose, almost without his willing it, to touch the piece of knobbly wood beneath his shirt.

"I suspect that the Plume part of the Pirran Pipe is of no use to Aurons," he said. "They have shown no interest in it, and its power does not seem to affect them. Yet as we approached the dome, and the Auron part of the Pipe was near, Penn was clearly as moved as I was."

Wearily he pulled off his sodden cloak, and sank down beside Kree. "We must pretend to trust them for now, in any case," he murmured. "We need their help. Our first task must be to gain the stem of the Pipe. After that, we will deal with what comes."

Penn hurried back into the room loaded with bundles and baskets. Her face was tense, her lips were strained into a smile that had no meaning.

"Here are rugs to keep you warm while you rest," she chattered. "And bread — freshly baked — with hot Molisk patties. I am sure you are hungry."

She put down a basket of flat speckled rolls and

a bowl of steaming objects that looked like green meatballs. Suddenly aware that they were ravenous, the companions helped themselves.

They ate with relish. The bread tasted of the sea, but was crisp and warm. The patties were delicately flavored, and melted on the tongue.

"This meal pleases you more than the soup?" Penn asked.

"Much more," Barda agreed, with his mouth full.

Penn's smile became a little more real. "It is written that Doran enjoyed Molisk patties also," she said. "They are our festival dish. The Piper ordered them to be prepared in honor of your visit. I am glad you are having them now. Before . . ."

Her voice trailed off, and she turned away.

Lief, Barda, and Jasmine looked at one another, the delicious food suddenly dry in their mouths. It was quite plain that Penn thought that the Molisk patties would be their last meal.

✳

Meanwhile, in Del, Sharn and Marilen looked down at the small body lying in the bed. Carrying Jinks back to his own chamber had been a grim task, but they had agreed that it was necessary.

"Only *we* know he was not as ill as he claimed," Sharn said, covering the terrible face with the sheet. "People will think that he died of his injuries."

"The poisoner may guess the truth," Marilen said soberly. "And now we must try to think who that person may be. A person who knows I am here, and somehow knows who I am. And who had the opportunity to poison my food. The cook, Amarantz — "

"Amarantz does not know you exist!" Sharn broke in. "She thinks your trays are for an old palace servant who can no longer manage the stairs. And in any case I would trust her with my life. She would never serve the Shadow Lord."

Marilen looked doubtful, but finally nodded. "Then it must be one of the guards on this floor or the library floor," she said. "The guards must know that I am a special, secret visitor, for I never go downstairs."

"But *they* do not go downstairs either, Marilen," Sharn pointed out, her heart sinking as she realized how few the suspects actually were. "Barda refused to risk them gossiping or being drugged, as happened once before. They are living on camping rations and sleeping in turns on this floor."

Marilen shook her head in frustration. "Then who can the spy be?" she demanded. "Doom brought the tray to me. But Doom cannot be suspected. Nor can Josef, surely, though . . ." Her brow creased.

"What?" Sharn demanded. "Tell me!"

"Josef was . . . different, in the library this morning," Marilen said hesitantly. "He looked cross and anxious. He rushed out, telling Ranesh to meet him in the kitchen to discuss an important matter. He has never done such a thing before."

Sharn hesitated, unwelcome thoughts rushing through her mind.

"Marilen," she said at last. "Do not take this amiss, but I must know. You and Ranesh have become . . . good friends. Is it possible that you have given him a hint of the reason for your presence here?"

Marilen blushed to the roots of her hair. "No, I have not!" she cried angrily. "Ranesh knows I am of Tora, certainly, but anyone who looks at me must know that. He has never asked why I am here, or what my future might hold, and I have never told him." She lifted her chin defiantly. "I have every reason not to do so!"

Those last words ringing in her ears, Sharn looked into the hurt, troubled eyes, and knew the girl was speaking the truth. She sighed, her heart very heavy.

"I am sorry to have caused you pain, Marilen," she said quietly. "But we must face the truth. Of all the suspects, Ranesh and Josef are the only ones who know you are here, and who were also present in the kitchen when your tray was being prepared."

"Then however difficult it may be to believe, Josef must be guilty," said Marilen in a hard voice.

"It cannot be Josef, Marilen," whispered Sharn.

"Why not?" Marilen snapped, suddenly reminding Sharn vividly of Jasmine. "Because he is old and frail? Because he says he saved *The Deltora Annals*? Surely we in Deltora have learned by now that wickedness can wear a smiling, deceiving mask?"

Indeed, thought Sharn, as they left the room of death, locking it after them. *But I fear, Marilen, it is a lesson that your own heart has made you forget.*

As they turned towards the stairway, they saw one of the library guards hurrying towards them. In his hand he held a folded sheet of paper, heavily sealed with wax.

"What are you doing away from your post, Follin?" Sharn asked sharply.

"It is my rest period, ma'am," said the guard. He thrust the paper into her hand with an air of relief.

"The old fellow—the librarian—gave me this soon after you left the library with the young lady, ma'am," he said, bowing distractedly in Marilen's direction. "He said it had to be delivered to you urgently."

Marilen stiffened. "A message from Josef?" Sharn said faintly.

The guard nodded. "He has been plaguing the life out of me ever since, ma'am, to carry it to you. But, as I told him again and again, I could not leave my post until my replacement came. Those were the orders, ma'am."

He looked at Sharn anxiously, plainly worried that he had made the wrong decision.

"Quite right, Follin," said Sharn, forcing a smile. "Thank you. Go to your rest now. You have earned it."

The guard made a clumsy bow, turned and lumbered away. With fingers that felt stiff and cold, Sharn broke the seal on the note and unfolded it.

Madam,

When I saw you in the library just now—so kind and so brave—I realised that I could no longer keep silent. My heart is sorely troubled. I must speak to you at once. Do not delay, I beg you.

Your wretched servant,

Josef

13 - Treachery

Sharn's heart was beating painfully as she ran up the stairs to the library. She dreaded hearing what Josef had to tell her.

Marilen was close beside her. Marilen had read the note also, and would not hear of being left behind. "It could be a trap, Sharn," she had said fiercely. "You must not go alone! And in any case, I want to face him."

There was no help for it. Whatever Josef had to say would have to be said in front of Marilen.

And perhaps it is for the best, Sharn thought despairingly.

She found Josef hovering by the library doors, watching for her under the stern gaze of the guards on duty. The old man's face crumpled in relief as he saw her approaching. And at the sight of Marilen, tears sprang into his eyes. He did not seem to notice how coldly the girl answered his greeting.

"I have set Ranesh a task on the other side of the library," he whispered, leading the two women through the huge, echoing room. "I would prefer that he did not hear us."

He ushered them into his own small chamber, and closed the door. His hands were trembling as he turned to face them. Plainly, now that the moment had arrived, he did not know how to begin.

"What is troubling you, Josef?" Sharn asked quietly, though her mind was boiling with fears.

Josef's mouth quivered. He took a deep breath. Then he said the last thing Sharn expected to hear.

"I have betrayed my trust," he muttered. "I let my pity for an old friend and protector sway me. And in doing so, I did great wrong." He bowed his head in misery.

"Why, Josef! What do you mean?" exclaimed Sharn, very aware that Marilen was holding her breath.

"I wished only to comfort poor Amarantz. To tell her that Lief was sure to return to the palace," whispered Josef. "So — I wrote upon her slate that he would certainly return, that he *had* to return, because his Toran bride was here."

Marilen made a strangled sound.

"*What?*" gasped Sharn, gripping the girl's arm.

Josef's eyes suddenly filled with tears. "The mes-

sage was only for Amarantz," he choked. "But then —
suddenly — the giant, shaved-head woman, Lindal,
burst into the room with the man, Jinks. They might
have seen the message. I think they did."

"Ranesh was in the kitchen, too, Josef, was he
not?" Sharn asked quickly.

"Ranesh?" Marilen's face was scarlet.

Josef looked confused and fearful. "Do not
blame Ranesh for concealing what I did, madam," he
cried. "Ranesh knows nothing of it! I had wiped the
slate clean by the time he arrived, and I did not tell
him later. I was too ashamed, and fearful of his anger
at my betrayal of our precious secret."

He bowed his head. "It is unforgivable," he
mumbled. "Why, Lief himself entrusted us with the
lady Marilen's care. He did not say who she was,
of course. But the palace was buzzing with the news
that he had gone to Tora for a bride, and naturally,
when Ranesh and I met her, we put two and two together."

"Naturally." Sharn's head was spinning. Palace
gossip. Of course! How could they have left this out of
their calculations?

The blush had slowly faded from Marilen's
cheeks, leaving her deathly pale. "I am going to my
bedchamber," she said stiffly to Sharn. "I have . . .
tidying to do, as you may recall."

She bowed shortly to Josef and left the room,
walking very quickly.

Josef looked after her with anguished eyes. "Will she flee — back to Tora?" he whispered.

"Perhaps," said Sharn slowly. "She has had a great shock."

"Ah, I would give anything to take back what I did!" Joseph moaned. "I have been in torment, in terrible fear that some harm would befall her. But that, at least, has not happened."

Sharn made no reply. She was too occupied with her own thoughts.

"I am ready to go," Josef added miserably.

Sharn looked up. Josef was standing before her, a small cloth bundle in his hand. For the first time she noticed that the little room had been stripped of every personal possession.

"Josef — " she began.

The old man hung his head. "If you feel you can trust me not to disgrace myself again, I will return to my old home," he mumbled. "I would prefer it to a dungeon, though there is not much to choose between the two. But I will do whatever you — "

"Josef, do not be absurd!" cried Sharn. "There is no question of your going away."

He stared at her in disbelief.

"No question!" Sharn repeated. "You made a mistake, certainly. But surely we can all be allowed one slip?"

Josef's lips trembled. "The results of my . . . slip

. . . could be grave," he said. "The man Jinks — I do not think he can be trusted. And Lindal . . ."

"Jinks is dead," said Sharn abruptly. "Lindal is with Doom. There is only one person I must see to settle this."

Josef gaped after her as she hurried out of the room.

✳

Sharn was panting when she reached the kitchen door. She stood quite still for a moment, her hand on the knob, trying to calm herself. Then, to her surprise, she heard the muffled voice of Amarantz, and the sound of her own name.

"Sharn is upstairs, but she will be back at any moment. Wait here for her, I pray you. And try one or two of these, to please me. They are a new recipe. No doubt you are hungry from your journey."

"Indeed we are," boomed another voice — a voice Sharn knew well. "I could eat my old horse, if we did not need him to pull the caravan. Come on, girl!"

There was a loud scraping of chairs.

Sharn threw open the door, taking in the scene in an instant. Two huge figures were sitting at the table. One was Doom's friend Steven, the strange Plains pedlar who had been such a good and powerful ally in the time of the Shadow Lord. The other — was Lindal!

And taking his place beside them was Doom himself, wearily pulling off his coat. But Sharn had no time, no space in her mind, to wonder why Doom and Lindal had returned, or how Steven had come to be with them. Her gaze was fixed on the platter towards which all three were reaching — a platter heaped with small, golden-brown cakes in silver paper cases.

"No!"

She sprang forward. As they shouted in shock, her arm crashed down on the table, sweeping the platter away from them. The platter fell to the floor, smashing on the stones, cakes bouncing and rolling away.

Amarantz, her face pale as parchment, fell to her knees, scrabbling to pick them up.

"Sharn! What is it?" roared Doom, astounded, almost angry.

Sharn could not answer. She was gasping, dizzy with relief. If she had been a moment later . . .

She steadied herself on the edge of the table and made herself look down at the old woman crawling on the stones of the kitchen floor.

Amarantz's eyes met hers. And suddenly it seemed to Sharn that something else was watching her from behind that familiar, faded blue. Something alien. Something cunning. Something wicked.

Her stomach churned with sickness. She shrank back, shivering.

And then, horribly, Amarantz began to laugh.

"Fools!" she cackled. "Do you not know that you will never defeat me?"

With an oath, Doom leaped to his feet, his chair crashing behind him. Steven rose more slowly, gripping the edge of the table. The muscles of his arms and neck bulged as though he were lifting a great weight. He trembled all over. His eyes flickered from gold to brown as Nevets, the savage brother he carried within him, struggled for freedom.

"No!" Lindal ordered, putting a huge hand on his shoulder. "Nevets, we do not need you here. Go back!"

The terrible shuddering quietened and ceased.

Shoulders heaving, Amarantz crouched toad-like, watching them. "What joy it would have been to have sent you the way of the poor little bride, Doom!" she croaked. "And your friends, those ugly freaks of nature, with you. But, ah well, this feeble body is nearly worn out as it is. I will see you another time, Doom, in another place."

She pressed her clenched fist to her mouth.

"Stop her!" Sharn exclaimed urgently.

Instantly understanding, Doom leaped forward.

But it was too late. The poisoned cake was already in the old woman's throat, and she was swallowing it whole.

"Soon we will be everywhere!" she hissed. "Very soon . . ."

Her face changed, her eyes rolled back. With a

terrible shriek she clutched at her stomach and fell sideways, her feet kicking, her head beating horribly against the stones.

As Doom, Lindal, and Steven stood frozen with horror, Sharn ran to her. She could not help it. For whatever hideous force possessed the old woman, this was Amarantz, the friend of her youth. She could not let her die horribly, alone.

She took the jerking body in her arms and held it tightly. For a long moment there was no change. Then suddenly the eyes returned to normal. They stared at Sharn vacantly for a single moment, then seemed to focus.

"I am here, Amarantz," Sharn whispered.

The eyes grew puzzled. The cracked lips opened. "Sharn?" Amarantz murmured. "Oh, Sharn, I had a terrible dream. Such a terrible dream."

Sharn nodded, stroking the wet forehead, her eyes brimming with tears.

"I dreamed that the Grey Guards came to the pottery, and we were all taken," sighed the old woman. "And I — " Her eyes suddenly widened, filling with terror.

"Do not fear anymore, Amarantz," said Sharn quickly. "The dream has ended now. Ended."

"Yes." The faded eyes grew peaceful once more. The lips curved in a half smile. And then the breathing stopped. For Amarantz, the nightmare had truly ended at last.

"What was that she said of 'the poor little bride'?" asked Doom urgently.

"She thought she had poisoned Marilen. But she was wrong," said Sharn.

She laid the old woman's head gently down and brushed the wisps of grey hair from the bloodstained cheek. Then she thought . . . she thought she saw something moving in the hair that trailed on the ground. Tears were blurring her eyes. She rubbed them, looked again, then jerked back with a scream of horror.

A long grey worm with a scarlet head was crawling from Amarantz's ear. It slithered out onto the floor in a trail of slime and writhed there, its tail lashing in fury.

14 - Leap of Faith

His face twisted in disgust, Doom strode forward and stamped on the evil thing, grinding it into the stones.

"What was it?" screeched Lindal.

"A new piece of Shadow Lord devilry," Doom muttered. "Amarantz was taken to the Shadowlands, it seems. And at some time — perhaps not long ago — *that* vile thing was put into her brain, and she was sent back."

He looked down at Amarantz's crumpled body.

"At least we now understand what has been happening here," he said. "Why we are plagued by assassins and spies — all of them once good people."

There was a short, fearful silence. One thought was in all their minds.

"There could be thousands of them," said Lindal roughly, putting the thought into words at last.

"No." Doom's brow was furrowed in thought. "The words were, '*Soon* we will be everywhere.' For some reason, the real invasion has not yet begun."

"I think — I think that is because the process is not yet perfect." Sharn was controlling the trembling in her voice with difficulty. "It still causes . . . damage."

As her companions stared, puzzled, she took a deep, shuddering breath.

"Do you not see?" she said. "Amarantz said she had been deafened by a beating, but that was a lie. At the last, when she was herself again, when the worm had begun leaving her because it knew her time was ending, she could hear me clearly. The worm had been blocking her hearing, as well as controlling her mind."

"Yes!" Doom's eyes blazed. "And this explains many things. The babbling woman with the knife. The old guard who could not walk — "

"And — of course — the man Pieter, who put the scorpion in Lief's bedchamber, was tormented by agonizing headaches," Sharn exclaimed. "He was another — imperfect experiment." Suddenly the horror was too much for her. She covered her eyes.

"The Shadow Lord is no doubt working to correct the fault in his process," muttered Lindal. "And when he is satisfied . . ."

"Ah, you are as gloomy as Nevets, girl!" growled Steven. "Are you trying to make us lose all hope? I suspect you have a worm in your own painted skull."

"My only headache is you, Steven!" Lindal retorted. "I am simply being realistic. The Shadow Lord — "

She broke off as the kitchen door swung open. Marilen walked in, her head high, color burning in her cheeks. Her defiant eyes widened as she saw Doom, two huge strangers, and the body of Amarantz on the floor, but she did not hesitate. Ignoring everyone else, she spoke directly to Sharn.

"Please do not blame the guards because I am here. They had no orders to stop me. You all relied on my obedience for that. Well, I am tired of being obedient!"

"Marilen . . ." Sharn began, astonished. But Marilen had not finished.

"I came to tell you that, whatever you might think, I am certain that Ranesh is guilty of no wrong," she said clearly. "Also, that I am determined to stay here, whatever the future may hold. But I will no longer cringe upstairs in hiding and in ignorance of what is going on in the palace."

Lindal snorted with laughter. "Is this 'the poor little bride'?" she whispered piercingly to Steven. "She has grown a few muscles, it seems."

Marilen's color brightened even further but she tossed her head and turned to Doom. "No blame will attach to you, or to Lief, if anything happens to me," she said. "This is my decision, and mine alone."

"The decision is not yours to make, Marilen," Doom said grimly. "It is not only your father who fears for your safety."

Marilen met his eyes without flinching. "The decision *is* mine, Doom," she said. "I will be a prisoner no longer, and that is final!" She glanced at Steven and Lindal, then looked back to Doom and lifted her chin. "Discuss it with my father, if you wish," she added, with an unmistakable air of triumph. "He and Zeean are coming to Del."

Sharn gave a muffled gasp. Steven and Lindal looked at her curiously,

"The letter came this morning," Marilen said. "I should have read it at once, but — " Again she glanced at Steven and Lindal. "But something happened which drove it from my mind. Zeean and Father will be here in a day or two."

"Well," said Doom, his face unreadable, "I am glad that I have returned in time to greet them."

"Doom, why *have* you returned?" cried Sharn, suddenly recollecting.

"Lief and Barda are no longer in the Hills," said Doom. "They have followed Jasmine into the caverns under the earth."

Sharn stared at him, joy and fear mingling on her face. "Jinks *was* lying?" she gasped.

"Of course!" said Marilen quietly. "Did I not tell you?"

"My mother's bees brought us the tale," Steven put in. "The story took time to spread to them, but it began, I gather, with vine-weaver birds in the Hills. I could not make head nor tail of it, for I had heard that Lief was in Tora. So I came to find out and, lo and behold, met Doom and Lindal on the road."

"Under the earth . . ." Sharn shook her head. "So Jasmine is truly trying to find a secret way to the Shadowlands! And — and Lief and Barda are with her?"

"So it seems," Steven nodded.

"But Doom, you must go after them!" cried Sharn. "You must stop them! They cannot save the prisoners alone! All that will happen is that Lief will deliver himself — and the Belt of Deltora, Doom! — into the Shadow Lord's hands!"

"The Belt cannot be taken beyond Deltora's borders," Doom said. "We know this, and Lief knows it too."

Sharn stared at him, unable to understand his calm. "But what of the Pirran Pipe? Lief was so sure it was the only way to defeat the Shadow Lord on his own ground."

"Perhaps Lief knows something we do not," Marilen murmured.

"Perhaps he does," said Doom. He looked at the girl thoughtfully for a moment, then turned back to Sharn. "It was not an easy decision to return to Del,

Sharn," he said gently. "My whole instinct was to continue. Then it came to me that it was Lief, Barda, and Jasmine who restored the Belt of Deltora, and that they did it alone, without our help or protection."

Sharn's eyes were blinded with tears. "You are saying that we should trust them."

"I am saying that we *must* trust them," said Doom. "Our place, our task, is here — especially now. All we can do is keep faith. And wish Lief, Barda, and Jasmine well, wherever they may be."

✳

Lief, Barda, and Jasmine were in a place, and facing a challenge, that not even Doom could have imagined. They were following Lief's plan. They were climbing the cavern wall that jutted beside the dome of Auron.

One of the raft-dwellers' old patched boats floated below them. The Piper himself sat in the stern. Penn was with him, looking up anxiously. At their feet lay what remained of a great coil of rope, slowly unravelling as the three companions made their perilous climb.

"The hand-holds are growing farther and farther apart," gasped Barda, hauling himself up to a new ledge.

"You can stop now. We are already above the height of the dome," said Jasmine, who was climbing nimbly above him, the rope trailing behind her. "I will go on and attach the rope."

She continued climbing, aiming for a lump of rock that jutted out high above them where the cavern wall curved to meet the roof.

Flattening himself against the rock beside Barda, Lief looked down. Far below, slightly to his right, the boat, small as a child's toy, rocked beside the band of seaweed. The great coil of rope had completely unravelled. Now the rope hung loosely down the rock face, its knotted end swinging, rising steadily as Jasmine climbed.

And looming before him, rising from sluggish, milky waters, was the rounded shape of the dimly glowing dome. Arach crawled in the shadowy filth heaped at its base, feeding, spinning, watching.

The sound of the Pirran Pipe rang in Lief's ears. He closed his eyes, fighting it down.

"Very well. It is as secure as I can make it," Jasmine hissed from above.

Lief looked up. Through the dimness he could see that Jasmine had pulled her end of the rope from her waist and looped it over the jutting rock, tying it firmly.

She tugged at the rope to test it. Then, without a sign of fear, she leaned back over the terrible drop, curved her body so her feet touched the rocky wall, and began running downward, the rope slipping through her hands.

In moments she had reached the ledge where Lief and Barda stood.

"Ready?" she asked casually.

Barda took hold of the rope, his hands gripping it firmly just below Jasmine's own.

"Promise me, Lief," he muttered, "that if this should go wrong, you will get back to the rafts and return to Del, however you are able. We cannot risk — "

"It will not go wrong if we follow Lief's plan," snapped Jasmine. "I am sure the rope is long enough, and the fastening will hold. The most important thing is to push off the cliff-face as hard as we possibly can, so that we swing out fast and far enough to cross the gap. And when I say jump, Barda, you must jump. At once!"

Barda gritted his teeth. "And if I land safely on the top of the dome, but cannot hold myself in place?" he muttered.

"Then you will slide all the way down to the base and fight Arachs," said Jasmine calmly. "But if not, you will simply wait while I return with Lief."

There was nothing further for Barda to say. With a grim nod, he tightened his grip on the rope and bent one knee so that the sole of his boot was planted firmly against the cliff-face. Then, on the count of three, he and Jasmine launched themselves into space.

Lief held his breath as they swung in a great arc towards the dome, two small figures at the end of a rope that looked impossibly frail. Time seemed to stop. The milky sea crawled beneath them. Their shapes showed dark against the dome's dull glow, swinging up, up . . .

"Now!" shrieked Jasmine, and her voice echoed weirdly from the rock. *Now . . . Now . . . Now . . .*

Barda let go of the rope and sailed through the air. He landed on the dome flat on his belly. The surface of the dome shimmered but did not bend.

Jasmine was already swinging back, her small body hurtling towards the wall with terrifying speed. Lief stood ready to catch her, to cushion her so that she would not smash herself to pieces against the rock.

It was all over in seconds. In seconds, Jasmine was back on the ledge, gabbling instructions. In seconds, Lief was taking Barda's place, grasping the rope, pressing his foot against the wall, thrusting himself forward at Jasmine's signal.

Then he was flying, cold air rushing against his face, ears strained for Jasmine's call.

The dome was huge, filling his view. He felt himself swinging upward. His brain filled with the singing of the Pipe. Louder. Louder . . .

"Now!" shrieked Jasmine.

Lief let go of the rope. His body sailed up through the empty air, up over the dome. His eye caught the flutter of Jasmine's clothing beside him. He could see Barda stretched motionless below.

Then he was falling. The dim glow of the dome

rushed up to meet him. A warm, shimmering haze surrounded him.

He was aware of nothing but sound. Sweet, pure music poured through him, possessed him. It was blind instinct that made him reach for Jasmine's hand, clutch at Barda's shoulder, as he began to slip through the haze, and the magic of the Pirran Pipe drew him in.

15 ~ The Isle of Illusion

The grass was velvety soft under Lief's feet. Above his head arched a sky of perfect blue. Soft purple hills misted the horizon. The air was warm, and fragrant with the flowers that bloomed beside a rippling silver stream. The shadows under the trees were dappled with sunlight.

Pirra.

The birds seemed to sing the name. The stream babbled it. The leaves whispered it, rustling in a gentle breeze that seemed to breathe magic.

Lief felt hands tugging at his arm. Heard Jasmine's voice calling him from far away.

"Lief! Wake! We are inside the dome."

The blue of the sky shimmered uncertainly, like water. The trees wavered.

"Lief, behind you! Look!" Jasmine's voice was

sharp, urgent. It could no longer be ignored. Unwillingly, Lief turned.

A large crowd of people stood silently watching them. One, wearing the tall, stiff head-covering of a Piper, was dressed in purest white. The rest wore fluttering robes in soft, light colors. Many had flowers in their hair. They looked like the Aurons of the rafts, but they were taller, their faces were less sharp, and their skin was golden brown.

And behind them, rising high above the tops of the tallest trees, seeming almost to touch the sky, was a glittering spire of glass. It flashed so brilliantly in the sunlight that at first Lief saw it only as a vast, shimmering column.

Then, as his eyes cleared, he realized that it had a shape. It was a vast statue of a woman — a Pirran woman, wearing the headdress of a Piper. And he knew without doubt that the woman was Auron the Fair, who had long ago made music so beautiful that her audience wept.

The statue's long robe fell straight to the ground in a thousand glittering glass pleats as sharp as razors. Its fixed, unseeing eyes gazed serenely towards the purple hills. Its tall headdress glared like a white flame against the blue sky. And embedded in the centre of the white flame, perfect and untouchable, was the stem of the Pirran Pipe.

Lief stared, aghast. No hands could have formed

that vast image. It could only have been created by magic.

"No wonder we are here, in the center of the island instead of at the edge as we expected," Barda muttered. "The mouthpiece of the Pipe pulled us to where it wanted us to be."

"We will never climb that statue. We would be cut to ribbons in a moment if we tried," Jasmine said. "You will just have to persuade the dome-dwellers to give us the stem willingly, Lief. They look gentle enough. Surely they will listen to you."

But Lief was silent, fighting despair. The statue had clearly been created to seal the stem of the Pipe away from every danger for eternity. Those who had made it would never willingly give up their prize. Never.

"Greetings, strangers."

Lief forced his dazzled eyes downward, tried to focus on the figure standing before him. It was the man dressed in white. His arms were outstretched in welcome. The people behind him were also smiling, their robes fluttering like the petals of flowers ruffled by a gentle breeze.

"I am the Piper, Auris," the man said. "I cannot guess how you have come to our land, but know it must be for a good and beautiful purpose, since nothing evil can dwell here. On behalf of the people, I bid you welcome to Pirra."

Welcome to *Pirra*?

Lief glanced at Barda and Jasmine. Both were struggling to keep their faces blank.

Auris was waiting courteously. Lief wet his dry lips. However hopeless this situation seemed, however sure he was that the dome-dwellers would be enraged by his request, and certainly would not grant it, he had to try.

"Thank you for your gracious welcome, Piper," he said carefully. "I am Lief, King of Deltora. I have come with my companions, Barda and Jasmine, to beg a favor of you."

Auris's brow furrowed slightly, and it seemed to Lief that the sweet, sunny air flickered.

Then Auris's face cleared. "Ah," he said, bowing and smiling. "Of course. Deltora. The realm beyond the mountains. You must forgive me, your majesty. For a moment the name escaped my memory. We of Pirra do not feel the need to travel. As I am sure you can well understand."

He lifted an elegant hand, gesturing at the beauty around him.

"Indeed," said Lief politely.

"A favor, you say?" Auris murmured.

Lief took a deep breath, glanced once again at Jasmine and Barda, willing them to be patient, and mentally crossed his fingers for luck.

"Many of our people are prisoners of the Shadow Lord, who is your enemy as well as ours," he said, keeping his voice low and calm. "The only thing that will save them is the Pirran Pipe, the stem of which you possess. We already have the mouthpiece, given to us willingly by the Plume people. This was how we were able to enter your magic dome so — "

"Stop!" The Piper's eyes had glazed. The people behind him had begun flitting around so frantically that they seemed blurred. And the light — the light was flickering, dimming . . .

"There is no need to fear us!" Lief exclaimed hastily. "We could not take the stem by force, even if we wished it. But I beg you will listen. We have journeyed far through the caverns, and faced many terrible dangers, to find your island."

There was a low rumbling like distant thunder. The trees, grass, and flowers quivered, then began to droop, as though their colors and shapes were melting into the trembling air.

Auris clapped his hands over his ears and screwed his eyes tightly shut. "You are speaking gibberish! Your words have no meaning!" he shouted. He was breathing heavily. His face had turned as white as the belly of a fish. The crowd behind him was surging like a troubled sea.

"Do not listen to them! They are deluded fools!" he panted, plainly speaking as much to himself as to the people. "There are no caverns. No dangers. No island. No dome. There is only Pirra, where all is beauty, all is peace, all is truth—"

"*You* are the one speaking gibberish, Piper!" Jasmine burst out, unable to keep silent any longer. "There is *nothing* true in this place."

"No!" Auris's eyes flew open and seemed to bulge in his head. "Stop—"

The thundering sound grew louder. Lief looked around him. Everywhere trees, flowers, grass, and sky were shuddering, dissolving. Everything was melting, changing . . .

But . . . but this was not just a result of the Piper's anger, surely. This was something far more serious. It was as if . . . as if . . .

A terrible thought struck Lief, shaking him to his core. Suddenly he remembered the parchments Penn had shown him. He remembered the one thing that had puzzled him about them. He remembered Penn's anguished eyes, Penn's words:

I have done all you require of me, Piper, and it has cost me dearly.

Yet what had Penn done but tell the history of her people's exile? Why had it cost her so dearly? Just because she feared for three strangers' lives?

Or because, in the telling, she had broken the law she held most sacred?

Truth is all-important.

What had Penn said when Barda asked her why her ancestors had been expelled from the dome?

They were dangerous . . . They were sick of pretense.

Dangerous? Why *dangerous*? Unless . . .

"You can make all the thunder and lightning you wish, Auris, but you *will* hear me!" Jasmine shouted. "This is not Pirra! It is just an island protected by magic and filled with pictures. And you know that! I can hear it in your voice!"

There was a splitting, cracking sound, as though the heavens themselves were breaking apart.

Auris shrieked.

And Lief's skin crawled as he understood at last. Penn had not lied. But she had not told the whole truth, either. And whatever the Piper claimed, Penn knew that this was the same as lying.

Auris and his people were swaying, backing towards the statue as though for protection. "Foulness is in your mouth!" Auris howled at Jasmine. "Your mind is crude, your heart is mean and shrivelled. You are a savage, whose eyes are not fit to see the beauty of Pirra!"

"Jasmine, do not answer! Let him be!" Lief cried urgently. "Jasmine, the raft-dwellers *knew* this would happen. They are *using* us — to break the illusion and destroy the dome! The dome depends on belief! Doubt cracks it. Doubt will destroy it!"

But Jasmine was not listening to him. She was moving after Auris, shouting at him, beside herself with anger. "I am not a savage, and *this is not Pirra!*" she shrieked. "You pretend not to know that, but you do, you *do*! Outside this pretty dream of yours, there are monsters crawling and breeding in filth! There are caverns, and a great sea, and thousands of people who live in darkness because you — "

Thunder rolled and crashed above them.

"You have been sent by the unbelievers!" Auris screeched, his bulging eyes dark with terror. "You are spies for all that is wicked and faithless! You have come to destroy me!"

And with that final word, the surging, fading crowd around him simply vanished, the flickering colors and shapes draining away into the grass like the phantoms they were.

Auris screamed — a scream of pure anguish that chilled Lief's blood.

"What has happened?" Barda roared over the cracking of the thunder. "The people! Where have they gone?"

"They never were," Lief shouted back, his stomach churning with horror. "They . . . were part of the illusion. He is alone here. Who knows how long — "

"One by one the last of them failed me and died," cried Auris. "But I kept the faith! Alone I kept Pirra alive, harnessing the magic of thousands to keep its beauty perfect. Then you came. Spies and traitors! Saying what must never be said, speaking of things that must never be admitted — "

There was a flash of dazzling light and an earsplitting crash. A jagged black crack opened in the sky, zigzagging down to the trembling horizon like a bolt of lightning.

Auris shrieked and fell to the ground at the base of the statue. Desperately he stretched out his arms to it, his bony fingers clawing the air.

The split groaned and widened as the magic trapped for so long within the dome began escaping with rushing fury. Brilliant rainbow light could be seen through the gap as the cavern walls outside exploded into life, and colors dimmed for centuries gleamed.

Lief, Barda, and Jasmine threw themselves to the ground, gripping the earth desperately as the force howled around them, tearing at the rags of trees, the faded tatters of flowers, grass, distant purple hills . . .

Then, suddenly, there was utter silence. But it was not the peaceful or exhausted silence of an ending. It was heavy and tense, as though everything was holding its breath. Waiting . . .

Cautiously, his skin prickling, Lief raised his head. The vision of Pirra had been swept away. Only the huge glass statue remained, rising into thick, still air which seemed to have been drained of color. Auris lay facedown at the statue's base, the tips of his fingers just touching the knife-like folds of the robe where they met the ground.

Everything was bathed in a weird half-light. The hills on the horizon had disappeared. Great branching clumps of fungus, tall and thick as ancient trees, hunched where trees once stood. Tiny ferns and mosses covered the clay and clustered along the banks of a deep and silent stream.

In the distance, the jagged tear in the fabric of the dome was now a gaping wound. At the top, it shone with rainbow light. But lower down it was deepest black.

That is strange, Lief thought slowly.

"Lief!"

Startled, Lief turned to see Barda scrambling to his feet and backing away to stand with his back to the nearest clump of fungus. Barda's eyes were fixed on the tear in the dome. Jasmine, too, was jumping up, reaching for her dagger.

"What — ?" Lief began. Then he saw their faces change, and heard, behind him, a distant scratching, tearing sound.

He spun around. And realised why no light had been visible through the lower part of the hole in the dome. Something had been pressing against it. Something huge and black that was now ripping its way through the gap, leg by spiny leg.

Arach!

16 ~ Terror

With a low growl, the Arach forced itself fully through the gap in the dome. It rose on its back legs, huge, dwarfing the towering clumps of fungus that dotted the horizon.

It lurched forward abruptly, and to his horror Lief saw that another Arach was pushing through the gap behind it. Rainbows shone briefly through a tangle of black legs and a bloated body. Then the second Arach was through the hole, which was quickly blocked by a third.

"They are escaping from the light!" exclaimed Jasmine.

Of course! Lief thought. The Arach came from caves. They live and breed in dimness. They cannot bear bright light. Now that the caverns are lit by magic once more, the dome is the only place left for them to hide.

For the dome had not been brightened by the rainbow brilliance that shone behind the tear in its fabric. It was as though the half-light that hung above the island stifled the brighter light, and prevented it from entering.

Five Arach now loomed on the horizon. And more were coming. The first arrivals had begun moving forward. Their massive bodies swaying on their long, spiny legs, they were feeling their way, moving awkwardly on the unfamiliar, solid ground.

"They are coming this way," Jasmine exclaimed. "Perhaps the statue attracts them. Or perhaps they can smell prey."

"That is not a pleasant thought," said Barda grimly. He looked thoughtfully at his sword. Large and heavy as it was, it seemed as small as a needle compared to the approaching beasts.

"We cannot fight them, Barda," Lief muttered. "Any more than we could fight the Sand Beasts in the Shifting Sands, or the Glus in the Maze of the Beast. We would not last a moment!"

"What else are we to do but stand and fight?" Jasmine hissed furiously. "You have seen them run, Lief. They would catch us in an instant if we tried to flee! Are we just to lie down and wait for them to eat us?"

"We must hide," said Lief. "The light is poor. We must hide and hope they pass us by so that we can creep away."

"Hide?" Jasmine exclaimed, looking around at

the low ferns, the sparse clumps of fungus. "There is nowhere to hide!"

Lief pulled off his cloak. "There is," he said. "Just as there was, not long ago, in the River Broad when an Ak-Baba was overhead. Just as there was in the Shifting Sands when Grey Guards were approaching. Have you forgotten so soon?"

Jasmine's green eyes flashed. "I have forgotten nothing," she said abruptly. "I thought you had, however."

Lief stared at her, hurt and confused. He could not understand her meaning.

Barda cleared his throat. "If we are to hide, we should do so at once," he said. "The creatures are moving slowly, but their strides are huge. They will be upon us very soon. What of Auris?"

Lief tore his eyes away from Jasmine's and glanced over to where Auris lay beside the statue. He thrust the cloak into Barda's hands. "You and Jasmine take cover," he said. "If he still lives, I will fetch him."

"Keep low! Take care!" Jasmine called softly after him as he began to run.

Obediently, Lief lowered his head. At least she cares whether I live or die, he thought. But why did she say that, about my forgetting our quest for the Belt? How could I ever forget?

Auris was rigidly still, and his eyes were closed. But as Lief drew near enough to the statue to feel its strange, radiating warmth on his skin, he realized that the last of the dome-dwellers was not dead, or even unconscious.

Auris was chanting under his breath — so softly and rapidly that Lief could not catch the words.

"Auris," Lief urged, touching his arm. "Auris — come with me. There is danger here."

Auris screwed his eyes more tightly shut, but made no other sign that he had heard. He did not lift his head, or move his fingers from the hem of the statue's robe. Did not stop, for a moment, his frenzied whispering.

Lief glanced nervously at the approaching Arach. The creatures were closer now. There were at least ten of them, crawling in a wedge-shaped pack with the first, and largest, in the lead.

"Auris!" he said sharply. He tried to pull the Piper away from the statue, but the thin fingers immediately clutched at the razor-sharp glass and gripped it tightly. Blood ran in streams into the ground, but still the whispering voice did not pause.

Lief bent closer, straining to hear.

"Thespellmustholdthespellmustholdthespell . . ."

One phrase, endlessly repeated.

"Lief!" Barda and Jasmine were beckoning urgently from behind the fungus where they had taken cover. Lief could hardly see them. As always, his cloak had taken on the color of its surroundings. It was disguising them perfectly.

He turned and was shocked to see how close the

Arach were, how far they had crawled in just a few moments. They had quickly become used to the solid earth under their feet. They were moving steadily, confidently.

They still had not seen him. But any moment . . .

Desperately, hissing warnings and commands, Lief tried again to drag Auris free. But the Piper's bleeding fingers gripped the warm glass like steel bands, and his babbling chant did not cease.

It was no use. In despair, Lief left him and crawled to where Jasmine and Barda crouched, anxiously waiting.

"He will not move," he said, creeping under the cover of the cloak with them.

"It is his choice," Jasmine answered calmly. "Perhaps he thinks the magic of the statue will offer more protection than a hiding place."

Lief shook his head. He had a lump in his throat which made it hard to speak. "I do not think so," he said. "I think he is using the last of his power, and the power of the Pipe, to try to hold on to all that remains of his world."

He had a sour, burning taste in his mouth — the taste of defeat, anger, and guilt. He thought of Penn and the Piper. Were they still watching from their boat beyond the seaweed band? Or were they already hastening back to the rafts, delirious with joy because they had regained for their people the light and magic so long denied them?

"For all the Piper of the rafts knew, there were thousands of people inside the dome," he muttered, his eyes on the approaching Arach. "Thousands, whose lives would have been destroyed by what he did. By what *we* did, in ignorance."

"He was fighting for the lives of his own people," said Barda in a low voice. "Like any good commander, he seized a chance for victory when it came."

Lief thought of the Piper's glowing eyes as he spoke to Penn about the visitors.

They could be our salvation.

"And like any good commander," Barda went on, even more quietly, "he knew that sacrifices would have to be made in the cause. Unfortunately, *we* seem to be the sacrifices in this case. The beasts are not going to pass us by."

The Arach were almost upon them. They had slowed as they neared the statue, and now they had stopped completely.

"It is the warmth," breathed Jasmine. "They stayed close beside the dome not just because of the food, but because it was warm. They like the statue for the same reason. They will probably try to nest around it."

Lief felt sick. Was it so? Were they condemned to crouch here, with no chance of escape, helplessly watching the slaughter of Auris? Knowing that the second part of the Pirran Pipe was lost forever because of something they themselves had done?

He watched with horrified fascination as the largest of the Arach moved closer to Auris's motionless body.

The creature was gigantic. Monstrous. Its eyes bulged from its glossy black shell, gleaming red. Its fangs slowly opened and closed, dripping venom.

Its two front legs reached out delicately, took Auris in their grip, and tugged. Auris's hands tightened on the glass. He did not stir.

"No!" Lief whispered in agony. He tensed himself to rise.

Barda's hand clamped firmly on his wrist. "Be still! We cannot help him! There is still a chance we can get you out, Lief. You, at least."

"That is not important anymore," Lief hissed back. "All that matters is — "

But at that moment, the Arach lost patience. With a low growl, it tore Auris away from the statue, and lifted him high into the air.

Auris's shriek of terror and despair chilled Lief to the bone. Cold sweat broke out on his brow, and he began shivering violently. He wanted to cover his ears, but his hands were rigid. He wanted to look away, but he could not move.

The beast rose on its hind legs and pulled its victim closer. Auris screamed and screamed again, writhing in an agony of fear. The monster's red eyes watched him closely, almost as if it was enjoying his terror. Then suddenly its fangs lunged forward and sank into his neck, mercifully ending his struggles.

The spiny, clawed legs instantly began tearing the limp body apart, shredding it exactly as they had shredded the boat.

The other Arach closed in, scrabbling for a share of the prize, fighting over every dripping scrap of flesh that fell from their leader's jaws.

Sickened, Lief at last managed to look away.

And only then did he see what had been right in front of his eyes since the moment Auris was plucked into the air.

The statue's arms were rising. As Lief watched, astounded, the hands covered the serene face. Then — suddenly — the glass was no longer clear and gleaming. It had become thick white.

Lief pressed his hand over his mouth to stifle a cry. Glancing sideways, he saw that Jasmine and Barda were also staring in amazement.

There was a strange, grating sound. Then, with no further warning, the statue simply crumbled, collapsing in an earsplitting, thunderous shower of shattered glass.

"Beware!" Lief shouted, pulling Barda and Jasmine with him to the ground.

They lay there under the cloak, eyes tightly closed as jagged fragments sprayed upward, then fell again, pelting the ground like deadly hail. They heard the Arach bellowing, the cracking sound as shooting glass cracked the beasts' shells like darts.

And then, at last, all was still once more. Cautiously Lief lifted his head. His mind filled, echoing, with the sound of the Pirran Pipe. The Pipe's stem was there, somewhere, buried deep in shattered glass. It called to him, beckoned him. But he held himself rigidly, knowing he could not stir.

The two Arach which had been closest to the statue lay where they had fallen, their legs kicking and tangling uselessly. But the others, despite small cuts and cracks in their shells, had been injured only enough to drive them into a fury. Growling, they rose onto their back legs, their front legs pawing at the air.

Barda cursed under his breath.

But Jasmine was looking up. "The dome," she said softly. "The dome . . ."

There was a low, sighing sound. And then the dome — simply melted away, disappearing like mist.

The light was blinding, filled with rainbows, glittering, dazzling. Lief, Barda, and Jasmine buried their faces in their arms. The Arach shrieked and scurried frantically away, leaving their two injured fellows to die where they lay.

And Penn, standing panting in the place which once had been the gap in the dome, a bone spear clutched awkwardly in her hand, sobbed part in frustration, part in relief, for there was nothing now for her to do.

17 ~ Peace

Much later, in Penn's little hut on the rafts, all was the picture of peace. Light streamed through the window, bringing with it the sounds of rejoicing. Tresk and Mesk bobbed lazily in their bowl. Kree, cradled in Jasmine's arm, cautiously tested his healing wing.

Lief, Barda, and Jasmine sat around the stove with Penn and the Piper, the cheers of the raft-dweller crowds ringing in their ears. A huge platter of Molisk patties and a basket of warm bread lay between them. Filli sat on Jasmine's shoulder, nibbling sea berries which made his tiny nose wrinkle with surprise and pleasure.

Even Fury and Flash lay quietly in their cages, side by side. Their adventure with the Arach seemed to have changed their minds about the wisdom of fighting. Together they had faced a terrible enemy, a spider far mightier than either of them could ever have imagined. For now, they had decided that peace was a blessing.

"So. The Arachs have gone back to the caves where they came from," the Piper said, biting into a patty with relish. "They could not bear the light and the cold. I told you, Penn, that it would be so."

Penn glanced at Lief, Barda, and Jasmine. Her food lay untasted on its plate. She, at least, was still not at peace.

It would be a relief to her, Lief knew, if the matter hanging between them was put into words.

He was very aware that the stem of the Pirran Pipe, retrieved from the pile of shattered glass on the Isle of Auron, was at this very moment firmly tucked inside the Piper's robe. He knew it would not be wise to anger the Piper now.

But he had to speak his mind, for all their sakes.

"You used us, Piper," he said. "We suspected that you were using us as tools to obtain the stem of the Pirran Pipe. But you were doing much more than that. You were using us as a weapon to destroy the dome."

"To destroy the thing that was sucking the life from my people?" the Piper said mildly, licking his fingers. "Yes, I did. Would you not do the same for Deltora?"

Lief hesitated.

"Of course you would, Lief," Jasmine said

sharply. "You can be cold and calculating enough when you believe the good of the kingdom requires it."

"What do you mean, Jasmine?" Lief exclaimed, startled by the sudden, bitter note in her voice.

Jasmine shrugged. "If you think a secret should be kept, for example, you keep it," she said shortly. "Even from those it most concerns."

She looked down at her hands to avoid Lief's eyes. She was furious with herself. She had not meant to speak so rashly.

She had tried not to think of Faith, the little sister who was a prisoner in the Shadowlands and who Lief had tried to prevent her from discovering. She had tried not to think of the highborn Toran girl Lief had brought in secret to the palace to become his queen.

Most of the time she was successful. But now and again she remembered, and the knowledge jabbed at her heart like a spear, making her lash out in anger and pain.

Lief felt his face grow hot. He remembered Jasmine's hasty words on the island.

I have forgotten nothing . . . I thought you had, however.

Was it possible that Jasmine had guessed the secret he had kept at such cost to himself? The secret that was like a crushing burden?

No, surely not. He and Doom had been so careful!

He glanced at Barda. But Barda had turned to

look out the window, as though there was something of great interest happening on the silent street.

Jasmine simply suspects there *is* a secret, Lief told himself. She feels the barrier that hidden knowledge always creates between two people who have always spoken the truth to one another.

Lief felt it himself, and he hated it. He longed to tear the barrier down. To end the terrible, aching loneliness it made him feel at moments like this.

But he knew he could not. Not until all was safe. Not until Deltora's future had been secured.

He became aware that the Piper was regarding him curiously, and his blush deepened.

"It is sometimes necessary for leaders to do things they would prefer not to do," the Piper said, as though he were speaking to himself. "Sometimes they have to put aside their own wishes, even their own deepest longings, for the greater good of all. It is . . . not pleasant. Especially when their actions anger those they care about."

Jasmine did not raise her head. But Lief could see that she had heard. He prayed that she had also understood.

"You think, no doubt, that I am evil," the Piper went on, in the same even tone. "You think Penn tricked you, on my orders. You think I used you as tools to destroy the dome. You think that I cared nothing for your lives, or the lives of the people who may have lived on the island."

"It did occur to us," said Barda dryly.

The Piper shrugged his narrow shoulders. "It is true that I forced poor Penn to do what she did," he said, glancing at the history-keeper, who had bowed her head. "She was sorely distressed by the task. Like all raft-dwellers she respects truth above everything else. I suggested that she let you *read* our history, so she would not have to tell it."

"But the history was not complete," said Lief. "The two parchments Penn gave us were torn, the first at the bottom, the second at the top. They were once part of the same document, I think. You tore a section from the middle before giving the story to us. Is that not so?"

Penn nodded miserably. Without speaking, she crawled to her feet and went over to the hanging baskets. She slid a fragment of parchment from the back of one of them, returned to the stove, and thrust the scrap into Lief's hand.

The dome could only remain whole, however, while all within it believed in the illusion and shut out any doubting thoughts. Because they denied that the island was Pirra, and spoke aloud of the caverns and the dome, our ancestors continually threatened the dome's existence.

"If I had allowed Penn to show you the whole parchment, would you have helped us?" the Piper asked, turning his cold little eyes on Lief.

Lief hesitated. "We needed the second part of the Pirran Pipe," he said finally. "We would have entered the dome, even if the truth was known to us."

"Perhaps," agreed the Piper. "But perhaps you would have been so careful in what you said that the dome would have remained closed, and my people would have continued to live in growing darkness. I could not take that risk."

He sighed. "So I am guilty of the first charge you have laid at my feet. But I am not guilty of the others."

He took some bread from the basket and bit into it. "I knew the dome-dwellers would not harm you, for blood may not be spilled inside the dome," he said thoughtfully, with his mouth full. "And I did not think that you or anyone else would have to face the Arach. I thought the dome would shatter, the light would return to the caverns, and the Arach would flee to the dimness of the caves at once."

"But that did not happen," said Barda gruffly. "Auris kept the spell alive. He held the dome, damaged as it was, in place with all the force of his will. Only his death ended it."

"Indeed." The Piper shrugged. "I had not counted on that. But as soon as we realized what had happened, Penn and I called the guards. Then we entered the dome ourselves, even before the guards arrived, to do what we could to aid you."

He took another bite of the bread, and glanced at Penn. "What use we could have been, I do not know," he said, chewing. "As I told Penn, we were almost certainly going to our deaths. But she insisted. Fortunately, the man Auris expired in time to save us all."

Lief shuddered as a vision of Auris's terrible death rose before his eyes. He glanced at the Piper with dislike, then looked away, repelled by his coldness.

And yet, he thought . . . for all his seemingly uncaring words, the Piper *had* entered the dome. *Had* put his own life at risk.

Lief looked again at the small, wrinkled Auron, who was chewing his bread with every appearance of enjoyment. Whatever he pretended, the Piper was not without feeling. Not without honor or courage. He was just a being who preferred to keep his emotions locked within himself. It was his way of surviving.

"We never dreamed there would be just one soul left on the island," Penn burst out, breaking her silence at last. "We knew there would not be a large number, however. The dome-dweller colony could never have thrived. Fewer and fewer children were being born to the tribe, even at the time our ancestors left it."

The Piper nodded, swallowing. "Children are not good at living a lie. Children have too much energy, are too impatient, and ask too many questions," he said.

He glanced slyly at Jasmine. "Some people, indeed, keep these qualities long past the age of childhood," he added. "That, I think, is a good thing. But it is not always comfortable for those who love them."

In the tense silence that followed, he calmly finished eating. Then he brushed the crumbs from his hands, and fumbled in the folds of his robe.

"Here is the stem of the Pirran Pipe," he said, drawing out a small piece of carved wood and handing it casually to Lief. "Use it as you will. We would be glad to have it back when you have achieved your aim, but for now we can do without it."

Lief took the stem of the Pipe in trembling hands. As he touched it, his whole body tingled, and the Pipe's music rang in his ears. He took the mouthpiece from the inside pocket of his shirt, and screwed the two pieces together.

"Thank you," he managed to say.

The Piper allowed himself a small smile. "You are welcome," he said. "In fact, it is no great sacrifice. After all, we have done without our part of the Pirran Pipe for a very long time. For now, the magic that lives in every Auron, and which has now been returned to us, will be more than enough. Thanks to you, the island is ours once again. What more can we ask?"

The music in Lief's mind rose and fell, sweet and filled with longing. He looked up at Barda and Jasmine. He saw their eyes fixed on the magical object in his hands, and knew that they, too, could feel its power.

One more effort . . . one more adventure, and the Pirran Pipe would be complete.

And then?

And then, thought Lief, we will be ready. Then we can go, for good or ill, to the Shadowlands.

THE

SHADOWLANDS

Contents

1 The Forbidden Way .... .301

2 Keras .... .310

3 Song of the Pipe .... .319

4 The Grey Zone .... .327

5 In the Shadowlands .... .337

6 The Wild Ones .... .345

7 The Beast .... .353

8 Claw .... .362

9 West .... .372

10 The Mounds .... .381

11 The Factory .... .390

12 Discoveries .... .400

13 The Tunnel .... .410

14 The Shadow Arena .... .421

15 The Trap .... .430

16 Reunions .... .439

17 Secrets .... .447

1 - The Forbidden Way

The narrow channel through the rock disappeared into thick darkness, echoing with the hollow sound of lapping water. A broad band of bright pink and yellow seaweed floated across its entrance.

Lief had no need to consult the little map in his hand to know that this grim tunnel was the Forbidden Way — the only path to the island of Keras, and the third part of the Pirran Pipe. But still he looked down at the map and the arrow drawn by the Piper of Auron.

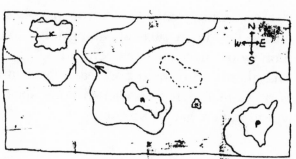

The map had been soaked, marked, and dam-aged, but against all odds it had survived. Like us, Lief thought, looking up at Jasmine and Barda.

They were both sitting very still, staring at the dark crack in the rock. They no longer had to squint against stinging spray. The Auron guards who were towing the boat had ordered their great eels to slow.

Because Auron boats were narrow, with no room for two to sit side by side, Barda was alone on the cen-tral seat, holding the boat's single paddle. Jasmine was at the front of the boat with Kree, whose injured wing was still weak, perched on her shoulder and Filli chattering beneath her collar. Lief was in the back.

"Once we are in that tunnel, there will be no turning back," Barda muttered. "We will have to stay alert."

Lief nodded. Certainly, Doran the Dragonlover, the first explorer of Deltora's underworld, had passed through the Forbidden Way. But that had been hun-dreds of years ago. Many things might have changed since then.

As the boat's prow nudged the first strands of bright weed, the Auron guards released their hold and moved away. Only Penn, the Auron history-keeper, stayed close beside the boat, speaking softly to the gi-ant eel on whose neck she was perched.

The guards were wild and fearsome, with their clothes of animal skin and wicked bone spears. But they would not cross that bright weed barrier, the ancient Auron warning of danger, unless ordered to do so by their leader, the Piper. And no such order had been given.

"We will give you a boat and guide you to the edge of our territory, but we can help you no farther," the Piper had told Lief, Barda, and Jasmine as they ate their final meal in Penn's little hut. "No Auron may enter the Forbidden Way."

"It is our most ancient law," added Penn, anxious to soften the Piper's bluntness. "Should Aurons enter their sea, the Kerons would attack."

"The Plume people said the same of you," Jasmine remarked lightly. "They said you would kill us on sight."

"The Plumes are lying savages!" snapped the Piper, his eyes sparks of pale fire in his wrinkled face.

Lief and Barda glanced ruefully at each other. They knew that there was no point in defending the Plumes. The old hatred between the Pirran tribes was too strong to be shaken by the arguments of three strangers.

But Jasmine was looking at the two fighting spiders, sleeping peacefully together in their new, large cage. United by fear of a common enemy, Flash and Fury had put aside their bitter rivalry and now wrestled only in play. As a result, they were to stay with Penn, who had grown quite fond of them despite their fearsome looks.

"Even Flash and Fury have decided they have

more in common than they thought," Jasmine said. "But the Plumes, Aurons, and Kerons cling to their bitterness. It is hard to believe that once you were all Pirrans."

"That was long ago," muttered the Piper. "Pirra is the Shadowlands now, and the Plumes and Kerons are to blame. If they had accepted the lady Auron as Piper, the Pirran Pipe would never have been divided, and the Shadow Lord would not have been able to take our land."

Penn's brow creased. She, at least, was clear-sighted enough to admit to herself that the followers of Auron had been just as stubborn as the followers of Auron's rivals, Plume and Keras. The three groups had shared equally in the rash decision to divide the Pirran Pipe.

Now, as the boat rocked gently in the swell caused by the coiling of the great eels, Lief looked up at Penn's anxious face.

The history-keeper had insisted on accompanying them as far as the Forbidden Way, carrying the fire that would light their torches. She had been cheerful on the journey through the rainbow sea, but now her fears showed clearly in her eyes.

Holding her flare high, she urged her eel to the front of the boat and lit Jasmine's torch. Then, silently, she moved back to Lief.

"Farewell, Penn," Lief said. "Thank you for all you have done for us."

"I have done nothing," Penn answered, dipping the flare till it touched the torch Lief held up to her. "But what you have done for *us* can never be repaid. I pray that you — "She bowed her head, unable to continue.

"Never fear," said Barda heartily. "We will live to share Molisk patties with you again, Penn."

"I hope it will be so," Penn whispered. "May Auron protect you."

She murmured to her eel, which obediently moved behind the boat and nudged it forward. The boat slipped over the band of weed and into the mouth of the tunnel.

At once, Lief's mind filled with the sweet, piercing music of the Pirran Pipe. The sound was so loud, so overwhelming, that it seemed to him that Barda and Jasmine must surely be able to hear it, too. But he could see by their faces that they could not.

He stared, transfixed, into the darkness ahead. His mouth was dry, his head ringing with sound. Dimly he realized that he was clutching the cloth bag that hung around his neck, under his shirt. There the mouthpiece and stem of the Pipe lay hidden.

The last piece of the Pipe was calling to them out of the darkness. Calling . . .

Stop this! You must be alert, be ready . . .

Lief forced his hand over the side of the boat, scooped up some water, and dashed it into his face. He gasped as the icy liquid splashed on his hot skin.

The spell was broken. The music faded away, leaving a strange, sad emptiness behind it. Lief blinked rapidly as his eyes cleared.

The light was dimming rapidly. The walls of the passage were racing by. Lief twisted in his seat to look behind him, and was startled to see that the passage entrance was already just a narrow slit of light in the distance.

"What is happening?" Jasmine exclaimed. "Why are we going so fast?"

"Some sort of current is pulling us along," Barda called uneasily. "I am hardly paddling at all, and yet . . . "

"It is the Pipe," Lief managed to say. "I — feel it."

In moments the boat was skimming along in darkness, the passage walls lit only by the flickering yellow light of the torches.

The walls flashed with rainbow colors, which soon gave way to purest green. But above, where the torchlight did not reach, there was only thick black.

Suddenly Kree squawked as Jasmine jerked in her seat and slapped at her neck. "Something just fell on me," Jasmine exclaimed.

"A moth, no doubt," said Barda, concentrating on steering the boat as it raced along. "I have seen a few of them around."

Then he slapped at his own neck. Something had fallen onto the skin there, and was clinging.

Lief felt a tickling on his hand. He looked down and saw a winged, slug-like creature squirming there. He shook his hand, but the creature did not fall away. With a start, he realized that it was biting him — burrowing its head into his flesh.

And it was growing. Its body was swelling as he watched. Filling with his blood.

"Leeches!" he shouted, shaking his hand again, filled with disgust.

He saw Kree fluttering from Jasmine's shoulder as she scrabbled at the collar of her jacket, trying to pull off two leeches that were hanging from her neck. He saw with horror that more of the loathsome creatures had already landed on her hands.

"Beware! Above!" shouted Barda.

Lief looked, and his stomach heaved. The air high above them was teeming with flying leeches, streaming in thick, whirring clouds down from the darkness.

Wildly he waved the torch above his head. Dozens of slimy, winged bodies sizzled in the flames. But still many of the leeches swerved around the fiery barrier to settle on his hands and arms, to feed and swell.

And these were only the forerunners. Thousands upon thousands were following, spiralling downward.

"Jasmine, Barda! Get down!" Lief shouted. Recklessly he cast his torch into the water, then tore off his cloak and threw it across the boat to make a canopy.

In moments the companions were lying face down beneath the cloak, holding it awkwardly in place. A pattering sound began as the first cloud of leeches rained down on their shelter, sensing the warm bodies beneath it. The pattering increased, became a relentless pounding. The cloak began to sag.

Lief's arms and hands were trembling with the effort of holding the cloak in place. The leeches that had been clinging to him before he took shelter, and the few that had found a way to creep under the cloak since then, were hanging like bloated sausages from his wrists and the backs of his hands. He gritted his teeth, forcing down the wild, urgent need to pluck them off.

The loaded cloak began pulling away from the boat's edge. Panic-stricken, Lief heaved at the fabric, trying to tug it back into place. But already leeches were pouring through the tiny gap, fastening onto his hands, slithering into his sleeve.

The cloak bulged and slipped again. The gap at the side of the boat opened further. Leeches poured through in a whirring mass.

We are finished, Lief thought suddenly. After all we have been through, we are lost — defeated by the smallest creatures we have ever faced.

It would have been almost funny, if it had not been so vile.

Even as his hands struggled hopelessly to close

the gap, his mind flew to Del. He would never return. Marilen's worst fears had come to pass.

Yet I regret nothing, Lief thought. I did what I had to do.

A strange peace flowed through him. And with that peace came the music of the Pirran Pipe, piercing him with its exquisite sweetness.

At last, Lief surrendered himself to it. He let himself drift in the tides of sound. His eyes closed.

And so it was that he did not notice that emerald light was suddenly shining through the fabric above his head. He did not notice that the drumming, pounding sound had ceased. He did not hear the soft splash of water as the boat skimmed lightly across a rippling green sea, drawn safely and surely to land.

2 - Keras

When Lief came to himself, the voice of the Pipe had faded and a great weight was pressing down on him. He pushed violently, and at last struggled into dazzling emerald light. Then Barda and Jasmine stirred beside him. As they sat up, the boat tilted under the shifting weight of millions of dead leeches.

The boat was rocking gently in shallow, pale green water that lapped on a sandy shore. Beyond the shore was a forest of fungus trees in soft greens and browns.

"We are on Keras!" Barda said slowly. "We must have reached the end of the Forbidden Way. We came out into the light, and all the leeches died."

Suddenly shuddering, he scrambled out of the loaded boat, Jasmine and Lief close behind him. They plunged their arms and faces into the shining green water over and over again, as if to wash even the memory of the leeches away.

When they felt clean again, they waded to shore, heaving the boat after them. They pulled the craft onto the gently sloping sand and upturned it, emptying it of its vile cargo. Then Lief reclaimed his cloak and they moved on, into the green shade of the forest.

A sandy path wound through the trees. They began to follow it. Now and then there was the sound of a creature scuttling in the sand, but there was no other sign of life. The silence was eerie.

"So, we are in the territory of the emerald," Barda said, in a casual but very loud voice. "Above us is Dread Mountain, where our friends the Dread Gnomes live."

Lief realized that Barda was telling any unseen watchers to be wary of attacking them. Barda sensed, as he did, that the forest was not as deserted as it seemed.

They reached a clearing closely hemmed in by trees. Here the silence seemed thicker. The back of Lief's neck prickled. He looked rapidly around, but nothing stirred.

Jasmine's eyes flicked down to the great gems that studded the belt at Lief's waist. The ruby and the emerald were undimmed.

"The gems cannot be relied upon to give warning down here," Barda muttered.

"So you have told me," said Jasmine. "But why

is it so? The gems first came from deep within Deltora. Surely they should be *more* powerful here, not less."

"Who are you? Why are you here?"

The companions jumped back, drawing their weapons. The whispering voices seemed to have come from all around them. But the clearing was empty.

"Answer!"

Jasmine drew a sharp breath and nudged Lief. Following her eyes, he looked up. A fiery sword hung above his head, point down. Two more swords hung over Jasmine and Barda. Sweat broke out on Lief's brow. Clearly, the questions had to be answered, quickly and carefully.

"I am Lief, king of Deltora, the land above," he said clearly. "My companions are Jasmine and Barda. Many of our people are enslaved in the Shadowlands, and only the magic of the Pirran Pipe will save them. The Plumes and the Aurons have each lent us their part of the Pipe. We have come to beg the people of Keras to do the same."

There was a moment of great stillness. Then, abruptly, the swords vanished and a large group of people appeared out of thin air.

Like the Plumes and the Aurons, the people were small, with pale eyes, long noses, and large, pointed ears. Their garments were shimmering green, and a few, strangely, had yellow hair on their heads.

One of these, a woman wearing a Piper's tall

312

headdress, moved towards the visitors. Green moths with glittering wings fluttered about the headdress like a moving crown. A boy with a bony, eager face and a mass of spiky fair hair crowded close behind her.

"Greetings, cousins!" the woman said in a low, musical voice that held a hint of amusement. "I am Tirral, Piper of Keras. Please lay down your weapons."

As Lief hesitated, there was a soft, rushing sound. The next moment his sword, Barda's sword, and Jasmine's dagger were all lying at Tirral's feet.

Jasmine and Barda lunged forward, but Lief flung out an arm to hold them back. He had seen what they had not. At the moment they moved, the green moths fluttering around Tirral's head had changed to shimmering arrows, pointed at their hearts.

Tirral, who had remained utterly motionless, smiled.

"Forgive our caution, cousins," she said. "You claim that the parts of the Pirran Pipe you carry were given to you, but it is far more likely that you took them by force."

"It may be more likely, but it is not true," said Lief, slowly dropping his arm. "Keep our weapons, however, if it makes you feel safer."

Barda and Jasmine, their eyes on the hovering arrows, stepped back reluctantly.

The arrows shrank and changed back into

moths. "Thank you," said Tirral calmly. "It would have troubled us to injure kinsfolk. Especially kinsfolk who have done what is proper, and brought with them a fine gift."

"Gift?" growled Barda suspiciously.

"Such a great quantity of bait, heaped on the shore!" the eager-faced boy cried. "Ah, thanks to you we will have fresh-caught Seawing for weeks to come!" He smacked his lips. "Seawing are delicious! And there is nothing they like better than leeches from the entrance to the Keras sea. If only we could — "

"Gathering the leeches is a dangerous task, and we do it rarely," Tirral explained, cutting him short.

"If we lit the tunnel — for just a few moments — " the boy began.

"We cannot light the tunnel, Emlis," said Tirral wearily, as if they had had this argument many times before. "The darkness and the leeches are our protection from the Aurons. Are we to risk daring our enemies to attack us for the sake of a little bait?"

"I am surprised that you need bait for fishing, Piper, since your magic is so powerful," said Jasmine pertly.

Tirral smiled. "There are many ways to catch a fish," she said. "And if the fish you want rises to a simple bait, so much the better. Please follow me."

She turned on her heel and moved away, ushering Emlis firmly before her.

"I hope that *we* are not the fish in this case," muttered Barda as he, Lief, and Jasmine followed, with the other Kerons close behind. "Are we guests, or prisoners?"

"It is not far to go, cousins!" called Emlis, craning to look at them over his shoulder.

"Why do they call us cousins?" said Jasmine, rather too loudly. "We are no kin of theirs!"

"But you are!" said Tirral, stopping where the path ended in a dense clump of trees. "Do you not recall your history?" She turned to face them, and touched the wisps of fair hair that showed beneath her head-covering.

"The Girl with the Golden Hair!" Jasmine exclaimed, astounded. "Alyss and Rosnan! You mean . . . ?"

"Certainly," said Tirral. "After they settled on Keras, Alyss and Rosnan had many children. Those children grew up to marry Kerons, and have children of their own. And so it went on through the generations."

"Most of us have some above-worlder blood running in our veins," Emlis broke in. "Even those who do not bear the sign of the golden hair as I do." He ran his fingers through his wiry hair with obvious pride.

Tirral sighed. "And so we greet you as distant cousins, as our ancestors greeted Doran the Dragonlover, long ago," she said. "Doran was not surprised. It was the tale of Alyss and Rosnan which had brought him to the caverns in the first place."

"We were led here by the same story," Lief murmured.

"And of *course* Alyss and Rosnan stopped on Keras!" cried Jasmine. "The emerald cavern is the last before the grey place where they feared to go."

"But who would have thought that after so long there would still be a trace of them here?" Barda exclaimed.

Tirral shrugged. "Blood is blood, no matter how thinly it is spread over the ages," she said. She raised her hand. The trees blocking the path vanished to reveal a large group of startled, guilty-looking children.

"Bad little fish! Did we not tell you to remain hidden in the fruit store?" scolded Tirral. "What if we had been a band of savage Aurons, come to eat you alive?"

She sounded very fierce, but hid a smile as the children scattered.

Now the companions could see that the clump of trees had concealed a village. Without speaking, Tirral led the way through the broad, tidy streets.

The village was large, light, and pleasant. The houses were made of green fungus wood, thatched with dried seaweed. Fish swam lazily in ponds in almost every garden, and the children who had been shooed from the village entrance peeped from behind the garden walls.

At last they reached a large open space, in the center of which a fire burned brightly in a deep cradle of stones. Woven mats were spread on the ground around the fire.

"This is our meeting place," Tirral said, sitting down on one of the mats and signaling for Lief, Barda, and Jasmine to join her. "Here Alyss and Rosnan told their story to our ancestors."

"Doran sat here, too, in his time," put in Emlis, throwing himself clumsily down beside her. "It was Doran who brought the fire that burns here still."

The other Kerons who had been gathering by the fire were all whispering and watching the visitors with interest. But none was as eager as Emlis. Quivering with excitement, he gazed at the visitors, drinking in every detail of their appearance. "That is the Belt of Deltora, is it not?" he breathed, leaning closer to Lief. "Doran said much of its power."

Tirral glanced at him with affectionate irritation. "This is my son, Emlis," she said. "He has more above-worlder blood than most of us, I think, for he longs to travel, and knows Doran's tales by heart. Your arrival has pleased him greatly."

The young man blushed and he ducked his head, muttering awkwardly.

"Now!" Tirral raised her voice slightly. "You are

our kinsfolk and, according to Keron beliefs, it is our duty to help you if we can. Our part of the Pirran Pipe is precious to us, but we can well survive without it if we must. Our own magic is sufficient for our needs."

The people around the fire murmured solemn agreement. Lief's heart began to pound with excitement.

Then, with a stab of dismay, he saw Tirral's face hardening.

Whatever she says of Keron beliefs, she does not want to give up her treasure, he thought. She has found a way to refuse us. A way her people will accept.

"The Pipe will not be lost," he said quickly. "It will be returned to the caverns, I swear it!"

Tirral went on as if he had not spoken. "But also according to our beliefs," she said, "if you borrow something from us, swearing to return it, I may demand something of you to keep as a token of your oath. A thing that is as close to your hearts as our treasure is to ours."

She smiled broadly, showing all her white, pointed teeth.

3 - Song of the Pipe

L ief, Barda, and Jasmine looked around at the silent people by the fire. All were nodding seriously. Clearly, Tirral was speaking the truth.

But it is a trick, Lief thought. She is going to ask for something she is sure we will not give. Glancing at his companions, he saw that Jasmine's hand had crept to her shoulder, where Filli and Kree huddled silently. Barda was frowning, thinking, no doubt, of the sword that had been his faithful companion for most of his life.

Lief thought of his own most precious possessions — the sword forged for him by his father, and the concealing cloak woven by his mother's hands. How could he survive in the Shadowlands without them?

He waited in hideous suspense as Tirral turned to him, her eyes glittering. At last she spoke. "I ask for

. . . that pretty jewelled belt you wear, King of Deltora," she said.

"Mother!" cried Emlis, aghast.

A great, dizzying wave of heat swept over Lief. He heard Jasmine and Barda crying out in amazed anger and the watching people exclaiming, but he felt only sick — sick with relief. He hung his head, knowing that he must not let Tirral see his eyes.

Finally he allowed himself to look up. "Very well," he said. Ignoring Barda and Jasmine's startled protests, he unclasped the gleaming belt and handed it to Tirral.

The watching people gasped in awe. Many jumped to their feet and rushed to crowd around their leader, eager to see the famous belt more closely.

But Tirral's face was a study in baffled rage. Never for a moment had she thought Lief would agree to her demand. Like all Kerons, she had grown up with Doran's tales. She knew how vital the Belt of Deltora was to the safety of the world above.

"Lief, what are you thinking of?" Jasmine whispered furiously.

"Three things," Lief whispered back. "First, we will be in the Shadowlands very soon. Second, the gems in the Belt of Deltora cannot be taken beyond Deltora's borders — a fact that Tirral clearly does not know. And third, this is the safest place I can think of to hide something of great value."

Jasmine's expression changed abruptly. She had

been living in the present for so long that she had actually forgotten that if Lief was to go into the Shadowlands he would have to leave the Belt of Deltora behind.

But Barda's face was like thunder. "Lief," he muttered. "Are you saying that you actually intend to cross the border with us?"

"Of course!" Lief stared at him, astonished. "Have I not always said so?"

Barda shook his head furiously. "Whatever you said, I was sure that when the time came you would come to your senses. Are you mad, Lief? You cannot go into the Shadowlands! You and the Belt are the only things that stand between Deltora and the Shadow Lord. Have you no sense of duty?"

Duty? Lief's fists clenched.

What had his life been over the past months, but a rigid devotion to duty? Had he not worked till his eyes were burning, hidden himself away from everything and everyone he loved? Had he not kept secrets, suffered being criticized, misunderstood — even hated — because the safety of the kingdom was his first responsibility, and enemies were everywhere?

Passionate words trembled on his lips. He longed to unburden his heart at last.

No! You must not weaken now. Especially now . . .

Lief clenched his teeth, fought the hasty words back. "The Pirran Pipe first called to me when I did not even know of its existence, Barda," he said. "I know that I was intended to find it, and carry it on this quest. I will not abandon it now."

"Then I wish we had never seen it!" snarled Barda.

Jasmine was looking worried and uncertain. "Truly, the risk is very great, Lief," she murmured. "Perhaps . . ."

"Jasmine, do not join Barda against me!" Lief cried. "I cannot act against my nature!" Or my heart, he thought miserably. Jasmine, do you not see? Pirran Pipe or no Pirran Pipe, how could I let you go, and not follow?

He became aware that the people clustered around Tirral were drawing back. Tirral was weighing the belt in her hands, bitter contempt mingling with the anger on her face.

"This is not a fair exchange!" she exclaimed loudly. "The belt is all but powerless!"

"Mother, that cannot be!" Emlis burst out, blushing with shame for her. "Doran told us! The Belt of Deltora is as powerful as the Pirran Pipe!"

"In the world above, perhaps," snapped Tirral. "Here, it is just a jewelled trifle."

But the crowd murmured restlessly and, as Tirral looked around, biting her lips, Lief breathed a sigh of relief. Much as she might want to, the Piper could not go back on her bargain now without seeming dishonorable and losing her people's trust.

Stiffly, as though every movement was paining

her, Tirral took from the folds of her robe a small shell box. At the same moment, Lief lifted the red cloth bag containing the mouthpiece and stem of the Pirran Pipe from beneath his shirt.

Tirral opened the box and held it out. The end-piece of the Pirran Pipe lay inside, nestled on a bed of silk. It was very small. Its strange, carved surface gleamed faintly green in the emerald light.

She looked up at Lief and their eyes locked as the music of the Pipe flowed around them.

The people fell silent. They, too, could hear the music. But Jasmine and Barda fidgeted, glancing at one another, for they could hear nothing at all.

Dazed by the music, Lief drew the partly completed Pipe from its covering. Then Tirral handed the endpiece to him, and he fitted it into place.

The music stopped abruptly, as though shut off by a tap.

"It has ceased to mourn," whispered Tirral, and suddenly glistening tears sprang into her pale, cold eyes.

Stunned by the sudden silence, Lief stared at the magical object in his hands. It was shining with a subtle radiance, as though lit from within. Here, at last, was the Pirran Pipe — whole and perfect for the first time since the warring tribes of Pirra divided it and stilled its voice. And complete, it was transformed.

"But, it has changed!" Jasmine breathed in awe.

"It glows! And surely it is bigger than it should be."

It was true. The endpiece of the Pipe had been the smallest part of all, and should have added very little. But now, complete, the Pipe seemed far larger and stronger, far more strange, more beautiful, more thrilling than it had before. It was as though it was greater than the sum of its parts.

But it was silent. Waiting. Waiting for warm breath to bring it fully to life. Waiting for the skilled and loving touch that would call its music back from the ghostly realms in which it had grieved for so long, and let it sing in the present.

And I cannot do it, Lief thought, with a pang of sadness. I would not know how to begin. And even if I had the skill, it is not fitting that I should be the one.

He looked up at Tirral. Saw the longing in her glistening eyes. Suddenly knew what should be done. He held out his hands, the glowing Pipe held loosely between them.

"You are the Piper, Tirral," he said softly. "Will you play?"

※

And so, for the first time since the world began, the pure notes of the Pirran Pipe rang out in the caverns of the secret sea, while the people of Keras listened, their rapt, upturned faces wet with tears.

The music caressed the rippling waters, echoed

from the gleaming rock, echoing, echoing until the air itself seemed to quiver with its beauty and no walls could contain it.

It flowed into the Forbidden Way, where the leeches heard it and cringed in the darkness. It sang in the opal sea, where the great eels raised their dripping heads from the water and swayed to the sound.

The Aurons building on their island looked up from their work, transfixed, as the sound drifted to their ears. Their Piper's ancient face did not change, but his body trembled all over, as if shaken by an icy gale. And Penn, packing manuscripts in her little hut on the rafts, clasped her hands in joy and wonder.

The song of the Pipe echoed through the rainbow caverns where the mud grubs burrowed deep to escape it, and the sea moles leaped and played. It filled the Glimmer with its beauty and flowed on to the ruby sea, and Plume.

Nols, tending the grave of the warrior Glock, gave a cry when she heard it. She scrambled to her feet and ran to the shore where awed, silent people were wading knee-deep, waist-deep, into the scarlet water, gazing towards the sound.

The music floated on, faint and haunting, till it reached the farthest corner of the golden sea, where Clef and Azan, fishing in their tiny boat, dropped their nets and sat spellbound. Then the last, tiny shadow of sound rose high above their heads, through the topaz haze. And carried by the cool, soft breeze, it stole into the golden dragon's enchanted sleep, bringing with it soaring dreams of sunshine, great winds and high mountains, magic and vanished glory.

4 ~ The Grey Zone

Tirral sat silently through the celebration that followed her playing of the Pipe. There was food, drink, and laughter around the fire, but she joined in none of it. Only when the Kerons brought out their small pipes of fungus wood did she raise her head.

The sweet, breathy music was worth listening to, indeed. And to the companions' surprise, the sweetest tunes of all were played by Emlis.

When they congratulated him, as he put down his instrument and came to sit beside his mother, Emlis bit his lip. "Playing has always brought me joy," he said. "But now I have heard the Pirran Pipe I know that the sounds I make are just a pale reflection of what music can be."

Awkwardly he wiped his pipe on his sleeve and

held it out to Barda. "Perhaps you would play for us now?" he asked. "I long to hear above-worlder music."

Barda laughed. "It is very like your own. But I am sorry, I cannot play for you — and neither can my companions. None of us is musical."

"What?"

Tirral's high-pitched exclamation cut startlingly through the music and laughter. Silence fell.

"Are you saying," cried Tirral, "that you cannot even *play* a pipe?"

"We cannot play music as you do," Lief agreed, with sinking heart. "But it is the magic of the Pirran Pipe that counts, not the skill of the player. A single note will be enough to stay the Shadow Lord's hand."

"You cannot know that!" Tirral cried. "In ancient times the Pipe was only played by Pirra's finest musicians!"

Her face glowing with renewed hope, she appealed to the silent people around her. "Our beliefs do not require us to give or lend to a cousin if the cause is pointless, Kerons! Is that not so?"

Heads nodded reluctantly.

"Well, then!" Tirral cried. "What could be more pointless than to give the Pirran Pipe to those who cannot even *play* it?" She gazed around triumphantly.

"It does not matter!"

Everyone jumped as the high, nervous voice

broke the silence. Everyone stared as Emlis stepped forward, blushing to the roots of his golden hair.

"It — it does not matter if our cousins cannot play the Pipe," Emlis stammered, meeting his mother's angry stare defiantly. "It does not matter because — because I can play very well. And I am going with them!"

✳

Much argument followed, but there was no point at all in Tirral's raging, or the companions' protesting. For the people of Keras, Emlis's announcement had removed the last objection to the Pirran Pipe's being taken to the Shadowlands.

"So you have won, and I have lost," Tirral said bitterly, as she returned the companions' weapons to them. "I have lost not only the Pirran Pipe, but my son. You have won the right to destroy them both, as well as yourselves. I hope your victory brings you joy."

Her face was ashen. The moths around her head were barely moving.

"Tirral — " Lief began. But already the Piper was turning and walking rapidly away.

"It is not *our* fault that her son is coming with us," hissed Jasmine. "It is all her own work! If she had let us go in peace Emlis would never have thought of the idea."

"Yes he would," Barda said shrewdly. "That

young man is as anxious as we are to escape this island. I think he saw his chance and seized it with both hands."

"But he does not realize what he is doing!" muttered Lief.

"No," growled Barda. "And do we?"

※

Within hours, two longboats rowed by silent, craggy-faced leech-gatherers were setting out from the north side of the island. Lief, Jasmine, Barda, and Emlis sat in the stern of one boat. In the other were the frozen-faced Tirral and two of her closest advisors.

Green water stretched ahead, gradually darkening to grey. The horizon was shrouded in darkness.

Kree clucked uneasily.

"The Grey Zone," Jasmine said, staring at the ominous horizon.

Emlis nodded. Fear mingled with excitement on his thin face, which was almost covered by the hood of the thick, dull green leech-gatherer's cloak he wore.

"It is not too late to change your mind, Emlis," muttered Barda, who was sitting beside him. "This is not one of Doran's tales. It is real, and deadly."

"I cannot change my mind now," said Emlis. "You need me. They will not let you take the Pipe without me."

"Your skin is not fit for the world above, Emlis," whispered Jasmine, leaning forward. "The sun will burn you. The light will blind you."

Emlis shook his head stubbornly. "The cloak will protect me from the sun. And I am not the first Pirran to leave the caverns. Doran told of seven who did so, in the time of Alyss and Brosnan."

"They all died, Emlis," said Barda brutally. "They died, and never saw their homes again."

"They were killed by above-worlders, not by the sun," Emlis said, his voice trembling. "And in any case, they were Plumes, and the Plumes are as foolhardy and stupid as the Aurons are wicked."

"Plumes and Aurons are not stupid and wicked!" cried Jasmine. "They are your own people! Your kinsfolk! Far more closely related to you than we are."

The leech-gatherers who were paddling their boat turned and frowned ferociously. One made a low sound in his throat. The other bared his teeth unpleasantly. Jasmine pressed her lips together and returned their stares without flinching until at last they turned to face the front and began paddling once more.

Emlis hunched his bony shoulders. "I beg you, do not argue with me any more," he mumbled. "This is my one chance to fulfil the dearest wish of my life. To see a world that is not my own. If I die in the attempt, that is surely my choice."

Barda ran his hands through his tousled hair in despair. "Three of them," he muttered under his breath. "Three young hotheads. By the heavens, were not two bad enough?"

❋

Gradually the emerald light failed and within an hour the fleet was paddling through a grim realm of grey. They were far beyond the scope of Doran's map now. Beyond Deltora's border.

When they looked up, all they saw was swirling darkness. They knew that far above them towered the treacherous peaks that clustered behind Dread Mountain — iron-hard rock filled with dank, secret caves where hideous beasts like the giant toad Gellick thrived.

The boat was moving more slowly, and the rugged faces of the leech-gatherers had become strained and watchful.

Ahead loomed an ink-black shadow. The cavern beneath the Shadowlands.

"When are they going to leave us?" Jasmine murmured.

"We must go to the edge of the Shadow," one of the leech-gatherers said unexpectedly, without turning around. "So the Piper says. And there we stop, praise be to Keras, and send you up, to the evil place above."

"Send us up?" Lief blinked, confused. He had imagined that the Kerons were going to show them a secret way to the surface. But this sounded like . . .

"The magic of seven may not be needed for the task," said the leech-gatherer, "but we thought it best to be on the safe side. Who knows how deep the rock is, up above. For all your strange ideas, we would not want you caught midways, would we now?"

His companion chuckled grimly.

Lief felt Jasmine shudder, and knew that she had been gripped, as he had, by a nightmarish vision of being trapped in the midst of solid rock.

"Do not fear," said Emlis. "Our ancestors sent Doran to the surface without harm many times."

"That was long ago," muttered Barda, who was looking rather sick. "And I presume Doran was not sent into the Shadowlands."

"Oh, no!" Emlis agreed. "Doran always left the caverns in a place to the west of Keras. He said that in the land above, just at that spot, there was a great waterway and boats to help him make the journey home."

"The River Tor!" Lief exclaimed. "So that was how Doran did it so secretly. He would reappear in the brush below Dread Mountain. Then he would walk down to the river and wait for a boat. There would not have been so many pirates then."

"Or Ols," said Jasmine. Kree squawked nervously on her shoulder, but she did not turn to him. Her eyes were fixed on the mass of darkness looming before them.

The Shadowlands. Soon, very soon, she would be able to begin the search for Faith, her lost sister. And Lief and Barda would be beside her.

Jasmine had not forgiven Lief for trying to keep

knowledge of Faith hidden from her. But after all they had been through together since entering the caverns, her anger had lost its bitter edge. Now she felt sure that Lief had kept Faith a secret only out of a desperate wish to keep her, Jasmine, from harm.

He was wrong to deceive me, Jasmine thought. But he did it for reasons he thought were good.

Her eyes stared, unfocused, at the growing Shadow ahead. Waiting for Lief in Del was his bride-to-be — that well-read, noble Toran girl who would make a fitting queen, and one day bear a child to wear the Belt of Deltora after Lief. But Jasmine was here with Lief now. And she was his friend — his true friend.

And that is enough, Jasmine told herself. That is how it must be. For what do I know of palaces and politeness and fine clothes? Nothing at all, and nor do I want to. Lief knows that.

Filli whimpered softly beneath her collar, and she raised a hand to comfort him, unconsciously drawing her own comfort from his warmth.

"The first time Doran came to the caverns, he did not reach Keras," Emlis was chattering meanwhile to Barda. "Some Plumes found him drowning in the topaz sea. They saved him, but sent him straight back to the surface! That is how stupid Plumes are!"

He broke off and glanced guiltily at Jasmine, but she was still staring fixedly ahead.

"The Plumes thought Doran would forget what

had happened," Emlis said. "But a song they sang as they paddled their boat stayed in his head and made him remember. So he returned. And *this* time he — "

His eager voice broke off in a squeak.

Darkness had fallen like a curtain. The water surrounding them was black as night. They could see nothing. They could only hear the sound of the water lapping and the small craft that surrounded their longboat bumping together gently.

"It is time." Tirral's trembling voice floated in the darkness. "Now is the last chance for you to change your minds. Will you return with us to Keras, and safety? Lief . . . Barda . . . Jasmine . . . *Emlis*?"

There was a long pause.

"Very well." Tirral's voice was rigidly controlled now. "I have one piece of advice for you, and I urge you to attend to it, for I feel its worth in every bone of my body. Shadows have sunk deep into the soil of Pirra now. Whatever the Plumes and Aurons may think, Pirra is lost forever. It can never be reclaimed."

"We know this," Lief said. "And neither the Plumes nor the Aurons expect — "

"I have not finished," Tirral snapped, speaking over him. "Listen! The Shadow Lord's power is far greater now than when the Pipe kept him from Pirran soil. Played well or ill, the Pipe will stay his hand only for a time, and only if he is taken by surprise. Keep its magic for when it is most needed."

"We will," Lief, Barda, and Jasmine murmured together.

"There is nothing to do, then, but to wish you well," said Tirral from the darkness. "Put your arms about one another. Close your eyes. Think of nothing."

Feeling as though he was in a dream, Lief moved into the center of the boat. He knelt down on the hard, wet boards, spread his arms wide, and gripped his companions tightly. He bent his head, forced his mind to go blank.

"Good fortune, cousins." The rough voice of one of the leech-gatherers rumbled low in the silence. Then . . .

Cold, freezing cold. Rushing darkness. Sick dizziness, unbearable . . .

There was a sudden, terrifying stillness. A bleak, bitter smell. A rapid, thumping sound, very close, mingled with the moaning wail of wind. And Lief opened his stinging eyes, took his first, gasping breath, in the Shadowlands.

5 - In the Shadowlands

Lief lay very still, slowly realizing that the thumping sound he was hearing was the pounding of his own heart. He was sprawled face down on hard earth. Wind was sweeping over him, a draft that seemed neither hot nor cold, carrying with it the bitter smell he had noticed before.

Cautiously he raised his head, blinking in the sullen light. Jasmine was crouching beside him, Kree on her shoulder. Barda was crawling to his feet not far away. Emlis, swathed in his cloak, was still on the ground, curled in a small ball.

With a chill Lief realized that they were in the open, on a windswept plain pocked with gaping craters. Barren white clay, as parched and cracked as a dry riverbed, stretched in front of them as far as the eye could see. Thick grey clouds boiled low overhead, hiding the sun.

The Shadowlands

The land was dead. Dead as bleached, white bones.

Lief's eyes burned as words from *The Tale of the Pirran Pipe* sprang unbidden into his mind.

Long, long ago, beyond the Mountains, there was a green land called Pirra, where the breezes breathed magic. . . .

Pirra, once a land of beauty, sunshine, and flowers. The ancient home of the Kerons, the Plumes, and the Aurons. Now . . . this wasteland.

And this is what Deltora might have been. Still might be. If you were wrong, Lief. If you were wrong . . .

Lief shook his head, trying to shut out the voice in his mind, the tormenting voice of his own conscience. But it would not stop.

You should have let Jasmine go. You should have remained in Del. That was your duty. Your duty . . .

Jasmine was pulling at his arm. "Lief! We must take cover, quickly," she hissed. "There are — things here. Coming closer."

Lief tore his gaze from the barren horizon and looked at her. Her eyes were startled, wide, almost black.

"People? Beasts? Ols?" he asked quickly.

"I — do not know," Jasmine whispered. "Things." She shuddered. Filli whimpered in his hiding place under her jacket.

Barda had scooped Emlis from the ground and was hurrying towards them.

"Do not just stand there!" he said roughly. "If an Ak-Baba should sight us, we are finished!" He grabbed Lief by the arm and swung him around.

Only then did Lief realize that they were not marooned in the middle of the vast plain, as in his confusion he had thought. Behind them, rising like a great, jagged fence, were the mountains, their cruel peaks piercing the cloud, their foothills edging the plain. The great bulk of Dread Mountain hulked in the background, spreading away to the west.

Of course! Lief thought, sprinting towards the bare, forbidding foothills with the others pounding close behind him. The Kerons spirited us to the surface just inside the Shadowlands border. Of *course* the mountains are here! What was I thinking of?

He heard Emlis waking, protesting, demanding to be put down. Well, that was one good thing. Barda would have his hands free to climb, at least. Lief swerved around the first of the grey boulders that lay at the edge of the plain and began to scramble rapidly upward, aiming for the shelter of the larger rocks he could see farther ahead.

Then, suddenly, a white flash of pain exploded behind his eyes as something slammed against his brow with shocking force. He staggered backwards, arms spinning wildly, fighting to keep his balance. Through the ringing in his ears he heard muffled cries of alarm, then, with relief, he felt a firm hand on his back. Barda was supporting him, pushing him back on his feet.

Trembling, he sank to his knees. Barda, Jasmine, and Emlis crouched beside him, pressing closely together so that the great boulder hid them from the plain.

"Lief, what happened?" he heard Jasmine whisper.

"Did you not see?" he mumbled, pressing his hands to his aching head. "Something hit me."

"No!" she whispered back. "There was nothing there. You just jerked backwards, suddenly, for no reason. One minute you were running, the next — "

Barda drew breath sharply. He picked up some pebbles and threw them at the empty air in front of them. Astounded, Lief saw the pebbles stop short in midair, bounce slightly back, then fall to the ground.

"An invisible wall!" Jasmine breathed.

"Yes," Barda said grimly. "I thought it strange that the mountains were unprotected. The Shadow Lord has sealed the border in his own way, it seems."

As he spoke, they saw movement near where one of the pebbles had fallen. A small, brown striped lizard with bright eyes had scuttled into view.

"But it came from uphill!" whispered Jasmine excitedly. "From behind the magic wall. I saw it! Is it only humans who are stopped by the shutting spell?"

Lief felt ill. He had thought of another explanation, and he could see by Barda's grim face that Barda had thought of it, too.

The lizard's tiny forked tongue flickered in and

out for a few moments. Then, abruptly, it turned and scuttled back uphill. When it reached the invisible wall it stopped dead and fell back.

"Yes," Barda said slowly. "That is what I feared. The spell does not stop people or creatures coming in. It only prevents them getting out."

He, Lief, and Jasmine looked at one another, the words hanging heavily between them. Then Lief began struggling to rise.

"Stay still," Jasmine hissed, catching hold of his arm to hold him down. "You must rest. You hit your head — "

"No!" Lief gritted his teeth and pulled against her restraining hand.

Jasmine's grip tightened and he fell back with a groan, his head swimming. "You said — you said something was coming!" he mumbled. "We must — "

"Do as you are told for once, Lief!" said Barda grimly, drawing his sword. "We are as safe behind this rock as anywhere, at present. And whatever Jasmine can hear, I can still see nothing."

The little lizard was scrabbling frantically at the invisible wall now, running along it for a short distance, then turning and running the other way. Every now and then it would raise itself and push with its front legs at the empty air, its tail thrashing frantically.

"But — but why does the Shadow Lord not protect his border?" asked Emlis in a high, trembling voice. "He has many of your people! Does he not fear that an army — or a small group such as yours — might cross the mountains and invade his territory?"

"That is what he *hopes* for, I would say," muttered Barda. "He has left the way open, after all."

"But why?" asked Emlis, his voice rising to a squeak.

The lizard fell back, exhausted. Instantly, an orange, spiny beetle-like creature sprang from a crack in the clay just behind it. In the blink of an eye the orange creature had seized the lizard, bitten off its head, and dragged the still twitching carcass back under the earth.

"Does that answer your question?" asked Barda dryly.

Emlis stared at him, open-mouthed.

Lief turned his face to the rock, his stomach churning. Then he saw it. A mark had been scratched laboriously into the rock's hard surface. He stared, hardly able to believe his eyes.

"The sign of the Resistance!" he breathed, tracing the mark with his fingers. His heart was pounding.

Another Deltoran had sheltered here. A Deltoran who had somehow escaped from captivity and made for the mountains, only to find the way to freedom barred. A Deltoran who had used, perhaps, his or her last strength not to weep and curse fate, but to scratch a message of defiance on the rock.

The despairing confusion that had clouded Lief's mind ever since arriving in this dread place seemed suddenly to lift. Suddenly he was able to think again.

Barda was touching the sign now. "It is not fresh, but it is not very old, either," he said slowly. "A year or two at most, I think."

Lief was remembering another Resistance sign he had seen marked on rock. It had ended a message written in blood on a cave wall in Dread Mountain.

Doom had written that message: Doom, the only Deltoran captive ever known to have escaped from the Shadowlands. And he had escaped from . . .

Kree gave a low, warning squawk. "The light is changing," Jasmine whispered, reaching for her dagger.

Lief and Barda looked up quickly. The low, tumbling clouds were stained with faint, sullen scarlet, and the whiteness of the plain was dimming.

"Surely something as small as a lizard would not have sounded a border alert," Barda muttered. "Such things must happen often."

"It is the setting sun," said Lief, looking to the west, where the clouds glowed more deeply. "Night is falling."

They were silent for a moment. They had been in

the caverns so long that they had almost forgotten that the days in the world above were ruled by the movement of the sun.

"Doran said sunsets were glorious to see," said Emlis, gazing with disappointment at the clouds. "Doran said they were like red and orange fire blazing in the sky."

"Not here, it seems," Barda growled.

Jasmine was peering not at the sky, but at the plain. "Look," she breathed, pointing.

The plain was coming to life. Legs scrabbling, long feelers waving, spiny orange beetles were emerging in the thousands from the cracks in the clay.

6 - The Wild Ones

L ief looked down. The cracks in the earth near his feet were full of movement, though so far nothing had ventured to the surface.

"I do not like this," Barda said. "We had better move on. Those insects are small, but there are many of them, and they are meat-eaters. If they are hungry enough — "

He did not complete his sentence, but he had said enough to make everyone stand hastily.

"Which way?" Jasmine looked desperately left and right.

"West," Lief said instantly, turning to face the dark red glow that was the setting sun.

"Why west?" Jasmine demanded. "If we are to find the Shadow Lord's headquarters in time — "

"What?" Barda interrupted, staring at her in disbelief. "What madness is this? The Shadow Lord's *headquarters*? Why, that is the very place that we must avoid at all costs!"

"But — but the slaves!" Jasmine stammered, flushing hotly. She had betrayed herself. She had forgotten that her companions knew nothing of her plans.

She was sure that Faith was somewhere in or near the Shadow Lord's headquarters. The little girl had been secretly using something she called "the crystal" to call for help. And where could such a magical object be, except in the Shadow Lord's main stronghold? Somehow, Jasmine had to convince her companions to seek it.

Should she admit her secret at last? Tell Lief and Barda what Faith had said?

Almost immediately she decided she could not risk it. Not here, on this windswept plain, where every gust of wind brought the scent of danger. She had kept the secret too long for that. This was no place for argument, for loss of trust, for the angry words that she knew would burst forth from her as soon as they questioned her.

No, Jasmine thought. I have played a lone hand this far. I must continue doing so until the time is right.

"The slaves must be scattered all over this cursed land!" Barda was growling. "Why do you think — ?"

"Wait!" Lief suddenly looked rapidly from side to side. "Where is Emlis?"

Shocked, Jasmine and Barda swung around. Emlis was no longer behind them. He had disappeared.

"But — but he was *here*! Standing beside the rock!" spluttered Barda.

"Well he is here no longer," Lief said grimly. "He must have wandered away while we were arguing."

It was growing darker by the moment. Quickly they separated and, calling in low voices, searched the immediate area. But Emlis was nowhere to be found.

They came together again at the large boulder, all of them fearful and angry.

"I cannot believe this!" Barda ground his teeth in fury. "What game does the young fool think he is playing?"

"We will have to go on without him," Jasmine snapped, burning with impatience. "There is no time to waste. And those insects are massing in their millions!"

Lief squinted over the plain. The clay, darkened by the setting sun, was now the same color as the beetles. The insects would have been perfectly camouflaged except that they were so many. The ground seethed with them, rippling like water driven by the tide.

The ripples seemed particularly large at one spot, beside the nearest crater. It was as though waves were breaking over a large rock lying there.

My mind is still half in the secret sea, Lief thought. Then, suddenly, he leaned forward, peering intently through the gloom. Why would the beetles crowd so closely together just at that place? It was almost as if . . .

Hideous understanding shot through him like a thunderbolt. He shouted and sprang forward.

He could hear Jasmine and Barda chasing him, hissing to him to stop, as he ran out onto the plain, crushing dozens of beetles with every thud of his flying feet. But there was no time, no time to stop, to explain. No time to tell them why his stomach was heaving, his heart was racing . . .

In moments he had reached the heaving mass of beetles by the crater and was plunging his arms into its midst. Then, panting and shuddering, he was hauling the limp, bleeding body of Emlis from the ground.

Exclaiming with horror, Barda and Jasmine began beating the clinging insects from Emlis's shredded garments, and tearing them from the raw, bloody flesh beneath. Around their feet, thousands of beetles scuttled in panic, fighting one another for space as they squeezed back into the cracks in the clay.

Emlis was groaning feebly, trying to speak.

"How did this happen?" shouted Barda. "Was he so mad as to walk out — "

The words dried in his throat. His eyes bulged. As he raised his sword, Lief and Jasmine swung around to look at what he had seen.

Shapes were rising out of the crater — ragged, shambling shapes with bared teeth and glowing eyes.

Clawed hands reached for them. Low growls and piercing howls rose in a terrifying chorus of baffled anger.

Half carrying, half dragging Emlis, Lief turned and stumbled back towards the hills, beetles scattering before him. Barda and Jasmine backed after him, their weapons held in front of them to fend off the ghastly creatures crawling in ever greater numbers from the crater.

The creatures were like humans — yet hideously changed. Some were covered in hair, with fangs and tusks protruding from their gaping mouths. Some had shrunken limbs, long tails, and scaly skin. Others had humped backs covered in gleaming shell, twisted, insect-like legs, and spiny fins for arms. Roaring and howling, they began to spread out, encircling the fleeing companions like a pack of animals closing in on prey.

Lief, Barda, and Jasmine reached the rock marked with the sign of the Resistance and, speechless with horror, turned to fight. The creatures were coming at them from all sides. There would be no escape.

Then, suddenly, a shiver seemed to run through the savage horde and it stopped dead. There was a long, low rumbling like distant thunder and at the same moment the dim light brightened.

Instinctively, Lief looked up, and a cold shiver ran down his spine. Instead of the rising moon, which he had expected to see, another shape was forming in the sky. Huge and menacing it shone like cold white fire against the greyness of the clouds.

Moaning and whimpering, the creatures were falling to the ground, covering their eyes.

"Now! Run!" hissed Barda, heaving Emlis over his shoulder.

Together they left the cover of the rock, broke through the ring of creatures cringing on the ground, and began to run along the line of the hills, towards the west.

After only a few moments, they heard the sounds of pounding feet behind them and a terrible chorus of baying, grunting, and howling. The creatures had recovered from their fear at the rising of the mark of the Shadow Lord, and were in hot pursuit.

Not daring to look back, the companions raced on, swerving around boulders, stumbling over the rough ground, buffeted by the relentless wind that gusted across the plain. Then they saw, not far ahead, something barring their way. A long, rocky outcrop jutted out into the plain, gleaming in the terrible light from the sky.

"Over the top!" Barda panted. "We — cannot risk — going around it. Must not let them — get in front of us."

They reached the barrier and leaped upward, scrambling to the top and sliding down the other side.

Lief tumbled to the hard ground, jarring his shoulder painfully. As Jasmine landed beside him, he jumped to his feet and reached up to Barda, to take Emlis's weight. Then he heard Jasmine shriek his name. He swung around, clutching Emlis in his arms, and saw something that made his blood run cold.

Not far ahead of them was another outcrop, higher than the one they had just climbed. And from its shadow, something was emerging — something huge and dome-shaped that gleamed with the same dull sheen as the rocks. Its vast body rippled and bulged horribly as it moved, as though the thick, smooth skin clothed flesh that was nothing more than quivering jelly.

As it crawled farther into the light, Lief gave a strangled gasp. He heard Filli squealing in terror and Kree screeching, heard Barda's muttered curse. Ringing the beast's body like the swollen beads of a hideous necklace were dozens of heads, each one with glassy, staring eyes and a lipless mouth from which hung a long, thin, dripping tongue.

The companions flattened themselves against the

rock. The sounds of howling and pounding feet were growing louder. Their pursuers were closing in. To turn and climb back the way they had come would be to deliver themselves straight into the pack's hands.

But the beast was moving towards them. It was gliding effortlessly over the rough ground on hundreds of tiny legs that were almost hidden beneath a fringe of skin hanging from its body like a ragged skirt. Its many eyes had swivelled to fix on the intruders. Its tongues were lengthening, curling and quivering ominously.

"We must split up and try to get around it," muttered Barda to Lief and Jasmine. "You two go right. I will go left, with Emlis."

But the moment they took a step, there was a hiss and tongues shot forward like striking snakes in both directions, missing Barda and Jasmine by a hair. They shrank back against the rock. Clearly, they were not to be allowed to move.

The beast's body rippled and seemed to swell as it glided closer, its blank eyes gleaming.

7 - The Beast

Shoulder to shoulder with Barda and Jasmine, Lief faced the beast. It undulated before them, its tongues flickering and curling, its body flattening and spreading, rising slightly on the side that faced the rock.

It is preparing to engulf us, Lief thought.

His legs felt weak. His heart was pounding. His sword hand was slippery with sweat. Sweat was running down into his eyebrows, too, and as he cautiously raised his free hand to wipe it away, his arm brushed the Pirran Pipe hidden beneath his shirt. Into his mind flew the promise he had made to Tirral.

The Pipe will not be lost. It will be returned to the caverns, I swear it!

Lief licked his dry lips. That vow, it seemed, had been worthless. As worthless as *all* his promises — to the Plumes, to the Aurons, to Marilen . . .

Do not fear, Marilen. You need do nothing but wait.

The wind moaned around the rocks, like the ghostly voice of his own despair.

"The Pipe, Lief," Barda gasped beside him. "The Pipe! Use it!"

Lief hesitated. The Pipe might indeed stop the beast. It might give them a chance to escape. But the moment it was played, the Shadow Lord would become aware of it, and of them.

They would lose the advantage of surprise. They would be hunted down mercilessly, without ever finding the prisoners, let alone setting them free.

He forced himself to slide his hand under his shirt and loosen the drawstring at the top of the red cloth bag. The tips of his fingers touched the Pipe, grasped it . . .

A warm tingling ran through his hand, along his arm, through his body. It was like new blood rushing through his veins, strengthening his trembling legs, stilling his racing heart.

He straightened his shoulders, took a deep breath, suddenly alive again. Through the eerie wailing of the wind he heard the angry sounds of the pack on the other side of the outcrop.

Suddenly he knew what he must do.

"We are here!" he roared at the top of his voice. "Come and get us!"

"Lief!" screamed Jasmine in terror.

Howls and screams of rage filled the air. There

was the sound of frenzied climbing, the rattling and scrabbling of claws.

"Flatten yourself against the rock!" Lief shouted, pushing Barda and Jasmine back. "As hard as you can! Ready — "

Growling shrieks sounded above them, and the next moment savage figures were throwing themselves blindly, heedlessly, over the edge of the outcrop. Screams of triumph became shrieks of terror as the attackers realized their mistake too late. Twisting and howling they thudded down on the billowing body of the beast, puncturing its skin with claws and tusks, rolling to fall sprawling onto the clay.

Dragging Emlis with them, the companions began edging along the outcrop, towards the open plain. They began slowly and carefully, never taking their eyes from the beast. But it was no longer interested in them. Swelling and spinning, clear fluid bubbling from the gashes in its skin, it was striking out at the new intruders, at the attackers who had dared to injure it.

Hissing, a dozen tongues darted out, curling around the writhing figures on the ground. Other tongues flicked upward, reaching for the creatures still teetering on the edge of the outcrop. The tongues snatched the nearest off their feet to drag them, screaming, to their doom.

The companions had nearly reached the end of the outcrop. Now was the moment of decision. Should they run out onto the plain and risk whatever new horror might be lurking there? Or should they make for the second outcrop, which meant crossing the perilous space in which the beast still spun and hissed?

Lief looked back, and his stomach seemed to turn over. The beast's body — its torn, rippling body — was coming apart! The heads around its sides were tearing themselves away from the billowing mass, dragging great chunks of flesh with them.

Staring wild-eyed, Lief heard Barda give a choking cry, and Jasmine gasp in understanding. Then, suddenly, he, too, saw the truth. The extra heads ringing the monster's body did not belong to the monster at all. They belonged to its young — smaller versions of itself that the beast carried in pouches around its vast body.

The young were crawling away from their injured parent now, leaving gaping cavities behind them. Each one was as tall as a man, and four times as broad. Each was eager to drag in the prey it had captured with its curling tongue, and to feast.

Their ears ringing with the howls and screams of the captives as the monsters engulfed them, the companions sprinted across the gap. They reached the second outcrop, swung around it, and pelted towards the scattered boulders that marked the edge of the plain.

Panting and trembling, they took refuge behind the largest stone they could see. Emlis was moaning in pain. Barda put him down and together the companions cleaned and dressed his wounds as best they could, using ointment and bandages given to them by the Kerons.

For a long time none of them spoke of what they had just escaped. The memory of it was too raw. But at last, when Emlis lay quiet, Barda found his voice.

"I am sorry," he mumbled. "It is no thanks to me that we are safe. I thought we were finished. I could not think — could do nothing but despair. And still I feel numb. I do not know what has happened to me."

Lief glanced at Jasmine. Her face was pale and shadowed. Filli was hiding beneath her jacket, only his nose visible. Kree, his feathers ruffled, hunched on her shoulder.

"You feel it, too, Jasmine," Lief said quietly.

She nodded shortly. "I have been trying to fight it, but it is impossible," she muttered. "It is as if . . ." She swallowed painfully. ". . . as if I take in fear with every breath. As if the very air of this place is poisoned."

With a start, Lief remembered the strange, bitter smell he had noticed on the wind when first they reached the Shadowlands. He had grown accustomed to it, and had not thought about it for a long time. But now he realized that Jasmine had hit upon the truth. The wind was the Shadow Lord's way of sapping the will of those who entered his realm. The bitter scent it carried was the stink of despair.

"You are right!" he exclaimed. "But we *can* fight

it." He pulled out the red cloth bag. Carefully he slid the Pipe from its casing and held it out to Barda and Jasmine. As they clasped it, he could see their faces change. The strange, hopeless expressions disappeared, their eyes brightened, their mouths grew firm.

"Why — it is miraculous!" breathed Barda.

"See if it will help Emlis, too!" Jasmine urged.

They placed the Pipe between Emlis's pale fingers. And sure enough, after only a few moments the young Keron's eyes flickered open. He stared up at the companions in bewilderment, then gave a start and struggled to sit up. The Pipe began to slip to the ground. Lief grabbed it before it fell, and put it back into the red cloth bag.

"Where are we?" Emlis was gabbling. "What happened? The creatures . . . they seized me, carried me, and then — " His eyes widened with horror as full memory flooded into his mind.

"Stay still, Emlis," said Lief quickly, tucking the red bag inside his shirt once more. "Gather your strength. We must move on very soon."

"Indeed," Barda muttered, glancing over his shoulder at the outcrop, which was still too near for comfort. All was silent behind the outcrop now. Lief repressed a shudder. He did not want to think about what was happening there.

Jasmine was also looking back, but for a different reason. "Our way to the east is barred now, unless we want to risk crossing the beast's territory once more," she said, frowning. "Why were you so intent on moving west, Lief?"

Lief leaned forward, eager to explain. "Because I remembered Doom," he said. "Doom escaped from the Shadow Arena. From there he went straight through the hills into Deltora, and was pursued up Dread Mountain by the Grey Guards. So . . ."

"So the Arena must be very near the border — and near the western slopes of Dread Mountain!" exclaimed Barda. "Yes! Why did I not think of it? If we keep moving west, we should find it easily."

"And surely the Shadow Arena must be where many of the prisoners are," said Lief, turning to Jasmine. "If they are to be put to death as the bird told you . . ."

He paused, and Jasmine nodded uneasily. It had not been a bird, but Faith, who had told her that the prisoners were in danger.

It does not matter, she told herself. The truth is the truth, whoever tells it.

Barda clambered to his feet. "West it is, then," he said. "Not that we have a choice. I, for one, do not wish to cross that beast's path again." He glared at Jasmine, daring her to disagree.

But Jasmine had been thinking rapidly. Lief was right. The Shadow Arena had to be near the border, and near Dread Mountain, too. And she had remembered something else. Poison for the Grey Guards' deadly blister weapons had been carried through a pass that led from Dread Mountain into the Shadowlands.

No one would move glass jars of lethal poison any farther than necessary. So almost certainly the factory where the blisters had been made was close to the pass, on the Shadowlands side.

The Shadow Arena *and* the factory. Both very important sites. Both near Dread Mountain. It made perfect sense for one of the Shadow Lord's main bases, at least, to be in the same place. And Faith, perhaps, very near.

She bowed her head so that Barda would not see the flash of hope in her eyes. "Very well," she murmured. "If you think it right, we will continue moving west."

Barda frowned at her suspiciously. Jasmine was not usually so agreeable. But he did not waste time in questioning her. He was already helping Emlis to his feet, anxious to be gone.

Lief stood beside them and peered out onto the plain. It was flooded with light, but no moon, no stars could be seen through the thick cloud. The mark of the Shadow Lord dominated the sky, burning with cold white fire.

"We will have to go carefully," he murmured, turning to look at the ragged line of rocks that straggled away to the west. "There is little cover. If we are seen — "

"You have been seen already, you fool!" croaked a harsh voice at his feet. And before he could move or speak, claws had seized his ankles, and were dragging him down.

8 - Claw

Scrabbling helplessly at the hard earth, Lief felt the scrape of stone on his legs. With a surge of panic he realized that he was being dragged feet-first into a hole that had opened beneath the rock.

Desperately he flung his arms forward. Gasping with shock, Jasmine, Emlis, and Barda seized them, trying in vain to hold him back. He tried to kick, but the scaly talons that gripped his ankles merely tightened their hold and pulled more strongly. He felt as if he was being torn in two. He yelled in pain and terror.

"Shut your mouth or you will kill us all!" barked the harsh voice.

There were grunts and curses from below. Then, suddenly, Lief felt another pair of hands seize his legs and heave. His arms slipped from his companions' grasp, and he slithered under the rock, falling with a thud onto hard ground.

Instantly he was lifted up and slammed against a wall, a vast hand around his throat. Dazed, half-strangled, he saw that the rock had not been a loose boulder at all, but part of the roof of a large cave. A torch flickered on rocky walls and floor. Water trickled in the shadows. A small group of strangely ill-assorted beings was peering at him.

There was a bearded scarecrow of a man whose hands were scaly claws, like the talons of a bird of prey. Beside him stood a woman — young and tall but gaunt with sunken eyes, the brand of the Shadow Lord burned cruelly into her brow. And pinning Lief to the wall, scowling, filthy, with an iron band around his neck, was — Glock!

Lief gaped at the brutish face snarling so close to his own. This could not be! He was dreaming! Glock was dead — dead and buried in a hero's grave on the island of Plume. Had an Ol taken the shape of Glock to deceive them? A Grade 3 Ol, that could mimic even the warm touch of a human being?

But if that was so, surely the Ol would pretend to recognize him, would greet him by name, in Glock's voice. No flicker of recognition showed in this man's eyes.

The enormous paw around Lief's throat tightened as Jasmine thudded through the hole in the cave roof, with Barda and Emlis close behind. His companions' weapons were in their hands. They sprang forward, then saw Lief pinned against the wall and froze.

"Move another step and I will snap his neck like a twig!" growled the being who looked like Glock.

"Put down your weapons," snapped the talon-handed man, stepping forward. "We are friends!"

"You may call dragging our companion into this place the act of a friend, but we do not," growled Barda, raising his sword a little.

The man put his head on one side and regarded him curiously. "Brianne, close the trapdoor!" he ordered over his shoulder.

Frowning furiously the tall woman went to do his bidding. "You were a fool to bring them here, Claw!" she said sharply, as the light in the cave abruptly darkened. "Did I not tell you?"

"Was I to leave them to the Wild Ones?" the talon-handed man drawled. "You were glad enough to be saved when *you* were wandering the plain, Brianne. I tell you, I heard them talking! They are harmless."

The being who looked like Glock spat disgustedly. "Harmless? You are mad! At best they are decoys, at worst, spies. Look at them! Do they look like escaped slaves? They show no sign of the Sadness."

"And they came from the east, Claw," Brianne exclaimed. "All the slaves are in the west. With our own eyes we saw them trekking across the plain, chained together and under heavy guard, with Ak-Baba flying overhead. With our own ears we heard the guards taunting them, telling them they were going to

the Shadow Arena. How could these four have escaped?"

Jasmine drew a sharp breath. Lief could imagine
what she was thinking, and it was all he could do to
keep his own face expressionless. He had been right.
All the slaves were being herded into the Arena. Some
terrible plan was afoot. They had to get away from
here, and quickly.

Lief met Barda's eyes and blinked. Barda's
mouth tightened very slightly.

"Well, strangers?" Claw said crisply. "You have
heard my friends' opinions. Explain yourselves!"

"We do not have to explain ourselves to you,"
Lief gasped. "We do not desire your help or your company. We merely wish to go on our way."

"Indeed!" said Claw, bowing mockingly. "And
why should we allow you to do that?"

In seconds he had his answer, for before he could
blink Barda had sprung forward, and Barda's sword
was at his throat.

A strangled groan burst from Lief as the powerful hand that gripped his neck tightened viciously.

Barda merely smiled. "Will it be a life for a life,
then?" he asked Claw casually. "I can well do without
the lad, who is far more trouble than he is worth. Can
your friends do without you?"

Lief's attacker growled angrily. Brianne, stone-
faced, folded her arms to conceal her trembling.

"Your point is well made," said Claw, apparently

365

entirely unmoved. He raised his voice. "Let the boy go!"

Lief felt the choking grip slacken. Then his captor stepped away from him. Lief slid down to the cave floor, points of light dancing before his eyes, the breath rasping in his bruised throat. As Emlis and Jasmine ran to him, Barda pushed Claw over to join them.

The other cave-dwellers faced them, not daring to move.

"I fear our relationship has started badly," said Claw calmly, as if he was in conversation at a polite social gathering. "This is a pity, for I think we will have to help one another, very soon. You do not act like escaped slaves, certainly. But I do not think you are Shadow Lord creatures either."

"What are they then?" snapped Brianne. Then, suddenly, her hand flew to her mouth and her eyes widened.

Claw nodded, without taking his eyes from Barda. "They are proof of what I said the day the red clouds swept back over the mountains and the Wild Ones screamed and trembled at the Enemy's fury. Deltora is free. Somehow the Belt of Deltora has been restored, and the heir to its power found. Our visitors have come across the mountains from Deltora."

Barda's face remained expressionless.

The corner of Claw's mouth twitched with something like amusement. "You do not trust us," he said.

"Perhaps things will improve if we introduce ourselves. I am known as Claw, for reasons that must be plain. My real name, however, is Mikal, of Del."

He saw Lief's eyes widen, saw Jasmine and Emlis glance swiftly at his talons. He smiled without humor.

"You are surprised," he remarked. "Did you think I was some strange oddity from a land far away? Oh, no, my friends. I am a citizen of Del — or was, before Deltora forgot me. I lived and worked at the pottery. Perhaps you know it?"

He waited, and receiving no response, went on. "When I came here with my family, the Enemy made some — improvements — to my appearance. The Enemy enjoys such . . . experiments."

He stretched out his talons and flexed them thoughtfully. "These are strong, and serve me well," he said. "I escaped the Factory before the Enemy had quite finished with me. I am one of the lucky ones. Others are not so fortunate. Your small companion in the hood has already met some of them on the Dead Plain, I think, when they used him as Scuttler bait. We call them the Wild Ones."

He smiled grimly.

Lief heard Emlis whimper softly, felt Barda tense, and Jasmine's hand seek his own. Sick with horror, he stared at Claw, forcing himself to face the terrible truth. The savage creatures who had stolen Emlis — those hideous half-beast, half-human beings who prowled the arid plain — were his own people. Maddened, hopeless victims of the Shadow Lord's evil.

Satisfied by the effect of his words, Claw waved his hand at the tall woman. "Brianne is the newest member of our group." His mouth twisted in a mocking half smile. "Often do I regret the day I brought her in. She is as stubborn as a donkey, and has been a thorn in my side from the first."

The tall woman glared and straightened her shoulders. "Brianne of Lees," she said abruptly.

A memory tweaked at Lief's mind. Brianne of Lees. Where had he heard that name before?

But Claw was speaking again. "Brianne escaped from the Shadow Arena. Only the third Deltoran ever to have done so, it is said. What happened to the first, I do not know. But the second is here."

He gestured towards the hulking figure scowling beside Brianne. "This is the last member of our party. The last, and greatest, according to his own account. Gers, of the Jalis."

"Gers!" Jasmine burst out, staring.

The man Claw had called Gers stuck out his jaw and clenched his enormous fists. "You find the name amusing?" he growled. "Fight me, then, weakling, and see if you are still smiling when the fight is done!"

"There is nothing wrong with your name!" Jasmine cried. "It is just that — that you look like — exactly like — a . . . a friend of ours."

"A Jalis called Glock," added Barda, never moving his sword from Claw's throat.

Gers's face grew very still. "I had a brother called Glock," he said slowly.

"Do not listen to them, Gers!" Brianne exclaimed. "They are the Enemy's creatures! They are trying to deceive you!"

Gers's eyes narrowed. "I will not be deceived. I *had* a brother. He was one year my elder. But he is long dead. I saw him struck down on the field of battle when the Jalis made their last stand against the Enemy. Just before — before we were taken." His huge hand moved to finger the iron collar around his neck.

"Glock may have been struck down, but he did not die," Jasmine said, very moved. "He lived to play a great part in forcing the Shadow Lord from Deltora, and died a hero's death in — "

Barda cleared his throat and Jasmine broke off, realizing that she had nearly said too much.

" — in — in our arms," she finished lamely. As Gers frowned suspiciously, she quickly slipped Glock's talisman from around her neck and held it out to him.

"Glock gave this to me, just before he died," she said. "Do you know what it is?"

Gers's eyes widened. "Our family's talisman!" he mumbled, his lips barely moving as he stared at the small, faded bag. "The wooden charm of a goblin killed by one of our ancestors. A stone from the belly of a Diamond Serpent, and two more from a dragon's nest. Herbs of great power. And the flower of a Gripper. Never did I think to see it again."

Jasmine glanced at Lief and Barda. Her face showed that she, at least, was convinced. Again she held out her hand to Gers.

"Take it," she urged softly. "It is yours by right, and Glock would want you to have it. He gave it to me because there was no one else, and we had fought side by side. It is no longer complete, I fear, for the thing you call the charm of the goblin is gone. But perhaps you will be glad to have it, in any case."

The big man stared, still making no move to take the little bag. "What did Glock say when he gave you this?" he muttered.

"He said — " Jasmine's voice trembled slightly, but she clenched her fists and continued. "He said, 'You have the heart of a Jalis. Take my talisman from my neck. It is yours now. May it serve you well.' "

Gers wet his lips. " *'Take my talisman from my neck. It is yours now. May it serve you well,'* " he repeated. "Those are the words! The words that are always said when the talisman is passed on."

He turned to Claw. "She speaks the truth!" he said, his rough voice husky with emotion. "She bore arms with my brother. And if he said she has the heart of a Jalis, she does indeed."

He faced Jasmine again, bowed low, and took the

talisman from her hand. "One day, I hope, there will be a time when I, too, will bear arms with you," he said. Clearly it was the greatest compliment he could offer.

Jasmine smiled. "Then leave this place now, and journey with us to the west, Gers," she said in a low voice. "The time has come."

9 - West

Within the hour, the companions were moving westward once more. But they were not travelling overland, in the way they had expected. They were crawling through a tunnel below the earth. And they were no longer alone. Not only Gers, but Claw and Brianne, too, were with them.

Lief was glad enough of the cave-dwellers' help and their company, but he had not expected it. The cave-dwellers still did not even know their visitors' names. After her dramatic announcement, all Jasmine had told Gers was that she and her friends were intent on freeing the slaves in the Shadow Arena.

She had said nothing of the Pirran Pipe, so the quest sounded foolhardy indeed. Lief understood that it might appeal to Gers, but he had expected Claw and Brianne to be more cautious. There was something, however, that Lief had not considered.

Claw said flatly that the cave was no longer safe.

"You will not admit that you have come freshly from Deltora, my friends, but I am sure you have," he said. "You have passed through the shutting spell that guards the mountains. The Enemy has been alerted. At any moment Grey Guards will be here in swarms, sniffing you out. The sooner we leave here, the better."

Gers merely grunted agreement, but Brianne's face filled with angry despair as she turned away to fill a water bag.

His face filled with pity, Emlis drew Lief, Barda, and Jasmine aside.

"Why can we not tell Claw that his fears are groundless because we came to the Shadowlands from below?" he whispered.

"That must be told to no one!" Lief whispered back. "However all this ends, the Shadow Lord must not learn of the caverns. Your people must not be betrayed."

"But we can trust Claw and the others, I am sure of it!" Emlis hissed. "They would not tell."

"They may not tell willingly," Barda agreed grimly. "But whether they come with us or stay here, they could be captured at any time. There are many ways of making a captive speak, and the Shadow Lord knows all of them."

Emlis looked horrified.

"That is why I told Gers so little," Jasmine murmured. "The less others know of our business, the safer we will be. And the safer *they* will be also, Emlis, for what they do not know, they cannot be forced to tell."

She glanced at Lief, surprised that he had not yet spoken. Lief's head was bowed. He seemed to be in the grip of some strong feeling.

"Do you not agree, Lief!" she demanded.

"Of course," he said, looking up and meeting her eyes. "We could relieve our own minds by burdening these people with our secret. But if we do, we could be condemning them to die despising themselves for betraying their friends and their country. We must keep silent. But I agree with Emlis. It is hard."

Before Jasmine could answer, Gers lumbered past them and disappeared into the shadows at the back of the cave. Claw followed with the torch. The companions heard the grating sound of moving rock. Then, as Claw held the torch high, they saw that Gers had moved a large stone aside to reveal a small, dark tunnel.

"This tunnel leads to another Resistance cell, further west," said Claw. "We have not used it since the day of the Shadow Lord's wrath, but it will be safer than the surface."

He saw the companions hesitate, and raised his eyebrows. "We will go first, if you wish," he said.

"Gers and Brianne first," said Barda. "You, Claw, between us."

Claw nodded shortly and ushered Gers and Brianne into the tunnel. Clearly they were used to it, for they entered without hesitation. Jasmine went next, then Emlis and Barda. When it was Claw's turn, he took a last look around the cave and smiled bitterly.

"When I came to this place, it was a mere hollow under the rock, just large enough for me to hide in like a wounded animal," he said softly. "Then I heard water trickling below. Mad with thirst, I dug. I found the cave, and the water. The water comes underground from Deltora — from Dread Mountain, I think — for it fights the Shadowlands despair we call the Sadness. This place has been a refuge to me for a long time."

"I am sorry we have been the cause of your leaving it," Lief muttered, his conscience pricking him.

Claw's smile broadened. "There is nothing to be sorry for. As soon as I saw the mines being abandoned and our people herded west, I knew that the time for hiding was at an end for me. While I could pretend that hiding served a purpose — pretend that saving a few people or killing a few Guards struck a blow against the Enemy — I could bear it. Now . . ."

He extinguished the torch, and followed Barda, with Lief close behind him.

❋

The tunnel was dark and narrow. Claw's people spoke little, and on the seemingly endless journey through cramped, musty blackness there was plenty of time for Lief to wonder if they were being led into a trap.

But at last the forward movement stopped. There

was another grating sound as a stone blocking the tunnel was heaved aside. Then a long, low groan echoed back through the tunnel.

"What is it?" Lief heard Brianne whisper. "Gers!"

There was no answer. The forward movement began again as first Brianne, then those following her, joined Gers in the cave beyond the stone.

Lief heard a muffled cry, a torrent of whispers, then — nothing. With a feeling of dread, he crawled through the narrow opening after Claw.

No one had lit a torch, but the cave was not dark. Cold white light streamed through its roof, which had been broken open like an eggshell. A thick layer of dust covered the remains of a few pathetic possessions scattered on the floor. Charred bedding. A broken bowl. Some scraps of clothing.

The Shadow Lord's mark had been burned onto a rock wall spattered with blood.

It was clear what had happened here. Discovery. Attack. The very air seemed to reek of fear.

Lief moved stiffly to Barda, Jasmine, and Emlis, who were standing motionless under the hole in the roof near the burned remains of a rough ladder.

"Hellena," moaned Brianne, falling to her knees and pressing a tattered blue shawl to her cheek in an agony of grief. "Pi-Ban. Tipp. Moss. Pieter. Alexi . . ."

Claw's thin lips were pressed together. He was so still that he seemed scarcely to be breathing.

Gers spat on the mark of the Shadow Lord. "It is

fortunate for us that the Guards were too busy destroying to make a search," he muttered. "They did not find the tunnel. The rock was still in place."

"That does not mean they did not find it," Claw said grimly. "This plainly happened months ago, but they may still be waiting up above, like cats at a mouse hole."

Brianne stood up, tall and straight, her gaunt, scarred but still beautiful face icy cold. "I hope they are," she said, and her fingers caressed the dagger at her belt.

It was then that Lief suddenly remembered where he had heard her name before. It had been on the road to Rithmere. Brianne of Lees had been spoken of as a great athlete, a Champion of the Rithmere Games. It was said that she had gone into hiding, to avoid sharing the wealth she had won with her village.

That story had been false. Wickedly false, for it had made her own people hate her, as no doubt she had been told by Guards only too eager to cause suffering. Lief wished he could tell her that her people now knew what had happened to her, and mourned her loss. But he could not speak. Not yet.

Jasmine murmured to Kree, who fluttered up to the hole in the roof. They saw the bird's black shape outlined against the sky, yellow eye gleaming. Then Kree flew back to Jasmine's shoulder and gave a series of low squawks. Jasmine's face grew alert.

Gers cursed under his breath and felt for his talisman. "Do you see that?" Lief heard him mutter to Claw. "The bird is speaking to her!"

"So it seems." Claw's keen eyes regarded Jasmine and Kree with interest.

"Kree can see no Guards," Jasmine said. "But there is a large building a little to the west."

"That is the Factory," said Claw. "We must pass it to reach the Shadow Arena." His voice was low and even, but as he spoke a nerve twitched beside his eye and he unconsciously flexed his talons.

Gers glanced at him. "Better that we begin while it is still night, then," he growled.

Claw nodded shortly. Then, without another word, he strode to stand under the hole in the roof and jumped, catching the rim of the hole with his talons and hauling himself up into the open air.

Jasmine, Barda, Lief, and Brianne followed, immediately turning to catch and lift Emlis as he was heaved upward by Gers. Gers himself came last, grunting and swearing with the effort, enormous hands grabbing for support, heavy legs kicking against the cave wall.

When finally he lay grumbling on the cracked clay, the companions were free to turn west, to look their fill at the long, dark mass that hulked in the distance.

The Factory sprawled almost to the mountains'

edge. Flame belched from its tall, thin chimneys, turning the boiling cloud above to scarlet. The very sight of it filled Lief with dread.

He turned to Jasmine and saw that she was staring fixedly at the shape ahead, her green eyes calculating, her mouth set with determination. Lief felt a stirring of unease. Why would Jasmine look like that?

They began walking in single file, keeping low, moving quickly through the open spaces between the scattered rocks. The chimney flames ahead leaped high, guiding their way. Their ears strained for sounds of danger, but all they could hear was a dull, low rumble that grew louder and louder with every step they took.

The flames grew closer. The rumbling sound grew more penetrating, till the air seemed to tingle with it, and the very earth under their feet seemed to vibrate. A ghastly sweet-sour smell gusted towards them on the wind.

Now Lief could see the brutal shape of the Factory, very close. He could see a broad road running beside it, leading west, then disappearing around a great hill. He could also see the source of the terrible odor. Enormous, shadowy mounds of garbage lay between the road and the mountains.

"Those mounds will give us good cover," Barda muttered to Lief.

Claw turned. His face was gleaming with sweat.

His eyes were glassy. His lips were fixed in a smile that looked more like a sneer. "Good cover," he repeated. "Oh, yes. I found them so."

Then, abruptly, his eyes widened. "Gers! Brianne!" he cried harshly.

Lief spun around and saw, leaping towards them, a monstrous green man-shape with massive bowed shoulders, clawed hands, and a lashing tail. The creature's snake-like scales gleamed, its hideous lipless mouth split in a savage grin, its orange eyes burned.

Lief knew what it was. He had seen its like before, on Dread Mountain. It was the Shadow Lord's creation, bred to fight. The ultimate killing machine. A vraal.

10 ~ The Mounds

The vraal's terrible curved, knife-like claws were spread. Its tail lashed and broken clay sprayed up behind its cloven hoofs as it sprang forward. In seconds it would be upon them.

"Run, girl!" roared Gers to Jasmine. "Do not try to fight it!"

Jasmine did not need the warning, any more than Lief and Barda did. They had tried to fight a vraal once, and once was enough. This beast gloried in battle. It cared nothing for pain, did not know the meaning of fear or retreat.

Jasmine turned and ran, making for the garbage heaps. Grabbing Emlis between them, Lief and Barda pounded after her.

Hissing with fury because its opponents would not stand and fight, the vraal gave chase. The rusty broken chain that still swung from its iron collar rattled and clinked, but the vraal did not mind that. It was used to the sound. It had lived with it ever since it had escaped from captivity.

To the vraal, the sound of the broken chain represented freedom.

Freedom to kill and feed where and when it liked, instead of at the bidding of its masters.

Freedom to prowl the plain, so open, so different from the narrow confines of its cell beneath the Shadow Arena.

Freedom to prey on the man-beasts who ate scuttling beetles, the ragged slaves who dug in the holes in the earth and the grey masters who tasted bad, but who gave reasonable sport before they sank screaming under claws and teeth.

These enemies were different. The vraal could tell by their scent as well as their actions that they were not the same as the enemies it had been forced to fight of late. Fresh, rich blood still ran through their veins. Fire still burned in their hearts.

These were enemies worth killing. They were like the enemies in the old days of the Shadow Arena, strong and alive, brought in fresh every day to fight and die.

But these enemies were not fighting. They were running. Running into the hills that stank like the long-dead meat the vraal ate only when it was starving.

The vraal's nose was keen and delicate. It disliked vile smells as much as any human. It also knew that its hoofs, well fitted for almost every other surface, would not serve it well on the loose, crumbling mounds. But it hesitated only for a split second before bounding forward into the muck.

Its enemies could only hide for so long. In the end, it would find them. Soon it would be light, and the building that hunched beside the vile hills — the building that belched fire — offered no refuge. The vraal knew from experience that humans would rather die than enter it.

The cave-dwellers had scattered, burrowing into the mounds until they were invisible. Years of hiding had taught them to go underground immediately when threatened. Barda, Emlis, Lief, and Jasmine, however, had not been so quick. And now they could hear the vraal slipping and scrabbling close behind them.

With Jasmine in the lead, they stumbled through the dimness, often sinking knee-deep in vile, oozing waste, trying to put as much distance as possible between themselves and the beast before they attempted to stop and hide. But the vraal's sounds were growing louder. Instead of falling behind, it was drawing closer.

Then, suddenly, as they plowed around the side of a hill, the Factory loomed before them, windowless and grim.

Jasmine has led us the wrong way! Lief thought,

panic-stricken. How has this happened? Jasmine has always been able to find her way, even in the dark, and she did not hesitate for a moment. It is as though she *wants* us near the Factory. But that cannot be!

At that moment Emlis caught sight of the Factory also, squeaked, missed his footing, and slipped, cannoning into Barda.

The big man staggered, his feet digging deeply into the side of the hill. The loose surface began to slide. Then a whole section of the hill broke away. The companions were swept helplessly down with a mass of tumbling refuse to land, shocked and winded, on top of a low mound right beside the roadway.

Half covered, almost overwhelmed by the stench, they lay motionless, terrified to move.

Lief could no longer hear the vraal. Cautiously he cleared mess from his face, slid his eyes sideways, looked up, and saw it. It had climbed to the top of a mound just beyond the one that had collapsed. It was standing motionless, a fearsome silhouette against the paling sky, peering down, searching for signs of movement.

"I smell ticks!"

Lief's heart seemed to stop. The slurring voice had come from right beside his ear. He forced himself to turn his head.

A ghastly face was lying close to his own. A white-eyed face that seemed half-melted, its features blurred and twisted. As Lief recoiled in horror, the lopsided mouth grinned hideously and words dribbled from it again.

"Deltoran ticks! Do you hear me, Carns?"

Lief heard Jasmine's sharp gasp and Emlis's high, panic-stricken whimpering, which was quickly muffled, probably by Barda's hand.

"Stay still!" hissed Barda. "It cannot hurt us. Do you not see? It is half dead."

"Ticks, yes, Carn 2," croaked another voice, very near.

"The Perns claim them!" This time the voice was bubbling from below Lief's shoulder blade. "The Perns will kill the ticks and please the master. He'll see we're good for more years yet."

Something moved on Lief's chest. His stomach heaved as he saw that it was a hand, a fumbling hand with bloated fingers overflowing from the arm of a stained grey uniform.

Then, suddenly, there was movement beneath him and all around him, and it was as if his eyes suddenly cleared and he saw for the first time what surrounded him, what lay thick below him. The mound was a mass of bodies in grey uniforms, piled one on top of the other.

Sagging, misshapen heads nudged upward. Feet spilling from split boots jerked helplessly. Sprawled, flabby limbs twitched. Dissolving hands flapped and scrabbled. And slurred voices rose in a hideous, mumbling chorus. "Kill the ticks! Get them and please the master! Show the master we are not . . ."

The vraal's head twisted towards the sound, the movement. Its burning eyes seemed to flash. Its mouth split like a red, gaping wound studded with white teeth.

As it leaped forward, Lief, Jasmine, Barda, and Emlis sprang up, tearing themselves free of the feebly grasping hands, which were trying to hold them back. Kree swooped, stabbing with his powerful beak at a Guard reaching blindly for Jasmine's ankle.

"Black bird! Report — black bird and girl!" rasped the Guard. The cry was taken up by his neighbors and whispered over the mounds, echoing horribly from hundreds of dry throats. *Black bird, black bird and girl . . . report to the master, the master . . .*

Breath rasping in their chests, sick with fear and horror, the companions stumbled down to the road and began to run.

Glancing over his shoulder, Lief saw that the vraal had reached the mound from which they had just escaped. The mound was still heaving with the movement of the dying Guards. The vraal was standing at the top, its tail lashing, its claws extended.

Lief knew that the beast was relishing the moment, looking forward to the chase, the kill, the certain victory. In seconds it would be upon them. In seconds . . .

"Lief!" Jasmine shrieked.

Lief looked ahead. Jasmine was standing in front of a metal door in the Factory wall. She was holding it open. Barda and Emlis were already hurrying inside.

With a roar the vraal sprang. Before it had hit the ground, Lief was pounding towards the door. He reached it, shoved Jasmine inside, leaped after her, and swung the door shut just as the vraal crashed against it.

The companions stood panting, their backs to the door, as the beast threw itself against the metal, hissing and roaring. They were in a square room with closed doors on all sides. One of the doors, the one to their right, bore a large, black-painted symbol.

Jasmine ran to the door, pressed her ear against it, and listened intently.

Lief looked around him. There was nowhere to hide. The room was completely empty. The walls were hard, smooth, gleaming white. The ceiling shone with cold light that seemed to have no source.

Like Fallow's chamber in the palace, Lief thought. Instantly he cursed himself, and tried to block his mind.

Too late. Already memories of that other gleaming white room were flashing through his mind, bringing with them weakness and terror. He felt cold sweat break out on his forehead. He fought the memories back.

It was no use. His brain was seething with pictures, with sounds.

Alone and in secret, trusting in the protection of the Belt of Deltora, he had tried with all his might to destroy the dangerous, evil thing Fallow's chamber contained.

It had been a desperate, agonizing battle. He had fought it alone, as he knew he had to do, and he had lost. In the end, exhausted, weak, and sickened, he had had to be content with having the room bricked up and setting guards to prevent anyone entering its hallway. Then he had tried to wipe it from his mind, forget it existed.

But he could not forget. The knowledge of the core of darkness that lay hidden in the palace's heart continued to torment him.

He never spoke of it. Only one person knew what he had been through in that sealed room, and that was Marilen, for there could be no secrets between them.

Marilen. . . . Into Lief's mind swam an image of the girl as he had last seen her — shivering, wrapped tightly in her cloak, her fearful face raised to his as she bade him farewell.

He clung to the image. Clung to it like a lifeline,

using it to pull himself free of the swirling mass of fears and memories that threatened to engulf him.

He realized that Jasmine was tugging at his arm. Whispering to him urgently. Something about hiding. About —

There was a mighty crash, and the metal of the door bulged inward as the vraal thudded against it once more.

"Lief! Guards are coming!" Jasmine panted, as Filli squeaked frantically on her shoulder. She dragged Lief towards the door that bore the black symbol. It was open, and Barda and Emlis were already slipping through it into the room beyond.

"There is no one in there," Jasmine gabbled. "And I think the sign means it is forbidden to Grey Guards. That might give us some time. Make haste!"

Now Lief, too, could hear thudding footfalls and shouting voices coming towards them from somewhere deep in the building. He hurtled through the open door, with Jasmine close behind him.

11 – The Factory

As Jasmine pushed the door shut, Lief stood with Barda and Emlis staring, amazed, at the vast hall they had entered. It was as hard white and as brilliantly lit as the room they had just left, but it was far, far larger. It was filled with a low humming drone and a slow, thick, bubbling, popping sound, like the sound of cooking porridge. The air was slightly steamy and very warm, and there was a strange odor that reminded Lief a little of the smell of hot iron.

The room was filled with long metal containers on short legs. The containers were neatly spaced, one behind the other, and each stretched almost all the way across the room. From the door, Lief could not see what was inside them.

He took a step towards the closest one, then

froze. Heavy boots had pounded into the room on the other side of the door. Rough voices were shouting.

"The door's bent. Something's been trying to get in. A gang of Wild Ones, no doubt. Get a look, Bak 3."

There was the sound of the metal door unlatching. Then there was a yell and a thundering crash as the door was slammed shut again.

"Vraal!" several voices shouted amid the shuddering thumps and bangs of the beast attacking the door again.

Amazingly, the Guards still had not caught the companions' scent, and had not guessed that the vraal was pursuing intruders. Lief felt Jasmine touch his arm. She put her finger to her lips and beckoned. Then slowly, very quietly, she began to move farther into the room.

"It's not going to go away!" shouted a voice from the other side of the door. "Call the Perns!"

"No! We can handle it on our own!" another voice objected. "We have the new sparking rods, haven't we? Now's our chance to use them!"

The Guards were still concentrating on the vraal.

When they have driven it away we can escape, Lief thought. But Jasmine is right to move. We are too exposed standing here. We must find a safe place to hide while we wait.

He tiptoed after Jasmine, with Barda, who was half-carrying Emlis, following closely.

But as they reached the first of the metal contain-ers, they all stopped dead. The container was divided into ten separate sections. Inside each compartment was what looked like a thick, slowly bubbling soup. The stuff was greyish white in color, and filled with strangely shaped lumps.

"What *is* this?" Barda muttered, wrinkling his nose.

"It does not matter," whispered Jasmine, dodg-ing around the corner of the container and moving on. "Do not stop. There is a door at the back of the room. Let us — "

Her hand flew to her mouth and she made a choking sound.

Lief hurried to her side with Barda and Emlis. And when he saw what Jasmine had seen, his stom-ach turned over.

The compartments in the second tray were half full of the simmering grey-white soup. But floating in the liquid were smooth, grey, featureless objects with heads, bodies, arms, legs . . .

Barda cursed under his breath. Emlis hid his face in his hands. Jasmine's face was distorted with horror. "Dead people!" she choked. "Dead bodies dis-solving . . ."

"No!" Lief had been moving along the tray, and he had seen what the others had not. Two words en-graved on the metal side.

CARN POD

"They are not dissolving," he said huskily, as he moved back to his friends. "They are *forming*. These are Grey Guards. They are not born, but *grown*! Here, in the Factory!"

He stabbed a shaking finger back towards the engraved words. "We know that Grey Guards are always in groups of ten. Ten identical brothers, with the same name, who work and fight together. Do you not see? Every one of these trays is a pod! This is the Carn Pod."

Barda gritted his teeth. "The Carns are out in the garbage mound, Lief! How could they be here also?"

"Because — " Lief began.

Then, suddenly, the door at the back of the room began to open.

Like a flash, the companions crouched behind the container.

". . . just a wild vraal, it seems," a young woman's voice said. "The Baks will take care of it."

"Or *it* will take care of *them*," an older male voice sneered in reply. "The present Baks are already ten days past their fail date. They are starting to make mistakes. And even without that, the Bak model was never up to standard, in my opinion."

Footsteps sounded on the hard floor. Peering through the legs of the containers, Lief saw two pairs of white-booted feet pacing slowly across the back of the room, inspecting the last row of compartments. He also saw that the door had not swung shut, but still hung half-open.

"These new Baks are almost ready," the woman said gently, after a moment. Her voice seemed familiar to Lief, but surely that was impossible. She was clearly a Shadow Lord servant.

"Not before time," the man snapped. "I told you! Guard supplies are running dangerously low. When we come to the Carns, you will see how bad things are. We had to dispose of the old Carns weeks ago, while the new ones were barely formed!"

Lief felt Jasmine and Barda's eyes upon him and knew that his companions had at last understood. Grey Guards, made only to serve, made to be cruel, unquestioningly obedient, without a trace of warmth or pity, had only a limited life. When they began to wear out, they were simply thrown away and replaced with identical models.

No wonder this room is forbidden to them, Lief thought. Blindly obedient they might be, but even *they* might react badly if they saw their replacements steadily growing in here.

The white boots turned and began to move back across the room again. The newcomers were inspecting another row of emerging Guards.

Cautiously, Lief, Barda, Jasmine, and Emlis began crawling forward, keeping close to the containers. Moving was a risk, but it was a risk they had to take. If they remained where they were, discovery was certain.

Fortunately, the inspectors were too interested in their work, and their conversation, to notice the tiny, shuffling sounds from the other side of the room.

"These Perns are growing more slowly than the charts predict," the woman commented, as the feet reached the end of the second-last row.

"Well, it is not my fault!" exclaimed her companion. "The power was cut twice yesterday." His voice took on a complaining tone. "It is all the fault of the Conversion Project! It has taken too many materials and far too much of the master's attention of late, in my opinion."

Conversion Project? Lief paused, holding his breath, listening hard. The inspectors had moved forward to the next row and had started pacing slowly back towards the companions' side of the room. It was dangerous to wait, but he had to hear this.

"You seem to have many *opinions,* 3-19," the woman said, her soft voice hardening. "If I were you, I would take care."

"What do you mean?" the man asked peevishly.

"Why do you think the Conversion Project became of first importance to the master, you fool?" snapped the woman, finally losing patience. "It is because the recent disaster in Deltora made him lose faith in the whole idea of Grade 3 Ols. In *you* and your kind, 3-19!"

Lief's heart thudded. The being called 3-19 was a Grade 3 Ol! An example of the most perfect, the most dangerous, of the Shadow Lord's evil shape-changers. Able to mimic humans so perfectly that they could live among them without detection.

Who — or what — was the other speaker then? He burned to see what the two looked like, but did not dare lift his head.

"The master has begun to think that the Grade 3s were a mistake," the woman was continuing. "Too like humans. Prone to pride, curiosity, weakness, and disobedience. And you, 3-19, seem to be proving his point!"

With that, she strode rapidly ahead of her companion. Lief slid forward and ducked hastily out of the side passage just in time to avoid being discovered.

He could see the crouched forms of Barda, Jasmine, and Emlis a few rows ahead of him. He could also see the white-clad legs of the mysterious woman, farther towards the back of the room.

With a thrill of horror, Lief saw that a corner of Emlis's green cloak was trailing into the passage. If the woman looked ahead, looked down . . .

But she seemed to be in no mood to notice her surroundings. One of her feet was tapping impatiently as 3-19 hurried to join her, murmuring apologies and explanations.

". . . did not mean anything by it," Lief heard the Ol say. "I would never question the master's judgment."

"I thought that was exactly what you *were* doing!" snapped the woman, moving into the next row of emerging Grey Guards. "The Conversion Project is the way of the future, 3-19. As you will find out, very soon."

"Soon?" gulped 3-19, thoroughly frightened now. "But I thought — "

"All errors in the process have been corrected," the woman said coldly. "Do you see any fault in *me*?"

There was a moment of stunned silence.

"I — I did not know you were one of them," faltered 3-19 at last.

"Well, I am!" snapped the woman. "Now! Explain to me why these Krops seem thinner than they should be."

They were moving towards the other side of the room once more. Lief, Barda, Jasmine, and Emlis slid out of hiding and began crawling forward as rapidly as they could.

In moments they had drawn almost level with the two inspectors, who by now had almost reached the end of the Krop Pod. Now was the most dangerous time. One by one the companions crossed the gap between containers. They would be in clear view of the two standing at the far end, should either of them turn.

But neither did. Glancing sideways as he scooted from shelter, Lief caught a brief glimpse of two white-clad figures, one tall, one short and slender, standing close together at the end of the container. The short one was consulting a chart. The tall one was bending to turn one of the knobs mounted on the container's shining metal.

Then the figures were out of sight once more as Lief scuttled on after his friends, past the last few pods and across the back wall to the open door.

Keeping low, Jasmine peered cautiously through the doorway. She turned and nodded to the others, then crawled through the opening. Barda and Emlis went after her. But as Lief followed, noting that the room beyond the door was some sort of workroom, he heard the Ol speak again, very timidly.

"The master's plan — "

"The master has many plans!" interrupted the woman sharply. "And none of them are your concern."

Jasmine was beckoning urgently from the other side of the room, but Lief could restrain his curiosity no longer. As soon as he could, he stood up and peered cautiously around the half-open door, back into the pod room.

The two figures had begun their inspection of the next row of Guards. The shorter one, the female, was consulting the chart. The tall one was walking behind her, glowering.

His thin, sour face was the face of Fallow.

Lief gripped the edge of the door till his knuckles turned white. That is not Fallow, he reminded himself desperately. Fallow is dead. That creature, 3-19, simply wears the same face. But still his breath came fast and his stomach heaved with loathing.

Then the female figure looked up from the chart and half turned towards her companion. Bright white light illuminated her delicate face, her pale blue eyes.

Lief stared for a split second, then shrank back behind the door, numb with shock.

12 ~ Discoveries

arda, Jasmine, and Emlis were clustered in front of a narrow door on one side of the workroom. Skirting a long white table cluttered with jars, measuring jugs, and a pot of bubbling green liquid set over a low flame, Lief ran noiselessly to join them.

"There is nowhere to hide in here," Jasmine whispered. "We will have to go farther." She paused as she noticed the expression on Lief's face. "What is it?" she muttered. "You look as if you have seen a ghost."

"I have," Lief whispered back. "That woman — the woman in the pod room — is Tira of Noradz."

Barda and Jasmine gaped at him, horrified.

"Who is Tira?" Emlis asked, looking from one to the other.

"A friend who once risked her life for us," said Jasmine, swallowing hard. "We knew her people had been brought to the Shadowlands. We hoped to find her, to save her. But — "

"But it seems she does not want to be saved." Barda clenched his fists. "She has become the Shadow Lord's creature. What have they done to her?"

"The answer is in there, I think," Jasmine said slowly. She moved aside and pointed to a notice on the door.

CONVERSION PROJECT NO ENTRY

There was no sound from behind the door. Lief tried the knob. It turned smoothly. He pushed the door open a crack and peered into the room beyond.

At first, all he could see was a haze of soft pinkish-red light. He blinked, and the room slowly came into focus. It was another, much larger, work-room — huge, silent, and empty. The strange red light glowed from the walls, ceiling, and floor. On the wall facing Lief there were two vast doors, firmly closed.

A wave of dread swept over him. Jasmine was pushing him from behind, urging him on, but for a long moment he resisted her. Everything within him was crying to him to stay where he was. He clutched at the Pirran Pipe beneath his shirt and at last gained enough strength to stumble into the room.

Many work tables jutted from the sidewalls, each one stretching about a third of the way across the room, each one fitted with a set of broad leather straps. Lief's mouth went dry as his imagination suddenly peopled the room. The helpless victims strapped to the benches. The cold, white-clad figures working over them, carrying out their master's orders.

Doing . . . what?

The broad strip of floor in the middle of the room was bare, but scars on its hard surface showed that it had not always been so. Something heavy, large, and square had once stood in the exact center. Shallow ruts, like the tracks of cartwheels, showed that the object had been pulled out of the room by way of the double doors.

There seemed nothing to fear, yet Lief's whole body quivered as he moved towards the marks on the floor. He knew without question that evil itself had been in this red-lit room.

The others felt it, too. Emlis seemed to have shrunk within his cloak, his small face pinched, and his teeth slightly bared. Barda was breathing hard, as though he had been running. Jasmine's face had paled. Filli had disappeared beneath her collar, and Kree was like a black statue on her shoulder.

Instinctively they all avoided stepping on the marks on the floor. They edged past them, pressing against the ends of the work tables, their eyes turned away.

They reached the double doors and, after listening carefully and hearing no sound, ventured through.

A surge of evil power hit them full in their faces, stopping them in their tracks.

They were in a dim, red-lit space with double doors on every wall. The space was completely bare except for a huge, square metal box that stood in the center, where the dented tracks in the floor ended. The box was as tall as Jasmine, and had wheels on its base and a trapdoor at one end. Its hinged lid was open, hanging flat against one of its sides. Clearly, it was the object that had been moved from the workroom.

Evil radiated from it like heat. But the feeling was cold, a deathly cold that seemed to chill their blood, freeze their very bones to ice. Emlis began to whimper.

Lief forced his hand upward and grasped the Pirran Pipe. A little warmth stole through his fingers. He took a step forward.

"Stop!" hissed Jasmine, clutching his arm. "Lief, no! Do not go near it!"

But Lief had to know. He had to see what was inside the box. Clutching the Pipe more tightly he moved forward, Jasmine stumbling behind him, trying to hold him back.

He reached the box and, gritting his teeth, looked over its edge.

At first all he could see was a squirming, pinkish mass. Then his throat closed as he realized what he was looking at — thousands upon thousands of long, pale worms with scarlet heads, thrashing and writhing in a bath of red slime.

And the worms sensed him. They began rearing, trying to reach him, their wicked scarlet heads straining upward, their tails lashing.

With a choking cry Lief jerked backwards, crashing into Barda and Jasmine, who were directly behind him.

He did not need to ask them if they had seen. Their appalled faces told him that they had.

"We have to get out of this place," Barda hissed. He pointed at the double doors to their right. "That way! By my reckoning, the rubbish mounds are on that side. There may be another door . . ."

"No!" Jasmine was shaking her head, pointing to the doors ahead. Barda glared at her, and her pale face flushed scarlet. "We must go on!" she cried desperately. "There must be prisoners here."

Lief looked from one to the other — and at Emlis, cringing behind them.

Jasmine wanted to come here, all along . . .

The thought drifted into his mind, stuck there. He knew it was true.

"Jasmine, who — ?" he began bluntly. He had

just enough time to register Jasmine's startled, guilty expression when a noise from the workroom made him break off.

It was the sound of voices and ringing footsteps. Tira and her companion had finished their inspection far sooner than he had expected.

". . . it cannot be helped!" Tira was exclaiming. "You heard the message. We are needed at once! The Conversion Project is about to be put into action."

The companions glanced around frantically. There was nowhere to hide. Barda grabbed Lief's arm and made for the right-hand doors, with Emlis shuffling after him. After just a moment's hesitation, Jasmine followed.

They swung into chill darkness. The doors had no sooner closed behind them than they heard someone entering the room they had just left.

"Ah, my beauties!" Tira's voice cooed. "Your time has come! I have just had word of it."

There was a creaking sound, then a slam and four clicks as the lid of the box was swung closed and locked into place.

"What is happening?" Jasmine whispered in panic. "What are they going to do with those . . . *things*?"

"Ssss!"

The hiss was startling in the dark silence. Lief, Barda, Jasmine, and Emlis jumped violently and spun around.

Behind them, its roof covered by a tangle of heavy cloth, was an iron cage on wheels. Inside the cage, something moved.

"Help me!" croaked a voice. "Free me, for pity's sake!"

The companions darted silently to the cage. Its door was fastened with a heavy padlock. Peering out through the bars was a gaunt, wild-eyed Dread Gnome, his face just visible in the darkness. "I am Pi-Ban," the gnome gabbled. "Pi-Ban, once of Dread Mountain. Are you the cause of the panic? Did Claw send you? Where are Brianne and Gers?"

Barda grasped two of the cage bars and heaved with all his might. But even his great strength was not enough to bend the thick, rigid iron.

Wordlessly, Jasmine held out her dagger. Lief snatched it and began trying to use its point to open the heavy lock. "Claw did not send us, exactly, Pi-Ban," he whispered. "But we know your name. We know you are one of the people who were taken from the Resistance cave to the east of this place."

"Where are your friends?" Jasmine asked urgently, as Barda began to work on the bars again. "Where are the prisoners kept?"

The gnome groaned, his eyes fixed on Lief's hands. "The dungeons are below ground level," he said, his lips barely moving. "But they are empty now. Moss, Pieter, Tipp, Alexi, Hellena . . . one by one they were taken away. It began the day we were captured, with Moss. It ended yesterday, with Hellena. Only I remain."

"But . . . but surely there are other slaves here?" Jasmine's voice was tense.

"There *were* others, at first," said Pi-Ban. "Many, many others, young and old. Some in the dungeons with us. Some — the quieter, more obedient ones — used to clean and carry. But they, too, are gone now."

"These — these quieter ones," Jasmine said quickly. "Were there any young girls among them?"

"A girl called Tira, for example?" Barda panted, pausing for a moment in his struggle with the cage.

The gnome raised his haggard face. "Is Tira the one you came for?" he asked tiredly. "Yes, I knew her. A gentle creature, with eyes like the sky. She was one of the Noradz — strange, timid folk dressed in black who cleaned the hallways and brought food and water to the dungeons. At first we thought they served the Shadow Lord willingly, but it was not so. They were prisoners, as we were."

Barda nodded grimly and attacked the bars again, as though his enormous hands were tearing at the Shadow Lord himself. Lief was frowning over the lock, lost in concentration.

As if unable to bear watching them any longer, Pi-Ban turned and paced to the back of the cage. He grasped the bars and sank to his knees, staring out into the darkness.

Jasmine edged towards him and kneeled down so that she could talk to him face to face.

"I heard of another girl who might be here, Pi-Ban," she said in a low voice. "Younger than Tira — a child — with black hair and green eyes, called Faith."

She held her breath as Pi-Ban frowned thoughtfully.

"Faith. How strange that you should mention that name," the gnome murmured at last. "I heard it for the first time only a short time ago, when Guards brought me up here. They were Baks, and in worse tempers than usual. Three of their pod had just been slaughtered by a vraal, which was pursuing a fourth into the desert. They had been ordered to abandon him in order to escort me. I told them I was pleased to hear it. That earned me a bruise or two."

A savage white grin shone briefly through the tangles of his matted beard, then he sobered once more. "They told me I was to be taken to the Shadow Arena, and that Faith had gone before me," he muttered. "They seemed to think this would torment me, because I knew this girl. But I do not."

He looked at Jasmine shrewdly. "She is of great importance to *you*, however, that is plain. Who is she, this little girl with black hair and green eyes like your own? And why do you take care to ask of her while your friends cannot hear?"

Her mind whirling, Jasmine turned quickly away from him.

"I cannot do it, Barda!" Lief muttered from the front of the cage. "The lock is too strong. We will have to find another way."

At that moment there was a loud sound from the room they had just left. Doors were being thrown open. There was the pounding of marching feet.

"Guards!" growled Barda.

"Go! Make haste!" Pi-Ban hissed. "There is another pair of doors behind the cage. I think they are a way out."

"No!" Jasmine whispered desperately, standing fast. "We cannot go now!"

"You must!" The gnome raised his tousled head proudly. "If I am to die, I wish to die as a Dread Gnome, not as a coward who drags others down with him. Get out! Save yourselves!"

But already it was too late. The double doors heaved. Dull red light shone through the gap. The Guards were coming through.

13 - The Tunnel

L ike lightning, Lief, Barda, and Jasmine leaped for the cage roof, swinging Emlis up behind them. They burrowed under the layers of cloth and lay still, peering out cautiously, their hearts pounding.

"Time to go, scum!" jeered one of the Guards. He approached the cage and jabbed a heavy stick through the bars. There was a shower of sparks, and the companions heard Pi-Ban groan and fall heavily. The Guards bellowed with laughter.

Two white-clad figures strode through the doors — Tira and the Ol called 3-19. The Guards fell abruptly silent.

"You are to go with the cage, 3-19," Tira said crisply. "I will follow with the Project."

"There is only one prisoner," 3-19 objected. "He can walk in chains. The cage is not necessary."

Tira's eyes narrowed. "It is not for you to say what is necessary," she said in a low, dangerous voice. "This prisoner has been kept especially for this moment. We cannot risk escape. He is not to be harmed, so watch the Guards carefully."

3-19 nodded, his thin face sour.

"We Baks do not need an Ol to tell us what to do," mumbled one of the Guards.

"Silence!" Tira shouted. She spun around and returned to the red-lit room where another pod of Guards stood, five on each side of the metal box.

3-19 cleared his throat. "You heard!" he said to the Baks. "Take your positions!"

As the Baks sulkily spaced themselves around the cage, he strode past them and threw open the second set of doors. Faint light flooded into the room, bringing with it the foul smell of the mounds.

Lief lay rigid, fearing that at any moment they would be seen, but there was no cry of alert. The Guards were staring resentfully at 3-19, whose eyes were fixed on the way ahead.

"Forward!" shouted Tira from the other room.

"Move!" 3-19 muttered to the Baks.

"We must pull down the covers first," one growled.

With a sickening thud, Lief realized that the pieces of cloth beneath which he and his companions were hiding were flaps designed to be pulled down over the sides of the cage.

"There is no need for the covers, you fool!" snapped 3–19. "It is night! The prisoners will see nothing."

"A travelling cage must be covered," the Guard said stubbornly. "Those are the orders. We Baks always . . ."

"You Baks are overdue for the scrap heap, and the sooner you are there the better!" spat 3-19 in fury. "Move!"

Muttering darkly, the six Baks put their shoulders to the cage and heaved it into the foul-smelling night. Behind them rumbled the great metal box.

Pi-Ban lay dazed and mumbling. Lief, Barda, Jasmine, and Emlis were clinging desperately to the lurching cage roof. Each of the Shadow Lord servants was occupied with his or her own thoughts of resentment or triumph.

And so it was that no one saw three shadows creep from the shelter of the mounds and follow.

✳

At first, all Lief could hear was the rattling of the cage, but after a while he began to pick up voices from below.

"We deserve more respect," a Guard was grumbling. "We gave the alert! *We* were the ones outside, fighting the vraal. *We* were the ones who heard those wrecks on the scrap heap calling."

Lief felt his scalp prickle. He listened intently.

"The Ol said we should be on the scrap heap ourselves, Bak 3," another Guard said.

"The Ol is a fool!" snarled Bak 3. "You *know* we don't have a fail date like other pods, Bak 9. We were told that from the first, and warned not to boast of it to the others. Have you forgotten?"

"No," Bak 9 mumbled. "But the Ol said — "

"Forget what it said!" Bak 3 snapped. "The master would never dispose of us! Why, *we* gave him the news he was waiting for — the news of the girl and the black bird. Why else are we going to the Arena now?"

Lief's heart thudded violently. The Shadow Lord had been waiting for Jasmine. He had been expecting her. It was news of *her* that had caused this haste.

The suspicion Lief had been fighting ever since they arrived in the Shadowlands reared its head once more and this time he faced it squarely. Jasmine had a secret — a dangerous secret. She had led them to the Factory. She had refused to escape, when escape was still possible.

He burned to turn his head, to whisper to Jasmine, ask her to explain. But he did not dare. The slightest sound or movement might betray them.

Through a gap in the cloth he could see that the cage was rounding the hill he had seen from the Factory. The Guards panted as they hauled the grating wheels into the curve.

Then, all at once, the road had straightened again. Now it was running right beside the mountains. Ahead was a vast, lighted Arena. There was the sound of a great, murmuring crowd.

"Faster!" shouted Tira from behind, her voice sharp with excitement. "Stop in the tunnel, 3-19! The Project is to go into the Arena first. Do you hear me?"

"I am not deaf!" barked 3-19. "Guards! More speed!"

"We are not deaf either, Ol," growled Bak 9.

The cage began to move faster. The noise of the crowd grew louder. Then suddenly the light dimmed, and the cage creaked to a halt. Lief saw dark stone and guessed that they were in the entrance tunnel that led through the walls of the Arena.

He felt a wave of sickness, heard the sound of heavy wheels, and realized that the metal box was being moved past the cage so that it could enter the Arena first.

"Wait here until you are summoned, 3-19!" Tira's voice echoed from somewhere ahead.

"Is the woman in red the slave Faith?" 3-19 asked curiously.

Lief felt Jasmine tense.

"Of course not!" Tira snapped. "She is the way of the future, as I am. The slave is chained below the platform. Perns! Forward!"

A drum began to beat — a deep, throbbing sound like a great heartbeat. The crowd fell silent.

414

Lief had to see what was happening. Cautiously he tweaked a little more of the cover aside.

The metal box, with Tira walking before it, was being pushed through a vast archway not far ahead. It was moving from darkness into blazing light. The light of the Arena.

Lief knew that there must be tiers of seats circling the Arena, but he could not see them from where he was lying. Neither could he see the vraals, whose growls were mingling with the beating of the great drum. But he could see the ground clearly. Everything within the frame of the arch was as clear as day. It was like looking at a vast, moving picture.

Grey Guards holding sparking rods lined the path along which the metal box was passing. The path led to a huge platform ringed with white columns. Someone wearing a long red robe was standing there, too far back for Lief to see clearly.

Behind the Guards were ragged people, pressed closely together. The peoples' shoulders were bowed, their eyes haunted and despairing. Most bore the Shadow Lord's brand on brow or cheek. They stood dully watching as Tira and the metal box passed them by.

Lief's eyes burned as he saw among them the black-clad people of Noradz, the hulking figures of hundreds of Jalis, some palace guards. Others he did not recognize. But he knew who they were. Farmers from the northeast, the west, and the Plains, gladiators from Rithmere, fishing folk from the coast, Resistance fighters, citizens of Del . . .

Deltorans, all of them. Beaten, worked, and swept by the wind of despair until they had no heart or hope left. They believed they had been brought here to die. For many, perhaps, death might seem a relief from the misery of their slavery.

But they will not die, Lief thought grimly. And they will be slaves no longer. They will not!

But there were so many. Uneasily Lief fingered the Pirran Pipe beneath his shirt. The Pipe's moment of testing was near. Would its magic give them time to rally the people? To get so many thousands out of the Arena? Would it break the shutting spell blocking the mountains?

The box had nearly reached the platform. And the light in the Arena was changing to a dull, angry red.

Dawn.

A movement caught Lief's eye. The Baks were stealing closer to the archway. 3-19 was looking resentfully after Tira. No one was watching the cage.

"This is our chance to get down!" Barda muttered.

"No!" Jasmine whispered urgently. "We must stay here. How else are we to reach the platform safely?"

"The platform?" exclaimed Barda, aghast. "Why —"

Lief was sure that Jasmine had her own reasons

for wanting to get to the platform. But he, too, believed that the center of the Arena was where they should be.

"The Pipe must be played where the Shadow Lord can hear it clearly," he whispered. "And the people must see us. Emlis, as soon as we reach the platform, I will pass the Pipe to you. Be ready!"

Emlis squeaked frightened agreement.

"This is a reckless plan, Lief," Barda growled. "The people have had no warning. They will not know — "

"Shh!" breathed Jasmine.

Lief froze. Then he heard what Jasmine had heard before him. At the back of the cage there were tiny noises. Whispering voices. A clink as someone lifted the cage lock. A grunt of effort and a muttered curse.

Then something tapped Lief's foot.

"Get down, you fools!" rasped a harsh voice. "We cannot release Pi-Ban, but you at least we can save."

Claw!

"No. We are staying with the cage," Lief whispered.

"Are you mad, boy?" Claw hissed.

"There is no time to explain," said Barda rapidly. "If you wish to help us, get into the Arena. Tell the people — as many as you can — to be ready to fight their way out. When it is time, they will know it."

417

"If we try to save them all, they will be slaughtered," rasped Claw. "And we with them. A few we might — "

"Tell them to make for the pass behind the Arena!" Barda broke in. "Now move away, Claw, for pity's sake. The Guards will turn and see you!"

"The pass is sealed by the shutting spell," Claw said.

"Leave that to us," said Barda. "Just tell them!"

"You are mad!" muttered Claw. The talon resting on Lief's foot tightened briefly, then slipped away.

They heard more whispering. Then silence. Claw, Brianne, and Gers had vanished into the shadows.

"Will he do it?" Jasmine murmured.

"Who can say?" said Barda grimly. "And I fear we are as mad as he claims! For all we know, the Pirran Pipe will trouble the Shadow Lord no more than a buzzing fly."

"Look!" Jasmine whispered.

A red-clad woman was walking forward on the platform, her strong face and smooth silver hair now clearly visible.

"Hellena!"

The despairing, unbelieving cry had come from below them. From Pi-Ban.

3-19 swung around. "Return to your posts!" he spat at the Guards furiously, then turned back to the Arena.

The red-robed woman had also heard Pi-Ban's cry. Her lips curved in a cool smile.

Lief stared, horrified. Hellena had been a member of Pi-Ban's group. She was the friend for whom Brianne had mourned so bitterly. Yet now her eyes gleamed in triumph as the Perns slid the metal box up a ramp and onto the platform. She was revelling in evil. Like Tira.

The Conversion Project . . . the way of the future . . .

"There will be no vraals released today," Hellena cried in ringing tones.

Howls of disappointment rose from the audience — howls that changed abruptly to wails as thunder cracked and a ghastly chill swept through the Arena.

The Baks cringed beside the cage. "The master is present," Bak 3 whimpered.

"Today a new era begins!" Hellena cried. "After today, nothing will stand in the master's way. Wherever he lays his hand, all will bow down before him and do his will. As you will see."

She raised her hand. "Bring Faith!"

Two Guards came up to the platform dragging between them a small, struggling, black-haired girl whose green eyes flashed fury.

Jasmine caught her breath.

Lief's heart seemed to stop. Barda cursed softly.

The child on the platform, her small face so like Jasmine's that the two could only be sisters, was scan-

419

ning the crowd, her eyes filled with fearful hope.

"This is the sister of one of the master's most vicious enemies!" shouted Hellena. "But, like the gnome who will be joining her — a gnome I know to be the worst of traitors — she will soon bow willingly before the master."

The audience roared.

"We are about to be summoned," gabbled Bak 9 fearfully. "The master will think we have disobeyed our orders. Dawn has broken, and the cage is uncovered."

Lief tensed, the child Faith suddenly the last thing on his mind. Surely disaster would not strike now, when they were so close!

The other Baks shuffled their feet nervously. "The Ol said — " one began.

"Curse the Ol!" snarled Bak 9. And without further warning the six sprang up onto the sides of the cage and ripped the covers aside.

Emlis, suddenly exposed, rolled in an agony of terror and fell. He hit the ground and lay still. Lief, Barda, and Jasmine struggled to rise, to draw their weapons, but they had no chance. The Guards recovered from their shock in an instant. The sparking rods thrashed down, down . . .

Lief saw Jasmine crumple and fall back, Kree with her. He saw Barda hit once, twice. Then he himself felt a fiery jolt on the back of his neck. Agony shot through him. Then all was darkness.

14 - The Shadow Arena

L ief came to his senses slowly. Something was thumping, thumping, every thunderous beat sending shooting pain through his head. He was lying on a hard, jolting surface that was jarring his aching bones . . .

He forced his eyes open. His head was jammed against cold bars. He could see nothing beyond the bars, because thick fabric hung over them on the outside.

It took some time to remember what had happened and then to realize, with cold horror, where he was. He was in the cage, and it was moving through the Arena. The sound he could hear was the beating of the great drum.

Barda and Jasmine were stirring beside him. Pi-Ban was crouched by Barda's head, his face the picture of despair.

Lief felt for his sword, but of course it was gone. With a thrill of terror he moved his hand to his neck, and relief rushed through him as he felt the cord unbroken and the Pirran Pipe still hanging beneath his shirt.

Rough voices were muttering somewhere near. Lief realized that they were the voices of the Guards who were pushing the cage on his side.

"The Ol will try to claim the credit."

"Let it try! When the covers come off, its face will show its surprise. The master will understand that it was the Baks who brought him the three, and that the Ol knew nothing of it."

"That scrawny Wild One that was with them — "

Emlis! thought Lief, looking wildly around the cage. Then he remembered. The last he had seen of Emlis was when the little Keron fell from the cage in the tunnel.

Another Guard was speaking. Lief closed his eyes, straining to hear. As he listened, his heart sank.

"The Wild One was damaged. It crawled away to die. Forget it. It is the three the master wants. Boy. Big man. Girl with black bird. We had fine luck, Bak 3."

"And what a fool the Ol will look!"

Low, sly guffaws.

Wincing at the pain in his head, Lief hauled himself to the front of the cage. At the corner, the cover flaps gaped apart. He squinted through the gap.

422

Ahead, the Ol, 3-19, stalked straight-backed towards the platform where Tira waited, her face like thunder. Beside Tira stood Hellena, one hand holding Faith's chain, the other resting on the lid of the metal box.

Behind the Grey Guards lining the path pressed the mass of dull-eyed, ragged people. And beyond, rising out of sight, were tiers of seats crowded with onlookers — onlookers of every shape, color, and size.

The audience seemed to be shimmering, shifting, wavering . . . Lief rubbed his eyes.

Then he realized that his eyes were not at fault. There were a few Ra-Kacharz on the benches, some pods of Guards, and a rabble of Wild Ones. But most of the audience were Ols — Grade 1 and 2 Ols, whose shapes kept changing, melting, and re-forming as he watched.

Here, of course, there was no need to deceive. The lower-grade Ols did not have to hold one shape if they did not wish it. They could change at will, for their own entertainment or use.

He focused on one pair as their horned, goat-like heads dissolved into gaping fish-faces, their hands became fins, their color changed from brown to silver-green, their bodies swelled. This crowded the pair beside them, two women in red bonnets. The women hissed angrily, and for an instant showed their true shape — white and formless, with gaping toothless mouths and eyes like coals. The next moment the white shapes shrank and narrowed, becoming writhing snakes with human faces.

Sickened, Lief looked down again. At the slaves, standing so still and so silent.

And then — then he saw something strange. No one appeared to be moving, but it was as though ripples were passing through the crowd.

He pressed his face against the bars. Yes! The same tiny actions were being repeated by one person after another. A small turn of the head. Lips moving, so slightly that it would be impossible to see from a distance that words were being said.

A message was being passed among the slaves. And Lief was sure he knew where the message had begun. With Claw, Brianne, and Gers, mingling with the crowd at the edge of the Arena. Whispering the same words over and over again.

Watch the platform. Be ready to fight. Get to the road behind the Arena. Pass it on.

"The word is spreading," said Barda's voice in his ear. "We must stop it!"

Lief turned. Barda was behind him, looking over his head into the Arena. The big man's eyes were deeply shadowed. A great red burn marked his brow where a sparking rod had struck him.

"It is too late to stop it now," Lief said.

"But everything has changed, and plainly Claw, Brianne, and Gers do not know it!" Barda whispered urgently. "They must have been hiding outside the tunnel when we were captured, and saw nothing. If they can see the cage covered now, they no doubt think it is all part of the plan."

Lief felt for the Pirran Pipe and slipped it from its casing. Tingling warmth flowed through his fingers, and a strange peace stole over him. "Nothing has changed, Barda," he said calmly. "You cannot cage a sound. When we reach the platform, I will play the Pipe exactly as planned. Not as Emlis might have done, but as well as I can."

"Whatever else the Pipe may do, it will not melt iron bars, Lief," said Barda grimly. "The others may escape. But we will be trapped."

Then so it will have to be, Lief thought. Claw, Brianne, and Gers can lead the people to freedom as well as we can. But he said nothing.

Looking around for Jasmine, he saw that she had also woken and crawled to the front of the cage. But she had not come to join her companions. She was crouched in the other corner, peering through the gap in the covers there.

Trying to catch a glimpse of Faith, Lief thought. The sister she has been seeking all along.

He moved to Jasmine's side, touched her hand. "Jasmine," he whispered. "Why did you not tell me of Faith?"

Jasmine turned on him, her eyes dark with misery. "Tell *you*? How can you ask that?" she said in a low voice.

Lief stared at her, aghast. "What — what do you mean?" he stammered.

Jasmine clenched her fists. "Do you still try to deceive me, Lief, even now?" she hissed. "Do you not understand? I *know*. I know what you did!"

"What?" Lief asked wildly.

The word was no sooner out of his mouth when the cage's front wheels hit the foot of the ramp with a thump. He, Barda, and Jasmine were thrown violently backwards. The Pirran Pipe flew out of Lief's hand and began to roll towards the back of the cage. He snatched for it frantically and managed to catch it just as the Guards, grunting with effort, tilted the cage and began to haul it upward. Another second and the Pipe would have slipped through the bars and been lost.

His heart beating fast at the near disaster, Lief crawled back to the front of the cage.

Forget everything, he told himself. Everything except what must be done. He felt a familiar dread chill and knew that the cage was nearing the metal box. He gripped the Pirran Pipe more tightly.

"Attention, slaves!" Hellena cried. "I have something of importance to tell you! Listen well!"

Lief reached the cage corner and peered through the gap. Tira was standing right beside it, with 3-19.

"Why is the cage covered?" Tira muttered furiously to 3-19, glancing nervously upward.

"The Baks did it," said 3-19 sullenly. "By the

time I saw their disobedience, the summons had come and it was too late to take the covers off."

"You are an incompetent fool!" Tira spat. "How glad I am that the master has finished with you and your kind."

She turned away and 3-19 glared at her, his long fingers twitching as though he longed to fasten them around her slender neck.

Tira had moved to stand beside Hellena. Hellena raised her arms.

"Once I was a deadly enemy of the master," Hellena cried. "I freed his slaves. I killed his servants. I confess it. And my companion was once the foulest of rebels — a creeping, deceitful spy who secretly helped the master's foes!"

Tira lifted her chin. "I confess it!" she said loudly.

Lief heard Barda's soft groan behind him, but did not look around.

Hellena's cold, glittering gaze swept over the Arena. "Now, we are both free of doubt, fear, and evil thoughts. Thanks to the gift the master has bestowed on us, we are not only his servants, but his eyes and ears as well."

Lovingly, her hand smoothed the metal box. "Like us, you deserve death, slaves. But the master is merciful. You are all to share his gift. Soon your struggles will be at an end. You will belong to the master, as we do."

The audience cheered wildly. The slaves on the floor of the Arena were deathly still. Hellena smiled coldly.

"There is no need to fear, slaves, whatever rumors you may have heard," she said. "The Conversion process has been perfected. It is safe, efficient, and simple. Once released, the carriers of the master's gift will find their own way to you. They are slim and very fast. The process will take no time at all."

She touched her ear. "A brief moment's pain — here — and the master will be with you always. Your Conversion will bring you freedom. You will return to your homes, mingle with your people, and do the master's will gladly."

Lief's skin was crawling. At last he understood what had happened to Tira and Hellena. He understood what the hideous worms were — what they did. He saw the Shadow Lord's plan.

The master has many plans . . .

Into Lief's mind sprang a terrifying picture. Thousands of prisoners set free by the Shadow Lord, returning to Deltora, received with joy and welcome. Thousands of prisoners who looked and sounded exactly as they had before, but who carried the Enemy within their brains, guiding their every thought, their every deed.

Thousands of prisoners, in whose keeping, safe in bags or pockets, were more of the deadly scarlet-headed worms. So that at night, while their families and neighbors slept . . .

Hellena had begun speaking again. "Though there is no escape from the master's gift, it is best if you do not struggle," she said. "With the help of the slave Faith and the gnome who once fought side by side with me against the master, I will show you how easy it can be."

She turned to the Guards. "Remove the covers!" she ordered.

15 - The Trap

The covers were swept from the cage. Light streamed in, mercilessly exposing the four people who had sprung to their feet and backed against the bars. Lief heard 3-19 shouting in anger and the Baks' loud, triumphant explanations. He saw Tira and Hellena looking up with shining eyes at the red smoke swirling in the tower above them, and the dark shadow within it.

Lightning cracked the boiling clouds. A thunderous gale crashed downward, throwing Lief and the others off their feet, pinning them down. The cage shuddered, its wheels bent by the force of the blast.

Gasping for breath, unable to move, pressed down, down by the howling wind, Lief heard the screams of the slaves writhing helplessly in the Arena, the cries of Tira and Hellena, the grunts of the Baks and the Perns on the platform as they struggled to rise.

430

Screeching, the seven Ak-Baba swooped down-ward, riding the gale, talons outstretched, hooked beaks gaping. The columns that ringed the platform trembled and came to life. Ols! Hissing white flames with darkness at their hearts, with gaping, toothless mouths, hollow eyes, and clutching hands, they rose and stood against the force of the wind. And with a grating crash, stone doors slid into place, sealing the Arena.

Then Lief knew that not only Jasmine but *all* of them had been expected. The Enemy had not known how, or where, they would appear. But he had known they would come. He had prepared for it.

There was one thing, though, that the Enemy had not expected. Eyes watering, almost deafened by the roaring wind, Lief began dragging the Pirran Pipe towards his lips. Slowly, slowly he forced his hand up-ward.

"3-19! The prisoners are down! They are ready!" Tira shrieked against the gale. "Open the Conversion Project!"

The Ol in the shape of Fallow walked to the metal box, moving easily, untroubled by the wind. He put his hand to the catch that fastened the trapdoor.

"3-19!" Lief shouted with all his strength. "Be-ware!"

The Ol turned its head to look at him blankly.

"Do not listen!" screamed Tira. "3-19! I order you!"

"You will be finished if you open that box, Ol!" Lief shouted. "With humans to do his will, your master will have no need of you. You and all your kind will lie rotting in the scrap mounds with the Guards."

3-19 hesitated, frowning.

"Baks! Perns!" cried Tira in fury.

But the Baks and Perns, scrabbling on the boards of the platform, could not move, any more than she could.

Lief's hand, clutching the Pipe, had reached his chest. He forced it on towards his mouth. He needed one more moment. One more . . .

Red smoke rushed from the tower, ferocious malice at its heart. Eyes blazed within the smoke. Shadowy hands reached out.

3-19 cried out in agony, crumpled, and fell. The trapdoor at the end of the box burst open. Scarlet-headed worms streamed out in a great flood, spreading, greedily seeking, into the cage.

Lief could feel them seething over his feet, his legs. Jasmine and Barda's panic-stricken cries were ringing in his ears. Kree was screeching despairingly. Pi-Ban gave a single, high scream. Lief screwed his eyes shut, concentrating all his strength on a final, desperate effort.

Then he had the Pipe to his lips. He blew. One pure, clear note.

The piercing sound rose and echoed around the

walls of the Arena, and on to the mountains beyond.

And with the sound, the stream of worms halted. The worms thrashed, twisting and dying like leeches of the Forbidden Way exposed to the light.

The red smoke recoiled in a clap of thunder that shook the ground. The gale died, and the Ak-Baba lurched in the skies. The Ols lowered their grasping hands and stood, swaying. The beings on the tiers of seats bent and groaned. The vraals howled in their cages.

The slaves in the Arena had been told to wait for the signal. What more of a signal did they need? They leaped to their feet and surged forward in a great wave. The confused Guards lining the pathway stumbled and fell, crushed beneath their weight.

But there was no way out. No way out of the Arena, sealed with doors of stone. No way to reach the pass to freedom. Nowhere to run. Nowhere to hide.

Gasping, staggering to his feet, Lief drew breath. The red smoke swelled and twisted above him, the shadow within it gathering strength. Again he blew, and again the piercing note echoed through the Arena, thunder cracked, and the smoke recoiled.

Lief saw Pi-Ban rising, wide-eyed, a shrivelled worm falling from his ear and onto his shoulder. He saw Barda and Jasmine hauling themselves up, clinging to the cage bars.

Outside the cage, the guards milled, confused. Tira and Hellena had fallen to their knees, staring with dazed disgust at the worms that had dropped away from them onto the platform. Faith stood alone, pale as a ghost.

"Faith!" shrieked Jasmine. "Get the keys to the cage!"

The child turned and looked, unsmiling. Her lips opened. Then came the voice — a low, deadly whisper that chilled the blood.

"There is no escape, Jasmine."

Jasmine stared, frozen. The voice whispered on.

"From the moment you looked into the crystal, from the moment you let me into your mind, you were doomed. I knew you would come to me. I had only to wait. But do not think I cared about you. You were only bait. I knew that wherever you went, *he* would follow."

Then the girl laughed, horribly. And laughing she shimmered, faded, and disappeared in a drift of red smoke, like the phantom she was.

Jasmine screamed and screamed again, clutching the cage bars in shock, grief, and horror. Shock that what she had thought flesh and blood had been a mirage. Grief for a child who had never existed. Horror as she realized how cunningly, how completely, she had been deceived.

Into Lief's mind flashed a memory. Tirral, speaking on the Isle of Keras.

434

There are many ways to catch a fish. And if the fish you want rises to a simple bait, so much the better.

Jasmine rose to the Shadow Lord's bait, and so did I in turn, Lief thought. How easy it all was! How easily he lured us into this trap. Using our weaknesses. Jasmine's loneliness and impatience. My love for Jasmine.

"For the Jalis!" The words roared amid the thunder. Then Gers was leaping onto the platform — Gers, leading a ragged army of his tribe. Some of the Jalis flung themselves, roaring, on the panicking Baks and Perns. Others set their great hands on two of the cage bars and heaved.

The iron bent like butter. Pi-Ban scrambled through the gap. Barda followed, half-carrying Jasmine. Then came Lief, the Pipe still pressed to his lips.

Again Lief had to draw breath. Again the red smoke writhed and lunged. Again it drew back as the Pipe sounded once more.

But the Enemy was gaining strength. Each time the Pipe repelled him, he drew back a little less. The seven Ak-Baba hovered around him, their unearthly cries mingling with the thunder. Within the smoke's core, malicious eyes were gleaming.

How long could the Pipe hold the shadows back?

And then, Lief heard it. Through the sound of the Pipe, through the rumbling of the thunder, came a faint, exhausted wail.

Lief swung around. But Jasmine had heard the sound, too. Jasmine and Barda had gone back to the cage. They were kneeling beside it, peering under its base, shouting to Gers.

Then the Jalis and Barda were heaving at the cage, tilting it while Jasmine slid underneath and emerged dragging a small figure in a green, hooded cape. Emlis!

Lief could not speak. Could do nothing but go on playing the Pipe. But he watched and listened as Emlis staggered to his feet.

Emlis was babbling of crawling under the cage in the tunnel, of clinging to the cage's underside as it was rolled to the platform. He was telling of being trapped when the cage's wheels bent beneath the force of the wind. Of being pinned, helpless, unable to scramble free, unable to make anyone hear him, until now . . .

Then Emlis was beside Lief, taking the Pipe from Lief's hand. Emlis was playing. And for the first time in countless centuries, the land that had once been Pirra heard the true song of the Pirran Pipe.

For as Ak-Baba shrieked and the red smoke shrank back into the boiling sky, as the Ols crouched, moaning, and the prisoners listened in awe, Emlis played like the Pipers of old. Emlis played on the Pirran Pipe the music of his own heart.

The exquisite sound filled the Arena, echoed from the mountains, rang on the Factory walls, and rolled on over the parched plain. In it was mourning for ancient beauties lost, anger at evil that seeks only to rule and destroy, fear for what might be. And then, a deep longing for home.

Not Pirra, despoiled, transformed, and gone forever. But the only home Emlis knew.

A home where deep waters rippled and soft sands drifted on peaceful shores. A place where the light was soft and cool, and the gentle, lapping sound of water filled the air. A place missed, and ached for.

Lief stood, transfixed. His heart seemed to be breaking as the music rose, pleading for rescue, crying for release.

Then . . . the Arena disappeared.

Cold, freezing cold. Rushing darkness . . .

And the next instant Lief was struggling in black, icy water, the panicking cries of thousands ringing in his ears.

What had happened? What new sorcery was this?

"Jasmine!" he screamed.

"Here!" Barda bobbed up beside him, supporting Jasmine and Pi-Ban. Lief took Jasmine from him, held her head above the water, felt the rush of Kree's wings.

"My music!" Emlis swam like an eel towards them. "My people heard it! They brought us home! The Shadow Lord will never know what became of us!"

"*Our* people will drown, Emlis!" choked Jasmine. "Oh, there are so many! Far too many for the Kerons to save in time. They will drown!"

Then Lief heard her gasp, and the next moment light flooded the darkness, pushing it back, back, as the magical music of the Pirran Pipe had made the Enemy shrink and retreat. And with the light came a rushing, rippling sound. Lief pulled himself around, shivering. He blinked, hardly able to believe his eyes.

For coming towards them was a vast fleet of boats. The shell-like craft of the Plumes, the elegant new boats of the Aurons, the heavy longboats of the Kerons, paddling together, scooping struggling people from the water, hauling them to safety.

Clef and Azan paddled furiously to keep up with Auron guards on twisting eels and stolid Keron leech-gatherers. Nols, Piper of the Plumes, rowed beside Tirral, Piper of the Kerons, as Tirral searched the black waters for her son, whose music had summoned them all.

But it was Penn, the Auron history-keeper, who lifted Lief and his companions from the water. And it was with her that they began their long journey home.

16 ~ Reunions

The people slept as they were carried through the caverns. Only Pi-Ban was woken, to wring the hands of Lief, Barda, and Jasmine, and then to be spirited up to Dread Mountain, above the emerald sea.

"I fear he will tell of his adventures, whatever my warnings," Lief murmured. "The Dread Gnomes are great storytellers, Penn."

"Pi-Ban will not tell," Penn said serenely. "He will forget with his first breath of the air above. Do you not know, Lief? You have read Doran's rhyme."

Lief bent his head, remembering. " 'Where timeless tides swamp memory . . .' " he murmured at last.

"Yes. The seas of the underground are the seas of forgetting," Penn smiled. "How do you think we have lived here in secret so long?"

"But in the Shadowlands we remembered," Barda objected.

"You had Emlis with you," said Penn. "And the minds of all of us were focused on you, besides."

"But when we return home, we will forget?" asked Jasmine, very grave.

Penn smiled, and took from her pocket three small, smooth stones. "Not if you keep these with you," she said, handing one stone to each companion. "They are soul-stones. All Aurons carry one. Doran carried his always, so it is said. And these are yours."

Lief, Barda, and Jasmine looked down at the stones. They seemed to change hue every moment — gleaming gold, red, green, blue, black, purple, and all the colors of the rainbow in turn.

"I cannot tell the real color," Barda said in wonder.

"That is because there is none," Penn said simply. "It is the eye of the observer that makes the difference. And so it is with people, we found, when the Pipe sang in our caverns for the first time, not long ago."

"That is how . . . ?" Jasmine began.

Penn nodded. "We on Auron heard the Pipe. Its song made us remember that once our people were one. We set out to see for ourselves, at last, the others of our kind, and to find out what had happened to you. At the Forbidden Way we met the Plumes, who had travelled north for the same reason. They did not seem as savage as we had feared. And so together we called to the Kerons, bidding them to light the tunnel and allow us entry to their territory."

"And Tirral agreed?" asked Barda disbelievingly.

Penn smiled. "After a time," she said placidly. "It seems that, like us, she and her people had been giving thought to the wisdom of keeping up old rivalries in times of trouble. We learned that her son had gone with you to the Shadowlands. Then, together, we all waited for the sound that would tell us that he, and you — and the Pipe — were ready to return. Together, at last, we heard it, and together we brought you back."

"Without you we would have perished," said Lief. "We owe you our lives."

"Without you, the Pirrans would have remained apart forever," Penn answered. "We owe you even more."

✳

The Pirran fleet skimmed through the caverns like leaves blown by the wind. There was much time for talk and for reunion, however, for many boats paddled for a time beside Penn's own. Clef and Azan came, their craft riding low in the water under the sleeping weight of Claw, Brianne, and Gers. Nols came, Tira and Hellena peaceful at her feet. And Tirral came with Emlis, who had thrown off his leech-gatherer's cloak with relief.

"My son seems taller than when he went away," Tirral said.

"He has grown in more than stature," Barda answered. "He has a great heart."

"When I am a little older — old enough to wear a leech-gatherer's cloak in comfort — I am going to be an explorer like Doran," Emlis said shyly. "I will explore and map the caverns. I will travel the seas of the Plumes and the Aurons, and unknown seas as well."

"Seas of soft purple," murmured Lief. "Black seas filled with stars. Caverns that glitter like diamonds."

"How do you know?" Emlis asked in surprise.

But Tirral put her hand inside her cloak and brought out something that gleamed in the magic light. She passed it to Lief. He stared down at it, almost as if he had forgotten what it was.

"I return the Belt of Deltora to you," Tirral said formally. "In exchange for the Pirran Pipe."

"Thank you." Lief hesitated. There was more he wished to say, but he decided it would not be wise. Very aware of Barda's and Jasmine's eyes upon him, he fastened the gleaming thing about his waist, and kept silent.

✳

At last, in the golden cavern of the topaz, it was time to say farewell.

"We have brought you to the place where the signs of life above are strongest," Penn said to the companions softly, as the fleet gathered around them. "From here, all your people can travel home."

"Lief! Barda! Jasmine!"

Lief turned and saw Emlis waving to them, not far off. He was still holding the Pirran Pipe.

The companions waved back. "And what of the Pipe, Penn?" Lief asked. "Will it be separated into three parts once more?"

"No," said Penn. "The Kerons will keep it for now. It was decided, before you returned, that if it should ever come back to us, it would remain complete. It will stay with each tribe for one full year, to be played morning, noon, and evening by the Piper as is the Pirran way. Then it will be passed on, in a great festival organized by the tribe who is giving it up."

Her eyes twinkled. "I daresay there will be much competition," she added. "The tribes will try to outdo one another, and every festival will be greater and more exciting than the last. But I, at least, will not complain. Festivals are far better than war. And no one enjoys a feast better than I do. Well — are you ready?"

Lief swallowed and nodded. "Farewell, Penn," he said. He took Barda's and Jasmine's hands in his own and closed his eyes.

"Farewell," he heard Penn whisper. And the now familiar darkness closed in around them.

✳

They opened their eyes on the light of Deltora. It was just past dawn. The grass on which they lay was still wet with dew. The sky was palest blue, faintly

443

streaked with pink. A breeze stirred the trees and brushed their faces, fresh and sweet.

Lief felt he had never seen such beauty.

He saw that they were in the gardens of the palace, near the stairs to the great entrance hall. Two palace guards were standing at the doors.

For an instant the guards stared, astounded, at the crowd that had appeared on the palace lawn from thin air. Then they turned and raced inside, shouting the news at the tops of their voices.

Jasmine raised her face to the sun. Kree took flight, stretching his injured wing, screeching joyously. Barda gave a great sigh.

All around them people were opening their eyes, sitting up, staring in unbelieving joy. In the blink of an eye, it seemed to them, they had been swept from the Shadow Arena to this beautiful place that looked and smelled like home. Most were convinced that they were dreaming.

But there, slowly climbing to their feet, were the three strangers who had stood on the Arena platform before them. One was the boy who had played the strange Pipe. Around his waist he wore something that glittered and shone. A belt of steel, studded with seven great gems.

The slaves who were no longer slaves stared in wonder, gradually accepting the truth.

Deltora had not abandoned them. They had

never been forgotten. They were free. And it was their king who had brought them home.

The doors of the palace flew open. People began to stream down the stairs, many still heavy-eyed with sleep but all shouting and opening their arms. The people on the grass stood up and stumbled to meet them. The two crowds met and mingled, loved ones and strangers alike embracing, weeping, and laughing for joy.

The palace bells began to ring, calling to the people of the city below. Jasmine touched Lief's arm. He looked down at her, his heart very full. She murmured something, but he could not hear her over the noise of the bells. He bent closer.

"I said, it is shame to me that I ever doubted you, Lief," Jasmine repeated awkwardly. "But Faith seemed so real. And she said —"

"The fault is mine," Lief said quickly. "I was a fool to refuse to speak of the crystal, to pretend it did not exist. I did tell you and Barda of it once, after I saw it in a dream in the Valley of the Lost. I thought you would remember."

Jasmine looked puzzled. "I think I did, at first," she said slowly. "But then I looked in the crystal, and forgot everything but the lie I saw there." She looked down. "I should have known that you would never deceive me."

Lief hesitated. This was the moment he had been

445

dreading. He glanced at Barda, who was stolidly pretending not to listen. He cleared his throat. "I *have* deceived you, Jasmine," he said loudly. "You, and Barda too. There is something — "

He broke off. Jasmine's hand had slipped from his arm. She was looking towards the palace.

A small group of people had appeared at the doors, looking eagerly out into the crowd. Sharn and Doom stood to one side, supporting Josef between them. On the other side was Stephen the pedlar, beaming, arm in arm with a strange, tall woman whose shaved head was painted with swirling designs. But in the center stood Ranesh, his face expressionless, Zeean of Tora, and a graceful figure wrapped in a long cloak.

Marilen.

17 - Secrets

His heart in his mouth, Lief took a step forward. Marilen saw him. With a final glance at Ranesh, she gathered up her cloak and walked slowly down the stairs, her head held high. Lief felt Jasmine and Barda drawing back from him as she approached.

The celebrating crowd seethed around them, but the four — the three companions and the approaching girl — had eyes and ears only for one another. It was as though they were on an island in time and space.

Her face glowing with relief and welcome, Marilen held out her hands. Lief took them.

"Oh, Lief, how I have longed for your return!" Marilen murmured. "How I wished I could tell you . . . all is well, Lief! All is well. We are safe."

Lief bowed his head, overwhelmed by thankfulness. He felt the girl's hands move away from his.

He glanced behind him. Barda was looking straight ahead, but Jasmine met his eyes with a determined smile.

Lief had a moment of confusion. Could it be that his companions already knew the secret he had kept from them so long?

But there was no time to think any longer. Marilen was waiting. The moment had come. He put his hands to his waist, unfastened the glittering belt, and let it fall. He heard Jasmine and Barda gasp.

Marilen pushed back her cloak. There was a flash of gleaming color. Then she was taking something from her own waist and handing it to Lief. Smiling with relief she moved quickly away to stand at a little distance.

The great jewels of the Belt of Deltora shone like stars under the morning sky. The exquisite links of steel gleamed warm in Lief's hands. He put the Belt on, felt its familiar weight, straightened his shoulders, and turned to face Barda and Jasmine.

They were staring, open-mouthed.

"The real Belt was safe in Del all the time!" Barda roared. "You were wearing a *copy*! All this time — and we did not know!" He scooped up the fallen belt and shook it in Lief's face. "*This* . . . this really *is* just a jewelled trifle!"

Lief nodded, shamefaced. "You have a right to be angry, both of you, but I beg you will understand," he muttered. "Doom and I made the copy in secret at the forge. We arranged our meetings using coded messages — just a simple code where each letter was replaced by the one following it in the alphabet and the numbers were treated likewise."

"So 'DOOM' would be 'EPPN,' " said Jasmine, remembering the note she had found.

Lief glanced at her curiously. "We used gems from the palace jewels that most nearly matched the real ones," he went on. "They have a little power of their own, as all great gems do, but compared to the talismans in the real Belt, they are worthless."

He smiled wryly. "Tirral felt no magic in the belt for very good reason. There was no magic in it!"

"You — you left the real Belt behind, to keep it safe," Jasmine stammered. "Your — your friend — wore it because — because she was the one you most trusted?"

"Because she was the one who *had* to wear it!" Lief answered. "In case anything happened to me." He beckoned to Marilen, who moved back to join them.

"Marilen is my distant cousin — my nearest relation on my father's side," Lief said, with a touch of pride. He laughed as Jasmine and Barda looked politely baffled. "Do you not see, you two?" he cried. "Marilen is my heir — the next in line to the Belt of Deltora."

"*What?*" Barda exploded.

"But — " Jasmine's voice caught in her throat.

She swallowed and tried again. "But I thought only the child of a king or queen could be the heir."

Lief nodded, unconsciously reaching for her hand. "The palace chief advisors encouraged that belief, because they were secret servants of the Shadow Lord," he said. "But when I thought about it, I knew it could not be true. It is far too dangerous for Deltora. My life was threatened from the moment I became king, and I had no child to wear the Belt after me, should I die."

It was such a relief to tell the story at last. The words, so long held back, tumbled from him in a stream. "*The Belt of Deltora* says simply that the Belt must be worn by Adin's true heir," he said. "It follows, then, that if a king or queen dies childless, the Belt will join with the next in line — a brother or sister, for example."

"But you have no brothers or . . . or sisters," said Jasmine, biting her lip as the last word brought back unpleasant memories.

Lief held her hand more tightly. "No. Or uncles and aunts, for that matter. It has been the royal habit to have one child only. By chance, Adin's heir had only one child, and this became the tradition — one the chief advisors insisted upon."

"It suited them very well, no doubt, to have the fate of Deltora hanging on one frail life in each generation," muttered Barda.

"Yes!" Lief said. "And they had done their work

so well that at first my attempts to find an heir seemed hopeless. But then — " He glanced at Marilen. "But then I remembered that Adin himself had several children."

"All of them married Torans," said Jasmine slowly. "Jinks told me that."

"Exactly," Lief said, wincing at the name of Jinks, as did Marilen, for a different reason. "So I knew that if I looked long and hard enough, I would surely find myself an heir in Tora, no matter how distant a relation he or she might be." He smiled slightly. " 'Blood is blood, no matter how thinly it is spread over the ages,' as someone said to us not long ago."

"So you searched the library books and parchments for clues," murmured Jasmine. "Family histories, records of marriages, children born . . . all those hours of work!"

"I had to secure Deltora's future before I could do anything else," Lief said. "And I had to do it in secret. Doom and my mother were the only ones I told. They knew how vital it was. They knew that Deltora's safety must never again depend on the life of just one person."

He smiled. "Marilen is a descendant of Adin's second son. When I found her, I knew I had my heir at last. It is true that when I have a child, that child will take her place as first in line — "

"That time cannot come soon enough for me!" Marilen broke in fervently. "When Lief told us in Tora that through my mother's family I was his heir, the news seemed more like a curse than a blessing."

Lief smiled at her fondly. "But still she agreed to leave her home, family, and friends and come to Del — "

"To wear the real Belt of Deltora if you went into danger, so that if something ill befell you, it would shine at once for her!" Jasmine burst out, finishing for him. "And all the time we thought — everyone thought . . ."

She pulled her hand from Lief's and put it to her burning face. Her head was spinning. So much that she had thought was not true. So many things she had seen one way, she now saw in another. Lief shutting himself away in the library. The parchment labelled *The Great Families of Tora*. The secret visits to the forge. The taking of the royal jewels. The visit to Tora itself . . .

"I know Lief wanted to tell you and Barda of me, Jasmine," Marilen said softly, seeing her distress. "But he had sworn to my father that only Sharn would know who I was, aside from Doom."

"The more people who knew Marilen was next in line, the more danger there was for her," Lief added. "If the Shadow Lord heard even a whisper . . ."

Jasmine swallowed and nodded. "Then why do you tell us now?" she managed to say.

Marilen smiled delightedly. "Because *now* all is well!" she exclaimed. "Lief had time only to trace the line of Adin's second child. But Adin and Zara, his wife, had *five* children in all. Zeean and my father examined the parchments Lief brought to Tora. They have discovered many more of Adin's descendants, not only in Tora, but in Del, too, and indeed all over the kingdom!"

She clasped her hands, her eyes sparkling. "Soon everyone will know that a threat to Lief is no longer a threat to the whole of Deltora. There will be no point in killing him — for that reason, at least."

"So I will no longer have to live in the palace, shut up like a prisoner!" exclaimed Lief with great satisfaction.

"And neither will I," said Marilen, equally happily. "If Lief should die childless, I will take his place. If I should die in my turn, there will be another to take *my* place — and another, and another, and another! The Belt will always find an heir, and Deltora is safe."

"What is all this talk of dying?" cried Barda clapping Lief on the shoulder and smiling broadly. "Though I confess I could strangle Lief myself when I think of the terrors I suffered, fearing for him and that lying belt!"

Marilen laughed. "I am so glad, so *glad*, that all this has ended in happiness," she said.

Jasmine nodded, still finding it difficult to think in different terms of Marilen. "This time must have been hard for you," she said, rather awkwardly.

"Indeed it has," Marilen said frankly. "I faced no

real danger compared to you, however. I had the Belt of Deltora, so I knew Lief lived, for it never shone for me. And the gems aided me. Once, the amethyst dimmed when my food was poisoned. I saw it, and knew something was amiss."

Her face broke into a smile. "Besides," she added, "if I had not come here, I would not have met Ranesh!"

She looked around to where Ranesh still stood alone on the stairs, forlornly looking after her. "I must go to him," she said. "I have much to explain. To him, and to poor Josef, too."

With another smile, she left them.

Lief raised his eyebrows. "So," he murmured. "Marilen and Ranesh." He glanced at Jasmine. He had sometimes had fears about Jasmine's feeling for Ranesh.

But Jasmine's smile as she met his eyes was very real. A great peace descended on Lief's heart.

Then Marilen turned around. "By the by, Lief," she called, "it seems that everyone believed I had come to Del to be your bride. Did you know?"

Lief's astounded expression was her answer. She laughed, and went on her way.

Lief swung round to Jasmine and Barda. "Had you heard this tale?" he demanded.

Barda remained expressionless, preserving wise silence. Jasmine's cheeks were burning again, but she shrugged. "Palace gossip," she said carelessly. "But you are far too young to marry. I always said so."

Lief was speechless.

Barda caught sight of Tira wandering towards the stairs, looking lost. He muttered something and strode off towards her.

"Of course," Jasmine went on, beginning to smile as she and Lief walked slowly after him. "Marilen would have been an ideal choice as a king's bride. Well read, beautiful, polite, elegant, at home in palaces . . ."

"When the time comes," Lief said, determinedly drowning her out, "I will follow Adin's example and marry for love." He glanced at her. "If the woman I love will have me, of course."

"She probably will," said Jasmine. "When the time comes." She slipped her hand into his.

A tumult of shouting and cheering began behind them. A great crowd was surging up the road from the city to join the crowd already thronging the lawn. The people on the stairs were laughing and beckoning. The bells were still ringing. Lief's heart swelled with joy.

And now, he thought. Now, at last, we can begin.